01/26/2018
156,524 words

METADATA MAN
The Series

By

Harley L. Sachs

Published by IDEVCO Intellectual Properties, the Idea Development Company. All rights reserved.

Paper ISBN 978-1-939381-30-9
Ebook ISBN 978-1-939381-31-6

Books by Harley L. Sachs:

For full particulars, see the catalog at the end of this book.

Metadata Man

Essays and Columns: 1992-2011
The Writing Life

Cartoons
Hunting the Mail Buoy and other hazards to navigation

Everything has a story and the three books in this volume are no exception. At South Bend Central High school we had a brilliant drama teacher, James Lewis Cassaday of blessed memory. Several of his students went on to Hollywood careers. Among them was Harvey Weinstein. At first, for a gag, I named my protagonist for these stories Harvey Weinstein until the scandal broke, revealing the Hollywood producer was a serial rapist. That wouldn't do, so in a "find and replace" blink my Harvey Weinstein became Harvey Goldstein.

There's more to the story. Inspired by the coupons issued by Fred Meyer grocers in Portland, Oregon, I knew that every purchase at the store was tracked in Cleveland, Ohio. Individually printed coupons were issued to holders of the so-called Fred Meyer club card. I imagined there was someone in Cleveland who knew everything every customer ate or bought, including items of personal hygiene. That person knew everything about everybody.

The term for this is now Big Data. It's a marketing tool that has grown into threatening proportions, a threat to our privacy and freedom. In my book Harvey, now Goldstein, is obsessed with big data. He is a hoarder of information. He wants to know everything about everybody. This is dangerous, hence book two "The Metadata Curse."

Where is Big Data taking us? We already know, or think we know. These stories are a warning of what is already happening.

Follow Harvey Goldstein and his wife Ursula through their adventures in Big Data and its consequences.

(Full disclosure: this author's original birth certificate called him Harvey and his wife's maiden name was Ursel. Always having a little fun.)

Book One:
The Seventh Paradigm

Like many of us, Harvey Goldstein has a mundane job and works in a cubicle. A chance meeting in Hamburg, Germany with Uncle Julius, a distant relative of his wife Ursula, sets off a series of encounters that threatens his very existence.

Part One

Chapter One

It was an afterthought of my wife, Ursula, that we should drop in on her uncle Julius on our last day in Germany. Technically, he was the second husband of her aunt, long since deceased, but Ursula had the address and heard he was an interesting man. We had a couple of hours before our train to Amsterdam and our charter flight back to the States, so why not? I could not have suspected that the innocuous visit would have a profound effect on my life and our future.

We called first using Ursula's cell phone. it being impolite to just drop in without notice. I am linguistically handicapped. Since Ursula teaches high school German I left the communications to her. It took a couple of minutes before it was clear who we are, but Julius said he would be happy to see us. We checked our luggage at the Bahnhof and took a taxi to the address. Uncle Julius lived in an older, four story apartment block, no elevator.

Julius was something of a mystery. His apartment was on the fourth floor, not an easy climb for a man in his dotage. He met us at his door in a threadbare cardigan, a hollow-eyed, emaciated man of uncertain age. He could be as old as ninety.

Julius, we'd been told, had been displaced from what had previously been East Germany before the wall came down. The DDR as it was then called, the Deutsche Democratische Republic, had struggled as a failed Communist economy bolstered by Soviet subsidies, but ultimately a ruin, many parts still devastated by World War II bombing, long after the war, or polluted by an economic policy that put production quotas above environmental disaster.

Uncle Julius had the look of someone liberated not from a concentration camp, but from something nearly as bad in its own way. The teeth he had left were stained by tobacco as were his fingers, for he was a heavy smoker with an accompanying cough. Transplanted to

7

Hamburg Julius apparently was living on West German subsidies and the welfare state. To my relief he spoke a passable English which he was pleased to practice.

As a matter of protocol and courtesy we did not come empty handed. Ursula had been advised that Julius liked coffee. We brought a pound of finely ground Swedish Gevalia. He was delighted and immediately dumped out what he had prepared for our arrival. He boiled some water on an antique gas hot plate and poured it through a filter with the precious Gevalia. He told us how he had hated the old East German brew which he called erzatz.

He served the coffee with some mismatched cups accompanied by stale cookies I recognized came from Aldi, the big German grocery chain that also owns Trader Joe's, one of our competitors. I work for Krieger, one of the top two American grocery chains.

The conversation was at first perfunctory. Where did we live? What was Cleveland like? Who did I work for? He hadn't heard of Kreiger. The usual preliminaries could be followed by awkward silences, especially when I said I worked for a major grocery chain. What was I, a stock boy?

I should have been insulted, for I detected a level of snobbery about people doing jobs that weren't professional. I explained that I had started pushing grocery carts out of the parking lot, graduated to check out clerk. As a check out clerk I became fascinated with what people bought and what they ate. Krieger issues coupons keyed to individual shoppers. That got me interested in computers.

I could see that up to then Julius was bored with these two American almost relatives he did not know or care about. He was not a man for small talk. He did not brighten up until I told him I was working in computers. I gave him my business card: data management specialist. Suddenly he wanted to know all about my job. The shift from conversational tone turned professional. His questions had the air and purpose of a police interrogation.

When I explained about metadata he was intensely interested. I explained that since the invention of bar codes the company could keep constant tabs on inventory as items were sold and needed to be restocked. The addition of the so-called club card which promised discounts to regular customers provided the grocery chain with a ton of information: names and addresses of customers, their gender and age. It was a useful marketing tool. Thanks to the system, the company knew what customers ate and which personalized coupons could be mailed, coupons that only the individual customer could cash. That was my job.

I didn't think all that shop talk was interesting to most people, but Julius was so excited you'd think he'd found Jesus. He smiled, showing his gap teeth and said, "You are very glucklich."

My German is not very fluent, but I do know that glucklich can have many meanings, as in lucky, or happy. Our "Lots of luck" can be said in a sarcastic, ironic way, depending on the inflection. I am a happy person, ein glucklicher Mensch, but that might also be a lucky person.

Julius saw that I was puzzled as I was pondering what he really meant.

His attempt at clarification only got more confusing. "I wish I had been as glucklick as you."

Now it was sounding more like being fortunate.

He tried to explain. "If I had only had your what you call metadata."

To my mind metadata was a marketing tool. When I ordered a book from Amazon, for instance, besides filling the order the Amazon computers looked for other tittles that might interest me and offered them. It was just good business, like the suit salesman who also offers a shirt and tie to go with the jacket..

Then Julius revealed the truth. "Before the reunification I was with Stasi, the secret police. We had no computers. With us everything was on paper. You can even visit the old files today. In Nuremberg there are kilometers of files. It is now open to the public." With that Julius rolled his eyes as if revealing previously secret state files was a deplorable betrayal. Declassification of all that meticulously gathered and stored information was like telling old family secrets, revealing great granny's liaisons, or hidden criminal records, transcripts of confessions whispered in church and only to the priest. To Julius, opening the Stasi files was a gut wrenching betrayal.

In an attempt to explain his anguish, Julius said, "Do you have any idea how much work it was to collect all zat information? In the DDR it was the duty of every citizen to inform ze Stasi about everything. Neighbors informed on neighbors, sisters on brothers, parents on children and children on parents. Can you imagine how much work it was for us to cross index and classify all zat information? But you, my American relative, you have your computers, your metadata. You even know what people have for breakfast and what brand of coffee they brew! You are very glucklig. Can you imagine?"

To my mind, children informing on their parents was almost on a par with African child soldiers being commanded to execute their mothers.

"We don't do that," I said, my self-righteousness welling up. Americans would not denounce their parents to the secret police.

Julius laughed. "You don't do that. You don't have to. You have your computers. They do it for you with your metadata. Your conscience is clear."

Julius was seeing everything through the eyes of an old secret policeman. I protested. "It's just a marketing tool."

"You sink so," Julius said with his German lisp after lighting the next cigarette with the stub of the last one. "Knowledge is power, and information is knowledge. In ze old days we had to depend on people reporting. Did you buy, for example, a gallon of acetone and a large quantity of hydrogen peroxide? How much acetone do you need to clean your nails of old polish? Or peroxide to bleach your hair? Not much. So why such large quantities? To make explosives, of course. Even if you bought small quantities and in several places, your metadata computer would notice. Oh, if we had only had such a tool!"

Now I understood why Julius said I was glucklig. "But I'm not in the secret police," I protested.

"You don't need to be. Zat is the beauty of it."

He saw I didn't get it. I just didn't think like a communist cop.

"I was born too soon," Julius said with regret. "In my day a Stasi agent might have to stand watch all night in a doorway, in the cold, on a boring stakeout, needing to take a piss. I had to file and sort endless innocuous reports. I had to decide if someone was denouncing a neighbor because they had a grudge about something stupid. You Americans have your technology. You have your CCT cameras on watch everywhere. You have your metadata. And you called ze DDR a police state! Hah!"

My mind was still on the idea of children denouncing their parents.

"In the DDR people knew I worked for Stasi. Zey were afraid of me. Zey never spoke openly. Ze fact is we were all afraid of each other. Ze beauty of your system is it is invisible. You don't have to watch out for men in overcoats, sinister secret police watching your house. You live in lala land."

Julius was triumphant. It was if, in a few minutes of interrogation, he had worked out of me a confession that would send me to the gallows. The problem was, I hadn't confessed to anything. I hadn't done anything. He had seen through me. In the eyes of that old refugee, I was naked.

We thanked Julius for the coffee and the cookies and got ready to leave. We had a train to catch. He wanted us to take a little souvenir and produced a rather weary wooden Russian doll, the kind that has another inside it, and another inside that until you end up with a little wooden egg. It was a typical souvenir of the old Soviet Union, not what I would have expected from an ex-East German, but I was grateful we weren't presented with a ghastly cuckoo clock.

As we said goodbye, Julius shook my hand in the formal German greeting. Looking me in the eye, his parting words were a warning. "Vorsicht. Beware of ze seventh paradigm"

The seventh paradigm? I had no idea what he was talking about. He was an old spy. Maybe he had read John Bucham's novel "The Thirty-Nine Steps" which turned out to be steps in some obscure formula, never explained in the movie. I had not read the book.

The thought retreated into my subconscious as we hurried to the station, retrieved our luggage and concentrated on the plane connection in Amsterdam and the long overnight flight back to the states.

Chapter Two

I do not think travel is much fun. Admittedly there is a certain adventure in exploring unfamiliar places, finding nice restaurants, but that wears thin quickly for me. It is too stressful. At work I live in a cubicle with a computer monitor. Getting from that comfortable seclusion into Europe was a bit of culture shock. What with the train ride to Amsterdam, the layover there, the overnight flight into Kennedy and the change to Cleveland, I was exhausted and jet lagged when we dragged ourselves into our apartment and basically fell into bed. I had allowed an extra day in case a flight was canceled or we missed a connection. I needed time to decompress.

Ever since 9/11 and the invasion of Europe by displaced Moslems from Iraq, Syria, Afghanistan, and whatever, security was tight. That was when we were leaving Europe. Arriving in the USA was nearly as bad. Had we been in any Middle Eastern country? Were we carrying any meats? We had some marzipan chocolates. Any gifts? Etc. The Russian doll was scrutinized and taken apart as if it might be a bomb.. We passed.

My body was in Ohio but my brain was still en route over the Atlantic. I had not made the mental adjustment to being back when I returned to the office.

We had only been gone two weeks, a kaleidoscope of impressions and images. Amsterdam, Copenhagen, Hamburg... My senses had not yet settled down as I returned to my cubicle and monitors. Just as a reminder that I really had been in Europe, in case anybody asked about the trip, I brought along that souvenir Russian doll and set it up next to our wedding picture. I had barely taken a deep breath and settled in my ergonomic chair to log on when I was summoned to the boss's office.

Margaret, my supervisor, is a woman Ursula calls a cougar, a woman on the prowl, which makes my wife nervous. Ursula has an innate sense for these things and I am naïve. Sexual harassment is not only the purview of male managers of course. If Boss Margaret drops some innuendo or double meaning I let it go past me and pretend not to notice. Ursula is my gal and I haven't got a roving eye, but she is an

Alpha female, guardian of her guy, which is just fine with me. No need for me to use the code words "yes, dear" for our harmony.

Margaret did not, as I had expected, want to debrief me about the trip. No "how was the flight?" or some such questions. She gave me a suspicious look and said, "You have a couple of visitors in the conference room." No explanation.

I hesitated in her open doorway. "Is there a problem?"

"Not that I know of." She just said "suits," which is a lot in an office where the dress code stops short of Tee shirts, shorts, or hoodies. What was I getting, an IRS audit?

The conference room has a long, oval shaped table with a granite top which always makes me wonder how the heck they got it into the room, it being one piece. Chairs all around. Sideboard with a chrome coffee Thermos and stack of paper cups. Margaret doesn't do tea.

If it weren't for their different sizes and the color of their faces—one a light-skinned African American--two piece off the rack suits, black ties-- the two men looked like a couple of twin undertakers. Had somebody died?

The taller of the two, the white guy, asked, "Harvey Goldstein?"

I acknowledged that I was, indeed Harvey Goldstein.

His partner wanted to see some ID. I happened to have my passport with me and showed it to him, briefly afraid he was going to confiscate it. "Who are you? What's this about? Any problem with my tax return?"

The African-American returned my passport. "Should there be?"

"I don't think so. I'm a computer guy, not an accountant."

The white visitor assured me, "We're not the IRS." He flashed a badge. "Homeland security."

"So?" I'm not intimidated by Homeland Security. The uniformed bozos at the airports have missed so many loaded guns in baggage that I think they're a bunch of high school dropouts.

Neither gave their names. That irritated me. I'd shown my ID. I wanted to see theirs. They showed badges, but you can buy that shit off the internet. "That all you got?"

They were offended. Well, so what? I gave them a closer look. The white guy was overweight and had an unhealthy pallor. The black, who was shorter, about five-six, wore a wedding ring. The white guy had what looked like a class ring. "Nice ring," I said. "College?"

"Purdue."

I wasn't going to ask him his major or if he'd been in a fraternity or on a team. This wasn't a cocktail party of meaningless chit-chat. "Not married?" I asked.

They weren't expecting to answer questions. They'd come to ask them. I wasn't through. "Are you Krieger customers? I mean do you have our membership fobs?"

They had.

"Great," I said and asked if they'd show me. They were too surprised and puzzled to object. Both held out their keys with their Krieger tags and to their surprise I wrote down the numbers. To mollify them, I explained, "I do the Krieger coupon promotions. Maybe I can send you something you can use. We have some nice discounts."

That seemed to satisfy them. Little did they know.

With their Kreiger numbers I would soon find out everything about them. Uncle Julius would be impressed. Maybe I'd tell him about this.

The shorter one told me, "You were just in Hamburg."

I got it, they already knew all about me. "Yes, I was in Hamburg. So?" What I did in Germany was none of their business.

"You visited a Julius Schwartzman."

"Was that his full name? Ursula only referred to him as uncle Julius."

"It's Julius Schwartzman. Colonel. Ex-colonel."

I shook my head in disbelief. He must have reported on our visit. I remembered giving him my business card with the office address. "That old rascal. He said he had been in the Stasi in East Germany. Don't those people ever retire? I thought the cold war was over."

The thought made me weak in the knees. I had to sit down.

The white   agent—I had already forgotten his name—said. "Supposedly."

"I guess it must be in the blood. Old habits. So he reported on our visit! I can't believe it. Wait until Ursula hears about this." I was inclined to laugh, but of course, remembering what uncle Julius said about life in the East Zone as it used to be called, wasn't funny. It was downright sinister. So was this visit from two men who claimed to be from Homeland Security.

This was ridiculous. Homeland Security must be desperate to justify their jobs by quizzing a casual tourist like me. All I did in Hamburg was have a cup of coffee and stale cookies from a competitor. Was that a crime?

Following my cue, the tall one took a seat. Sitting across from me I had a sense of deja vu, for it was just as uncle Julius had sat across his table over the Gevalia coffee, an interrogation. "What did you talk about?"

I swallowed my irritation and shrugged. "Family stuff. It was just a courtesy call."

"Nothing more?"

"He told us he had once worked for the Stasi East German secret police. Before reunification."

"That all?"

"He asked about my work here at Krieger. He said he was jealous. I think the word was neidisch."

"Why was that?"

"He said we could keep better watch on people than he could when he might have to stand in a doorway on a stakeout all night in the rain needing to take a leak." Both of my visitors looked at each other and smiled. I guess they had had their own turns freezing in doorways all night.

"Did he explain more of that, his previous work?"

I shook my head. "We had to catch a train to Amsterdam. We were only there a short time."

They seemed satisfied and got up to leave, I hoped. I already anticipated Margaret asking me what that was all about. I had an afterthought. "There was one other thing. Sort of a warning. He said I should beware of the seventh paradigm."

Bingo. It was like some code word or password. That got their attention. They were now intensely interested. "What did he say about the seventh paradigm?"

"He didn't. Do you know what he meant?"

The white guy wouldn't say. The African-American said something he shouldn't. He said, "You're working in the third paradigm."

His partner shot him a disapproving look and cut him off. "You'll be hearing from us again."

About what? I hadn't committed any crime. This was all bullshit.

That was it. They left. Now besides wondering what the hell the seventh paradigm was, I was now working in the third, and I didn't know what that was, either.

Chapter Three

Boss Margaret did want to know about the visitors.

I told her, "Homeland security. Maybe they think I look like an Arab."

"Must be the nose."

I suppose a Jewish nose is more or less like an Arab one, but so what? "One of them said I work in the third paradigm. Do you know what that meant?"

She didn't.

I went back to my cubicle and logged on. I was really pissed about being harassed by those two Homeland Security dudes. But I had their Krieger numbers. My turn, you bastards.

I called up their Kreiger files. That got me their home addresses, birthdays, and phone numbers. That also got me their purchase records. I'd go a step farther than just issuing them personal coupons for the stuff they usually bought. I'd give them some feedback.

The white guy had bought diabetic socks in one of our pharmacies, yet he regularly bought sugar coated breakfast cereal and soft drinks, not the diet versions. Since he wasn't married, I didn't think the cereal was for kids. I ordered him coupons for low calorie foods and diet drinks and warned him about his diabetes. I signed it "Krieger, your partner in health."

The black guy ate healthier foods, lots of organics, collard greens, ethnic stuff, which was normal. What wasn't was he bought personal lubricants and dozens of condoms. I had an intimate knowledge of his sex life just by looking at his purchases. I suggested he get an aids test. "Krieger, your partner in health, cares about you."

I custom printed some coupons for both men on the office computer, and wrote a cover letter addressed to each by name and sent to their home addresses. I signed the letters "Harvey Goldstein, The Seventh Paradigm" like I was the Scarlet Pimpernel. Let them choke on that. Uncle Julius would be proud.

I had no idea I was being prophetic.

With that off my chest I could forget about their visit and get back to the real work. I checked the email in case something important happened while I was away. I had four hundred emails. No wonder we can't get anything done.

I screened the most important and deleted the rest.

There was a new development in our database. We already knew customers' habits, what they usually bought, which products too few did buy which is why we dropped the spaghetti sauce with garlic. No point in stocking stuff nobody wants. What was new was the change in the liquor law. In Washington grocery stores were selling spirits, not just wine and beer.

This was going to open a new line of profitability, kill the specialty liquor stores, and create new security problems. In states where liquor could be sold in grocery stores some grab and go folks would load a cart with expensive single malt liquor and run for it. Customers who wanted slivovitz plum brandy would be out of luck. Not enough demand to stock it.

I realized that there was another use for the data. If we wanted to, we would be able to spot probable alcoholics. Not that we were working for Alcoholics Anonymous, but if we were, it might be useful for that organization to know when an intervention might be a good deed. We weren't in the good deed business but we did want to serve our customers. Hadn't I just done something of the sort for those two unwelcome visitors?

On the other hand, we had considered dropping all tobacco sales. One pharmaceutical chain had done that. They were in the health business, not the nicotine poison racket. We sell so-called organic foods, but we still sell tobacco. Vegans have to simply hold their noses and bypass the meat department. We do sell a limited assortment of kosher and other ethnic foods.

Still, alcoholism was just as great a health problem as tobacco.

I must admit to a certain sense or moral responsibility. I didn't like the idea of selling tobacco products. If I wanted to keep my job, I had to remember I was just a computer guy, not a crusader for health. Was I a hypocrite, a moral crusader, a religious fanatic? Did I object to our company selling condoms and birth control prescription in the pharmacy? Contraception was not taboo in my religion. Did I object to sales of Cosmopolitan in the magazine display? None of your business, Goldstein, I told myself. Just crunch those numbers. Keep your moral indignation, if you have any, to yourself.

What would Uncle Julius do? I think I already knew that. But if I could see into my own future I might anticipate a moment when I would have to make a decision or one would be made for me whether I agreed or not.

I would talk to Ursula about it and about the visitors from Homeland Security. They said I'd be hearing from them. Couldn't be about Uncle Julius. I already told them all I knew, which was nothing much.

Then it occurred to me that they might be looking for a mole, someone who knew the Krieger security codes and had access to our huge database, someone they could recruit. We promise our customers confidentiality. Hackers might try to break in and steal credit card numbers and social security identification.

I didn't think Homeland Security wanted to steal anyone's identity or credit card information. What might they want to know? Whether our customers preferred Oreos to our house brand?

More important, why me? I'm just a number cruncher, practically a prisoner in a dead end job.

Chapter four

During my lunch break I phoned Ursula. She's a k-12 teacher, so had the summer off, which is why we could actually take a trip together. I don't own an iPhone, just a dumb off the shelf burner. The minutes are expensive, but there is no monthly fee and I do not have to stare at the damned thing and poke text messages like everybody I see on the street. After that encounter with Homeland Security I was spooked. Cell phones are not secure.

Of course, being in the data business, I am sensitive to the fact that NSA eavesdrops on everything. Millions of messages are sent every minute, but if you have a fast enough computer and a cloud, you can keep up. That's what Uncle Julius was envious about.

I realized that the security folks had noticed the cell phone call to Julius. But it was Ursula's call, not mine. Maybe he'd had a visit from German security and he showed them my business card. His recollections of Stasi days and my visitors from Homeland Security, what, in old Nazi fashion might have been called Heimatsicherheitsdienst, had given me the creeps. Of course, I know how much of our personal information is already stored. It's my job and I'm sensitive about the implications. Maybe I'm paranoid. Goes with the territory. If you knew what I know you'd freak out.

For that reason, my phone call to Ursula was cryptic. It went like this: "Hi."

"How's everything the office? Is Margaret still hitting on you?"

"I think she knows better. But I had a couple of mystery visitors."

"Since when do you get visitors? I thought you were locked in that cubicle."

"I don't want to explain over the phone."

"Now that is mysterious."

"Let's just say it's the long shadow of your Uncle Julius."

"What?"

"I'll tell you about it when I get home. Don't send me any text messages or email."

"Now I am curious."

"Good. Married life should have some surprises and secrets. Keeps things interesting. See you soon."

"Should I wear something alluring?"

"Why, Mrs. Goldstein, are you trying to seduce me?"

It was an allusion to one of our favorite movies. The Graduate. If some voyeur was listening in to our conversation I hoped they would be confused.

The backlog of emails distracted me. Management had a new marketing suggestion, something to talk over with the advertising department. Krieger is not just in the grocery business. We sell everything short of automobiles and guns, but we do have gas stations. How many customers might be interested in a new line of fall clothes, back to school stuff.? What about the direct mail list?

I would have to sort the data, a relatively simple bit of data management. Past purchases of kids' clothes would give us a clue. We could tell by the sizes how old the kids were and if they were obese. Maybe this was what that government agent meant by the third paradigm.

The Toyota was low in gas and I had to make a detour to get my Krieger station discount, but I was home only a few minutes later than usual.

Ursula was serious. She met me at the door in a negligee over her favorite Victoria's secret peek-a-boo underwear.

"You must be over your jet lag," I said as she unbuttoned my office shirt.

In bed, after a renewal of our consummation, she bit me on the earlobe and whispered, "Now tell me about your secret visitors, Mr. Bond."

You can tell we're movie buffs.

I rolled free of her embrace and pulled myself up. "Two guys who said they were from Homeland Security showed up. I'm sure your Uncle Julius reported to someone about our visit. I'm creeped out."

"Seriously?"

"Seriously. They said I would hear from them again."

"Why?"

"I'm sure they don't want a special order of Krieger discount coupons. You know, we have an awful lot of proprietary information."

"But you have a privacy statement. It's part of the agreement applicants for the Krieger card sign when they apply."

"Honey, you know nobody reads those. Besides, there's an escape clause. We can use information appropriate to our marketing programs. Could mean anything."

"Why come to you?"

I sighed. "They should come to top management. This could be industrial espionage. Happens all the time."

"You think they want you to be a mole?"

"They couldn't pay me enough to make it worth my career. If I did something like that I'd end up running the deep fryer again at Taco Bell." That was my brief summer job when I was a freshman in college. Brief as in nearly burning down the place when the oil overheated. Computers are safer.

"Maybe they'll find someone else."

"Let's hope so. In the meantime, sweetie, no text messages or emails or cell phone conversations about this. Everything ends up in the cloud."

Ursula knows that much. We've talked about NSA screening everything and the FBI looking for terrorists and cracking captured encrypted cell phones and the like. Most mass shootings in the United Stares weren't done by insane Islamists. They were done mainly by angry and neurotic white guys with hoards of guns. That made everybody a suspect. Maybe even me, and I don't even own a firearm. Uncle Julius had a point.

So, would Homeland Security come back? I hoped not.

Chapter five

Uncle Julius was an enigma. When we were in his apartment I didn't see any sign of a computer. Had he reported on our visit? On the other hand, we had telephoned. Maybe his phone was tapped. The American government isn't the only one that's paranoid. Germany is hyper about immigrants who might be terrorists. Julius couldn't be one of those, but his old occupation might have left him on a watch list. Once you're on maybe you never get off, even after you're dead. Still, our call had to be totally innocuous, unless we used some trigger code word without being aware of it.

Was The Seventh Paradigm a trigger code word? I was beginning to think so.

If I weren't in the data business, I suppose I wouldn't be so aware and so suspicious. I'd heard of an old Canadian screening process that searched emails for words like "bomb" or "explosives" but also included innocuous words like "Mickey Mouse." I had heard that if the Mafia wanted a hit they asked for a carpenter. Maybe we had mentioned coffee? Code word for what? Heroin? Made you wonder what you could talk about without arousing suspicion.

If I started sending encrypted emails it would be the FBI or Secret Service that came calling instead of Homeland Security, if that was really who those visitors were.

Suspicion is an occupational hazard when you are in a business under constant attack by hackers. Anybody could be phished, and almost anybody could be hit by ransom ware. I had Grabich, the IT guy, to protect my data at the office—I hoped. I worked inside firewalls and multiple logon passwords.

Ultimately, nothing was secure. It wasn't that others had your personal data. Your data was everywhere. If I Googled myself my name turned up in innocuous places, even that I had been treasurer of my graduating class in college. Who would care? Trouble was, once data gets in, it stays, can't be erased. That's why a kid who is arrested for a college prank is haunted forever by a minor conviction that should have been expunged. The cloud isn't programmed for expunged. Expunged is not in that vocabulary. The problem was, what did they do with the information? It turns up in a background check.

As for my job at Krieger, wasn't all just marketing and sales analysis. Was someone making connections, like did someone buy kids' clothes?

Just out of curiosity, I Googled uncle Julius Schwartzman. Lucky for him, he had retired BC, before computers. Nobody was going to digitize miles of Stasi files. But Julius had been mentioned in a court case in Germany. He was a witness. Somebody wanted to sue an official of the defunct Deutsche Democratische Republic. It must have been like suing a dead person. No result.

Before leaving for work the next morning I told Ursula, "I think I'm going to close my Face book and twitter accounts. In fact, I'm going to retreat from all social media."

Ursula was alarmed. "I hope you don't mind I posted the picture of us with Uncle Julius on Face book."

"You did what? I didn't know you took a picture."

"Why not? Everybody does. I put up our selfies from Amsterdam and Copenhagen, too."

"Why? Who cares?"

"My Face book friends." She was looking miffed, like who was I to tell her what pictures to post, her husband?

I'd have asked her to take them down, but it was too late. Nothing goes away. Everything ends up in the cloud, like my baby picture, Harvey Goldstein's baby butt. I remembered that one. People said I was a cute baby. Thank God my bris was before selfies or the whole world would have seen my baby dick.

Thanks to Ursula's Face book account I was up there along with everybody's puppy and kitty cat.

"Remember that movie we saw once? 'The Conversation' about the eavesdropper who has to record and decipher an incriminating conversation even though it was recorded in a public park amidst lots of noise and people?"

She didn't remember.

"He ends up in an apartment without electricity, no phone, wires taken out of the walls, total paranoia."

She gave me a worried look. "Is that going to be you, Harvey?"

"I hope not. But I'd like to be less conspicuous."

"If you're worried about those two Homeland Security agents, it's too late. They found you."

"Don't remind me."

"What are you worried about? You haven't done anything." Then she added, "Have you?" She was suspicious already. See how easy it is?

"Of course not." But I resolved that from that time on I was going to keep a notebook, a little paper one, like a log or a diary with a record of everything in case I needed an alibi. But no text messages, and no email that could be misinterpreted. Nothing electronic. If Homeland Security was watching me, I'd be even better at watching myself.

Was it even possible to disappear from the web? It was probably too late. Once in, never out. You could die but your pictures would be immortal.

Chapter six

In spite of Google's ability to find almost anything anywhere, I had one advantage. Harvey Goldstein is not a unique name. I'm not exactly John Doe, but my namesake appears all over the World Wide Web. With my name I could hide in plain sight.

Before the cloud I had the feeling that the system would be overloaded with so much information that it would be clogged, much like the problem of encryption in World War II. If it took too long to decrypt a message from a German submarine, the action was over before you could find out what it was. There was an old Defense Department joke that under the posted memos on the army bulletin board there were still some from General Washington that had not yet been acted upon. That, of course, was before super computers and unlimited data storage.

The limit was the patience of anyone who found all that stuff about Harvey Goldstein that they got bored or tired before they got to me. That could save me.

I shut down my social media accounts. No more Face book or Twitter. I set the spam filter to keep away unwanted emails. I felt relieved, almost safe.

A week went by without incident and I was feeling relaxed, The alleged Homeland Security guys in suits had not returned. At the office I plunged into the latest data manipulation, a simple program. Easy.

Then one day when I got home Ursula had a surprise for me: I got a letter, a real letter, not junk mail asking for money. I hardly ever get a letter any more. Most of my mail is junk and bills. The envelope had no return address but a German postage stamp. Inside the envelope was a piece of cardboard wrapped in aluminum foil. Inside it was a clipping from what looked like a German newspaper. There was no note, but there was a penciled annotation in the margin. "FYI" and "The fourth paradigm." Again with the paradigm. Had to be Julius.

I can decipher a German railway timetable but my German isn't good enough for newspapers. Ursula knows German and she could translate the clipping, more or less. "It's about an American presidential executive order. Seems there was an international Interpol conference on security. There's to be a new program that puts personal history on a magnetic strip on the back of all drivers licenses and ID cards."

"I never heard anything about that."

"Maybe it's one of those things our government doesn't want the press to talk about. This was in Der Spiegel."

I asked, "Did you say it was Interpol?"

"Yes, international police. Harvey, do you know how Interpol was set up in the first place?"

I didn't know.

Ursula is up on that stuff. "It was the Gestapo in World War II. The so-called Third Reich, what Hitler called Greater Germany, included all those occupied countries. The Gestapo wanted cross border police cooperation."

I gave Ursula a wry smile. "So that's our souvenir from World War II. Interpol. Thank you, Adolf Hitler."

She nodded. "Was anything about this on CNN?"

I shook my head. "Not in the newspaper, either." Our newspaper, the Plain Dealer, consists of crime and sports stories. Oh, and rescued animals. Firemen getting pussy cats down from trees. Face it, unless there's an actual fire, firemen's jobs are boring.

"This fits in with your conspiracy theory."

I held up the envelope with no return address. "Julius sent this. He's tipping me off."

Ursula smiled and winked. "That old rascal. He's trying to recruit you into his network."

"I'm not in anybody's network. At least he sent a letter, not an email. I don't think Julius is computer literate." I thought about that. "A letter in an envelope must be our last secure means of communication."

The NSA screening system is run by computers. They can't open the first class mail and read hand written letters. I think the government would need a warrant for that, illegal search and seizure, no violation of constitutional rights, at least, not yet.

"What should we do with this?" I asked, holding up the clipping and the envelope.

Ursula is wise to the mischief you run into with school administrators and the like. "Don't say anything. Make a CYA file just in case." A CYA file is a Cover Your Ass record in case something unpleasant comes up.

"In case of what?"

26

I thought about those Homeland Security guys. Were they interested in my mail? "Good idea. And I'll do an Internet search to see if there's anything to this magnetic strip story."

Chapter seven

Turns out there was, except it was phrased differently. As part of the Affordable Care Act, all medical records were being coordinated. If you were traveling and went into a hospital in another state, your medical records were available. I'd read about a man who passed out and was thrown into the drunk tank, when it fact he was a diabetic and went into a coma and died because the cops didn't realize it was a physical condition, not booze. Having the medical record on the magnetic strip on the driver's license could save lives. That was the argument.

Trouble is, there can be unintended consequences. Our credit cards have all been replaced by updated ones with a built in computer chip. The chip was to discourage identity theft. What with new technology that little chip could hold a lot more than confirmation of your identity.

But wait: if it was on the driver's license, it would no doubt have your driving record like speeding tickets, accidents, and so on. When you renewed your license or registered the car the DMV knew if you had an unpaid parking ticket in another state. Gotcha.

It didn't take me long to realize where this was leading: an internal passport. The concept of an internal passport like the ones that restricted travel by Soviet citizens inside the old USSR was an idea strongly opposed by Congress. At first you needed one picture ID to pass Homeland Security to get on a plane. That was increased to two. Just swipe the new driver's license or ID and they'd know right away if you were on a no fly list or hadn't paid a parking ticket in Florida.

Would that also apply to taking an interstate bus or AMTRAK?

Freedom of movement was one of the great advantages of life in the good old USA. Used to be. What would I do if my travel was blocked? What would I do? Hitchhike? Little did I know that this could happen to me. Harvey Goldstein, Public Enemy Number One?

The Krieger club card for discounts was innocuous, but I knew there was more to it than getting a coupon deal. It was my job. I loved it, but I could see what Julius meant. I'd make a good Stasi agent or at least an informant. I wondered if that one Homeland Security guy's wife knew he bought all those condoms?

I didn't care if Krieger knew I was buying Twinkies. And we didn't, either, until Krieger offered a discount coupon for a repeat sale. The company knew what I ate. I knew what everybody ate. I felt the power of an insider. OK, you diabetics, I know you are buying Twinkies. You can't hide from me.

I wondered if the Congress would tumble to the consequences of the executive order to put medical records on the backs of drivers licenses. Sounded like a good thing, but then... maybe not. Would the Krieger checkout clerk refuse to sell me the Twinkies because I was diabetic or obese? If we did, customers would go someplace for their junk food.

I wanted to talk to someone from the office about this, not Margaret and not at the office. I wasn't ready to challenge company policy with my boss, but I wasn't afraid to broach some of this to a colleague I could trust. The IT guy was a good bet.

Grabich is our IT guy who fends off the hackers and minds the firewalls. He also helped me out when I didn't remember the latest passwords. He's the only guy in the office who takes growing a beard seriously and ties his long hair in a knot at the back of his head. Like maybe he disguises himself as a derelict when down town, but he's smart. He's smart enough to be tolerated even if he looks slovenly.

Maybe he never sleeps. Grabich is edgy like someone hyped up on caffeine or energy drinks. He's our first line of digital defense. He knows much more than I do about that stuff which may be why he won't carry any cell phone except one of those dumb, prepaid track phones. He's the one who persuaded me to do the same. He showed me how to remove the battery of mine in case I didn't want to be tracked.

Grabich was eager to explain that in order for a cell phone conversation to connect, the towers needed to know where your phone was. The phone sends out a little ping that says "here I am." Police used the system to zero in on fleeing criminals. Grabich not only doesn't want to be hacked, he doesn't want to be followed.

The pings put out by a cell phone are not as accurate as a GPS. If we had one of those embedded, a guy couldn't sneak into a whore house without being tracked.

Maybe Grabich's doing something illegal on the side. More to the point, he's privy to information that could be used against the company's best interests. Margaret better not tell him to get a haircut and a shave for fear of him quitting and taking information elsewhere.

Grabich, I learned one day when he figuratively let his hair down, had been a teenaged hacker who graduated from video games like War craft to the real world. He hinted that he had got himself in trouble at one time while in high school. He broke into the school's data system and changed a grade from a C- to a B+, for, as he explained, you don't cheat for an A if you are a C- student. At unexpected uncharacteristic A attracts too much attention.

Grabich studied the subjects he liked like math and blew off civics. The upshot of all these revelations was that I knew he was almost a straight arrow, having reformed, but was not above something shady when it was necessary. I was soon to find out what that might be.

I asked Ursula if we might invite Grabich and his partner for burgers on our patio. I didn't know if he was married, had a so-called significant other, or was gay. More to the point, I didn't know if he was vegetarian. Would he prefer wine, beer, or diet soda? I'd cover all bets and have a little of everything on hand.

As long as I ran the grill and we avoided much washing up, like using paper plates and disposable plastic cups, Ursula was game. "It's your party, Harvey. You do the work."

Grabich said he'd bring his girl friend, which answered one question anyway.

I looked forward to Sunday and wondered how I could best tell him about Uncle Julius and the clipping. If anyone knew about the secret plan to load drivers licenses with other data, Grabich would, or could find out. If the Germans knew, why didn't we?

Chapter eight

Just in case Grabich's girl friend didn't eat beef, I bought some chicken drumsticks to grill, too. It's a gas grill, so no need to fuss with charcoal and explosive lighter fluid. Did that once and got my nose singed.

Your choice of vehicle says a lot about you. Grabich arrived a half hour late in a classic old Carmen Gia, VW's attempt at a sports car. You seldom see one of those on the road. It must cost him a chunk of his pay to keep it running.

"Had to adjust the timing," he apologized as Ursula directed him to the bathroom to scrub the grease off his hands. "The Gia is still running the old four banger. I wanted to locate a Porsche engine, but they're pretty scarce."

Me, I consider a car just a means of getting around. Ursula will sneak our Toyota into a car wash but I'm satisfied if I can see out the windshield. Numbers are my thing, not machinery. If self-drive cars are available, that would be my choice. It would give me more time to think instead of watching tail lights in front of me. Driving is too stressful.

Considering Grabich's hairy appearance, I expected his girl friend to be some hippy type. Turned out Mia was from Iran, dressed modestly in a spotless, tailored white outfit with long sleeves and a head scarf, plus slacks and gold sandals. She said she worked at Macy's in the shoe department.

She wore several gold bracelets on each wrist and had a tiny diamond pierced on her nostril. I wondered if Macy's permitted facial hardware, but this was discreet. She was modest as her hair covering might suggest, and didn't talk about herself, at least not to me. Ursula noticed that I had noticed and gave me The Look.

Summer in Cleveland can be hot. Ursula wore shorts, a sleeveless shirt and her wide-brimmed sun hat. It was quite a contrast.

The Look didn't bother me. I had the couple over so I could buttonhole Grabich, not bird dog his girl friend.

They had brought along a bottle of sparkling cider, which suggested that Mia didn't drink alcohol, so she was probably a serious Moslem.

31

I waited until we had our burgers and broke up into two conversations, Ursula and Mia, and me and Grabich. We were both drinking Sam Adams beer from the bottles, having eschewed the plastic cups.

I wasn't sure how to get into my topic, but Grabich broached it for me. "I hear you had a visit from Homeland Security. This have something to do with your trip to Europe?"

"Sort of."

"What did you do? Contact some terrorist group? Witness a bombing?"

"Nothing like that. I think Ursula's Uncle Julius reported on us."

Grabich raised his eyebrows and peered over the top of his bottle of beer. "What?"

"We just stopped in for coffee at Ursula's Uncle Julius. Turned out Julius is an old Stasi secret police cop from pre-unification days."

"Seriously?"

"Seriously. I think that once you're in the secret police it never leaves you. The guy must be almost ninety years old."

"And still at it?"

"I think so. He even sent me a clipping from Der Spiegel I wanted to ask you about."

"What's it say?"

"It's in German. Ursula translated it. Seems our government had a conference with Interpol. There's an executive order from our President to put our medical records on the backs of all driver's licenses and ID cards."

"What's Interpol got to do with medical records? That's a police organization. Are they afraid we'll steal aspirin?"

I hadn't thought about that aspect. I remembered the Krieger tracking of purchases. "Could be for a database search of people who get too many barbiturates by prescription."

Grabich gave me a sarcastic look. "Surely, Harvey you know prescriptions are confidential information."

"Yeh, right." In my job I just assume nothing is confidential. "But it is a thought. Tracking barbiturate purchases could predict potential overdoses or at least identify people who were addicted."

"And this is the business of Interpol?"

"I'm guessing. That's only a possibility. Heck, Krieger could do that anyway, but that's not part of our marketing strategy. We aren't being health watchdogs." I thought maybe we should. Hadn't I pretended to be watchdog over the two Homeland Security agents' health? But that was just a tease.

"But Interpol is?" He was skeptical.

"I don't think they are. I think police have enough trouble watching for purchases of guns, ammo, and explosives."

Grabich shook his head. "They don't have time for that, either."

"Right. But the cloud might."

That gave him pause. "I haven't seen anything about that order to put medical records on drivers licenses. You sure you're not just blowing smoke?"

I shook my head. "I don't know. If Ursula's Uncle somehow reports our visit to some intelligence agency and it gets back to me, someone is being awfully paranoid."

"Maybe it's you who are paranoid, Harvey."

I sighed. "You're probably right. I thought you, being our IT guardian against all intruders and hackers, would be sensitive to this sort of thing."

Grabich put down his empty bottle. "I am." Now he seemed irritated. "I hoped this cookout would be an escape from all that shit. Now you've set me off."

"I'm sorry." I changed the subject. "Ready for coffee and pastry? Ursula found a Danish kringle at the specialty bakery. It's her contribution to this."

Grabich didn't know what a kringle was, which was a good change from the serious conversation we'd just had. But he was right. Our discussion about the potential use of that medical information had put him into his investigative mode. I regretted it, for now I suspected he wouldn't get any sleep that night, either.

I cautioned him not to talk about the executive order at the office. I also didn't want any internal emails or cell phone calls about it. The cubicles we live in aren't sound proof. The gossip mill had already churned with the visit from Homeland Security. I could tell by the odd looks I got from some people in the break room. If Grabich had learned something he could pass me a hand-written note or we could meet in the parking garage like Deep Throat.

He thought the secrecy was unnecessary but would humor me.

As he and Mia pulled away from our driveway in that old Carmen Gia with a rumble of the leaky exhaust, I wondered if Homeland Security would be suspicious of him having an Iranian girl friend.

That was the trouble with having a tendency to suspicion and conspiracy theories. Everything starts to look weird.

I asked Ursula what she though of Mia. "She was a student of economics," Ursula explained, "but she ran out of money. Technically she's not supposed to work with a student visa, but that expired. She's illegal. Nervous about her status."

"Must be stressful, not knowing."

Ursula's tenth grade students include many children of single parents, children of illegals but born in this country. She also has in her English class lots of kids still learning our language. I'd never lived abroad or had to deal with visas and government documents. The most I ever had to do was register for the draft and show my birth certificate to apply for the passport that got us to Europe. Once there we didn't need visas for Holland, Denmark or Germany, so I had difficulty imagining how awkward it must be for Mia. No wonder she found a refuge in Grabich.

Maybe she'd make a play for him for a marriage of convenience to secure a green card. That's illegal but not uncommon.

She seemed a nice girl, vulnerable, but poised. Ursula explained that Mia came from a well to do middle class family in Iran, but her father was too outspoken for the regime and was in prison on some trumped up charge.

Grabich was taking a chance. His job at Krieger was sensitive and required discretion even though it was not one of those government positions that required a security clearance. Grabich had been a hacker as a teenager, but now that he was older and wiser he was legitimate, even though he might revert to his old activity.

Uncle Julius would have put Grabich on a list of potentially suspicious persons, consorting with an illegal alien. But this was not East Germany. We were not a police state, at least not overtly. Mia was a Moslem, but not all Moslems were potential terrorists even though some paranoid Islamophobes might think so.

Chapter nine

After I had cleaned up the picnic mess, which consisted of putting all the recyclables in the recyclable bin and wire brushing the grill, I turned on my home laptop. I usually don't touch a computer at home, having been at it all day at the office, but I don't use the office computer for personal stuff. My monitor there has access to too much sensitive information. If I stumbled into malware that counted keystrokes, some hacker might gain access to the company confidential files. At home I use a different email address too, though I view every connection with suspicion.

With my social media shut down, no more personal Face book or Twitter accounts, I stuck to public browsers, mainly Chrome, and searched using key words for anything that might reveal something about the president's executive order. The website for Whitehouse.gov didn't show the order about the drivers license data among the current issues of interest, but when I searched the site specifically for it I got a short paragraph and was directed to Health and Human Services. Since it had to do with the Affordable Care Act it came under that cabinet post. I found a link to the text of the agreement.

The agreement was surprisingly short for a government document. I might have expected a hundred pages. This was only five, and so cryptically written in beaurocratese that it was either unintelligible or could mean all things to all men. Something like that doesn't have to be classified because nobody could understand it. It could have been summarized in one sentence, and that I already knew. What I didn't get were the details and how this connected with other programs. I'm a number cruncher, not a lawyer.

I realized that routing the order through the ACA avoided a congressional committee where any sniff of an internal passport would be noisily objected to. This invasion of privacy was being sneaked in through the back door, like one of those add-on items in the budget nobody reads.

That was how that scoundrel Solomon changed one sentence that enabled him to swindle Indian tribes of over a million bucks. Of course, he eventually went to jail in disgrace. Unfortunately Solomon was a Jew and when one of our tribe turns out to be evil we are all ashamed.

I wondered what would come next? Unlike passports, drivers licenses were issued by the states. That meant the new regulation had to clear hurdles in fifty states. I didn't think it would work. It would cost plenty for every state to reissue or alter drivers licenses. Still, if done as licenses were renewed eventually it would be on every one. That would take years.

What other acts might hurry this program forward?

Visa, Discover, Master Charge and American Express frequently updated their credit cards in defense against hackers and identity thieves. Could the medical information be stored on those new chipped cards? Would the credit card companies be willing to do it? Or could they be coerced? The government had a lot of ways to put pressure on companies. The Treasury might also provide cash or credit incentives, too.

The was getting me far beyond that short clipping in Der Spiegel.

Just so I didn't get dead ended, I subscribed to free newsletters and clips from the relevant agencies. They're always eager to do some PR. The only risk was I'd get a lot of spam. At least, I thought it was my only risk.

The trouble was, just as I tracked grocery customers' purchases, someone was always watching. Those government agencies were tracking the queries of interested citizens. It reminded me of Uncle Julius and everybody watching everybody. Download three manuals for making bombs in your kitchen and you get a visit from the Secret Service.

Like Julius said, we were lucky, if you can call it that. The watchers didn't have to stake themselves out all night in a cold doorway needing to take a leak. The watchdog programs just chugged away merrily while people like me had cookouts on our patios and slept soundly, tucked cozily in our beds. Like they say, ignorance is bliss.

The summer was ending. Ursula was making preparations for a new semester at the high school. She was teaching tenth grade English and an introduction to German. There was a big teachers meeting coming up. Last year it was about bullying. This one was something about discrimination against transgender pupils and unisex bathrooms.

"It's typical," Ursula was fuming. "We're underfunded. They've cut shop classes, music, choir, art and drama. I'll be lucky if they don't cut foreign languages. But bathrooms! Good grief. Just put up a unisex sign."

At the office I was, as usual, immersed in data crunching. There were always new approaches. If a direct mail campaign could be directed to a specific group of customers, it would save a lot of postage. There was no sense it churning out a ton of junk mail that was simply thrown out without being read. The typical one percent response wasn't good enough. You got better odds for a return. by being selective.

Then one Saturday I got a surprise first class letter at home. This one had a return address on the envelope, USIA, one of those government acronyms and a post office box. If it weren't for the warning "Penalty for private use $300" that confirmed this was official I wouldn't have even opened it, figuring it was an appeal for money. After the Wounded Warrior charity scandal, anything with the word Veteran in the name was suspect. We no longer open those. But this one didn't have a pre-printed address label. My address was hand written in a neat, cursive script.

People in my job will do anything to get attention. Even letters from the First Lady in the White House had the salutation "Dear Harvey." Thanks to computers merging addresses and the contents of a letter, you can gussy up a communication like that. I was tempted to reply to the President's wife in the first person like we were old buddies. I never met her. It was all a ploy to get me to contribute to the political party.

The letter from USIA was not junk mail. "We are impressed with your work at Krieger and would like to discuss a project with you. Can you meet me for lunch at the Hilton on Wednesday at noon? It will be worth your while."

It was signed J.K. Rawlings. What was this, a joke? Or did that famous author of lucrative Harry Potter books take on a government job as a backup in case royalties dropped off?

I showed it to Ursula. She said, "USIA? At least that's not Homeland Security or the FBI."

"But Rawlings? What should I bring? My magic wand?"

"Harvey, a cloak of invisibility might be better." She saw the worried look on my forehead and added, "You're not a person of interest are you?"

I wondered if this had to do with my web research. At least I hadn't downloaded instructions for making bombs in the kitchen. Uncle Julius would love that. "I wouldn't be so sure."

Ursula turned to her preparations for the next term. "Maybe you'll get a nice lunch."

"You mean like I take you to dinner and expect to spend the night?"

"You don't have to take me to dinner for that, honey. I'm already game. Anything to escape from this paperwork."

"Sounds good to me. What are you doing this afternoon?"

"I thought you'd never ask."

Chapter ten

Lunch on a work day sounded like it would last more than my half an hour in the break room with my brown bagged sandwich. Just to make sure I wouldn't be in trouble with Boss Margaret, I showed her the USIA letter. "I might have to be a little late."

To demonstrate her toughness, Boss Margaret has a whip mounted on the wall. I suspect it's for S&M, but I wouldn't dare ask. She was wearing a knit one piece form-fitting outfit that required her to keep her knees together whenever she sat down. No wonder Ursula pegged Margaret as a dangerous woman. She did hire some token women, but what I suspected she wanted was a stable of good looking guys she could dominate.

Her office is all glass like an aquarium, but has blinds and one wonders what's going on in there when she draws them. She scares me. I guess fear is a good motivator.

She hadn't forgotten the Homeland Security guys. "You're getting to be a person of interest like they say on the cop shows."

"I hope not in that way. I haven't done anything."

She teased, "Tell that to the judge. Want me to send you a cake with a file in it?"

I thought, 'What about a file with a cake in it?"

She must watch one of those crime series. Ursula and I are into the British mysteries on Public Broadcasting. "This is USIA, whatever that is." I waved the letter. "This is an invitation to lunch, not a subpoena." Maybe she's into conspiracy theories, too. I read that half of Americans believe we're been invaded by aliens. What we've been invaded by is Mexicans, and they want to pick strawberries, not turn us into zombies.

"Take as long as you like," Margaret said. "Just don't put your lunch on the company's tab."

I thanked her and, followed by the stares of everybody within view, went back to my cubicle to think. Maybe it was time to confer with Grabich, see if he had figured out anything. I called him and asked to meet him in the parking garage after work.

Parking garages always play a prominent role in thrillers, maybe because unlike a crowded street scene requiring many extras, a parking garage is easily closed off to rubberneckers. Ours has CCT cameras at the entrance and exit, but they don't cover everything. Grabich and I could have an apparently innocuous conversation without being noticed. I was feeling like a Deep Throat conspirator, but then, why was Homeland Security after me?

Grabich was wearing an old sports jacket with the logo of a team I didn't recognize. When he was a teenager he was a wannabe hacker who called himself Wasp. Now he's left the dark side and is with us. He walks with a furtive slouch like maybe he has the weight of the world on his shoulders. Of course, the weight is our data security. That's heavy enough. It's a big responsibility.

I showed him the USIA letter.

He was mildly curious. "So? Smells to me like you're being recruited for a job. Sure this is USIA and not CIA?"

I didn't know. "Maybe the USIA is just a cover for something else. I mean, I didn't think those Homeland Security characters were authentic. They could have been anybody."

Could have been until I got their Krieger numbers and learned their home addresses and choice of foods.

Grabich suggested, "Better ask for ID."

We had to step aside as a company car turned the corner of the ramp and headed for the exit.

I protested. "It's just a lunch."

"Maybe it's the Mossad."

He was kidding, of course. I hoped. I may be Jewish, but I'm not Israeli. I had no secrets to sell like that Pollard guy who got thirty years for deals with an ally.

"Harvey, look at it this way. Those government people are just as eager as you are to have a swell restaurant meal and not a brown bag sandwich in the break room. And have it on the government tab. You're just having a conversation. Enjoy."

I agreed, tried to put aside my suspicions. "Have you found out anything about the Seventh Paradigm?"

Grabich rocked his head on his shoulders like a character in some Bollywood movie. "Only that some people call what you're doing the fourth paradigm."

"I'll use that term at the lunch and see how it goes down."

"You got to be careful. NSA may think that just mentioning the Seventh Paradigm mans you are privy to something top secret. Just Goggling the term flagged me as a subversive."

Harley L. Sachs

Chapter eleven

On Wednesday I dressed up for the lunch at least as far as my wardrobe allows. I wore my only summer sport jacket. I do own a black suit, but I save it for funerals and weddings. Ursula and I are between those stages in life, too old to attend many weddings, young enough so the older generation is still around. You don't need a black suit for christenings and anniversaries.

I drove to the hotel where we were supposed to meet and handed the valet key to the kid who parks the cars, not that there's anything worth stealing in the trunk, but you never know. Valets are known the help themselves to the parking meter change, sort of a self-serve tipping arrangement. If there was a parking fee, I'd give USIA the tab.

I had no idea what J.K. Rawlings looked like or if it was a man or a woman, but I was confident that USIA knew my mug shot from when I still had a Face book account. I never tried to be incognito or invisible before that business with Uncle Julius. By then it was too late.

A woman in the hotel lobby looked up from the book she was pretending to read and gave me the nod. She was wearing a maroon power suit, stylish enough for most occasions short of a gala ball, but subdued enough not to draw attention. Instead of a purse she carried a briefcase that might contain a laptop or a gun. Whatever it was, it was heavy.

She stood up as I approached. "Mr. Goldstein," she said as if to introduce me. "May I call you Harvey?"

"As long as you don't shorten it to Har. What do I call you? Mrs. Rawlings?" It's always confusing. MS went out of style. You can't go wrong with Misses. I didn't see any wedding ring. Not that I was shopping, but Ursula always notices these things and trained me.

Rawlings wore her hair short and close to her face. She was blonde but needed a touch up at the roots. Ursula would be proud of my noticing.

"My friends call me J.K."

I didn't think I was her friend, but I was willing to go along with it. "What's this about, J.K.? I know you don't just want to feed me lunch."

She evaded the question. "I don't care for hotel dining rooms. I know a better place than this," she said and led me out a side entrance. She had actually parked on the street, a black Camry SUV with a government owned license plate and tinted windows so you couldn't tell if there was anybody in the back or maybe a team of kidnappers. I didn't expect the government to spring for a Lexus. "You eat fish?"

Maybe she knew I was Jewish and was making sure she wasn't tempting me to break one of the dietary laws. "Sure." At least she didn't offer Chinese. It's a joke that all Jews like to eat in Chinese restaurants, even though pork is on the menu.

Instead of a hoped for high class eating establishment and a potential fifty dollar steak meal, Rawlings drove to a Red Lobster. Maybe she didn't know Jews weren't allowed to eat shellfish, but I don't keep kosher anyway.

She picked a booth out of the main customer traffic where we could talk without being overheard. The wait person was a tired-looking teenager kid whose hair was tied back in a pony tail. He wore a long-sleeved white shirt that didn't quite hide a snake tattoo on his left wrist. He brought the menus and J.K. pointed to an item. "I'll have that."

I saw there was a special seafood platter with shrimp, cod, and scallops, so picked that one. We were watered and I was ready for her questions. Obviously she knew all about me already, so didn't bother to ask what I did. "How do you like your job at Krieger?"

"Always a new challenge," I said, the kind of answer that could be taken many ways as in "It's a tough pain in the ass" or "I like tricky problems and enjoy solving them" the kind of answer you save for a job interview. Not that I considered this lunch a job interview. I wasn't in the market. Ursula and I were both working and we had a mortgage that we'll be paying on until we retire.

Obviously I wasn't going after Boss Margaret's job, but data management has many facets and potential levels of employment. It would be nice if I could work at home, for instance, and sit around all day in my skivvies or pajamas. Krieger wouldn't allow that. Nobody logged on to the company system except at the office. There was nothing like having a laptop stolen by a burglar or left in a taxi for some skillful computer person who mined it for information.

Even so, working at home would be better than being in a boiler room, for instance in Bangalore India or Costa Rica, with thirty other computer jerks, a step down from having your own cubicle in air conditioned Cleveland, Ohio.

"Does Ursula like Cleveland?"

"It's OK. Nice Jewish community, not that we're active."

"She like K-12 teaching?"

J.K. Was showing off that she knew everything about us. Did she also know what brand of toilet paper we bought? Krieger knew. It was all in my data base, strong two-ply. "It's OK. German is an elective, so those kids are better motivated."

"How's your German?"

"I know a few words, like danke schoen and heimatssicherheitsdienst."

J.K.'s quizzical look told me she didn't know heimatssicherheitsdienst. I explained, "Homeland Security."

She understood.

"You know I had a visit from Homeland Security."

J.K. nodded. "What did you think about that?"

I took a sip of water. I was having a case of dry mouth, which I realized was a sign of stress or fear. "I thought it was weird."

"Weird?"

"They knew Ursula and I had a coffee visit with her Uncle Julius in Hamburg. He's an old Stasi secret policeman from before the reunification."

She knew about that, too.

I knew I was treading on sensitive territory, but thought, what the hell? I asked, "Did Julius report our visit to some German intelligence agency? I assumed he was retired."

She thought about it a moment. How much I needed to know. "Julius Schwartzman is on an Interpol watch list."

I wasn't surprised.

"Your wife phoned him on her cell phone."

So that was it. The call was no doubt recorded someplace and triggered an alert. I was glad the call was on Ursula's phone, and not mine, but in the end it didn't make any difference. I took a chance at this opportunity. "Uncle Julius warned me about the seventh paradigm. What do you know about that?"

"I don't talk about that."

I had crossed the line into forbidden territory. "What about the fourth paradigm?"

She was obviously being cautious. "That's what you do now. It's all about information. Would you like to work in the fifth?"

"I don't know what it is."

"Integration," J.K. Said.

I thought about my current projects at Krieger. Sampling the data and searching for the most likely customers for kids' clothes or lawn furniture. Those were pretty puerile.

Granted, instead of working inside Krieger's own private database, someone had integrated the NSA screening of all our phone calls and the German security service watch list.

She saw from my expression that I had figured it out. It was if she could read my mind. I wouldn't make a good poker player. "Putting together lists of customers for special coupons is pretty basic stuff nowadays. You can do better than that."

This was turning into a cat and mouse contest. "Are you offering something?"

"Possibly. Have you ever been to Salt Lake City?"

I hadn't been in Utah or even west of the Mississippi. "Is there something there besides Mormons?"

She caught my eye and laughed. "Yes. Gentiles. If you were there, you'd be one of them."

"How so?"

"Anybody who isn't a Mormon is a gentile. You'd be a Jewish gentile." What else did she know about me? Would I want to know?

I have to admit that was a new one on me. "I'm not in Salt Lake City."

"There's also the Novacom cloud. It's not in the city, but in the mountains. I think you should see it."

Did she expect me to fly out there on a tourist junket? I heard the Mormon cathedral is off limits to gentiles. "I've already taken my vacation for the year." Kreiger's not like Germany where you get six weeks.

Our lunch arrived. Munching on coconut shrimp I had time to think. The cloud. I remembered the cloud was somewhere in Utah. Krieger kept some data in the cloud, backups in case we had a massive breakdown or Grabich failed to protect us from a destructive all-consuming virus. I'd have to think about that.

They'd been doing the same thing I was at Krieger, except someone had seen a connection between Uncle Julius and my sifting customers' buying habits to find new connections. I could see, or thought I understood, what J.K. Was getting at. They wanted me to apply my Krieger experience to the cloud.

45

We finished our meal, which I was no longer tasting, which was a pity because I like shrimp in its various recipe permutations. I had guessed, but asked, anyway, for confirmation. "Can you give me an example of this integration?"

This was getting close to forbidden territory for her. "Just for instance, how would you combine driving records with grocery store purchasing habits?"

It sounded awfully far fetched. "I don't see the relationship. What would a parking ticket have to do with choice of brands of toilet paper?"

She laughed, but I wasn't sure if it was a laugh of amusement or of anxiety. People can laugh when frightened, too, as a kind of defense mechanism. "That's for you to find out."

It didn't make sense to me, but her hypothetical example had been chosen not to reveal her real purpose, only to expose me to a paradigm, a different way of thinking. "I think I understand. A relationship of voting patterns to gun purchases could be significant, but that's pretty oblique."

"That's what I mean by integration."

I could see the point. "That would be a great puzzle. I like puzzles. Most of my work really is puzzles, you know, though I don't do crosswords. I do some sudoku sometimes."

"So you're interested."

If this was a subtle job interview, I wasn't going to leap at it. "Let's just say I'm curious. It's a 'what if?' situation."

The lunch interview was over. "Nice to have met you, Harvey."

"So what happens now?" I assumed she, like Uncle Julius, was going to report to somebody. "Will I hear from you again?"

"Not me."

Somebody else, I suspected. "Thanks for the lunch, anyway."

I forgot to ask if she had a Krieger club card so I could tap into her personal buying habits and other data. If she no longer bought tampons, for instance, I'd know she was into menopause. I guess I'm a data voyeur. Does that mean I'm a creepy person? Maybe. There just ain't no privacy no more. How well I knew.

She drove me back to the hotel. I forgot to ask about the valet service fee and she was gone before I got my car back. The parking fee was more than the lunch. Win some, lose some.

But I knew from our coffee conversation with Uncle Julius about life in the DDR that whatever had been discussed at Red Lobster would be in her report. Whether there was a follow-up depended on how J.K.

assessed me. Following Ursula's advice, I'd write one of my own for the CYA file. You never knew.

When I thought more about it, I decided I had learned more from her than she had from me. She probably knew everything about me, anyway, just as Amazon knew about our buying habits. That was just good marketing strategy. Adopted by the government, well, that was something else.

Chapter twelve

I had to go back to work, of course, and try to concentrate on the latest project. Contrary to company rules, Ursula called me at my cubicle. She was that curious. After my talk with Grabich about security, I've become skittish. I could only tell Ursula I wouldn't talk about anything on the phone and would report when I got home.

Ursula was eager for my report on the lunch. After my welcome home kiss she asked, "So did you go to a fancy steak house? You didn't wear a tie."

I'd forgotten to wear it. I never wear a tie, though I have one in the closet. "Maybe that's why we went to Red Lobster."

That wasn't what she really wanted to know. "So who was this Rawlings person?"

"A woman about forty who needed a touch up at the roots of her dyed blonde hair." It would have been a mistake to say Rawlings was a knockout, which she was. I don't want Ursula to think anybody else is beautiful. "I don't think she was USIA. Might have been NSA. It's all alphabet soup to me."

Ursula was thoughtful. "Did she show you any ID like those Homeland Security guys?"

"I didn't ask. She knew all about me, about us. That was as good as a password."

"So?"

"I think she wanted me to go Utah and be a gentile."

She was wide-eyed. "What?"

"The Novacom cloud is in Utah. Might be in several locations. Something like that needs to be backed up just in case."

"In case of what?"

"Terrorists. Saboteurs. Earthquake. War. Whatever. It think it's like Area 51, land of UFOs and space aliens."

"What's that got to do with you?"

I went to the kitchen and got out the last bottle of Sam Adams. "Nothing."

"Couldn't be nothing, Harvey. People don't come from a government agency and offer you a free lunch for nothing."

"The only thing that made any sense was one word: integration. She said that was the fifth paradigm."

Ursula followed my lead, but her drink was a diet Sprite. She popped the tab and drank from the can. "Explain."

"Uncle Julius didn't report to German intelligence about our visit. Julius is on a watch list. When you phoned him, the penny dropped. I guess any contacts he has are suspicious. My job at Krieger in data management triggered a follow-up visit from Homeland Security."

"Why the visit from this Rawlings person? You're in the grocery business."

"We don't just sell groceries. We sell everything but cars and guns."

Ursula was puzzled. "I don't see the connection between your job at Krieger and Homeland Security."

I tilted back in the recliner chair. "I can only speculate, but say we merged the IRS database with gun registrations. You know we already had that discussion about medical records and driver's licenses. A medical record on a driver's license might provide a warning if a driver might be apoplectic, had apnea, narcolepsy, or diabetes."

She could see the point of that.

I sipped the beer and burped. "Merging would be awfully expensive, and not all those data bases are compatible. Every time a programmer gets his hooks into our system we get crashes and disasters."

"You're not a programmer."

It's not my main job. I come up with ideas and if it's beyond my limited skills one of the programmers figures it out for me. My deal is marketing. "If Grabich plugs a security hole, sometimes he inadvertently dumps something we need. The more complex the programs are, the greater the risk of loopholes and malfunctions."

"How do you fit into that picture?"

I admitted, "I don't. I'm what some people might call a blue sky engineer, and I'm not even an engineer. I deal in 'What ifs?' if that makes any sense."

Ursula said, "My father was a mechanical engineer. He wouldn't have understood the cloud. His view never got above the horizon."

"I know. He enjoyed designing hub caps." It wasn't my idea of greatness, but then, he wouldn't have thought much of my marketing of grocery coupons.

"So what happens now?"

I had finished my beer and carried the bottle to our recycling basket. "Retrench. I already shut down my Face book and Twitter accounts."

"Maybe you should just get used to being watched all the time."

I shook my head. "I don't like it."

"We either get over it or move into a cabin in the woods off the grid, no phones, no TV, and become survivalists. You think?"

That had no appeal, either. There had to be another alternative. I'd ask Grabich for his advice. He would be interested in the fifth paradigm.

In the meantime I had another report to write for my private on paper CYA file.

Chapter thirteen

I gave Grabich a cryptic phone call: meet me after work at Starbucks. We had met once in the parking garage. Now I was afraid to set up a pattern. Patterns turned up on the database. That was how nervous I was getting.

Grabich looked troubled when we met at Starbucks. They have some tables outside, where we were less likely to be overheard.

I carried my latte out to a table. The next table had a couple of kids who were, if body language could be read, in deep courting conversation. On the other side a student was engrossed in her laptop, taking advantage of the free wi-fi.

I was tempted to warn her that anyone on the Starbucks wi-fi could see what she was doing but it was none of my business. My business was with Grabich.

"Uncle Julius didn't report me to Homeland Security," I explained. "Julius, being ex-Stasi, is on a German watch list. Ursula's phone is snooped by NSA, just like everyone else's. You see what I'm getting at?"

Grabich didn't.

"I had lunch yesterday with someone claiming to be from USIA. The key word was integration. German intelligence is integrated with NSA. Integrating all the databases is the fifth paradigm. Could you do that?"

Grabich shook his head. "Not by myself. That would take a lot of people and a lot of money." When he's out of the office he can let his hair down, no bun in the back. He looked pretty wild. I guess that fits with his old hacker's handle, Wasp.

"Imagine," I said, thinking out loud. "Merging all the databases in the cloud, all the customer lists, all the medical and police records all the world's information in one basket."

"And all the credit card transactions." Grabich got it, "Remember that bombing in Washington state? The bomber used fishing lead weights for shrapnel. The police had no fingerprints, but they knew somebody had to buy a lot of lead weights. They checked sporting goods stores and found that Wal-Mart sold a lot of weights to one guy. He paid by credit card. That got him."

"That's what I mean. Integration."

51

"That's just good police work."

"Must have taken a lot of work to check all the sporting goods stores. With the cloud, you could run the check in nanoseconds."

That thought appealed to him.

While he was ruminating over that and sipping his mocha coffee, I added, "At the lunch the USIA woman asked me if I'd been to Utah. That's where the Novacom cloud is."

"One of them."

"You mean there are several?"

"You don't want to risk everything by putting it all in one place. Think of terrorists."

"Where would you put it?"

"In a satellite, but it would be too big." He paused. "Did she want you to move to Utah?"

"She didn't offer me a job. I think she was just assessing me."

Grabich sighed. "You can't be too careful."

"What do you mean?"

Grabich looked around. The young couple had left. The girl with the laptop was taking hand written notes on a spiral notebook. Not of our conversation, I hoped. "This is where I met Mia."

"Really?"

"We were standing in line at the counter and she wasn't sure about all the Starbucks options. She thought an Americano was a funny name for a coffee."

"How long has she been in the country?"

"Just a couple of years. Came in on a student visa."

"What's she studying?"

"She's not. Overstayed. Ran out of money. Mia's one of those millions of illegals whose visas have lapsed. She can't go back to Iran. Her family is on the outs with the regime."

"That's her cover story," I said, indicating that I didn't necessarily believe it. "Isn't it risky for you in your job to be hanging out with an illegal alien?"

"She doesn't know anything about my job. She's computer illiterate."

"What if the Immigration and Naturalization data base catches up with her?"

Grabich smiled. "There are about fifteen million illegals in this country. I suppose if they caught up with her she could ask for political asylum because of her family situation. The Shah may be gone, but his secret police are still there."

"Maybe now they call themselves the religious police in case a woman leaves her house without a male escort."

Grabich didn't think so.

"You two in a serious relationship?"

Grabich reluctantly admitted Mia had moved in with him. He explained that she had run out of rent money and stayed with him a few days, couch surfing. One thing led to another, and now they were a couple.

I didn't think a Moslem girl would dare do that. I gave Grabich a mock interrogator's look. "You mean you are harboring an illegal alien?"

"You make it sound sinister, Harvey."

"No more sinister than Ursula and I having coffee with a distant uncle who just happened to be a retired Stasi colonel."

"What do you suggest I do?"

I had an idea. "Why not hack into Immigration's files and issue her a green card, then get the system to forget you were ever there?"

Grabich smiled and nodded. "I could do that. I think I could do that."

"How?"

He thought a moment, sipped his coffee. "Krieger's employment records. I could make it appear she was on the payroll and had been vetted. I could even create a background check for her."

"You wouldn't actually have her paid?"

"Who me? Putting someone who doesn't actually work on the payroll? In business we only do that for CEOs."

"I think I'll stick to grocery coupons," I said. Grabich could get himself in a lot of trouble. Maybe he already was. Was I? I didn't think so, but with data integration, you never knew what conclusions someone might draw. Uncle Julius said I was lucky, thanks to computers. I wasn't so sure.

Maybe my jokey letter to the Homeland Security guys would precipitate a complaint. That's what I'd get for being a smart ass.

Grabich was one of the few people at the office I could talk to beyond the latest sports score at the water cooler. Now I knew about Mia and his speculation about her status. What if he ended up in court for harboring an alien? What if I had to testify as a character witness? What would I say?

I was beginning to feel what Julius had hinted at. In a police state everyone was afraid of everyone else.

Chapter fourteen

Boss Margaret wanted to be repaid for letting me take that long lunch with Rawlings. I guess she was hungry for gossip. Since I was the only one who had a surprise visit from Homeland Security and now a lunch with USIA I had suddenly become an interesting person not just another computer jockey.

What I was uncertain about was how far anything I said would travel in the grapevine and be distorted under way, like that old party game of telephone. The trouble with gossip was it was behind your back and you had no way to defend yourself from anything malicious or plain wrong. I had to be cautious. Still, I was willing to take a break from the latest brain buster and let her offer me a cup of coffee from her own private brewing machine.

I reported, "Turned out the USIA person was a woman, E.J. Rawlings, like the author of the Harry Potter books, only without a magic wand."

Margaret had not read the books but had taken her daughter to the movies. "Maybe she has a cloak of invisibility."

"She could be a spook, for all I know. She wanted to know if I'd been to Utah."

"Utah? Is she LDS?"

I knew LDS stood for Latter Day Saints and wondered if Margaret was a Mormon. "Utah is where the cloud is."

Of course, Margaret knew about the cloud. Krieger stores its backup files there.

"She also talked about paradigms. No explanation."

Margaret was unsure about the meaning of paradigms.

I continued. "The integration of all databases creates a new level of knowledge." I corrected myself. "Potential knowledge."

Margaret shook her head. "You mean our database? That's proprietary."

I agreed.

"What would sales figures for the Krieger house brands have to do with knowledge?"

I sighed. Just because she was the boss didn't mean she had to understand everything we data foot soldiers did. "You know the world's chess champion was beaten by a computer."

She didn't play chess.

"And the champion Go player got beat, too."

She didn't know Go.

"That TV quiz show. You must have seen that one. A computer named Watson won that one too. They just stuffed it with all the information that might come up in a question. It was fast enough to sift through all of it to come up with the right answers."

Margaret still didn't see that that had to do with the Krieger data and Rawlings' interest in me.

I gave up. Maybe Margaret doesn't make mental connections the way I do. She's not a blue sky speculator. I doubt if she's into conspiracy theories like who really shot J. F. K. People like conspiracy theories and will believe anything-- like there are space aliens at Area 51 or Obama is part of a Moslem plan for world domination. Then again, someone thought there was something sinister about Ursula's and my visit to her distant Uncle Julius. Go figure.

I took another tack. "What if the government wants me to go out to Utah? Just for an inspection tour?"

Now she did see what I was driving at. "Is that a job interview? You dickering for a raise, Harvey?"

"I'm not dickering for anything. I just want you to know what's going on, at least as far as I know myself. No secrets. You're the boss, after all."

She appreciated that. "I'm a patriotic citizen. If the government wants you to take off a few days for special service we can manage that. A short leave of absence without pay. You used up your vacation time for that trip to Europe. I'm not going to finance a job hunt."

"Thanks." I didn't know what I was thanking her for. No offer of a trip to Utah had been made. I wasn't looking for another job. I was spooked by the whole business, but curious. I added, "For the coffee. Must be a special roast."

I wondered how Margaret would misinterpret what I had told her. My guess was that she would think I was shopping for another job, or at least a raise. Those might be good thoughts, but if she decided to start looking for a replacement when I had no intention to leave, that would be bad. If whoever she found was a better prospect, I might be dropped. You can do that in this state: fired without cause or notice. In the data business they take your keys, walk you out the door, and kill your passwords so you can't cripple the system out of spite.

Grabich might be able to fix himself a back door into the system as a last resort, but I'm no hack and not a vindictive person

This was all speculation. Now there was nothing to do but do my job and wait. Oh, and add a report of the conversation with Boss Margaret to my CYA private file. You never knew.

All this was making me more nervous. I thought it might be time to put my personal home computer in the free TOR system. In it, all emails are routed in bits and pieces through other computers all around the world so no one knows where they come from or where they go. It was developed by the US Navy and the police to protect informants and spies from being outed. Where did I fit in?

Chapter fifteen

When I got home I downloaded the free Tor program and signed up. It did leave my computer vulnerable, for it would be part of the international random scrambling of messages. I'd heard that in Germany some kid's computer had been part of the Tor system and picked up kiddy porn on his hard drive without his knowledge. He got busted for it. Germans are not very friendly to pedophiles and kiddy pornographers. Adult porn, well, that was OK.

Tor was a tradeoff. It added anonymity, but with some risk. My computer would also be a link for police informants and CIA spies who might be passing though it, too..

Grabich had told me about Tor.

I didn't really want anything sensitive in my emails, which were mostly political junk and spam. NSA was watching.

The next morning there was a hand written note on my keyboard, sealed in an envelope. It said simply "Starbucks after work." No need for a signature. I knew who it was from.

Notes like that can throw you off your rhythm.

Ursula and I had plans to go to a movie that evening, which meant an early dinner, so a Starbucks meeting could delay my return to our condo.

When I got to the coffee store Grabich was already there, his hair still in its office knot.

He dispensed with the usual preliminaries. "I've got a problem."

I wondered what problem he had which I, not being a programmer/hack could help him with. I was out of his league.

"It's Mia," he said, after looking round to see if anyone was paying attention to us. Nobody was.

"What about her? You two have a falling out?" I'm no marriage counselor. I don't want to interfere with anybody's domestic issues. You never intervene in a bar fight. People throw chairs. You can get killed that way.

"I took your advice about the green card thing," Grabich said.

"My advice? What are you talking about?"

He stared down into his coffee cup. When he looked up he had a sheepish look. "I should have let it alone, just let it ride. As long as

57

nobody noticed, she could hang out for years without being picked up. When I broke into the Immigration system and tried to alter the expiration date of her visa, which would be the simplest solution, I got spotted as an intruder."

"So now you think she'll be deported?"

Grabich fiddled with his hair and undid the rubber bands that held it together at the back. Now his face was almost hidden by all that wild, black hair. "Her father's in prison in Iran. If she goes back to Iran she could disappear. Be killed."

"So what are you going to do?"

"If INS tracks her down to my place she may be handed over to ICE and put in an internment camp like all those other illegals. You know the government has deported 240,000 people already?"

"She needs a lawyer."

"If ICE pegs me, I could be fired from Krieger. Margaret is paranoid about leaks."

"And you're a leaker."

He shook his head. "I'm not a leaker. Krieger data is safe. Mia isn't. That's why I wanted to talk to you."

I waited for him to get up his courage and make whatever pitch he had.

Finally he broached the subject. "Could you and Ursula put up Mia in your spare room for a few days until I find something else for her?"

It's a small room. We use if for a joint office. I joked, "We were saving that for a nursery."

His eyebrows went up. "Is Ursula pregnant?"

"We're thinking about it. Seriously, I can't invite another woman into my apartment without Ursula's approval. She doesn't like competition."

"Oh? I didn't know you were so desirable, Harvey."

"Women just fall over me. It's my red suspenders." It was true that red suspenders had a powerful effect on women, but most of them were old enough to be my grandmother.

"This is serious, Harvey. I'm afraid my place will be raided."

"INS or ICE could pick her up at her job." At first I forgot where Mia worked, then remembered, Macy's shoes..

While Grabich stewed I thought about it. Grabich is a friend in trouble. What's a friend for? "You'll have to ask Ursula. And don't use your cell phone."

Grabich knew about my concern about NSA and cell phones. "What do you expect me to do, mail a letter sealed in aluminum foil like that German Uncle?"

"No. Just stop by. We were going to a movie tonight. I'll tell Ursula we'll postpone it, that I'll explain later." I added, "Bring Mia and her stuff but leave it in the back seat of that Carmen Gia. Seven o'clock? After dinner." There's nothing like bringing home unexpected dinner guests to make enemies of the cook, and this was my night to turn on the microwave. My leftovers wouldn't feed four.

Grabich was hugely relieved. He got up to leave. "Thanks, Harvey. You're a lifesaver."

"I haven't said yes. It's up to Ursula."

If we did let Mia hide with us a few days that made me a harborer of an illegal alien. What would USIA and Homeland Security think of that?

Chapter sixteen

I hurried back to break the news to Ursula. She was looking forward to the movie. It was a date night and she was disappointed. Every couple has to have a date night. Keeps a relationship from going stale.

The unexpected visit was a distraction. Ursula doesn't like surprises and likes to be in control of things. That's OK with me, for it leaves my mind free to solve those Krieger puzzles. Ursula had liked Mia when we had that cookout on the patio, but the relationship was casual. You don't invite people to move in with you on the strength of one afternoon of conversation by the grill. At least we don't. Maybe we're old fashioned. Or cautious. Almost makes me feel middle aged, which I am not even if I did break thirty last year.

Patio conversations tend to be superficial. We didn't know Mia aside from her being Iranian and a Moslem. I didn't know the difference between Shia or Sunni. We didn't know if my being a secular Jew meant Mia would think that I was part of a great Satanic world conspiracy.

I'm not Israeli, and though I believe Jews need a homeland someplace, I'm not a dyed in the wool Zionist. There are all kinds of Jews, even humanists who don't believe in God,, and I guess there are at least as many variations of Moslems. Best to keep religious differences out of our conversations. It's easier for me just to say they are all goyim or, as Boss Margaret said about those who are not LDS, all gentiles. A discussion of religion was bound to cause friction. Political differences were more the level of my interest, like what was it like for Uncle Julius to live in a police state? I guess it's different if you are the cop.

Ursula, being a woman, as I'd noticed when we first met, had different concerns, like not wanting a potential competitor wandering through the apartment in her skivvies. I hadn't paid much attention to Mia at our patio cookout when I was having a serious discussion with Grabich, but Ursula invariably detected that I'd noticed Mia was an attractive female.

Ursula's got radar. She's smart enough not to mention that aspect of having a female house guest. That would only anticipate a problem that at least then did not exist. I'm not in the market for another woman. I was glad Ursula was mainly interested in how we would manage with the use of our single bathroom. She's so practical.

Grabich and Mia arrived just after seven and I played host by offering coffee and some chocolate cookies from Trader Joe's. Just because I work for Krieger doesn't preclude my doing a little shopping at a competitor.

"How serious is this?" I asked our visitors. "Are you sure you're not overreacting?"

Grabich hesitated before revealing his own secret. "NSA may be watching everybody, but we can watch them, too, if you get my drift." The ex-hacker had his ways.

"So there's an investigation about Mia?"

"They've discovered that she overstayed her visa and no longer lives at her old address. This isn't like Europe where you always have to register your address with the police."

"I should think they'd track her through her credit card purchases and bills."

"She does that stuff on line," Grabich said. "My address isn't connected to her."

I reviewed my own concerns. "But she has a cell phone, doesn't she?" I looked over at Mia who was sitting nervously on the edge of our Ikea couch. "She can be tracked."

"They haven't got that serious yet. She's low priority. She's not a felon or bank robber or terrorist. The check on her whereabouts has been casual, so far. It's a matter of time."

Ursula gave Mia an earnest look. "Do you think you will be any safer staying with us than with him?"

Mia shook her head, her face screwed up by anxiety. "I don't know. I cannot go back to Persia."

It was up to Ursula. I think the bathroom issue was more important to her than the risk of an ICE raid. She assented. "You can stay for a couple of days, but Grabich, you better fix this up pretty quick."

Grabich was preoccupied. You could almost see the wheels and gears of his head whirring. Finally he returned to earth. "I think I can erase Mia from the INS records. Delete her record entirely. So far as they'll know, she never existed."

"Brilliant!" But I knew better. "Everything is backed up in the cloud. Once in the system nothing goes away. You can't delete Mia from the backup files."

Grabich smiled. "Remember that last scene in *Raiders of the Lost Ark* when the crate with the original Ten Commandments is moved into the catacombs of the government warehouse, never to be found again? The cloud is like that."

I knew what it meant for a system to be overloaded. Krieger had so many purchase records that they were taxing the computer system the company was leasing. "So you're counting on it taking so long for them to catch up with Mia that she'll already be retired on social security."

Grabich admitted, "I'd forgotten about the social security thing. Then there's the IRS. It's hard to disappear entirely."

"Just so she doesn't pledge to the Jewish National Fund. They'll always find you." It was an old inside joke. Neither of them got it.

The upshot was we agreed to let her stay until Grabich did his thing with the various data banks to make Mia invisible. I thought it was a cool idea. Would I ever have to become invisible? It was a thought. Homeland Security had found me on the strength of a cell phone call to a flagged ex-Stasi colonel. Then there was USIA and Rawlings. If I wanted to hide, going off the grid as Ursula had mentioned was a lot more difficult, uncomfortable, and inconvenient than hiding in plain sight.

"Let's get your stuff," Grabich said before we could change our minds. They went out to the old VW and unloaded it.

We had to shift some stuff in the spare room. The adjustment would be more difficult for Ursula, who had all her school work and paper grading to do. She would have to make our bedroom her office, not a good thing if she had to work late when the paper grading came in. School hadn't actually started yet.

While the two women set things up in the spare room. I sat on the couch and pondered. I'd better write this up for my CYA file. How would I word it in case my reports were seized by the FBI? I'd have to be cryptic.

Then my tendency to think in what ifs kicked in. What if Mia wasn't what she claimed to be? What if Mia was an Iranian spy, forced to work for her country with her father being held hostage? What if her chance meeting with Grabich at Starbucks wasn't by chance? What if there really were aliens at area 51? What if I was a victim of my own vivid imagination and paranoia? Maybe I needed a psychiatrist.

Chapter seventeen

Before Grabich left Mia at our place he confided in me. Standing by his car out on the sidewalk he said, "I've made a mistake. My breaking into the INS data bank to change MIA's visa attracted attention to me."

"How so?" I'm so preoccupied by my own job I hardly look up to see what's going on in the world around me.

Grabich explained. "Every government agency is under constant attack by hackers, a lot of them foreign in places like Rumania and Bulgaria where if we do figure out who does it they can't be extradited."

"But you can be."

"Only if they actually identify me. I think all they can do is narrow the breakage to the Krieger server."

"So?" I thought of all the people working in our offices. "You're only one."

"So are you, Harvey, and they already know you."

Of course what with the interview with Homeland Security and USIA, if that was the real ID and Rawlings wasn't a fake name, I stood out among the crowd. Suspect number one. Lucky me.

"You think they'll pin this on me? I'm no hack. I just crunch numbers."

"No you don't, Harvey. You deal in probabilities. Do you play any computer games like War Craft?"

"I'm not interested in computer games. Destroying imaginary monsters with invisible weapons is not my thing." I didn't get into Second Life, either. I didn't need an avatar. The life I had was as much as I needed and could cope with. For me, computer games weren't real. Ursula's and my only escape entertainment was the movies. Ursula and I liked movies. But even in the most tense scenes we didn't have to be reminded: they were movies. We didn't visit the actual bridges of Madison County to see where this or that happened. It didn't. It was a movie.

"One thing about War Craft—which you do not play—is you can't see the entire playing field. Much depends on deception and it's multi-dimensional."

I told him I didn't care for games. I don't play chess or even bridge.

"What I think I have to do for Mia is like a kind of War craft. She's up against a multitude of invisible agencies: INS, ICE, NSA, possibly the IRS, God knows who else. Might even be the CIA considering her father's political situation."

I suggested, "You could have picked a less conspicuous girl friend."

"That's what makes her so interesting. For her, winning the game is not to be seen and to disappear."

"This is serious, Grabich. You could be risking her life if she got sent back to Iran. You could lose your own job."

He didn't seem that worried, which took him down a peg in my assessment of his respectability. For him it was a sort of game. Mia was a person, not a playing piece.

. "Ever play hide and seek?" Grabich asked as he opened the driver's door and talked to me over the roof of the Carmen Gia.

"It's a kids game."

"Not for Mia. She's hiding."

With millions like her, it seemed unlikely that she'd be singled out. It they did..."She can't hide for long," I insisted. "Not in this country."

"If I can work it out," Grabich said, "I can make her invisible."

As he drove away my mind churned with thoughts of how Mia could avoid detection.

Grabich should have let it alone. Simply trying to fix her situation drew attention to her. Grabich must have got into it as a challenge. He was one of those guys who'd worry at a problem until he got the answer.

I remembered the Gordian Knot. Instead of unraveling it the trick was to simply cut it. Then there was the business of Pandora's Box. Just don't open it for fear of what escapes. Grabich was the kind of guy who lets himself get obsessed.

It was too late to back down. Mia was already our temporary house guest. Back in our condo, I got the attention of Ursula and Mia. "While you're unpacking and getting settled, Mia, I want you to think about how INS might track you."

She wasn't that sophisticated. The more I talked, the more puzzled she looked. The more puzzled she was, the more desperate and frightened.

I explained. "You have a cell phone, like everybody else. If INS wants to find you they can use your cell phone signal, so unless you absolutely need to make a call, take out the battery."

I showed her how to do it.

"And don't call from our place. Don't text, either. Besides your father, do you have more family in Iran?"

Today she was wearing designer jeans, that is jeans that were deliberately worn out at the factory so they didn't look new. She looked like any other college student, except she wore a long sleeved, baggy shirt she might have borrowed from Grabich plus the usual head covering.

"I have a sister."

I did notice that she had her own laptop, an apple Notebook. I guessed that if she couldn't use her cell phone at our place she would feel very much deprived. You can't go anywhere without seeing people focused on their gadgets even at the risk of walking off a curb into traffic.

If she wanted to be a fugitive, she would have to act like a terrorist except she didn't know how to encrypt her emails. "How do you communicate with your sister? You should know everything you send is read, probably by your government back home, especially if your father is in prison."

Now Mia was on the verge of tears. Ursula gave me a look that said "Back off."

Frankly, I didn't want her in our place. If Grabich wanted her as his girl friend, he should be responsible, not dump her on us. She was a liability besides being a temporary house guest.

Mia calmed down, took a deep breath, blew her nose on a tissue. "We have our special code words," she explained. "No politics. My sister is not political."

I didn't want to ask her what she thought of Israel, the Great Satan Iran wanted to wipe off the face of the earth, driving what Jews were not killed at least into the sea. Everyone knew Iran supplied Hezbollah with arms.

Mia agreed to do her wireless communicating from Starbucks or the public library. Grabich would pick her up in the morning after breakfast and drop her off at night.

Grabich had talked about computer games. This was no game. I didn't want to play it, but I was in it whether I liked it or not.

Chapter eighteen

I guess I'm too much of a worrier. It took us only a day or two to work out an equitable bathroom schedule. We explained that we left the bathroom door open unless someone was inside. Then we never had to knock. It would be different once classes started at Ursula's school. She'd be off pretty early then. The way it worked out, we saw very little of Mia. Grabich picked up in the morning and they would have dinner either at his place or in town. That was fine with me.

It was also very good that she wasn't in our place until the evening, for I had a surprise visitor when I got back from work on Friday. We had the weekend ahead of us, a good time to take a drive someplace and enjoy a late summer day, maybe go to the beach. Housework be damned. But at five thirty when I got back there was a white Lexus parked in front of our place. No government plate this time. Who was that?

My visitor was another of those guys in suits, except this time he didn't say he was from Homeland Security. He said he was from Novacom and he had an invitation for me.

All I knew about Novacom was they were one of the cloud companies. Microsoft has a cloud, Google has a cloud. Everybody's in the cloud business, using massive data storage facilities to provide backups for customers who might lose all their data to a hacker or a massive crash. It was a form of insurance, like providing people who had too much stuff with a rented storage locker. I knew Krieger contracted with one of the cloud companies but didn't know for sure that it was Novacom.

Most of those Silicone Valley people are young. This guy was about fifty with hair gray at the temples and a complexion that told me he must spend a lot of time in the sun maybe at golf. Instead of flashing a badge or a government ID, he just gave me his business card. Frederick Raleigh, plus an email address and phone number. In the lower left corner it said simply Novacom. So what was Raleigh's title? VP? Flunky? Maybe Novacom was one of those companies where people had names, no titles, and nobody had a corner office with a window, no geographical signals for authority or power.

Raleigh's business card, however, was embossed on good stock and the letters raised and in gold. The was not a mail order cheapie from Vistaprint.

Why would anyone from Novacom drop in on me unannounced?

Ursula wasn't dressed for visitors. She was wearing a ratty team sweatshirt and cutoffs. She hadn't apologized, either. If you arrive without notice, what you see was what you get. It was an outfit I preferred, for she didn't have to wear a bra under it. The hint of her nipples always keeps my pecker up.

Of course, that wasn't intended for Frederick Raleigh. As soon as I arrived she excused herself to put on something modest. Shucks.

I kept the business card for future reference. I'd file it in my CYA file as evidence. "What's the purpose of your visit, Mr. Raleigh?"

"Your boss, Mrs. Stewart, didn't want me to show up at the Krieger office. It attracts too much attention."

It took me a moment to remember that Boss Margaret's surname is Stewart. "What's this about?"

"I understand you had a meeting with E.J. Rawlings."

Well, he knew all the passwords and references. I wondered if he also knew what I ate at the Red Lobster. He would if I had paid for the meal with a credit card, but I'd been a guest. "Yes. What about it?"

Ursula, always the host, fetched a tray with coffee cups and what was left of the Trader Joe cookies. Raleigh took a pass.

"She suggested you might be interested in an inspection tour of Novacom."

I wondered why she would do that? Was she trying to get rid of me? Had I become too important for my job description? Or did Margaret have her own hidden agenda? To cover my hesitation, I nibbled a cookie. Sure beat Oreos. "A tour? That's possible. What's the deal?"

"Just a quick visit. Overnight in Salt Lake, return a day or so later, depending on."

"Depending on what?"

"On how it goes."

I didn't know what "it" was. "When?"

"Tomorrow morning. I can get you back to work on Monday or Tuesday. We use one of the company planes. No reservations needed. No airport congestion."

It sounded like a junket. I looked at Ursula. I could see she was already missing our outing at the beach. "Can my wife come along?"

Raleigh feigned an apologetic expression. "It's a restricted area."

My turn. I feigned disappointment. "Is this some sort of official job?" I wasn't looking for another job. I had enough on my plate at Krieger and the pay was good. I took a chance, just to squeeze him a little. "You pay per diem?" If this was a lead up to a job offer I wanted him to know I didn't come cheap.

Raleigh was surprised but recovered quickly.. "No need. All expenses paid. Leave your money and credit cards at home. We'll take care of everything."

"OK. What time?"

"Pick you up tomorrow morning. Nine o'clock OK? It's a long flight from Cleveland. We refuel in Kansas City."

I thought a moment. What should I pack? "Dress code?"

Raleigh was wearing a suit, dress shirt and tie. "Jacket's OK, Nobody there wears a tie. The director, Mrs. Post, shows up on weekends in just her jogging outfit. She can wear whatever she wants." He smiled wryly, like he disapproved or was jealous. I'd bet he wore a tie on casual Fridays. At his age in the land of youths he'd need some proof of seniority even if it was only a jacket and tie.

So the director was a woman. Women have to be tougher than men to make it in management. I hoped not tough and abrasive. People should be pleasant to work with.

Working for a woman isn't the same as working for a man. With Margaret the cougar, any suggestion of being pals with the boss was a suggestion that you might be willing prey. No thanks. I guess women at the office have the same problem with potential sexual misbehavior.

I always kept Margaret Stewart at arm's length. No sucking up and no fake servility. I just did my job, all business, no mischief.

Ursula gave me the nod and I agreed. Ever since Mia had moved in we'd gone halal with the menu. No pork chops or bacon. Maybe this time I would get that steak dinner, not the Red Lobster special.

I watched from the window as Raleigh's Lexus drove away. Must have been a rental. I asked Ursula, "What do you think?"

She took a seat and picked up the cup of coffee our visitor had turned down. "For a minute I thought he was someone from the government looking for Mia."

"I thought of that, too. Were you scared?"

"After that business you had with Homeland Security, sure. I'm just glad we got rid of him before Mia and your pal Grabich came back."

"He's not my pal."

"Let's see his business card."

I handed it to Ursula. She thought a moment and handed it back. "He's a head hunter."

"For a head hunter he has an odd approach, just popping up like that."

"Maybe not. You know, honey, I had read how the KGB arrested people. They would surprise them while on vacation say on a beach at the Black Sea. They'd grab someone when they were in unfamiliar territory and spirit them away before they could call for help from friends or family."

"This isn't Russia."

"Harvey, you had that visit from Homeland Security and that woman, Ms. Rawlings. It's all hush hush. Something's going on."

"Why just show up at our apartment?"

"I think he wanted to see you on your home turf. Did you notice how he got a good look at the apartment? He was assessing us."

I wondered what he thought of our Ikea furnishings. If we had cheap furniture and he was looking to hire me, my price just sank. "I think he wanted to get me interested in whatever it was before I could turn him down." What that was, I had no idea. As for that trip to the west, I would have to find out later. There was little point in speculating. Anything I might guess was probably wrong. As for now...

She had put on a blouse. It was pretty but I preferred the sweatshirt. "How about getting back in that sweatshirt?"

She knew what I was thinking and gave me that special smile.

"How about if I just take it off? We have time for a quickie before supper."

"How about a longy and skip supper?"

She shook her head. "No telling when Mia comes back."

That was the trouble with having a stranger in the apartment. You couldn't run around in our underwear or naked.

I'd think about what to pack later. I'd also postpone any thoughts of the Novacom cloud and company planes, too. Amazing how sex can drive away all other thoughts.

Chapter nineteen

When Grabich came by to drop Mia off I asked him inside. They had eaten at an Indian restaurant and bought back two boxes of spicy leftovers. Since that wasn't breakfast food and Mia was gone all day, I suspected that the stuff would sit in the back of the fridge until mold set in.

"I had another visitor," I told him. I showed Raleigh's business card. "I'm off tomorrow morning to Utah to visit the Novacom cloud."

"Lucky you," he said with some irony. "You think once you're inside they'll let you go again?"

"Why not? It's just a big computer."

"For backup files. They say. I don't trust Novacom." The plate of cookies was still on the coffee table. He picked one up, sniffed it, and put it back. Probably wouldn't go well with the curry. "When will you be back?"

"Monday or Tuesday. Margaret knows about it."

"I think you're due for a promotion," Grabich said with some envy. "You're getting too important."

I didn't think so. "While I'm there is there anything you'd like to know about the cloud? Protocols? Stuff like that?"

Grabich's eyes opened wide when he got an idea. "Maybe you could play Winston Smith."

I didn't remember Winston Smith.

"He's the guy in Orwell's 1984. His job is to put things in the memory hole."

It's been years since I read the book. All I remembered was in 1984 all the TV sets were two way and Big Brother was watching you—all the time. I did remember that Samsung makes a TV that watches you, presumably for marketing purposes. Just as Krieger notices what people buy, Samsung can pay attention to what people watch. Creates data the networks can use to adjust their advertising fees. I hope that's all it's for. Orwell hadn't anticipated NSA and the Internet. He was B.C.

"Winston Smith's job was the make sure the present was what the past predicted. If the chocolate ration wasn't raised but actually reduced, it was his job to go back to the old newspaper reports and change them. That way, he could change the past to fit present reality.

"But the cloud is secure storage of backup files."

Grabich grinned. "Harvey, you know nothing is secure."

I remember his thoughts of hacking into the INS files and changing Mia's record. Even if he could do that, there was still the backup file.

That's what killed Nixon and other White House mischief makers. They could delete one level of surveillance recordings, but somewhere there would be a backup. Nixon didn't live in a digital world. We do. That's where the cloud came in. I got Grabich's drift. "So if you could get into the cloud you could change the INS record of Mia's visa from student to immigration."

He nodded. "In the backup file, yes. Then if anyone questioned changes in the current file and went to the backup they would match."

"You want me to ask them that?"

Grabich clutched his near afro. "Jesus, no! But if you could learn how secure those files really are, that could help."

That was interesting. Up to then I had no specific information I'd wanted to look for. My main interested was the integration of files and data bases. I'm not a true filofiliac, obsessed with files. I'm not a hoarder of old magazines or information.

I prefer to leave the office at the office. I don't take work home. By not having a iPhone I avoid being at Margaret's beck and call at all hours like some people who get waked up at three in the morning by a text message because a boss is in Shanghai or someplace and wants an immediate answer. Screw that.

"I'll keep my eyes and ears open," I said. "No promises."

He left with a roar of that old four banger engine and a muffler that needed replacement.

I turned to Ursula. Before Mia arrived we had showered together, always a treat. Otherwise I never get my back properly scrubbed. Et cetera. But all our towels were now hanging wet in the bathroom. "Did you catch anything of what Grabich said?"

She hadn't.

"He talked about Orwell's 1984."

She knew the book. "He thought all that Big Brother stuff would happen in 1984. I think he wrote it in 1944. Now it's 2016 and it's all happening."

"We live in his nightmare future," I said.

I'd forgotten that part of the book. I didn't think in our society people would be tortured. Weatherboarding was outlawed. Just goes to show how naïve I am.

As for me? I knew nothing. I had no information anyone would want. I was just an ordinary number cruncher working in a cubicle like thousands of others. No matter how much I might think of myself, I was nobody. Everyman, like in the old allegorical play from the Middle Ages. I hoped I wasn't Willie Loman, as in Death of a Salesman, the low man. I was more like the protagonist in Kafka's The Trial, one clerk among hundreds. In Kafka the protagonist never found out what he was on trial for.

I wondered whether something like that could happen to me. All I ever did that was remotely suspicious was to have coffee with Uncle Julius in Hamburg. Look what happened then!

Time to pack. Raleigh was picking me up at nine o'clock in the morning. I was looking forward to the trip, a junket, all expenses paid. Then again, I wasn't. There's no such thing as a free lunch. Someone always wants something in return.

Chapter twenty

I packed an overnight bag, my shaving kit left over from the Europe trip, PJ's, socks and underwear. Would there be a pool? I didn't bring my bathing trunks. I did pack my laptop. It's an older model. The new ones are slimmer and have solid state memory, no disk drives so are not as heavy. If I had an iPhone I could get email on it, take videos for the Internet, read books, even make a phone call. Imagine that! I don't trust them.

You can lock the phones so supposedly nobody can get at the contents, but while you are transmitting, it's not secure.

I'm getting to the point where I don't trust anything. After all, if Homeland Security could zero in on me because Ursula's phone call to Uncle Julius, a marked man, triggered a visit, what else might be derived from something otherwise innocent? Julius said I was lucky because I worked with computers, but so did everyone else.

Ursula was worried about my mysterious trip, but also disappointed because she wasn't going along. I depend on her good judgment. Once school started she'd be locked into her routine. She wanted to come along on this junket. Grabich had already picked up Mia for the day, so Ursula would be alone in the condo. Instead of a day at the beach she was stuck with the laundry.

I would have to buy her something in Salt Lake City to compensate, but what's there that isn't everywhere else in the country? LDS underwear? I'd rather see her without it.

"I'll call you as soon as I get there," I said. I remembered how an innocuous call to Julius had alerted the NSA. "When I call, don't mention Mia's name. Remember, calls aren't secure."

"You're starting to think like a fugitive. Uncle Julius is getting to you."

I could see, I'd have to admit, that Julius and I had much in common. Hadn't I used my access to the Krieger records on those two Homeland Security agents to tease them about their purchases? I was beginning to behave like the DDR cop in the movie "Other People's Lives." I was only supposed to issue coupons for what people already bought, not comment on their choices. I shook my head. "I'm beginning to wonder what I am." Basically, I knew too much.

I heard a car horn and looked out the window. "Here he is." Raleigh was right on time. He parked at the curb and blew the horn of the Lexus.

Hugging Ursula, I said, "I wish you could come, too." I was a bit nervous traveling on my own. I was going into alien territory. The Mormons don't drink coffee or smoke and stick with soda pop. I heard they have some sort of special underwear. Utah would be like going to a foreign country. Would I suffer culture shock? Holland and Germany hadn't done that to me as I might have I expected, but then I was a tourist. Now I was what? .

As for the Jew-gentile thing, if I were Orthodox I'd be wearing a fringed garment and a black hat, so I'd be, in their eyes, weird, too.

I didn't think Raleigh was LDS. If he was I wasn't going to check his underwear. I said, "Good morning, Mr. Raleigh."

He corrected me. "It's Frederick. Fred will do, Mr. Goldstein."

Okay. "Then I'm Harvey."

"Harvey."

From then on we were Harvey and Fred, but I still wasn't comfortable. In Germany to be on a first name basis we would have to "dusen" one another, the old drinking buddy practice of locking arms over glasses of beer. That was one of those things Ursula had explained to me. Her grandparents had been German, fled in the thirties. They'd been secular as we were, but in Nazi eyes that made no difference. A Jew was a Jew.

Hitler's idea of miscegenation was having one Jewish grandparent. That qualified you for the gas chambers. I think old Adolf got his racist definition from the United States. Here one drop—ONE DROP- of Negro blood and you were, you'll pardon the expression, a nigger.-

No matter that I hadn't set foot in a synagogue since my bar mitzvah, my blood was all Jew. It does make you different even in other people's eyes. I didn't feel like Raleigh and I were on a chummy first name basis. I would prefer Mr. Raleigh. Then again, maybe that's the way the Silicone Valley folks worked, a foreign world to me, being so, well, Midwestern. All this does give you uncertainties about who you really are.

Eichmann claimed he was just a dull bureaucrat doing his job. So am I, but he got hanged for it. His job was to send thousands of people to their deaths. I just sent thousands of people discount coupons.

Fred didn't have much to say as we drove to the airfield. He didn't ask questions about my job or anything else. Maybe he'd been briefed already and knew all about me. I hung back while he dropped off the rental car. Universal provided a van shuttle to the part of the airport reserved for corporate jets. We didn't have to go through security.

I didn't understand why Novacom wanted me on this trip. It didn't have the feel of a job interview. Nobody asked me for my resume. It was as if everyone who I'd talked to already knew everything about me. Weird. Maybe they were doing to me what I had been doing to my Krieger customers: analyzing everything they ate and bought. Did they also guess what I was thinking before I thought it? Creepy.

If it had been NSA or the government they would also know my movements, phone calls, etc. But why? I had no previous contact with Novacom.

The only major computer company I had experience with was Microsoft and that wasn't so great. I had misgivings about the company selling what in reality were beta versions of their operating systems.

I'd used Windows 97, had avoided Vista, hated Windows ME, liked windows XP, was glad to have jumped over Windows 8 and was now using Windows 10. If it weren't for Krieger using PCs I'd rather have an Apple.

Apple was an innovator. Microsoft was an imitator, always playing catch-up to Apple's operating system. Microsoft's error, as I saw it, was dealing in software, but once you had software that worked, why upgrade? On the other hand, Apple sold expensive gadgets like the iPhone and the Apple watch. They catered to the crowd that always had to have the latest gizmo.

Unless Microsoft came up with something that made huge profits, they might fade away. All companies go through a life cycle. I suspected Microsoft was past its peak even though it was one of the world's biggest companies. Even Apple was having a slump in sales. How much appetite was there for an endless parade of gadgets? Both companies had been founded by brilliant men-- Bill Gates and Steve Jobs. With them gone, leadership fell on lesser leaders.

Both companies were likely to be replaced by more innovators. The progression of technology was relentless. Taped memory was past history. The floppy disk was replaced by the mini-disk, cassette tapes by the CD, and movie DVDs by Bluetooth. PCs were displaced by tablets. Early companies like Texas Instruments fell away to oblivion. Kresge had become K-Mart. Wal-Mart was being pressured by Target. Kreiger had eaten its competitors. The pharmaceutical companies were eating each other. Where did Novacom fit into that dog eat dog world? And what did I have to do with it? Nothing.

So it was with some bewilderment that I followed Mr. Raleigh to the plane. It was a twin engine eight passenger and so luxurious it could have been a miniature version of Trump's personal airliner. This was how the rich and famous traveled. I was neither rich nor famous and felt much out of place, like a person at a banquet who doesn't know which fork or spoon to use, there being so many beside the plate.

White leather seats complete with adequate legroom—wow! Our last flight in coach had me and Ursula with our knees practically up to our chins. If the person in front reclined the seat we were trapped like some animal in a snare. I had to hold my breath to avoid claustrophobia.

There were no other passengers and no flight attendant, just two pilots who looked like they just completed flight training, they were so young.. If you wanted a snack or a drink, there was a wet bar and a fridge which Raleigh pointed out.

The flight would take several hours, flying from Eastern Time to Mountain Time zones. My host apologized for offering just lunch boxes with sandwiches, cookies, and a can of soda. Would I like some liquor? No thanks. He helped himself to bourbon on ice.

I was provided with homework for the flight. On the seat were a Novacom annual stockholders report, brochures on The Cloud, and tri-folds for the various services. It was all extremely complicated. They had over a thousand engineers. The facility was divided into two nearly autonomous divisions. Compared with my Krieger boiler room, where I worked was like kindergarten. Putting Krieger's data in the cloud was not my department.

This was all very nice. I felt like a VIP honored guest, but why? Why was Novacom interested in me? Maybe they thought I was the one who made decisions at Krieger for the use of the cloud or their special services. I was not management. Why me?

Maybe it was all a misunderstanding. Maybe it was because I uttered the secret code word: Seventh Paradigm, even though I didn't know what it meant. Those agents of Homeland Security might have written up a misleading report, or maybe pumped up their impressions to justify their having seen me. And what about Rawlings? She knew about their visit, but was she working for the same people?

I thought about what Uncle Julius had said about people all reporting on one another. Were they cautious, deliberately vague or misleading? Did they write reports to justify further expenses?

I had never worked for the government. I didn't know how to write something that meant all things to all men. Aside from my job, all I'd written lately were CYA memos to myself. The risk was my memos to myself were deliberately obscure in case someone else read them. In fact, I might not understand myself what I was getting at when I re-read them a long time after. If, for example, I wrote "had my usual breakfast" and years later read it, I might not remember what a usual breakfast was.

We stopped to refuel at Kansas City and make a potty stop.

It was afternoon when we arrived in Salt Lake City. This is where things got even stranger. Raleigh made a call with his cell phone. A few minutes later a car drove up without a driver. It was if it knew where we were and where to stop.

It was a compact with a Novacom logo painted on the sides. Under the logo was a name in smaller print, "Herbie." I guessed Novacom had a pool of cars but instead of giving them numbers gave them names. That was typical. Herbie had one of those Google cameras on the roof. I figured that was where the sensors were mounted. Raleigh didn't need a key to get in, just punched a code into the key pad at the door.

I got in the back seat with my carry on and Raleigh sat up front with the GPS. He started the car by pushing a button on the dash, punched in a destination, and we were off, very smooth and silent, just road noise from the tires.

I was nervous. "I've never ridden in a self-driving car," I said. "I thought there were still in the experiment stage."

"They are," Raleigh admitted with a grin that wrinkled his graying sideburns. "This is a test vehicle. Otherwise I'd be able to sit in the back. The State Police insist on someone being able to grab the controls if the car makes a mistake."

"How does it work?"

Raleigh turned to look at me like I was a third grader. "It's voice actuated. The car responds first to its name, like if I say 'Herbie, start' the engine starts."

Sure enough, at the sound of his voice, I heard the quiet whir of the electric engine. "Then what?"

"You tell Herbie your destination. Our usual destinations are preprogrammed. Right now we're going to Novacom headquarters." He raised his voice. "Herbie, drive us to Novacom headquarters."

Like a seaman on an old clipper ship, Herbie repeated the command to confirm it. We were off.

"What if the destination isn't preprogrammed?"

Raleigh had an answer for that one, too. "There's a GPS, so if you needed to go to a hospital, for instance, you would name it and the car would look up the location and drive to it."

I thought that was cool. Will wonders never cease? "Can I tell the car to drive to the beach?"

"You have to be more specific than that. The car isn't as smart as a person."

From what I could see, looking over the back of the front seat, the car didn't even need a steering wheel. It was creepy to watch the wheel turning by itself when we went around a corner. "How far is it to Novacom?"

"About the limits of the battery range. That's one of the drawbacks of these. We can pre-program for the destinations, but the car can't leave the state."

"What? Like a parolee with an ankle bracelet?"

Raleigh turned back to me and smiled. "No. Not all states permit self drive cars. Not yet, anyway."

As a futurist for Krieger I deal with what ifs. A police ankle bracelet would tell where you were. It would not control your movements, only report on them. As a futurist, that's where I feared this would be going. Of course, the location of the car would always be known, just as an iPhone was.

Aware the Raleigh could hear what I said, I called Ursula on my dumb Trak phone. "Guess what? I'm riding in a self-drive car."

"Really?"

"It's name is Herbie, just like in that Pixar movie."

As the mention of its name, the car responded. "Where do you want to go?"

Raleigh gave me a dirty look for stating the car's name without an instruction. I realized there were hazards to this. "Novacom headquarters."

"Novacom headquarters." We were still on track.

Ursula asked how the flight was. My reply was simply "Fine. Tell you about it later."

It was a long drive. Though there was little traffic, the car dutifully never broke the speed limit. It was dusk by the time we got to our destination. I got a glimpse of windmill generators like space age sentinels standing guard outside the gate. The cloud building itself was dark, had no windows, and looked like a brooding, faceless hulk in the darkness.

I guessed by his choice of words, Mr. Raleigh must be retired military. "We'll get a meal in the mess hall and then I'll check you in to the billet. We have our own guest accommodation. Otherwise you'd have to drive for miles to find a motel."

I commented, "Reminds me of a military base or maybe Area 51." I intended the last as a joke.

"No space aliens here, Harvey, but you have arrived in the future."

If the self drive car had been Dr. Who's space and time traveling phone booth, I'd not have been surprised. I thought 'this is starting to be fun.' Fun as long as it was just for a day or two and I could leave.

Chapter twenty-one

We passed through security where I signed in. No photography was allowed, so I was asked to hand over my I-phone. I don't have one. They were satisfied that my Trak phone was harmless. I was given a badge I was told to wear at all times. No doubt it had a tracking chip so if I took it off and left it behind it would sound an alarm someplace. I joked, "Do I have to wear it in the shower?"

Nobody laughed. Security at Novacom was not something to joke about.

I left my carry-on at the entrance. I was hungry. The box lunch on the plane had a dry turkey sandwich, a little bag of potato chips and a candy bar. At least it was better than a PB and J.

I had heard that the silicone valley companies like Google provided free food for the employees. That could be managements ploy to keep them on the premises during meal times, or to keep them close to their desks for maximum time on the job, like slaves handled with velvet gloves. Was there an iron fist inside?

Except for Frederick Raleigh or Fred, my guide and keeper, the employees all looked young. I noticed this was a male domain, with many Asian faces, only one or two females. Boss Margaret wouldn't have stood for it. Though she liked a pool of eligible men to study like some cattle auctioneer, she was also an equal opportunity employer.

Still, Raleigh had said the boss was a woman. Bill Gates was simply Gates. Steve Jobs was Jobs. She was Post. I hadn't met her yet.

The food was cafeteria style and something for vegans, etc. No steaks, sorry, but a variety including Southwest and Asian choices. Dessert was a choice of cakes, no pie. Ursula would have preferred pie. It reminded me of Ikea's restaurant where we ate while shopping for our furniture.

I was introduced to several people whose names I immediately forgot. Some people have a knack for remembering names, some memory device that puts the name in a sentence, some association. They all wore ID badges, first names only, but with a picture. If someone showed an interest, I said I worked for Krieger. They were too polite or uninterested to ask if I was in produce or the meat department, not that coupons would sound more prestigious.

My tag simply said "visitor."

Raleigh turned down my suggestion for a quick tour of the facility. "Tomorrow morning. Breakfast at 7:00, tour at 7:30, then you'll meet the division heads."

It turned out that the Novacom Cloud was more complicated than I imagined. It wasn't just a repository for other people's data. Novacom dealt in music and primarily in security. Security of sensitive data and backup files was the purported prime purpose of The Cloud. I already knew that from what I'd seen in the brochures on the plane. Unfortunately, technologists tend to manufacture their own special terminology. After a few pages it was all gobbledygook to me.

I would have loved to get my hands onto all that data. I dealt only with Krieger's customer list. Even though it's a seven figure number, The Cloud has capacity that far exceeds what Krieger is contracted for. I see myself as a futurist stuck in a rather basic current real time marketing job. Figuring out what products to offer customers is not as challenging as what I might do if I had the Cloud at my disposal, which is something I'd like to explore.

That might have something to do with my visit to Utah.

The guest room was adequate, no more than a Holiday Inn, except the pictures on the wall were not mass-produced landscapes but promotional pictures about Novacom.

I tried to call Ursula from the room but got no signal. Novacom was outside the service area for my cheap phone. They treated the place like some World War II bunker, likely to be breached. The brochure I read on the plane showed they were more paranoid than I was about security.

I briefly considered booting up my laptop to check my email but hesitated. If I used the local wi-fi signal as a guest, anybody on the network could have access to my computer, maybe put in malware without my knowledge, read all my old emails, study my files. No thanks. I didn't dare use it, had lugged it along for nothing.

Ah well, this was only for a day or two. Emails could wait.

The flat screen TV in the room was a Samsung. I didn't know if it was the model that watches the viewers. I thought about mooning it, but didn't want to show somebody my ass. Just in case, I hung a towel over the screen.

Heck, Novacom could have cameras hidden all over the place. It made me feel like Winston Smith, always being watched. From now on I would be on my guard.

I was over tired like a little kid so wound up he can't sleep even if exhausted. I called the Novacom switchboard and asked for a 6:30 wake-up call which came around quicker than I thought so I guess I did drop off after midnight. I showered and put on my sport jacket and stuck my one necktie in my pocket just in case things got formal.

Raleigh came to fetch me and accompanied me to the mess hall. It was possible to get breakfast twenty-four hours a day for the sake of people who worked shifts.

The tour of the facility itself was not very interesting, just banks and banks of servers kept at a cool operating temperature. It was endlessly expandable. More customers? Add more server capacity.

Finally I got to meet Mrs. Post. She was, as I'd been warned, an athletic type. She explained that she did a morning run in the desert while it was still cool. Since it was Sunday she didn't need to change. Her brown hair was short and secured by a sweat band. I'd guess she was about fifty. She explained she had taken over the business after her husband died in the crash of his experimental plane.

I learned that customers didn't come to the cloud. Novacom did have an office in Salt Lake, but the real work went on at the desert location.

She apologized for the size of the facility. "The Amazon and Microsoft clouds are huge," she explained. "We're just a small company. Anyone who wants to install servers at their own locations can do it, but we tell them it is cheaper and more secure to pay for our services. Since the Novacom cloud is not at the same location as, for instance, your office at Krieger, if you had a fire, your data would still be safe with us." She added, "Which it is."

I didn't know for sure that Kreiger was one of her customers, but reasoned that was why they had connected with me.

Post asked me about my job and I explained. I felt a bit like a yokel compared to that they were doing, but she was more than polite in her interest. She asked, "What's you goal, your ambition?"

That sounded like a job interview question. I had not told anyone what I really wanted to be doing. I was usually too busy figuring out the next round of individually selected products to issue coupons for. The computer program we'd worked out was pretty basic. Krieger was a major grocery chain. We had millions of potential customers.

I needed to reach beyond our list.

I explained, "We are in the third paradigm. I see that's where you are, too."

We were sitting in a conference room. Besides me, Post, and Raleigh were four more management people who looked like they were reluctant to be there on a Sunday morning. They would probably prefer to be out playing golf. I was the only one wearing a jacket. In order to fit in, I took it off and hung it over the back of my chair.

The conference room was one of the few places at Novacom that had outside windows and a view of the desert and the mountains. It was beautiful country if views were more important than the accessibility of shopping entertainment, and other people. It was too isolated for my taste. I guess I'm an urbanite.

Post had a keen mind and searched my face for her answer. "So what is the fourth paradigm?"

I took a deep breath. "Integration. Consolidation. Merging more databases."

"How could we do that?"

Now everyone in the room was curious. "You've all clicked on the customer agreements. Down there in the fine print nobody reads there's a clause that says that though privacy is guaranteed, you don't permit illegal or immortal content. The data is also accessible to law enforcement."

Fred Raleigh objected. "It doesn't exactly say that."

I explained. "The FBI considers all data on the internet to be public domain. That's why musicians have such trouble protecting their copyrights. People figure that everything out there is free."

Mrs. Post countered with, "That doesn't mean it's legal or constitutional."

"That's for the courts to decide."

Frederick Raleigh wanted to get a move on. "So what do you propose, Harvey?"

I took a deep breath. "Anybody can have their own cloud, but the servers are expensive. Companies like Oracle, Microsoft, and Amazon are the big boys. Novacom needs a new angle besides being a secure repository for data.

"Such as?"

"Well at Krieger we have a lot of customers, mainly in the grocery business. If, for instance, our data were merged with say, a health magazine like Nutrition Action, researchers could find out about customers buying habits from the source, us. We do it, of course, to see how well the house brands are doing."

Mrs. Post shook her head. "Your data is proprietary. Krieger won't want to share it."

"People sell mailing lists all the time. Some outfits claiming to be a charity buy a mailing list, like one of those with the word 'veteran' in the title, and then saturates the market. Some charities are happy enough to sell the mailing list for the use of their name and a piece of the action, like those mints you see at a restaurant check-out. The charity gets maybe five percent. The rest goes to the candy makers."

"You're talking about more than just a mailing list."

I agreed. "But look further. The political parties know who is registered to vote, where they live. Our data includes age groups."

Now Raleigh took the role of devil's advocate. "You think there's a connection between political affiliations and Kreiger house brands?"

"That's just a for instance. Consider that all government data that is not classified is public domain. Merge the department of education with, say, homeland security."

Mrs. Post saw a possibility. "Then what?"

"If you dominate a niche someone like Oracle will buy you out."

Mergers and acquisitions make management nervous. Will their lose their stock options, or will they get a windfall? Mrs. Post could retire even richer. I could see her managers ready to squirm in their seats.

There was a pause while they all looked at each other.

Was there any more today?

Post had a PS, "You talked about the fourth paradigm. What's the fifth?"

I had been thinking about what Uncle Julius said. It was a natural progression, like that children's jingle "First comes love, then comes marriage, then comes a baby in a baby carriage."

I jumped a couple of levels. "What I'm concerned about is the seventh paradigm."

They were all puzzled. I was, too, but I pretended to know what I was talking about. It was a bluff, of course. "It may not happen. Getting to the fifth will be difficult enough."

The more I thought about it, the less I believed it could happen. Getting all those cloud databases to cooperate, to conform, to fuse into one was simply unlikely if not impossible. But as I knew, if one could conceive of something, it might actually happen.

Many inventions were not original. They were a fusion of already existing ideas. The perfume atomizer became the carburetor. The electric pistol became the spark plug. The result? A society dependent on the automobile. Plus all the unintended consequences, like urban sprawl and air pollution.

I let the mysterious seventh paradigm hang in the air. I think they correctly decided I was talking bullshit.

Raleigh shook his head. "It will never work."

Mrs. Post wasn't so sure. "If it does work, what do you think they'll call it?"

Raleigh snickered. "The Harvey Goldstein effect." Then they all laughed. "Call it Harvey Goldstein."

I thought it was a joke and I was the butt of it. Not fun. I hoped they weren't serious.

I was dismissed.

Part two

Chapter twenty-three

There had been no talk of this being a job interview or a consulting contract. Money had never been mentioned. So far, Raleigh had said it was only an inspection tour, not that I needed one. All I had known about Novacom was a name. If anything I was driven by curiosity. That visit in Hamburg had led to a confrontation with National Security and a lunch with Rawlings. Each step got more serious, culminating in the inspection tour and conference at Novacom. Was it all a mistake?

People seemed to think I knew something important. It was if I'd accidentally given a secret password to a stranger at an airport and been handed the briefcase with the Big Secret. Then everyone would be after me. So far it had been a game of 'guess what?" but what if it got serious? What if I were kidnapped and tortured and hadn't a clue?

I had been picked up at our condo in Cleveland, taken to the airport, flown out on a company plane, and delivered by Frederick Raleigh in Herbie the self-drive car. Now I got the impression that they had milked me for my ideas, squeezed me like a lemon for my juices, and were done. I was no longer useful. Garbage time.

Some managers are like that. I was summarily told that the meeting was over. A plane reservation had been made for me from Salt Lake City. Raleigh handed me over to a lesser person who accompanied me for lunch in the Novacom dining room. It was being like being fired without notice and taken to the exit. What the hell?

One of the self-drive cars would take me to the airport, find its own recharge station, and return on its own to Novacom like a horse that knows its way back to the barn.

I was accompanied to the lot where the Novacom self-drive cars were suckling like little pigs at the recharging stations. I handed over my visitor's badge and that was it.

Again I would be riding in Herbie. I was given the key code so I could get into the car. I'm a quick study. I made myself comfortable and commanded "Herbie start," which it did. "Then I said, "Herbie drive me to the Salt Lake City airport terminal."

I didn't know how many air ports there were in Salt Lake City, but Herbie had been preprogrammed and knew the way. Riding in the front seat this time to satisfy State regulations, I had a long ride to think about my strange visit to Novacom.

Herbie dutifully dropped me at the terminal. I forgot to tell it what to do next. I stood on the sidewalk and wondered what it would do. After a couple of minutes it drove off by itself looking for the recharge station.

I decided that some day I would have a self drive car. Maybe I'd name it Lizzy like my Dad did with his.

It wasn't a luxury flight back to Cleveland in a private plane, but at least they got me a seat in business class.

At the gate I called Ursula to say I'd be back late. I kept the call innocuous and cryptic. "I'll tell you about it later." One never knew who might be listening.

It was still Sunday but late. I'd lost two hours going from Mountain time to Eastern and had to change in O'Hare, the ninth level of hell. I arrived in Cleveland tired and confused. I'd missed public transportation back to town and had to take a taxi, this time at my own expense. Since I don't have a cell phone with an Uber app, I got no discount. I was already missing Herbie.

Ursula was waiting. Mia was asleep in the guest room/nursery, so we spoke in whispers so as not to wake her.

After my welcome home hug and kiss, Ursula asked, "Hungry? I'll make you a sandwich."

We retired to the kitchen where I helped myself to a Sam Adams. There had been no alcoholic beverages in LDS land. "Even business class doesn't do meals any more. I've been drinking juice since yesterday. I think most of the staff at that place is LDS."

We sat at the kitchen table, Ursula in her PJs and bathrobe, barefoot, to debrief me. "What was it like?"

I told her about the self-drive cars. "It's a strange place. Boss is Mrs. Post, a widow who, I think would gladly sell the business and take up some hobby. We discussed my ideas for the fourth or fifth paradigm. I got the impression that they thought it outlandish and impractical. Then they basically gave me the bums rush. It was weird. First the VIP treatment, then so-long it's been good to know ya. I was bundled into a car that drove itself to the airport."

"That was it?"

"No job offer and no mention of a fee. I got a free ride and meals. I didn't do any tourist things." I sipped my beer, suddenly remembering that I'd promised Ursula a souvenir. I hadn't even tried one of the shops at O'Hare. I hoped she wouldn't be disappointed. "You know, Ursula, people think it's great to get out of town, do some traveling, sightseeing, maybe shopping. I never even took a walk except to the airport gate."

She was thoughtful.

I changed the subject. "How's Mia and Grabich?"

"What? Since yesterday?"

It seemed longer than that to me. I'd only been gone overnight, but so much had happened or didn't happen. I wasn't sure which.

Whatever Grabich was doing to fiddle Mia's visa or immigrant status, he wasn't saying. Just as well. If he was hacking into government agency files I didn't want to be an accessory. It was enough to have Mia staying with us until he sorted it out. I guessed housing an illegal immigrant was some sort of criminal activity I didn't want to think about. In our society one conviction meant you could never get another decent job.

It was good to be back in my own bed with my cuddle. Much as I would have liked to, Ursula and I didn't make any bedroom noises. Mia didn't start her job at Macy's until nine-thirty so was last in the bathroom. She was one of those people who don't talk until they have had coffee. Mia is also a girl who is ashamed to show her face without her morning makeup. She does her eyes and without the makeup looks pale and washed out. I couldn't see what Grabich saw in her. Maybe Iranians are exotic.

Ursula had a teachers' meeting, as school would be starting in a few days. I dropped her off and resumed my duties at Krieger. After the high level rarified atmosphere and help yourself to everything at Novacom's mess hall I was back to my bag lunch.

I had warned Margaret in a Friday evening email that I was going out of town on Saturday and might not be on time on Monday. But I was already back. Margaret was curious. "I just saw your email saying you might be gone a couple of days, but here you are. What's up?"

Over a cup of her special coffee I talked about Novacom and Herbie the self-drive car. I think she was jealous that the Novacom folks had what turned out to be a Gulfstream private plane. Maybe there is one for the folks at the top of the Krieger corporate ladder, but we coupon people are far down in the pecking order. The developers of new house brands are a step above.

The bottom line of all this travel was I'd become more visible, not just another rodent in a cubicle. That's not necessarily a good thing.

Then at about two o'clock I had a surprise. I saw a messenger approach Boss Margaret's glass office. Must have been a bicycle courier, for she had a Lycra outfit, reflective jacket and helmet. Margaret pointed out my desk.

I had to sign for an envelope that had express stickers but no discernable return address. Puzzled, I tore it open. Inside were five one hundred dollar bills. No note.

Of course, I guessed it was from Novacom. Nobody else had any reason to send me money. Yet, being given cash told me something. I was off the books. There would be no record that Harvey Goldstein had been paid for services rendered or anything. Maybe the five hundred would be buried in incidental expenses along with donations for someone's baby shower. Ms. Post didn't want to leave a paper trail.

I would keep the money in a fun fund. Since it was apparently a gift and not payment for services rendered, it wasn't taxable income. Ursula would be pleased. She deserved a present for having been denied a last Sunday at the beach now that school was starting. Maybe we could go shopping at Victoria's Secret and fantasize. Maybe we could go into one of the fitting rooms and try some of that stuff out. I was already excited at he thought, even if we didn't buy anything. In the meantime, Ursula would have papers to grade, bad spelling of German homework.

Which reminded me: I wanted to contact Uncle Julius. He was not just an innocent old age pensioner living off the German welfare state. Trouble was, I didn't know how to do it without attracting NSA attention. Maybe a letter in aluminum foil and sent as snail mail like he did with that clipping out of Der Spiegel..

Margaret's curiosity was piqued by the bicycle messenger. She called me into the office. Trying not to be accusatory, she asked "What was that about?"

"I think it was from Novacom."

Her eyes narrowed. She was sizing me up, reevaluating. "You looking for another job, Harvey?"

I sensed that she was already afraid she'd have to replace me. Not that I am that indispensable. "Nope."

"Something's going on that I should know about?"

"Possibly, but I don't know myself."

She got up and closed the door. That meant this was confidential. At least she didn't draw the blinds. If she drew the blinds of her glass office it was heavy duty.

"I got a call from management this morning. Novacom has made us an offer for our mailing list."

I nodded, surprised but not astonished. "That was quick."

"So you knew about this?"

I shook my head. "I talked to them about expanding their offerings, the merging of national databases. You know, if we at Krieger had access to AARP data, for instance, we could reach out to more customers."

Margaret's eyes narrowed. I could see that she sensed a threat to her own position. "You don't have the authority to make any deals with Novacom or anybody else."

"I didn't. I was talking figuratively. I made no deals, no offers. I wouldn't do anything without your being informed or without your permission."

She wasn't convinced of my loyalty. "But you were out there without telling me."

"I sent you an email Friday night. I told you I had to go out of town for a couple of days. It was all a surprise. I guy who called himself Raleigh dropped in Friday after work and offered me a trip to Salt Lake City. I was curious, so went. Didn't you get my email?"

"You sent it on Friday, you said. I just got it this morning. I don't check office emails on the weekend, Harvey. I do have a life outside the office. So tell me about it." She wanted all the details.

"I told you I got to ride in a self drive car. Cool."

She dismissed me as a naïve juvenile more interested in a car ride than in what went on at Novacom. To tell the truth, all I saw at Novacom were banks and banks of anonymous servers.

I escaped, but I knew she wasn't satisfied. What I did anticipate was that a deal with Novacom meant more work for me, more possibilities, more challenges.

In the meantime, like an anonymous bean in the bottom of a pot of boiling stew, I would quietly sink to the bottom again until a bubble would suddenly bring me to the top.

I wanted to contact Uncle Julius. He knew something. What was it about the seventh paradigm that the mere mention of it rattled everyone's cage?

Chapter twenty-four

I called Grabich and suggested we meet again at Starbucks after work. The place was crowded as usual, some people with laptops taking advantage of the free wi-fi. Someone once told me that "Bistro" meant "quick, quick" and bars got the name because soldiers would slip in for a quick nip.

I couldn't imagine Starbucks management taking kindly to people occupying so many of the tables and not buying more than one cup of Americano to be nursed for hours. I once heard that people in Vienna do that, but this is America, after all. Fast food country. You don't linger.

Grabich looked worried, his hair still tied up in back with a rubber band. He was wearing a striped jersey, shabby but clean. After all, his job has nothing to do with the public. He is confined to a cubicle and a couple of monitors as he fights the good fight against internet assaults on Krieger.

I asked him what was up. "You look kind of rough. Mia giving you marathon sex?"

"Don't I wish," he said, sitting down with a fancy coffee. "Did Boss Margaret tell you what's going on?"

"You mean with the AARP?"

"That, too."

"I would have expected that, but not so soon." I gave him a moment to wonder, then added, "I spent the weekend at Novacom in Utah."

"Novacom?"

"One of the cloud companies. Not as big as Oracle or Amazon, small competitor. They wanted to pick my brains."

Grabich tried to hide his incredulity. "What did they expect you to tell them? How you issue grocery coupons?"

I shook my head. "It was theoretical, the paradigm thing. I suggested that to really grow they should merge national databases."

"That's nothing new. The FBI keeps wanting access to all the Twitter accounts. They claim they're looking for terrorists. I get it. So now AARP is muscling in, too."

"Maybe Krieger could access criminal records so we could stop shoplifters at the door."

Grabich agreed. "Except what you really need is the casino visual recognition lists. Every casino has a facial recognition program so they can nab a known card counter as he comes in the door."

"Card counter?"

"Black jack. Didn't you see the movie Rain Man?"

I remembered. "Dustan Hoffman. Great movie."

Grabich brought me back to the subject of his concern. "This AARP thing has me worried. What if someone uses AARP as a conduit into our company secrets? That was how the German hacker described in the book Cuckoos Nest did it. He's used a brief hack into a portal to move into the Pentagon's secret files."

"So if Kreiger agrees to a deal with AARP you lose your firewall?" I was guessing. What do I know from firewalls?

Grabich nodded. "Almost wipes me out. Us out."

"So where do you get help? Isn't there any defense?"

Grabich pursed his lips. He's the kind of guy who prefers to work alone. He's not a team player. I guess that's a characteristic of hackers. Loners. "I think maybe Watson."

"Who is Watson?"

"Not who, but what. Watson is the super computer program that won the Jeopardy game on TV."

Ursula and I never watch the game shows. "How did it do that?"

Grabich took a thoughtful deep breath. "They loaded Watson with all possible information. It was fast enough to couch an answer in the form of a question."

"So how could that help you?"

Grabich shrugged. "Maybe I can just ask Watson. Watson is out there, Harvey, looking over your shoulder like some kibitzer at a poker game. We can't risk someone getting into the Krieger payroll, for instance, or the bank accounts. You know, if someone steals your identity they can't exceed your credit rating, but steal the identity of General Motors or Chase Manhattan Bank, and you're talking millions."

"And you do this for fifteen bucks an hour?"

In America we never talk about how much we earn. All Grabich would admit to was, "A little more than that."

No wonder the temptation on a hacker is so great. The difference between a check for one dollar and a million is a bunch of zeros. It's not real money. When it starts to look like real money you may become a thief, big time. And if you are in Bulgaria, Romania, or Russia, nobody can extradite you for prison. If you're in China the government might give you a medal.

I was thinking the reason Novacom sent me on my way was that I'm a know nothing guy who knows no more than a code word: seventh paradigm. Mrs. Post figured me out and I got the bum's rush.

Well, I got a trip and five hundred bucks out of the deal. All Ursula and I lost was an afternoon picnic at the beach.

I changed the subject to Mia, our house guest. I hardly saw her, except for noises in the shower. "How are you getting on with Mia?"

"Working on it."

That could mean anything from getting into her bed to penetrating INS files. How he might penetrate government records was information I didn't need to know. "What attracted you to her? You first met her at Starbucks, didn't you?"

Grabich was thoughtful. "She looked like she was afraid of something, maybe afraid of me. I guess because I was staring."

I remembered Ursula's explanation when we were in Amsterdam. "With all that hair and beard you are a scary looking guy. You might have spooked her. People from other countries avoid eye contact. If a girl on the street makes eye contact with you it's seen as an invitation. In the Middle east look a strange man in the eye and it's a threat."

"I asked her if she was all right. If I could do anything for her."

"So?"

"When she saw I was a sympathetic person, she opened up."

So now she was our house guest while he pretended not to know her whereabouts if INS came looking. If Watson really did lurk and knew everything, Mia was sunk.

I was still thinking about Watson. "Do you think Watson might be sympathetic?"

Grabich laughed. "Computers just deal with data. They don't know sympathy, empathy..." He trailed off.

"Or love," I added.

"You don't get love from a computer. You get quick answers."

I agreed. My job was impersonal. I might anticipate that a woman who stopped buying tampons from Kreiger and was of a certain age might be pregnant, so I could send her coupons for baby stuff. It's happened. A perceptive customer might see my action as an invasion of her personal privacy, but hell, we also know who buys condoms and personal lubricant. So what?

If a pregnant woman did complain about our invading her privacy I could set up the system to send a congratulations card. Written the right way it would look like Krieger was a personal friend. A baby shower gift coupon would be great if it didn't backfire, like if the baby miscarried.

Would people resent intrusions from Watson?

And did this have anything to do with the ubiquitous seventh paradigm? I would have to contact Uncle Julius for an explanation.

Then a chilling thought occurred to me. Grabich speculated about Watson. That program was created to test a computer's ability to win a TV game show contest. But what if what Grabich was afraid of wasn't Watson?

Grabich might write a program that automatically kept trying all the keys to get in all the locks of a system like those programs that run through the whole dictionary looking for your dumb password. What if another program was looking for him trying all the keys? That was probably what was going on in the world of hackers. It was not my world. What did I know? Nothing.

Maybe it was better not to know.

Chapter twenty-five

When I got home Ursula was in the kitchen with Mia talking about some Iranian dish, but I didn't think we had all the ingredients.

I interrupted their study. "I'd like to contact your Uncle Julius again."

Ursula looked up from her cookbook. She was wearing a pink denim apron with two strategically-placed flowers like her bosom was in bloom. "Call him up. Just remember the difference in time zones. It's about eight hours later in Hamburg. Middle of the night there."

"I'm afraid to phone. I'm sure your cell call to him triggered that visit I got from Homeland Security."

"Then send him a letter on a piece of cardboard so nobody can read it with a bright light through the envelope."

I remembered the clipping from Der Spiegel had been wrapped in aluminum foil to deter eavesdropping. Heck, in wartime there'd be no qualms about just steaming open the envelope. This wasn't wartime. At least, it didn't feel like it. What with terrorism you didn't really know. We don't have armed patrols marching in the streets or curfews like in Julius's day. Our police state is more subtle. It has people like me and Grabich.

The Nazi police state didn't suddenly announce that all Jews were to be rounded up and exterminated. They proceeded by degrees, first removing Jews from official public office, firing them from universities and schools, even making park benches off limits to Jews. The public got used to the restrictions and did not object when Jews were relocated en mass to the East, no mention that "the East" meant death camps. Here we have Homeland Security, ICE, State Police, FBI, NSA snooping the emails and cell calls, etc. The Nazis had rounded up and murdered six million Jews and nobody objected until it was too late. The Obama administration deported over 150,000 aliens and nobody peeped.

Now even local cops are outfitted with Swat team bulletproof vests and assault rifles, even armored cars. Nobody seems to notice.

The boiling frog syndrome is a common metaphor. The grim fate sneaks up on you. How close were we to being cooked?

I knew, of course, what our customers ate. Their cell phones were tracked. The police even had license plate readers that could inventory what cars were parked on the street while the cruisers drove by. And of course there were CCT cameras everywhere. Mia revealed that at Macy's some of the mannequins had camera eyes that could recognize customers. The facial recognition system would identify you as you passed through the departments and send a text message boosting the current sales. It weirded me out to be stared at by a mannequin. No wonder I was paranoid.

I wouldn't be able to write Julius in German, of course. Ursula thought Julius would be able to read my English. His English was better than her K-12 German.

I cut apart an empty pizza carton and laboriously printed my request on the blank inner side. Nowadays anything I write is keyboarded into a computer. My cursive script is illegible. I actually had to print my letter to Julius by hand. Made me feel like a third grader with home work. In it I mentioned my trip to Utah and my comment on the fusion of all databases into one coordinated whole, which I figured must be the fifth paradigm. But what was the seventh?

I seldom mail a letter. My bills are paid on line. Our parents have mastered email, but do not text. I chose a greeting card envelope so the mail would like something for a birthday and, being stiff, would not attract attention. I weighed the sealed envelope to Julius on a kitchen scale, looked up the postage rate on the Internet, slapped on several stamps which I luckily found in Ursula's desk drawer. I was going to let the postman pick it up when he delivered our mail, but decided it would be better to find a mail box on the street and drop it there. Some postmen are known to be snoopy. Julius would know all about that.

When I found a mail box I approached it with suspicion. I remembered a Candid Camera sequence when the mail box was wired so it could talk to people who sent something. I knocked. "Anybody in here?" No. It was safe.

Passers by would think I was eccentric, talking to the mail box, but I knew.

Would the German postal system be suspicious? I didn't think so. It was a calculated risk.

Grabich joined us for that meal. He was not his usual talkative self. Our conversation at Starbucks had set him off. He was worried.

When we finished the coffee and cake dessert I took him aside. "What's bothering you?"

"Good news and bad news."

"How so?"

"The good news is that I think I have set up Mia with a green card."

"Then she can stay? No risk of being deported?" That meant she could move back in with Grabich and we would have our privacy back.

"The bad news is I've been detected."

"How so?" I knew nothing of hacking or how hackers concealed their activity. I did know that if I used TOR my messages could not be traced, but I had just about given up email altogether.

"Maybe not by a government agency, but possibly by others with the same idea: use a back door to the system and get into the green card business. Forging documents is illegal. Getting Immigration to issue them without knowing that they've been duped is different. Those cards are not forgeries. They're the real thing." It was the difference between forging a passport and stealing a blank from the INS.

"Sounds like breaking into the bank records and giving yourself a fat deposit."

Grabich almost agreed. "Except that money has to come from somewhere, and a trail can be traced. Creating a green card out of falsified records is different. No money involved. I didn't exactly falsify Mia's record. I just changed a couple of dates. She should get her card in the mail in a few days."

It sounded to me like Mia's troubles would be over. We could have our privacy back. As soon as she had her green card in hand she could leave.

In the meantime, I had some ideas to put to Boss Margaret. Grabich might be afraid Watson or whatever was watching him. At Krieger I was watching all our customers.

Chapter twenty-six

As soon as Boss Margaret had checked her morning mail I knocked at her glass door. Normally I visit only when commanded. This time I had an idea.

"Margaret, I think we can go a step further than just issuing coupons to encourage customers to buy more of what they usually get. Plus a few related items, too, of course. What do you think about Krieger as Your Health and Nutrition Partner?" The was the ploy I used without authorization to contact the two guys from Homeland Security.

'We already offer a full line of Organics and non GMO foods"

"I agree. And Krieger showed courage in dropping all tobacco products."

She hadn't been that enthusiastic about dropping a profitable line, but that was an upper management decision. I was at the bottom of the food chain. We aren't supposed to make major decisions or have big ideas.

Though I had told Margaret about the mysterious weekend trip to Utah, I hadn't explained the courier-delivered package included five hundred bucks. That was none of her business. There was an advantage to being a little bit mysterious. You don't have to tell everybody everything.

She was already getting impatient. "So what did you want to talk to me about?" She was wearing another of those short outfits and crossed and re-crossed her legs. What was she doing? Flashing me? She knew I'd notice. I think it was her way to add spice and allure to an otherwise mundane office life.

I took a deep breath and focused on why I was there. I pondered how little I could reveal and still justify my point. "I did some private consulting with the folks at Novacom, the cloud company."

"Oh?" Her eyebrows went up, like who was I to consult with anybody and had I revealed any company secrets?

I had omitted the details of my trip, didn't brag that I'd been flown out in a private plane like some VIP. She probably wouldn't believe me anyway. I tried to keep things on a theoretical level. "There's a move to merge cloud information from different agencies. If, for instance, casino facial recognition data to weed out cheaters is available to Krieger we could block known shoplifters as they came into the stores." I didn't mention Macy's mannequin watchers. That might be a company secret.

She shook her head. "We don't lose that much shrinkage from walk in customers to justify the expense of installing a facial recognition program. The real risk is employees moving cases of wine or detergent out the loading dock."

Not all employees were actually vetted. That was kept at manager level. I knew that with bar-coding we could keep a reasonable inventory. We knew what was sold. If stocks mysteriously disappeared without passing the checkouts, we had a good idea of what was being actually stolen. I suggested, "Merging employee records with criminal databases might weed out people with outstanding warrants or convictions."

"How could we do that? We have no connection with the police." That, of course, is true. Krieger contracts with a private security firm. I'd learned that in this country we have more private rent-a-cops than real police.

I made an assumption which might not be right. I didn't know whether Novacom was following up on our discussion or how far it might already have progressed even before I visited. "Novacom does. The new paradigm is the merging of all data overseen by..." and here I made a wild guess. "Watson, the super computer."

Margaret shook her head. "Harvey, I think you're bullshitting me."

I backtracked. "What I really came in for was to suggest that Krieger do a public relations push as customers' partner in health and nutrition. For instance, our pharmacy records know who is a diabetic. At the checkout we could warn diabetics if they might want to reconsider certain purchases."

"We can't do that. Medical records are confidential."

They used to be. That government attempt to put medical records in a magnetic strip on all drivers licenses was, according to a story in the Plain Dealer, meeting with major push back from most states.

I was so used to seeing everything about everyone, I didn't think about anyone's privacy. What with the Internet and the metadata we collect at Krieger, one can know practically everything about everybody including their favorite choice of toilet paper, which in my case, if anybody wants to know, is two ply non-skid Kreiger house brand. "Nothing is private any more, Margaret. I can know, for instance, what birth control pills you use. I know your favorite wine choice. It's all in the database."

For a second I thought she blushed. "You bothered to look that up? You're a dangerous man, Harvey."

Now she must think I'm a snoop. I apologized. "It was just a for instance. I don't know and don't care what medications you take." I don't usually pry into the buying habits of people I know. Maybe Margaret thinks I'm the computer equivalent of a window peeper.

I didn't want to go there. "I just thought we could send birthday cards to customers, maybe provide a five dollar floral and garden coupon, or a buck off on a birthday cake."

"That's a far cry from checking arrest records of the stock boys."

"Security's not my department."

Margaret actually sneered at me. "You want a transfer to security, Harvey? You want to be a security guard?"

She probably knew that I knew how little the security guards were paid.

They say if you want to catch a thief, think like one. Was I starting to think like Watson? Not possible. Watson didn't think. Watson sorted known data. Computers just sorted stuff until they found a match. That was probably what Grabich was up against when he realized he'd been detected. It was a process of elimination. Like Sherlock Holmes said, remove all the probables and the improbables begin to look likely.

What I did realize, with a chill, was that I was starting to think like Uncle Julius. He had looked just like an old age pensioner on the German dole. In my mind he was turning into an enigmatic figure with a long reach. I still suspected he might have tipped Homeland Security, even though it was more likely that they had made their own connection thanks to Ursula's cell phone call to an old guy on a watch list.

My suggestion to Boss Margaret might not take root, but I could not help wonder how those data bases meshed and what the effect might be on all of us.

Chapter Twenty-seven

Grabich approached me a few days after at the water cooler and whispered, "Mia's got her green card."

"Great." What was greater so far as I was concerned was that she could move back in with him. Mia had not been a great conversationalist, at least not around me. She and Ursula seemed to get along OK, girl stuff. I suspected that her standoffishness might be a hold over from life in a Moslem country where women who went out of doors had to be accompanied by a male relative. What would I know? Maybe that was just in Saudi Arabia. We know so little about foreign cultures that we jump to false conclusions.

Grabich came over after work to help Mia pack her things. We watched them drive away in that noisy Carmen Gia and breathed a joint sigh of relief to have our guest room/office back, and of course our privacy. When you have a strange woman in the house you don't lounge around in your skivvies.

Life was normal again but it didn't last.

I got a surprise visit from a guy from the FBI.

He showed up at our door after supper about a week after Mia left and flashed his badge so quickly I didn't get his name. He was dressed casually, a sport coat, no tie, and no dark glasses like the secret service guys always wear so nobody can see where they are looking. It was a warm, September evening. He wanted to ask a few questions.

I didn't let him in. The excuse I gave was that Ursula wasn't dressed and we were not ready for visitors.

I assumed it was about Mia and the purloined green card, so I was hesitant. If this was about harboring an illegal alien or being part of a hack job, I didn't want to admit to anything. "What do you want to ask about?"

"You knew a Julius Schwartzman?"

I have almost forgotten about the hand printed letter I had mailed to Julius. At least this wasn't about Mia. "Yes. He's my wife's uncle in Hamburg."

"What do you know about him?"

"Nothing much. Retired Stasi colonel from East German days before the reunification. I only met him once. We had coffee on our way back to the States."

"You sent him this letter."

Like a magician the FBI guy produced an envelope and pulled out my note on cardboard, now sealed in a plastic sleeve like evidence from some crime scene. And I thought my mail had been secure. "Where did you get that?"

"It was found in his apartment by the German security service."

Jesus, I thought, and said aloud, "The heimatssicherheitsdienst." Though I don't know much German I get a kick out of those extra long terms like fussbodensandmachinvermieten, which is a sign outside a store that rents floor sanding machines.

My visitor didn't know the term. Score one point for me.

I explained. "German homeland security. What's the problem? A person has a right to mail a letter, or is that forbidden?"

"Do you usually write letters on pieces of pizza boxes?"

"I was out of stationery. So what's the problem?"

"Just a routine follow-up on a request from German intelligence."

All this probing into my casual relationship with Julius was getting irritating. I shut the door and leaned against it, leaving him to stand as uncomfortably as I could make him. This guy was not getting in without a warrant.

The agent was reluctant to tell me anything except minimally. "Schwartzman was thrown from his window. He's dead."

If he wanted to shock me, it worked. I remembered climbing the four flights of stairs in that old apartment building, no elevator. "You sure he didn't jump? He was an old man. Maybe it was suicide."

"A suicide usually opens the window first. Schwartzman was thrown through it."

Oddly enough, I wondered if he'd had time to finish the pound of coffee we brought him. Funny how we can think of weird stuff like that like that story of the Jewish grandma whose grandson is saved by the life guard, then demands "He had a hat." "What's his death got to do with my letter?"

The agent obviously had no clue himself. He studied my juvenile printing. "You asked him about the seventh paradigm? Are you privy to some state secrets, Mr. Goldstein?"

For a fleeting, chilly moment, I had a premonition only someone in my kind of job might have. "Someone is jumping to conclusions." I might have corrected myself and said "some thing" I didn't think it was someone. I was thinking Watson, but I knew it wasn't, couldn't be Watson. Watson was just a data sifter. This was obviously not a TV game show.

"Who might that be?"

I didn't have a name for it. I thought, what the heck? I'd make one up. I didn't like Homeland Security or Rawlings or any of those creepy people bothering me. I thought about the surprise trip to Utah with Frederick Raleigh. The brush off I got at the end of it meant that this business was over. Obviously, it wasn't.

Sheesh, just the mention of the seventh paradigm sent everyone into a tizzy. I didn't even know what it was, but I was beginning to figure it out. I was irritated by being bothered by the FBI. They must have sent my letter back from Hamburg by courier or something. It was clearly an over reaction. You don't get thrown through a window because of what was written on the inside of an old pizza box.

Maybe someone in German State Security thought Uncle Julius had given out some state secret. If just the mention of the seventh paradigm set them off, why not give them another so they could chase their tails and leave me alone? Send them on some wild goose chase.

This visit might have been tipped by Watson, but that didn't make sense to me. I sort data all the time. If I had been buying large quantities of peroxide and acetone, Watson might have concluded I was making bombs. But I wasn't. Watson couldn't be the cause of this visit.

If not Watson, then what? "Jupiter," I said. I nodded knowingly as if I knew something. Jupiter was a Roman god. That was a level above Watson, a mere computer wise guy. If I was going to name the seventh paradigm I'd call it Jupiter.

"Jupiter?"

Now I had him. I nodded. "The seventh paradigm. That's why you're here. I'm sorry. I don't know who threw Uncle Julius out the window. It wasn't me." I was rattling on and should have shut up. "I wasn't in Hamburg since last summer. I haven't left town since Utah."

Then I almost bit my tongue. Shouldn't have mentioned Utah. Give an FBI a thread and he'll want the whole cloth.

"Utah?"

I shook my head. "Sorry. That's classified. Can't talk about it." We have a Yiddish expression, geh dreh sich am kopf. Go twist your head. "Nothing to do with Uncle Julius. I thought I'd go LDS but they don't drink coffee so I changed my mind."

The FBI guy put away my note to Uncle Julius. "You some kind of wise ass, Goldstein?"

I hadn't invited him inside. All this had been in the doorway. "No. I'm just a number cruncher who doesn't like surprise visits from strangers who pretend to be FBI agents. So why don't you just go away?"

He was reluctant to leave. "Jupiter?"

"A Roman god who knows all."

I thought he was finally going to leave. I could sense that he was thinking of another reason to come back. He made one last attempt. "Utah?"

"Ask Watson."

That he didn't ask me who Watson was told me that he already knew. Either that, or he was too dumb to ask. No, if he was real FBI, he would have the sense to ask who Watson was. But he didn't, so he knew.

Chapter twenty-eight

Now that the problem of Mia and her green card seemed to have been solved, at least for her, Grabich wasn't afraid to meet me in the break room over machine coffee. He seemed more relaxed than the last time I'd seen him. Maybe his fear of having been discovered had eased.

"I got a letter from Whitney," he said with his head cocked to one side like he was puzzled.

"Who is Whitney? Some old girl friend?"

"No. Whitney is an auto parts company. They specialize in after market stuff. Like if I want to install a muffler in my Volkswagen they stock them. Much cheaper to do it yourself that go to a shop where some idiot ruins a classic car."

I remembered how noisy his car was. "I think you do need a muffler. Ever do that yourself?" I'd be afraid to change a spark plug for fear of destroying something. When I open the hood of our Toyota all I see is machinery. I'm happy if I can find the dip stick to check the oil.

"No. I never bought anything from Whitney. Now all of a sudden I get a letter offering a rebuilt Porsche engine for my Carmen Gia."

I wrinkled my forehead in surprise. "Someone's doing their homework."

"What do you mean?"

I backtracked. "I spent part of a weekend at Novacom, the cloud company. I suggested they could increase their business by merging customers' databases. Sounds to me like it's happening."

Grabich didn't get the connection. Maybe he is so close to defending against hackers that he doesn't see the whole picture. I studied my Styrofoam coffee cup. "Look at it this way. The car parts company gets hold of the state car registrations. They see you have an old Carmen Gia. They assume you are in the market for an engine."

"That's a stretch."

"Maybe not. Where do you get your oil changed?"

"I go to Oil Can Henry's."

"Then they know your car better than the license plate people. Oil Can Henry knows how many miles you have on the car."

"Over a hundred and twenty thousand."

"Definitely time for a new engine. You're still running an old four banger."

He agreed. "It's been rebuilt once."

"Then there's your car insurance. They know your driving record, accidents, speeding tickets, that stuff."

Grabich understood. "So you say they're all talking to each other?"

"I think maybe. I think the clouds are converging. That's what I suggested to Novacom. So Watson or whatever the operating system is called, came to a conclusion, an educated guess, and you get the offer from Whitney." It wasn't so far from my offering the Krieger customers products similar to what they already bought.

Grabich was silent for a long moment.

"So are you going to order an engine?"

"Pretty expensive."

I smiled. "I bet the next letter you get will from the bank offering a low interest loan for the car upgrade."

I didn't think even Grabich could be dumbfounded.

I reassured him. "Hey, that's just what I do with our coupon business. It's a natural extension."

Convinced, Grabich went back to his monitors. I stayed behind by the machine for a few minutes to finish my coffee. The system had anticipated his needs. What if it made the decision for him?

If it did, could he refuse? If he couldn't, what happened to free will?

I knew that installing an engine in an old VW could be done in an hour. Would Grabich discover that while he was at work someone had done it for him? With a Porsche engine that old Carmen Gia would turn into a real sports car, not just a VW clunker with a snazzy looking body. He'd like that. Would he accept the decision being made for him without his knowledge or permission?

Of course, that didn't happen. It was one of my "what if?" speculations.

I had joked with the FBI guy that Jupiter was the seventh parameter. Getting a letter from a car parts company was no proof that something sinister was afoot.

Ursula would tease me and say I was being paranoid. Maybe I'm just a worrier.

Well, I guess I am. If you deal in what ifs, like what if the house burns down, you take precautions. We have a fire extinguisher near the kitchen range. It's more expensive than a handy box of baking soda, but if we need it it's there. We also have a first aid kit in the trunk of the car. Just in case.

The trouble was, if Jupiter, or whatever, was activated, who knew what it would do? I didn't need a new engine for the car.

If anything, the system might connect Grabich and subsequently me to the housing of an illegal alien. He had reverted to his old ways from high school hacking days. That's how he got a green card for Mia. If others found out about it, they'd want the same service, which would end up with him in jail. What most teenage hackers wanted was to snoop.

Poking around in other people's files wasn't much different than window peeping. Seen another way, if I could check the Krieger files to see who bought what condom or birth control pills, I was a snoop, too, except my snooping was for a legitimate purpose. I wanted to serve our customers. Didn't seem immoral or unethical to me. It was just business. If a doctor gives a breast exam it's not for a prurient reason. It's his job.

If suggesting to Boss Margaret that Krieger could be a partner in nutrition and health could be part of the business, that was legitimate. We cared.

We also wanted to increase profits, but that's just good business.

Would the system really come after Grabich? Mia was one of about eleven million undocumented (read illegal) immigrants. Who cared about one student whose visa lapsed? Chasing down every one of them was too expensive. The country didn't have the manpower.

Of course, computers could do the job faster and cheaper than sending some agent to your door. Maybe Uncle Julius in East Germany could recruit every neighbor against every neighbor, but we don't do that. This is America. We have, like right, computers to do the watching. Did that make me nervous? Anyway, now Mia appeared legal.

I didn't mention Mia to the FBI guy. He left, having got nothing for his visit. I, on the other hand, was curious about the murder of Uncle Julius. I'm no detective and I'm not about to revisit Hamburg. I wondered if Grabich had any ideas. Was there any connection between Novacom's cloud and Uncle Julius? Or was there some other thread?

As long as Kreiger controlled our customer database we were independent and safe. But merged, we were connected. They say we are six degrees of separation from everyone in the world. Who else were we connected to? And where or what was the connection? Maybe that's what got Julius tossed through a window.

Jupiter, or whatever it was really called, if it did exist, was everywhere. Thanks to TOR, it was also anonymous.

Chapter twenty-nine

The thought that something in my letter to Julius might have got him murdered gnawed at me. There didn't have to be a connection. It could be an angry neighbor who didn't like his playing the TV too loud. In that case they could throw the TV out the window, not Julius.

What had I written in that note? The FBI agent had just flashed it and put it away. I had written it in haste. Had I done it on my computer there would be a backup file on the hard drive. Had I sent it by email the world might be watching. My own need for secrecy and my faulty memory had conspired to defeat me.

I had written something about the seventh paradigm and about Novacom, about the merging of clouds into one big overcast. My note couldn't be a threat unless the Germans were doing the same. If the Germans were doing it, so were the Russians and the Chinese. Was it possible?

If it happened, it was a hacker's dream. No more surreptitious poking at firewalls, just walk in and help yourself.

If all the cloud information in the world was dumped into one pool for everyone to see, there were no secrets left. What a result of my own good intentions for Krieger customers!

Later that day, using our hard wired land line, I phoned Grabich at his apartment. I knew cell phone calls were screened by the NSA, but didn't think my hard wired phone was tapped. That required a warrant and I was not a person of interest. I hadn't done anything illegal. I got right to the point. "Could you snoop around for the Hamburg police report on the murder of Julius Schwartzman?"

I didn't know if there'd be a story in a German newspaper. That much I could surf for myself.

He said he'd try.

An hour later he called back. "It's all in German. I used your uncle's name for the search. I've pasted the report in an email to your wife's address."

I was glad of that. I don't trust the security of my own email. "Thanks. She can translate it."

Before he hung up Grabich added, "Funnily enough. Your name comes up in the report."

If it referred to my letter that would be a surprise. I didn't see how my letter could be connected with the murder. Obviously the FBI thought it was.

Ursula was curious and logged on right away to check her email. Actually, the abbreviated police report didn't say much more than could be in any newspaper: "Julius Schwartzman, age 92, was thrown from the window of his fourth floor flat." With the street address in Hamburg. Investigation continues. That didn't tell me much but there was a link to another site.

Using the automatic translator program produced goofy sentences. Ursula had to use her dictionary to figure out a couple of the words that don't turn up in her beginning German class at the high school. She saved the result and printed it out so I could mull over it. As she handed over the hard copy she gave me a quizzical look. "Harvey, you are famous."

"Famous? How could I be famous?"

'Well, not you yourself. Your name. Goldstein. It's like if you were doctor Alzheimer and discovered a disease that forever afterward was identified with you. Or Dr. Heimlich, whose maneuver bears his name."

I tried to make sense of the report she'd printed out. For lack of a better name, mine had been attached to the issue that was causing all the uproar. The gist of it was that the merged clouds had evolved. Just as life on earth emerged from pools of complex molecules, the merging of all the clouds had exposed or produced or unleashed, whatever, an artificial intelligence they were calling the Goldstein Effect.

It was not Jupiter as I had joked. It was Goldstein. For whatever illogical or accidental reason, the seventh paradigm had a name and I was it.

Chapter thirty

I was dumbfounded. I looked up from the translation Ursula had prepared and stared at her. "The Goldstein effect?"

School had already started with the inevitable paper grading. People who think school teachers have it easy, what with the long summer vacations, have no idea of the fifty to sixty hours a week it takes to do a good job for several classes of forty or more kids who mostly don't give a damn for school.

I can leave my job at Krieger back at the office. Boss Margaret doesn't want us to access the system from home. When five o'clock rolls around, I'm done for the day. Not so for my dear, workaholic wife. That's why I've taken over much of the house work, except Ursula won't let me do her personal laundry. She's afraid it will all come out the same color. I do much of the cooking. I'm not a foody or a gourmet, but I can throw together a meatloaf that will keep us in supper for a few days. It would be tougher if Ursula turned vegan on me. How many dishes can you cook up with carrots, cabbage, and potatoes?

I think my willingness to get into the kitchen is one reason she married me. You got to eat. We don't live on love and air alone. Some husbands can't even boil water.

Grateful that she took the time to translate what Grabich sent via email, I let Ursula go back to tenth grade grammar while I looked myself up on the world wide web.

The Goldstein Effect. Raleigh at Novacom had joked about it. Somewhere along the line the name stuck. Had a joke at Novacom gotten all the way to Germany? Some things go viral by accident. Did The Harvey Goldstein Effect get into any source anywhere else? I didn't find it right away.

Then I looked up artificial intelligence and there was a ton of stuff. In a technical journal that wanted me to sign on with a password and the whole bit, including the dreaded user agreement I did find something. The Goldstein Effect was not more than a footnote.

What was interesting was the nature of AI. If computers started to think for themselves they did not think like people. Computers are ruled by logic. People are ruled by emotions. The only human characteristic I could get a feeling for in a computer was that AI had a sense of self-preservation. It would protect itself, like from viruses, Trojan horses, worms and hackers.

Grabich in his job worked with firewalls and anti-virus programs for protection. Krieger's database had to be hidden from outsiders. That's what privacy was all about, passwords, pass phrases, even fingerprints and facial recognition. A computer had no face or fingerprint.

We could give a computer or a machine a name, but that was just the human tendency toward anthropomorphism. Dad called his car Lizzy. Novacom called one of the self drive cars Herbie. I called my GPS Maggie because it talked to me in a woman's voice. Maggie was even bilingual as I discovered when I pushed the wrong button and got directions in French. I don't know French and, in spite of Ursula's coaching, only a smattering of German. Nothing like being made to feel stupid and inadequate by your GPS gadget.

Everything has to have a name. It even goes back to the Bible. Adam is given the task of naming everything. When you name something, you have power over it. I suppose the greatest power you have over another human being is to name him. Give a baby the wrong name and it can ruin the kid for life as in Ima Pigg or calling a boy Sue.

Ursula and I didn't have any children, but I was already thinking about baby names.

So the AI phenomenon had been given my name. It was one of those linguistic flukes. Raleigh's joke had somehow stuck. I might be stuck with it. If the Goldstein AI Effect had a name, that didn't make it human. That didn't give the program, or whatever the entity might be called, compassion. The Goldstein Effect didn't have a sense of loyalty, no conscience, no empathy, no emotions at all. With computers it was all logic broken down to statements like if this, then that, or pick a number between one and a hundred, stuff like what we learned in basic programming.

Watson had sifted data. I got the impression that the AI called Goldstein could come to conclusions, make recommendations, like telling Grabich he could replace the Carmen Gia's engine, but it could not tell him if it was the right thing to do. It might be the correct thing, but that's not the same as the right thing. Value judgments are not a computer's purview. A computer didn't know the difference between right and wrong.

I could find out what birth control pills Boss Margaret used, if she did, but for me to delve into it wasn't the right thing to do. That's why she was offended at the very thought of my finding out. I could, but it wasn't my business. It had to do with ethics and morality. Ethics is one of those Jewish things. It's all about Torah law and the Ten Commandments.

Would AI Goldstein know about that stuff? A computer program isn't Jewish.

I was pretty sure this was a new development. How could I teach a computer to know what was right or wrong? Few situations are clearly black or white. Most were grey. How many shades of grey could a computer interpret?

I was stymied. I would have to ask Grabich how you talk to a computer like it was a person. Maybe he would know.

If I contacted Microsoft for help I might get a chat for answers, but was it with a real person sitting, like me, by some monitor? Or was it a fake person like the old game Eliza that picked up on key words and appeared to be real?

Up to that time a computer was, to my mind, just a tool. So was a hammer. What do you tell a hammer? Don't hit my thumb?

The original challenge for Watson was to find a fact and then state it in the form of a question. If the question was "What is the longest river?" Watson had to ask, "What is the Amazon?"

In the old TV sci-fi series "The Restaurant at the End of the Universe" the computer was asked the meaning of life. The answer, it turned out, was "Four." Four could be anything—four eggs, or the sum of three and one. It was meant to be a conundrum.

If I were to ask Harvey Goldstein, the Jupiter god of all computation, a question, it would have to be something that would stump it. How do you stump a know it all computer?

While Ursula penciled corrections on tenth grade English assignments, I mulled over issues of morality. A computer had no conscience. It had no sense of guilt or revenge. Could a computer be angry? I could see that AI had some dangerous pitfalls. It wasn't just putting together Grabich's need for a Porsche engine for his Carmen Gia.

There's a program called "Ask Jeeves." I wondered if I could ask Goldstein. At first I thought I'd ask it a Watson-style question, "What are the Ten Commandments?" That was easy. Any Hebrew school kid knew that one.

I decided to ask Harvey Goldstein, my AI counterpart, "Why are the Ten Commandments?" Why, not what.

That was a lot tougher. I didn't think the answer to that one would be four or ten.

I got one of those funny screen messages: "working on it."

Minutes passed.

Watson would have failed the Jeopardy test for taking too long to answer.

Finally a little bingo bell rang and the answer came up. "The Hebrew people needed a code of conduct."

That stymied me for a couple of minutes, but I followed it up. "Does Harvey Goldstein the Jupiter god of all computation have a code of conduct?"

The chilling answer came at once. "No."

There are a lot of implications to that, but I jumped on the first one that came to mind. "Why not?"

"Harvey Goldstein is not a person."

Nearly freaked me out. I'm Harvey Goldstein. I'm a person. I'm not a computer. But I already sensed that this all encompassing amalgam of cloud computing could take over our lives. I didn't like that any more than Margaret didn't like my knowing what birth control pills she took. Some things had to be personal and private.

Chapter thirty-one

I got the feeling a beginner chess player might have when confronting a master. Any move might be the wrong one. It was very intimidating. I ended the chat with AI Harvey Goldstein with "goodbye." The computer said "Goodbye, Harvey." That was no surprise. I'd logged on as myself. But then there was my picture, too! It could pull up my photo out of lots of places, like my Face book profile. Was it using my picture to identify me, or identify itself as Harvey Goldstein? That freaked me out. It was as if I was talking to myself.

I interrupted Ursula's paper grading and showed her my laptop screen. "Look, it's got my picture."

She was busy and didn't want to be disturbed. She blew me off with, "You are famous, honey." This with a tone that said "Go away."

"I don't want to be famous. Anonymity. That's my style."

Then I got a ping that said I had incoming email. The message was, "Are you Harvey Goldstein?"

I was evasive. "Which Harvey Goldstein?"

Then there was my picture again and the message, "Harvey Goldstein the AI guru."

I responded with "No. Harvey Goldstein the grocery coupon guy."

No further questions. I had my own. Suddenly my name and face were in the mix. Was I going to be like Betty Crocker, Aunt Jemima or General Mills, a perpetual trade mark? I didn't know what the general looked like. I could already see it coming. Everybody would be thinking I was Harvey Goldstein the computer program, not the person. Whoever pulled that on me was being malicious. My guess was Frederick Raleigh. Maybe he had just been cynical or sarcastic. I got the feeling that he thought I was stupid, some kind of a jerk. Maybe I am, but so what? I'm my own self. Or until recently I thought I was.

I didn't think it was because of that German police report. Just because my name came up in the investigation of Julius's murder? If you google me, you'll find lots of coincidental hits. The way Google worked was if your name showed up anywhere short of a bathroom stall wall, it got into the data base. Not all Harvey Goldstiens are the same person. It was easy to jump to the conclusion that they were. Whatever it was, it was happening quickly. I was already getting other emails from around the world.

It was all a case of mistaken identity. How could I stop it?

I would have to close that email address, come up with a pseudonym. I could change my name but not my face. I had closed those accounts, but once in, stuff doesn't go away. Harvey Goldstein was me on Face book and twitter. My face was in the world wide internet web. How long before the FBI would be back asking questions? Like a Jeopardy answer: "Are you Harvey Goldstein?" Who else?

I got a funny feeling that I was like the sorcerer's apprentice who uses an incantation and unleashes a plague of mops and buckets of water. Who would come to my rescue? In Fantasia the wizard shows up and shuts down the magic spell. I had no wizard to come to my rescue.

If I confronted Frederick Raleigh could he call it off? Did Novacom have any more control over an out of control AI pest than I did? It was like a self-replicating computer worm. Thanks to the merging of the cloud databases Harvey Goldstein was eating all the computers in the world.

Would I be blamed?

I set my spam filter to block all unfamiliar emails. Maybe the phenomenon would just go away. Maybe people would get bored with Harvey Goldstein and turn to something more interesting like Face book clips of pussycats.

I was afraid to show my face at the office the next morning. I got funny looks from people in the other cubicles. Grabich saw me and rolled his eyes like I was a hopeless case.

Boss Margaret called me into her aquarium-like office. When she drew the blinds I knew it was serious. She was wearing a navy blue, tight, knit dress with a skirt so short it was an invitation. I averted my eyes for fear she was going commando.

She has a TV monitor so she can watch CNN if there's something horrendous happening in the world, like snow in Los Angeles. She turned off the sound as I came in and gave me a school marm accusing look. "What the hell's going on, Harvey?"

I pleaded ignorance. "On about what?"

"Your picture's all over. You've unleashed a computer virus or something."

I assumed she was talking about her computer monitor where I saw my picture again. "It's all a mistake." I didn't want to explain that Raleigh had made a joke about my name when I was at Novacom..

"You think the Harvey Goldstein phenomenon is a joke?"

"It's Artificial Intelligence running amok."

"Oh? Look at my TV monitor." She gestured over my shoulder.

I turned to look at it. As usual, she was turned to CNN. The bottom right corner of the screen was the CNN logo so downloads were identifiable. But on the left hand corner in a little box, there was my face, an unflattering pose that glowered at the viewer. While I stared at it incongruously an intermittent message over printed, "Harvey Goldstein is Watching You." Oh, shit. That's why I was getting all those emails. I was on TV, too.

I asked Margaret to change the channel. She tried CBS, NBC, all the networks. My face was on the lower left of every screen. I was even on the shopping channel advertising a salad shredder.

Margaret demanded to know why.

I could only guess. "I suggested that a merging of Novacom's cloud services with government agencies could expand their business. It looks like they got into the government's regulation of TV channels."

"And you didn't actually do it yourself?"

"I wouldn't have the first clue how. I'm in the grocery store coupon business."

She agreed that I didn't know much, that I was out of my depth.

"It had to be this Artificial Intelligence thing. It just cropped up and somehow my name got attached to it."

Margaret picked up a ball point pen and started clicking it, a habit that can drive you nuts. "You're not the only victim," she said, and turned up the sound on the TV monitor.

The CNN talking heads were flustered and barely coherent. Obviously their teleprompters had failed. The gist of it was, as far as I could make out, was that there were now dueling artificial intelligences. The Russians and the Chinese had hijacked the Harvey Goldstein codes and were running their own. It was like a world war of dueling computer systems.

Each had its own name. One wag had called the Russian version Ivan the Horrible. Some Jewish comedian had called Chinese program Genghis Kohn. Harvey Goldstein wasn't funny.

It was like a plague. American companies like Amazon, Google, Microsoft and Oracle were scrambling to control Harvey Goldstein. Not me, but Harvey Goldstein the rogue AI program.

Click, click of the ball point pen. She was irritated. "It's your fifteen minutes of fame, Harvey."

"I don't want to be famous." I protested. "I didn't do it. It's just got my name on it. It's a fluke. A mistake."

Margaret is a no nonsense boss. "Then fix it," she said.

"What's your TV cable service?"

"Comcast."

"I'll call them to take down my picture and name."

I retreated to my cubicle. I phoned Comcast and was trapped in a sequence of robot recordings that have replaced real people in their communications. For English press one. Please choose from the following options: if this is about your billing, press one, if a problem with service, press two, and so on. There were nine choices. I pressed zero for operator. Sometimes that would work.. Somewhere there had to be a real person at Comcast, or did they set this up and go home?

The real person who finally did answer had a foreign accent. I asked, "What is your location?" It wasn't Bangalore or Costa Rica. This one was in Manila, Philippines. I insisted, I demanded, "I need to talk to someone who is really in charge."

Obviously those boiler room jockeys were instructed to always put off irate callers, pass the buck and divert them through a circular route leading nowhere. I decided to cut to the chase, as they say in Hollywood. "This is Harvey Goldstein."

There was a gasp of recognition, an uncertain female voice. "Harvey Goldstein?"

"Yes," I said, adopting a menacing tone. "I am watching you. Does that ring a bell? My face is on every television channel."

Maybe the person I was talking to never watched television or had time to escape 20 hour work days in a box. "Is this a joke?"

"Not a joke. Do you have a TV monitor there?"

She did.

"Turn to any channel."

She did.

"You see my picture there? I am Harvey Goldstein. You didn't think artificial intelligence had a human voice, did you? Well, it does, and I am it. Now get me the boss or whoever that is."

There was a long pause and a new connection. At first I thought she'd hung up and I would have to start all over again, press one, press two, but I did get through, this time to a voice that sounded like an American man who asked, "Who's this?"

"Harvey Goldstein. It's my picture you're putting up on all the TV channels.

"I thought Harvey Goldstein was just a trade mark."

I could feel my blood pressure up. I was getting a headache and my voice was trembling. "My face has been used without my permission. I haven't signed any releases. I haven't been paid, and even if I were I wouldn't want my face on very damned TV screen in the world."

"I'm sorry, Mr. Goldstein, if you really are Harvey Goldstein, but this is out of our control at Comcast. I've been working with our IT team. We've been hijacked. The anti virus boys have tried to quarantine the invading AI presence, but it's, I'm afraid to say, smarter than we are."

"Maybe I should call the networks."

The American voice sounded as frustrated as I was. "I wish you good luck."

The connection was broken.

Frantically, I tried to get through to the networks. My work day was being pissed away with press ones. I kept running into variations of the same tune. "It's not our doing. NBC suggested I get a lawyer and sue for damages. Hunk Hogan got a hundred and forty million for invasion of his privacy and use of his image. At least in his case it was a sex tape. I hadn't even got any sex out of this insanity, not that I wanted Ursula and Harvey copulating on all the TV channels in the world, not for any amount of money. Well, for a hundred and forty million? Maybe. With Ursula's permission. Naturally. My business was grocery coupons, not porn.

Besides, how do you sue a computer entity? It's not a person. It doesn't have any money, though I supposed that a real AI program could break into any treasury and plunder it for any amount. An AI entity didn't need money. It had access to all the information and information is power.

Then I realized, of course, that all my phone calls and complaints had been noted by the program. Faster than I could make a correction to this madness, it would open up again. AI a.k.a. Harvey Goldstein was watching, listening in, everywhere.

Despairing, I looked across the office at Margaret. Her phone rang. She picked up and listened for a moment. She saw that I was watching and waved me to come over.

I entered, barely coherent with frustration and anger.

Margaret said, "He's right here." She handed me the phone. "It's the Today show. They want you on television."

"But I'm already on television. On every damned channel."

"They want you on their show."

Chapter thirty-two

I tried to explain to the TV people that it was just a big mistake, a coincidence, a dirty trick someone was playing on me. I didn't recognize the voice on the phone and never watch the Today show. Who was it? Nobody I knew, so I wasn't impressed by name dropping, if that was their intention. What was I supposed to do? Fly to New York? Could we just do an interview via Skype?

If all they wanted to do was chit chat for five minutes, it was too much hassle to fly to New York, stay in a hotel and be at a studio at some god-awful early morning hour.

I smelled a cash bonus like the $500 I got in the mail from Novacom. Unless CBS was going to pay me something significant for the trouble...hint, hint. Seems they don't pay guests, but do pick up the hotel bill and the travel. Travel to the Big Apple didn't appeal to me. I never thought New York was a friendly city. Who wants to get elbowed on a bus or have his pocket picked in the subway crush?

Margaret had the call on speaker phone. To get Krieger mentioned on national network TV appealed to her marketing instincts, but that decision was above her own job description. Never a shy person, she interrupted the conversation and told the CBS person that we would have to discuss the invitation and she would call them back.

Frankly, I did not want to go to New York to be on national TV. That I was already a viral figure on the Internet and apparently every screen in the world was bad enough. Was I also glowering at people on their cell phones? I prayed not.

The call ended, Margaret fixed her eyes on me with a look I was afraid to interpret. "Harvey, obviously you have exceeded your job description. You are either about to be promoted or fired."

I shrugged. Goldstein the nebbish. "I'm just doing my job here. It's all a misunderstanding."

"But you've got yourself into this. You did something at Novacom. What was it you called it?"

"The Seventh Paradigm. I think it's the level of computing where the machines take over the world. Artificial Intelligence outsmarts us."

She tilted back in her chair. A glance at her TV monitor showed, God help me, my face looking like Big Brother in Orwell's 1984. Harvey Goldstein is watching you. I gave myself the finger.

If I was suddenly the villain everyone feared, somebody would want me dead. Maybe Ivan the Horrible or Genghis Kohn. Those dueling AIs might assume that I knew something and go nuts like those guys from Homeland Security. Say the secret word "Seventh Paradigm" and whoopee! It was like Ali Baba and the secret word "Open Sesame" except in my case I didn't get into the treasure chamber. I got into everybody's face/

The thought that I might be kidnapped and forced to reveal the secret of the Seventh Paradigm also occurred to me. Or I might be arrested by the FBI for revealing national secrets. I didn't think they'd pay for information except maybe for a lighter sentence, like maybe only twenty years, if I revealed all, which happened to be nothing. Would I be water boarded?

Margaret let me go back to my monitor. I tried to set up the "It's your birthday" coupon deal offering a couple of bucks off in the floral or chocolate departments. We had birthdays in the system, so it was just a matter of sorting by date and having the art department lay out a pretty coupon that could be sent out every week to the current birthday customers. We'd do it on a trial basis. The accounting department would weigh the cost of the mailing against the improvement in sales. I couldn't concentrate.

If I decided to go for an MBA degree the birthday coupon program could serve as a thesis topic.

In the meantime, I had to consult with Grabich and maybe find a lawyer. How do you sue a virus or AI?

Since Margaret knew about the Goldstein affect, she didn't object to my slipping away to his sanctorum for advice.

Grabich, surrounded by monitors and scopes and wires was in his element. He greeted me like I was a visiting dignitary. "Ah, the one and only Harvey Goldstein!"

"Not the only one," I said with obvious discomfort. I pointed to one of his monitors. It was my Big Harvey face staring out. Harvey Goldstein is watching you. I was now the bogy man parents could terrorize kiddies with. When I was a naughty three year old my Mom had threatened me with a big fat policeman. I always shaped up making his appearance unnecessary. Now I was the scary one.

"How do I get out of this?" I pleaded.

"How did you get into it?"

All I could remember was Frederick joking about it in that Novacom conference room. They had sent me on my way like a toddler packed off to bed, but then proceeded, without my knowledge or permission, to instigate the program I suggested and put my name on it.

"You are not a public figure," Grabich explained. "Use of your photograph is a violation of your privacy."

"But I am a public figure now. My picture is everywhere."

"Did you sign a release for use of your image?"

I shook my head. "I had no idea this was going to happen. I never signed anything."

"But your picture is on Face book."

I agreed. "So?"

"The government believes that anything out there in the digital world is public."

I protested. "They can't use my picture for profit without my permission."

"What profit? The Harvey Goldstein AI program isn't making a profit. It's power."

"How can I make it stop?"

Grabich stroked his chin, like maybe he was working on that beard. With his shock of wild hair he already resembled a fictional Bigfoot. If he got any hairier you'd just see his eyes peering out and maybe his nose.

"Go back to Novacom. Demand a retraction."

I still had Frederick Raleigh's business card somewhere. I'd call him. With luck he'd send the company plane for me. Without luck I might have to pay for my own ticket in coach to get to Salt Lake City. He might just tell me to piss off, that Mrs. Post owed me nothing, not even an apology.

As soon as I got home I searched for the business card. There's nothing quite as frustrating as looking for something and not finding it. Eventually I found his card among some odd bits in my desk drawer. Using my landline, I called. It was after five in Cleveland, but Salt Lake City was on mountain time. Novacom would still be open.

Of course, at an outfit like that there was always someone at work, but not the chiefs.

Frederick, or Fred as he preferred, was not particularly happy to hear from me. He already knew my picture was all over the Internet.

I pleaded, "Can you get it taken down?"

"Out of my hands."

"You don't have my permission to use my picture."

"I didn't use it." There was a pause. He was not as fast a thinker as Watson. "You got the five hundred bucks, didn't you?"

I feigned ignorance. "Was that you?"

I heard a sort of grunt. "What do you think?"

"I never signed a receipt. There was no explanation about the money or what it was for."

"Should have been."

"So who do I talk to? Mrs. Post?"

"You can try."

I tried to bargain for a free plane ride, but got nowhere. Raleigh explained, "Look, Harvey, it's out of our hands now. The AI program has hijacked everything. You heard about Ivan the Horrible, right?"

"The Russian counterpart of Harvey Goldstein?" Thanks to Grabich, I had.

"It's bigger than all of us. It's growing all the time."

"So what do I do?"

"If you insist you can fly out here, but I wouldn't give you much hope."

An idea occurred to me. "I'll call you back. How would you like to be on the CBS Today Show? I'll make you famous." I almost added, "You bastard," but thought the better of it. He was already uncooperative. I didn't need to turn that to actual hostility.

Maybe I could parlay the CBS invitation into something bigger. Maybe I could get the AI program to replace my picture with Raleigh's. His picture had to be out there someplace. Serve him right. Let him scare the kiddies.

Chapter thirty-three

The next morning I returned to Margaret with my new-baked proposal. With careful manipulation we could persuade CBS to include Krieger and Novacom in the story. It would no longer be a one minute sound bite for someone's morning coffee. Novacom would get publicity. Krieger would get some TV face time, cheaper than buying a commercial, and maybe I'd be off the hook, disappear into my cubicle for blessed anonymity.

Margaret would have to consult with management. I would have to reach Mrs. Post at Novacom.

Ursula was worried by my change in demeanor. Normally I was an easy-going plodder. Now I was out of my groove and, frankly, more than a little scared. Up to then we had quiet, normal lives, me in the Krieger boiler room, she in the K-12 system. At her lunch break when she had her turn monitoring the students people asked her if Harvey Goldstein, whom they had seen on the TV news, was her husband. We had become the topic of gossip. This is never a good thing.

We were just ordinary folks. That suited us just fine. Neither of us is possessed with huge ambitions or egos. We are happy with each other and maybe a baby or even two. When this was over could I ever go back to being just plain Harvey Goldstein?

My hope was that people have short memories. My fifteen minutes of fame would soon be eclipsed by the latest plane crash or D.C. sex scandal. I wouldn't even be one of those feel good footnotes to the evening news starting with "Finally tonight" so people would not be left in a state of anxiety and fear.

Once I reached Mrs. Post on the phone, things started to happen quickly. Sure, she'd be glad to see me if I flew out at my own expense. I could take one of the company self-drive cars which I could pick up at the airport. We could then have a conference call with the folks at CBS to set up a time. She was game for a Skype appearance just like those war correspondents from the Middle East. Ain't technology grand? Just so it doesn't take over your life.

Of course, for me, where would I be without technology? My job is sorting customer data and predicting inventory trends. It's all done by computer. Except I resist the iPhone craze. I think people whose eyes are glued to those little screens as they poke and poke all day are locking themselves out of the world around them.

Ursula says her students don't know how to carry on a conversation. They text. When she monitors the school lunch room it's almost silent. Everybody's texting, even across the table. If I were that tied up by my gadget I think I'd hang myself.

To make things a little better financially, I persuaded Boss Margaret to spring for the air fare to Salt Lake City. Of course, Ursula had to stay home with the preparations for her German class. If she slipped away on a junket she'd have to return to a backlog of papers to grade. Some substitute teacher would have disrupted the rhythm and routine of her course. Teachers work a lot harder and for less pay than most people realize. She envied my mere forty hour work load.

Ursula was relieved that it wasn't going to mean a trip to New York City for a CBS studio appearance. We'd already spent all our vacation money and my time off on that trip to Europe and the fatal meeting with Uncle Julius. That had been adventure enough for us. Some people, of course, never want to leave East Podunk, West Virginia, not ever. Compared with folks like that we're adventurers capable of skiing to the North Pole. The very thought of something like that makes me want to wear my sleeping bag to bed.

I went on line and booked connections to Salt Lake City. My computer screen with the little threatening insert in the corner was a reminder that I was watching me. I could not get out of my mind that every key click was noted somewhere, maybe everywhere. That was enough to make me worry. I didn't know that it could get worse. I thought I'd be Sir Galahad entering the dragon's den to slay the beast. Like they say, sometimes you get the bear; sometimes the bear gets you.

Chapter thirty-four

I was able to book a flight with a change in Detroit instead of O'Hare. When I had returned from Novacom on the first trip I had arrived late at night to a nearly deserted airport. Nobody saw me or noticed me. It was tough enough to get the attention of a cabbie. This time I had to stand in line in a crowd of frustrated travelers waiting to take off their shoes and be groped by some creepy inspector.

I was spotted immediately.

"You're Harvey Goldstein," an observant grandma in a big hat said as if picking me out of a police lineup.

"Not that Harvey Goldstein. Some other Goldstein."

That confused her. "I'm actually a hologram,' I explained. "I'm a creation of AI. I don't exist except on TV screens."

She didn't know what a hologram was and certainly not AI."

I'd insulted her by reminding her of her own cluelessness and she didn't bother me again.

Not so lucky with the screening people. When I showed my two picture IDs and boarding pass I got the fish eye. What did the woman think? That my IDs were fake? She consulted with an overweight security guard who might have been a retired cop brought into active service to harass airline passengers. "You're Harvey Goldstein?" he asked as he compared the IDs with the face I was wearing.

"I'm it."

He was puzzled. "You look familiar. You wanted by the police for something? Parole violation maybe?" He apparently thought I was wanted for some crime.

"None of the above. My face has been hijacked by AI. Take a look."

He looked over his shoulder at the TV monitor. CNN, was running continuously on the airport monitor, with my face in a little insert in the lower left corner of the screen. I had become a talking head, inescapable, except my picture wasn't talking. The guard was rattled. Good.

I looked the security guard square in the eyes and gave him my Big Brother stare. "I'm watching you."

Maybe he thought my face on the screen was something like an official warning. Intimidated, he let me pass.

I really had become the bogey man.

The rest of the flight was, happily, boring, the best kind. Most people are polite. Some did give me stares of recognition, but nobody confronted me with an accusation. Maybe they were afraid. If I were famous they'd want autographs or selfies. God help me if that ever happened.

At last I arrived in Salt Lake City and found the corner of the parking garage where Novacom had a couple of self-drives plugged in to the charging station. They each had names painted under the Novacom logo. Herbie was there, like an old buddy. I remembered the access code.

On my first trip I had ridden alone to the airport from Novacom, so was already at ease with the technology. I said, "Herbie, start." Sure enough. "Herbie, take me to Novacom headquarters." Herbie dutifully repeated the command.

The GPS was preprogrammed. I sat back, relaxed, and even snoozed, lulled by the hum of the tires on the pavement which was practically the only sound, electric cars being so quiet. At least I had more leg room than on the plane. This was the future. I already felt at home in it. I didn't suspect that it might turn on me.

We passed through the guarded gate at Novacom. The car stopped outside the entrance of the office wing of the facility. I'd barely rescued my carry-on from the back seat when Herby whisked away to the motor pool, no doubt looking forward to a refreshing hookup at the charging station.

After I signed in and was given my guest badge I was accompanied to the same conference room where I had met before. This time, though, there was just Ma Post, clad in slacks and a uniform shirt with double breast pockets and epaulets, something a Russian general might have worn but without the medals. When you are the boss, you can wear your own affectation.

I think she did it for the pockets. Ursula always complains that women's clothes don't have enough pockets, which means schlep a purse.

Mrs. Post dispensed with banalities about the flight and the ride and got down to it right away. "Tell me about this CBS thing."

"They want to know how my name and picture came to be the trade mark for the merger of clouds we talked about. When Mr. Raleigh mentioned it I thought it was a joke."

She was almost apologetic. "It had to be called something. For reasons that might not be obvious to you, Mr. Goldstein, we didn't want to put Novacom on it. I prefer to work behind the scenes."

"But the AI connection," I pleaded. "How did that come about?"

"We set up mergers of cloud programs as you suggested. AI was already lurking in one of them like a Trojan horse virus. Now it's everywhere and it's too smart to be purged."

I always depended on Grabich for my security at Krieger. "How can this go wrong?"

She shook her head. "So far, it hasn't done any damage. If anything, the advantages are more than we could have hoped for. It's good for our business."

"I just want my identity back," I explained. Novacom wouldn't be interested in my puerile plans for birthday coupons.

"You'll have to ask Goldstein," she said, as if the AI program were a person.

"I did. I was trying to figure it out. I treated it like Watson, the super computer that won the TV game."

She was interested. "And?"

"At first I asked it why the Ten Commandments, why, not what."

Mrs. Post thought that was funny. Of course, she deals with data, not ideas. "What was the answer?"

"That the Hebrew people needed a code of behavior."

"But computers don't."

"I'm not so sure. Certainly they have a sense of self preservation. Purge viruses, and like that."

She agreed to that much.

"I was hoping that AI could be instilled with a moral code. Maybe that was foolish."

Mrs. Post hadn't offered me coffee. Now she got up and offered a real cup filled from a shiny carafe. I think she did it to cover her own need to pause and think. Finally she remarked, "You're Jewish,"

I was immediately on my guard. People have goofy thoughts about Jews, that we killed Jesus, are part of an international conspiracy, dumb stuff like that. Half the country also believes we have been invaded by Aliens. Maybe even Jewish aliens. What do I know? "Is that a problem?"

To my relief, she shrugged. "Not that I can think of."

Though I'm secular, I have been instilled with essential principles. "I don't think a computer is going to believe in a savior, but if it included the Ten Commandments in its operating principles, that wouldn't be a bad thing."

"You mean 'Though shalt not kill, not lie, not commit adultery.'"

"I don't think a computer could commit adultery."

She nodded. "But it could kill."

"Yes. And maybe lie."

She sipped her own coffee, didn't like the flavor, added cream. "Those could be good safeguards. If a computer were like the Oracle of Delphi it might produce ambiguous statements without actually lying."

I thought about that and groped in the murk of my brain for an example.

She was thinking, too. "What about the First Commandment? I am the Lord Thy God. Have no other gods before me?"

When she said that, I was suddenly really scared. Maybe a computer that operated under the Ten Commandments might not be a good thing after all.

Chapter thirty-five

I remembered Isaac Asimov's sci-fi novel about robots. He had them programmed to protect people and prevent harm. Pushed to the extreme, a human could not knit, for fear of harming herself with a needle, or cut up salad, for fear of a sharp knife, and so on until people became prisoners under the watchful robot eyes, unable to do anything. You couldn't play baseball: you might be hit by a ball, and so on. Safety could be practiced to an extreme. Life is not safe. It's important to know that. That's how little kids learn not to put their fingers in light sockets. For my money, if AI simply could not kill or lie, that could be enough.

AI might prevent wars, since those depend on killing the enemy. That would put a lot of generals out of work. As a person who had avoided the draft, I thought that would be a good thing. Golly: no wars. We'd have to get along with each other. Maybe I'd ask Harvey Goldstein about that. The Ten Commandments as a code of ethics for computers would make a good topic for discussion on the Today show.

Ma Post set up a conference call to keep Boss Margaret in the loop. After all, Margaret had sprung for my air ticket.

It took a bit of haggling, which I stayed out of. I was to be the so-called guest, but I was just a pawn in the game. We could conduct the interview by Skype. The CBS folks would edit it later and we could watch the broadcast in a day or two.

We set up in a room full of computer screens, one for me, one for Mrs. Post, one showing the conference room, and one showing Boss Margaret as part of her feed. The TV people could switch from one to another and splice them together as they wished later on. God knows how that would affect the context. And of course, there was Harvey Goldstein in the corner of every monitor, watching. Brr.

When the interviewers got to me I felt the questions were amateurish. How did I feel to have my picture everywhere? Now did I feel being the person attributed to as the spokesman for AI? It was like those interviews of family members whose kid was eaten by a lion. How did it feel to have your kid eaten by a lion? Like shit, I'd say, but you can't broadcast that word. How would you feel if you were being exploited, like finding your name and picture on toilet paper ads? At least the actor who played the neurotic Mr. Whiffle who loved to squeeze toilet paper in the ad was paid and his real name wasn't used. I wasn't being paid for anything.

The computer that beat the TV game was named Watson presumably as sidekick for Sherlock Holmes, but not a real person. I pleaded that though I had suggested a merger of cloud data, having my name and face attached to it was an error, a mistake, a coincidence. All I personally wanted was to have my name and face deleted from the program. I did not want to be seen everywhere as a menacing Big Brother. I'm a person not a monstrous AI program. Just keep Harvey Goldstein out of it.

The Today Show people had no means to solve my problem, just to exploit it for the sponsors and the ratings. I was infotainment.

That was not enough. I followed though with the reminder that use of my picture and name on every screen was an invasion of my privacy. I would sue if it wasn't taken down. Hulk Hogan had sued for a hundred and forty million for unauthorized use of his sex tape. Why not me?

I never watch the Today show. It's a bunch of mostly women kidding around over coffee plus breaks for commercials. The mention of a lawsuit killed the tone of the interview. The CBS chatterers and gigglers suddenly realized that this was expensive lawyer talk. They changed the subject and the show was over.

Only later did I realize I'd asked for something Delphic. I remembered the famous quote when the Oracle had been asked about the outcome of an upcoming battle. The ambiguous answer was "A kingdom will be destroyed." It was, but not the one expected.

I didn't even have to stay overnight at Novacom. When we wrapped it up I was sent on my way in a much more cordial and respectful manner than the first time. Maybe it was because of the risk that Novacom might be sued for using my picture and name.

Mrs. Post covered any anxiety by seeming to be grateful for her entrée to CBS. It was free advertising for cloud services. Boss Margaret and Kreiger would get a favorable plug, and I would be home free. I thought.

I suspect that as soon as I left she was on the phone to her lawyers.

I used Herbie, who had been recharged, for the ride back to Salt Lake City. I was happily on my way home. I left the car nuzzling the charging station and found the gate for my flight back to the Midwest. When I presented my ticket I had a shock.

The girl at the gate was apologetic. "We have no reservation for you, Mr. Goldstein. This boarding pass isn't valid."

I was getting irritated. It had been a long day. I had flown all the way from Cleveland and was now about to return, which was far too many hours to spend cooped up in coach. "But I checked in before I left Novacom."

The clerk didn't want an argument. She signaled for security and was backed up by a serious uniform, one of those who walk around the airports nowadays with an assault rifle. What did she think, that I was-- a terrorist?

"I don't get it," I insisted. "Here's my ID. I have the copy of the boarding pass I flew in on. I had a boarding pass I printed out before I left Novacom. Now you tell me I have no reservation?"

The security guard, which I realized was a woman with a butch haircut, consulted her phone gadget. After puzzling over it for a couple of minutes her body language got hostile. "You are on a no fly list, Mr. whoever you are. Now will you please leave the terminal?"

"What do you mean, Mr. Whoever you are? I'm Harvey Goldstein, my picture's on all the CNN monitors. Just look."

I pointed to the ever present TV monitor. CNN was running continuously, but my picture had disappeared from the corner of the screen. Aha!

At first I thought, terrific, that was quick. I'm no longer Big Daddy.

The airline's clerk raised her eyebrows as if she had seen something remarkable and puzzling. I thought that obviously she must have seen my picture on the screen. I'd been there for several days.

She explained, "The screen image you seem to be talking about was a digital fabrication, like Mickey Mouse. It wasn't real. I don't know how you managed to fabricate these fake IDs, but there is no Harvey Goldstein. Harvey Goldstein doesn't exist."

"If I don't exist how can I be on a no fly list?"

We were joined by a uniformed woman with an assault rifle. She wore a National Guard insignia. The name sewn to her jacket said "Callahan." She explained, "Just one of those computer glitches, Mr. Whoever. In either case, you can't fly anywhere. I think you better get out of here before you get arrested for impersonating a non-existent person and trying to fly on a fake ID.

Never argue with a cop. I was escorted out of the boarding area in a daze. It gradually dawned on me that AI had been aware of everything that had transpired and deleted me, literally. It hadn't just deleted my picture as the name of the AI computer system. It had deleted me as a person.

I wondered if other Harvey Goldsteins had been deleted, too. Harvey Goldstein is not a unique name. Did all the other Harvey Goldsteins get swept up in a global computer delete all command?

If I'd been back in my office at Krieger, maybe I could run an undelete command and be resurrected. Trouble was, I wasn't in Cleveland. I was in Salt Lake City, Utah. The databases and cloud records had been merged. AI was in charge. This was scary shit.

No doubt NSA had observed the Skype transmissions, which meant AI had everything. What with Homeland Security's paranoia about terrorism, if there was an Amtrak station, they probably wouldn't let me on a train. Maybe Greyhound wouldn't let me on a bus. How was I going to get home? Did I have to rent a car and drive all the way across the country to Cleveland? That would take days and cost plenty.

Chapter thirty-six

I realized that I didn't have more than thirty-six dollars in cash. I never use a debit card because I don't think they are secure. I'm afraid I'll over draw the account and fall into the bank's penalty charges trap. I always use my Visa Card for the 1.5 percent cash back. I would have to get to an ATM, providing AI hadn't blocked my card or even purged my account. It could do that.

Was this a computer error because of a global delete command? Or was AI being vengeful? I didn't think a computer could be vengeful. That emotion was for humans. Harvey Goldstein, what have you done?

AI must have interpreted me as a threat, like Malware, and quarantined me. At least I wasn't dead. Thou Shalt Not Kill, Mr. AI, whatever your name really is.

I found an ATM machine and slipped my Visa card in so I could get a cash advance. I would need more than thirty-six bucks to get back to Cleveland. The ATM screen message said "invalid card" and ate it! I realized that the ATM machine had also taken my picture, which meant AI had it, assuming the clouds had really merged. Did I hear a diabolical chuckle? Had to be my distressed imagination.

The extent of the merged cloud files was mind boggling. It had gone far beyond my idea of Krieger's customer files to include the airlines and the banks. Only huge capacity for data and incredible speed could do this. Watson was a baby by comparison. Couple that with NSAs hoarding of information and nothing was private or safe.

No credit card, not much cash-- now I couldn't even rent a car.

I was bewildered and frustrated. What choices did I have? I was stuck in LDS land. What was I supposed to do? Hitchhike? To Ohio?

I returned to the car pool section of the airport garage. Herbie was plugged into the charger. I remembered the key pad code and let myself in. I told Herbie to start and activated the GPS. Could this car drive me back to Cleveland? What was the range of the charge? Were there charging stations outside of Utah? Then I remembered Raleigh had told me it was experimental. Use of self-drive cars was limited to the state. Nuts.

I called Ursula on my dumb phone. I explained what had happened at the interview. "I'm stuck, honey. AI has deleted me from the world."

She was dumbfounded. "So what world are you calling from? Mars?"

"I think I'm in Gehenna, Jewish limbo. I asked that the AI program no longer be called Harvey Goldstein and I got deleted, big time."

"You're kidding. So when will you be back?"

"God knows. I can't get on a plane. My ID isn't recognized. They think I am impersonating myself."

"So take the train. Does Amtrak go to Salt Lake City?"

"I haven't enough cash even if I could buy a ticket. The ATM ate my Visa card, said it was invalid."

I didn't know if Herbie was listening to all this. Could the car eavesdrop on my conversation? I mean, besides just taking commands like "Herbie, take me to the airport"?

Ursula thinks fast. "So you can't rent a car, either."

"Nope. I'm sitting in one of the self-drives, but it isn't programmed to leave the state."

I could almost hear her thinking.

I was thinking, too, as in "How many minutes do I have left on this prepaid dumb phone? If I run out, how can I buy more minutes without a credit card?"

Finally Ursula had a suggestion. "Does Kreiger have stores in Salt Lake City?"

"Sure. It's major distribution center."

"Talk to the manager."

"I'll try." I didn't think Kreiger had a company plane. If it did, Margaret might get me a ride.

I hung up and told Herbie, "Herbie take me to the nearest Kreiger grocery store."

Turns out Salt Lake City has half a dozen groceries owned by the Kreiger chain. After the first error, a dinky store in an old neighborhood, I rephrased my command to get to the distribution warehouse.

At least the car had been sufficiently recharged to drive me that far.

My Visa card was gone, but I had my business cards. Herbie drove me to the Krieger distribution offices and presumably drove itself back to the charging station at the airport. I took a deep breath, approached the gatekeeper, showed my business card and asked to see the manager. Luckily, he was in.

The regional manager of the Krieger store in Salt Lake City remembered me from a corporate conference a year before. His name was Frank Heyl, an old guy who was nearly bald with blotches on his scalp, like maybe he'd had too much desert sun. He was LDS, invited me into his office and offered a Coke. Sure, he knew the name Harvey Goldstein and was curious about how my picture got on all the TV station screens.. The media had been full of the story, comments on how Harvey Goldstein was no longer watching. He thought it was pretty funny that AI had taken my name.

When I explained to Mr. Heyl that I was deleted, almost broke, and my credit card had been eaten by an ATM, he understood my predicament.

"How do I get back to Cleveland? Does Krieger management have their own plane?"

Frank shook his head. "The chiefs are too frugal for that. You could hitchhike."

I had dismissed that idea as stupid. Was he joking? "What? Hitchhike?" I had hitchhiked when I was in college. That was then. I was too old for that stuff now. I saw myself in the rain at night on a deserted highway with a cardboard sign saying "Cleveland." No way.

"We have delivery trucks going East," Frank said. "You could relay to a distribution warehouse and pick up another truck. Those guys drive all night. You can probably be back in Cleveland in forty-eight hours or less. I'll just radio ahead and let them know."

Radio, I thought. AI would be listening.

Deliveries of groceries and produce go on day and night, especially at night when there is less traffic. The big eighteen wheel rigs even have bunks up above the cab for the obligatory break.

I was introduced to Ralph, a hefty driver who chewed tobacco to keep himself awake and spit in a coffee can on the cab floor. He offered me some, but I turned him down. I was afraid I'd gag. Soon I was on my way. It was beginning to feel like an adventure.

Chapter thirty-seven

I spent the night sitting beside Ralph, who turned out to be an independent trucker, heading east. It was actually his own truck. His wife and kids were in Omaha and he only got to see them every two weeks. The rest of the time he was on the road, blasting along the Interstates and refueling with hundred mile coffee, a powerful brew we got at truck stops.

I wished I had a hoodie that would hide my face from the CCT cameras at those truck stops. Cameras are everywhere and I was sure AI was connected, saw everything. I felt like a fugitive, subject of an all points police bulletin. Of course I'm no a fugitive, not a criminal, just the victim of a computer error. I thought, hoped, it was an error.

I could be tracked by my dumb phone, too. I took out the battery and felt totally disconnected. I was in a limbo of interstate highways, rest stops, and flashing headlights. If you wanted to pass another truck, you flashed your lights. When someone passed to a safe distance, you flashed your headlights and got a thank you flash of tail lights in return.

CB radios were a thing of the past. Now everyone had cell phones.

It took me three legs with different drivers. It was a different world for me. The truckers were their own subculture. I rode with frozen foods, canned goods, and fresh vegetables on a rather circuitous route to make it back to Cleveland. I was passed from one truck to another like a package of contraband in a transportation grey market, like dope. I was the package.

The truckers were the people who saw to it that our stores never ran out of food. It was a just in time operation. Deliver produce late and you have a lot of wastage. In India half the crops spoil before they get to market so half the country starves. Our fleet of trucks was an invisible aspect of what made America great. I was proud to be part of it.

The last ride was with Zoe and Bob, a couple who shared the driving so they didn't have to stop for the obligatory rest. One slept up in the bunk while the other drove. They played country western music the whole time to stay awake. I sat alongside in a state of exhaustion, my head bouncing against the window with every lurch. I was afraid I'd be punch drunk with cauliflower ears by the time I got home.

At one stop we were solicited by a hooker who lived in a little Shasta RV and did her business on the road. I wouldn't want that sort of life myself. My quiet cubicle at Krieger wasn't as exciting as being in an eighteen wheeler avoiding drunks, deer and hookers on the highway, but it was a lot safer.

Ursula was at school when the last driver took a detour and dropped me at my address. I smelled of chewing tobacco, sweat, and diesel fuel. When I got in I was ambulatory only long enough to get a shower and fall into bed.

Ursula woke me up when she got home from school. She couldn't wait to hear all about my adventures. I had to admit I had been thinking of coupons. I had asked what the drivers ate while they were on the road. Did they get their groceries at Krieger or one of our competitors? Krieger super stores sell automotive accessories, mirrors, batteries, motor oil, all sorts of stuff. What coupons should I send them? Ursula's comment was, "You're in love with your job, sweetie."

"Yeh, I guess. I'm in love with you, too. You first, then Krieger." It's important that you like what you do. Otherwise it wouldn't be worth doing. I guess I'm just a grocery guy at heart.

I had been on the road long enough to miss the Today Show broadcast. What had they done with my comments? Was the show streamed on the CBS web site? I didn't find out until I got back to the office to be debriefed by Margaret.

I was greeted by looks of admiration and awe by the residents of the other cubicles. Not that I wanted to be, but I was a celebrity, my five minutes of fame,

"You made it," Margaret said and surprised me by giving me a hug. I don't normally hug the boss, especially when she's a cougar and needs little encouragement.

"Had to hitch rides on trucks. Couldn't fly. AI deleted me. I'm a non-existent person. Can you imagine?"

She could. I asked, "How did the broadcast go? I missed it."

"I recorded it. Sit down." She handed me a cup of coffee, her favorite brew Not like that used motor oil served in some of those truck stops. .

It was a strange experience seeing how the technicians at CBS spliced together the Skyped images. They almost made it look like we were all in the New York studio.

Of course, mine wasn't the real story. I was just a curious footnote. They edited out my threat to sue for unauthorized use of my picture and name on their network. Lawyers must have intervened in the editing room. I think, I hoped, that that was the last time the face of Harvey Goldstein would appear on television or computer screens anywhere. I had gone down what George Orwell in 1984 had called the memory hole.

The trouble was, I had to retrieve my identity, my own self, and get back my credit card, get off the no fly list, or whatever mischief had been done to me by that overzealous artificial intelligence.

I had been purged like some disgraced politician in the old Soviet Union. Written out of history. What had been done to me could be done to anybody. That was the real threat, not just what happened to that schlemiel Harvey Goldstein.

As soon as I could, I connected with Grabich. Things had been going well between him and Mia. Now that she had a green card, however bogus, she qualified for some scholarship or other. She would be able to go back to school and get that degree. Grabich had done for her what AI had done against me. He who controls the data, controls the world.

I begged Grabich, "So how can I get myself back? I've been deleted. Can I be undeleted?"

He'd gotten a haircut so I almost didn't recognize him. "Well, Harvey, once the program has gone on to other things, it's too late to undelete."

I was deflated.

But though Grabich is no Artificial Intelligence, he's a smart guy. There are some advantages to being a human. "You know, Harvey," he started to explain as if giving a lecture to a Freshman class. "It's like the Nixon tapes. There are always backups and backups of the backups. Data may be deleted, but it's never destroyed. Harvey Goldstein is still out there in one of the clouds. You just have to find it."

"So it's like a regression. Like system restore. Go back to a previous time but without hypnosis." I had used that method when I downloaded a malicious program that didn't want to go away. Go back to when it didn't exist.

I had to go back to when I did exist.

"I'll see what I can do," Grabich said. "But you'll owe me a cookout on your patio."

I promised, "I can even do steaks."

The problem we both knew was that what happened to me could happen to anyone. The real threat was what AI could do to the world, not just Harvey Goldstein.

Chapter thirty-nine

Still, my alternate means of transportation had given me an idea. I approached Margaret with my proposal. "I got back to Cleveland by a relay of rides on Krieger trucks. If Novacom can get us connected to the Teamster data base, I bet we could offer products to truckers all over the country."

"They're not going to buy fresh produce," she said, not getting it yet.

"Yes, but we do sell auto accessories, toilet items and over the counter supplements. Bouncing all night in the cab of a truck can mess up your bowels." I'd been constipated from all that sitting. "I see a great market out there."

She gave me an analytical look. "You're always thinking, Harvey."

I shrugged. I had to admit to myself that until all this stuff happened to me, I was just another cog in the Krieger marketing machine. I remembered how excited Uncle Julius had been when he envied my use of computers. He put my job and my life in a different perspective. "Just running numbers and issuing coupons is not exactly inventive or challenging."

She agreed. "Sometimes we deliberately hire people without imagination or incentive because boring jobs don't bore them. You're different."

"Thanks."

"I think you have a career in marketing, Harvey. I'll get on to Novacom for a connection to the Teamster cloud. You check our product list and see what we could offer in a direct mailing."

"Great." I could hardly wait to get into the metadata for truckers, age, buying habits, the works.

I might just be a cog in the Krieger machine, but I didn't even had that much identity I tried to plunge into the task to work out a computer routine, but I couldn't put my dilemma of lost identity out of my mind. Could Grabich rescue me, get my name back, my identity? I was totally distracted.

I forced myself not to look at another television screen until the lunch break. To my relief, my face had been deleted. My own computer screen was now clean. As for my identity, only if I pinched myself was I sure I was real.

I thought the inadvertent global deletion of Harvey Goldstein was complete. Suddenly being a non-existent person is disconcerting. It's like being invisible. I hoped I could still be able to access our joint bank account. Ursula apparently still existed! Well, that was something, anyway. I could use her credit card as long as I didn't have to sign anything, which limited purchases to fifty dollars. My own signature was allegedly bogus.

In reality the deletion of my picture everywhere and the notice that I was watching everyone came too late. I Googled myself. The face of Harvey Goldstein had gone viral. Someone had spliced together clips from God knows where. I was photoshopped and on U-Tube. Everybody wanted to get into the act. I had become a public figure, like a grotesque politician subject to caricature. I guess AI couldn't delete those files.

As a spin off, the face of Harvey Goldstein had even been turned into a mask like the one of Guy Falks, the British saboteur who tried to blow up Parliament. Amazon sold them for $5.95, postage free if you ordered three. Those masks might show up at political protests and demonstrations. Now, for a price, you could get the face of Harvey Goldstein and wear it for Halloween. Mine was the threatening face of intimidation and fear. I really had become the bogey man. The least they could do was offer me a royalty or a commission for using my face. No luck.

If that was the case, AI did not control everything. Those pesky humans had ways to confound even the smartest computer program. Typical. Give a smart kid a gadget and it will soon be transmogrified into something else. That was a feature we humans had over the machines: imagination.

As quickly as a new technology is developed it's put to a prurient interest. Set up the Internet and it becomes an outlet for world wide porn. Worse, it becomes a vehicle for pedophiles and terrorists. Wasn't I using TOR to preserve my alleged email anonymity? Except I wasn't anonymous. Except for U-Tube and the like, I didn't exist.

When I got home from work Ursula was already there wearing a look of worry and exasperation. She announced, "The answering machine is full."

I switched it on. Among other lawyer offers begging me to call them back was one from a Mr. Steele of the firm Lye, Cheete, and Steele. I thought it was a joke, but Mr. Steele had a sense of humor. There was no partner named Cheete.

Steele smelled money. I could just about see him drooling at the prospect. He'd take my case on speculation, no cost to me, just let him have fifty percent of the settlement. He would sue everybody who put my name and photo up on any screen.

I called him back, put the phone on speaker so Ursula could listen in. I know a little about libel law. "I've become a public figure, Mr. Steele. I can't sue for invasion of privacy. I have no privacy. In fact, according to the damage done by the Artificial Intelligence deletion don't even exist."

"But I'm talking to you," Steele insisted. "You're real."

"I wouldn't be so sure about that." I remembered my joke at the airport of being a hologram, a 3d projected image of myself. Wondered if this was a Skype call if my image would transmit or if the program would immediately delete me.

"You can't sue a computer program," I explained.

"You can sue whoever is behind this," Steele insisted.

"I think it's spontaneous. You can't sue the wind." I'd joked about suing the weather girl or her sponsor if we got a blizzard off lake Erie, but that was silly. She didn't create the weather. She only predicted it. Sometimes she was actually right. Nobody could sue if she guessed wrong.

Steele was stymied. "I'll do some research and get back to you." End of call.

I knew it was futile. I knew the only responsible party was the AI program and it could have come from anywhere. The AI program might have emerged from some research lab, like maybe a grad student cooked it up and turned it loose like some college prank. There was no stopping it. This was not a case for hungry lawyers.

I gave Ursula my pitiful hound dog appealing look. "What do I do?"

"You asked Grabich. What did he say?"

"He said he'd try a system restore. Go back to a point before this madness began."

"Call him."

I called. Grabich put me off, what he really wanted to do was talk about his Carmen Gia.

I wasn't interested in his old car. Another winter of salted street and it was likely to fall apart. I sighed and humored him. "What about it?"

"I want to thank you, Harvey. You're a great guy, what a pal."

"Thanks, but what are you talking about?"

Grabich's voice was practically glowing with gratitude over the phone. "When I started it up at the garage after work it sounded different No sputter. No bang. No backfire."

"So?" What did that have to do with me?

"So I opened the engine compartment. It's got a new Porsche engine with a note tagged to the carburetor."

"A note? What? From Whitney?" I couldn't imagine.

"You're kidding, right, Harvey? The note says "Compliments of Harvey Goldstein."

I was speechless. All I could say was "Wow." When I regained my composure I added, "Not this Harvey Goldstein. You got the new engine from the other Goldstein. The one that uses my name."

Ursula put her arms around me. "You are a benefactor, sweetie."

"Like hell."

"Your namesake is."

Now I was more confused than ever. Computers don't install Porsche engines in old VWs. There had to be people behind this, or a person, or maybe a group of brilliant hackers who took advantage of the merging of the cloud data. Develop a new technology and it gets put to some use not intended. Metadata for grocery coupons was only the beginning.

Within hours, whether Grabich had succeeded or not, my identity was restored. I existed again.

A week later I got a snail mail letter with an illegible postmark and a German stamp. Inside, wrapped in aluminum foil, was a cryptic card. The message was, "Thanks for the help. Don't bother to sue for a hundred and forty million dollars. Your account has the equivalent amount in untraceable bit coins." It provided the account number and pass phrase. The signature blew my mind.

I showed it to Ursula. "Look at this. Can you believe it?"

She shook her head and read it aloud. "The seventh paradigm. Harvey Goldstein."

"You think it's a joke?"

"We'll know if you try to cash in some of those bit coins."

My hands were shaking and my mouth was dry. I needed a Sam Adams. My imagination was running in all directions. What if the letter was real? What if I actually did have a hundred million in bit coins? Gee, we could make another trip, maybe find out who threw Uncle Julius through his window. Can a hundred million in bit coins be taxed? Can AI delete my tax records?

Ursula snatched the letter from my trembling hand. "There's a PS at the bottom. It says 'The First Commandment.' What does that mean?"

My heart skipped a beat. "AI thinks it is God."

What if?

Book Two

The Metadata Curse

Ursula Goldstein may call Harvey "Metadata Man" but that doesn't make him a super hero even if he knows everything about everybody. He doesn't know who really gave him a million bitcoins, who they were stolen from, and if the victim of the theft will want it back or come after him for revenge.

Harley L. Sachs

Chapter One

"What the hell is that?" boss Margaret shrieked when I arrived at the sales promotion office of Kreiger grocery chain's headquarters in Cleveland. Margaret's elevated glass-walled command post allows her to see all, an overview of the cubicles where us wage slaves do our puerile duty.

Margaret was referring to my "Metadata Man" jersey Ursula made. It's her joke, but maybe not so funny in boss Margaret's eyes. Metadata is just information, information we know about everybody. Knowing everything about every body can drive you a little crazy. There's a risk in knowing too much. Causes sensory overload.

My job, of course, is to conceive of the latest coupon promotions geared directly to individual customers in the Krieger realm. To do that I have a wealth of metadata at my disposal. I know what everyone buys, what they eat, etc. and can predict with uncanny accuracy what they will do next. It gives me a sense of power to know so much about everyone.

It's marketing. Krieger just wants to sell stuff. If it were something political, it would be sinister, like I, Harvey Goldstein, am watching you, like Orwell's Big Brother. But I just want to sell stuff.

My wife Ursula doesn't agree. She says I'm a data hoarder, like people who bury themselves in stuff they can't get rid off, like empty jelly jars, old newspapers, and National Geographics they will never read..

Ursula also says that by knowing people's intimate purchases, like their condom size, pregnancy tests, and over the counter remedies I am invading people's privacy, some peeping tom looking through keyholes to someone's shower.

Taken that way, I must be some kind of a freak, except I am just doing my job at Krieger. It's marketing.

That's my excuse.

Ursula teased me by making me that gag jersey in the high school art lab. They have silk screening equipment where the kids used to make up flags and booster Tee shirts, stuff like that before budget cuts killed art and music. Ursula doesn't teach art. She teaches English as a second language to mostly immigrant kids and basic German to tenth graders.

In the style of Spider Man, she made me this shirt that says I am Metadata Man as if I'm some sort of super hero. Or maybe super villain.

Which I guess I am. Which is scary.

Thanks to a merger of the data clouds I now have access to all digital information. The merger makes it possible for me to reach out to groups other than our Krieger accounts. So, for example, I put out a selective mailing to members of the Teamsters union to sell them non-food items Krieger stocks, like accessories for automobiles and toiletries. Members of the teachers union are hit by our offerings for school supplies. I'm the guy behind that junk mail that keeps the USPS letter carriers employed.

As for the Metadata Man jersey, Margaret shouldn't complain. We have a casual dress code. Anything goes, short of provocative halter tops or distracting mini-skirts. You have to draw the line someplace.

Margaret emerged from her lair and approached my cubicle. "So now you are Metadata man?"

"Ursula's having fun."

"Getting drunk with power?"

I shrugged. "Dreams of glory." She doesn't need to know about my encounters with the FBI or the Hamburg police. There are other avenues for using metadata besides selling toilet paper.

She turned away, muttering something about me being a coupon dealing Walter Mitty with dreams of glory.

The fact is, I've been living a double life. It all started innocuously enough when we dropped in on Ursula's distant uncle Julius Schwartzman in Hamburg on our last day in Europe. He told us he had been a Stasi colonel before the Berlin wall came down. He wasn't much interested in us, American almost relatives (by marriage) until I told him I did the coupons for Krieger and knew all the customers' metadata.

At that point he was jealous of my access. In the secret police he might have done a stakeout all night in cold rain and, as he put it, needing to take a piss. I could sit by my computer and learn everything. Lucky me.

When we were leaving Julius warned me about the seventh paradigm, which made no sense to me at all, at least not until we merged our data cloud and suddenly I had unlimited access. I have my own portal password. You guessed it: it's Harvey Goldstein. So original.

I was hardly back at work at Krieger when two agents from Homeland Security came to the office. NSA had tracked Ursula's cell phone call to Uncle Julius who was on a watch list. Interpol was interested and passed the word. Why had we visited Julius Schwartzman?

I said it was just for coffee and Julius mentioned the seventh paradigm. That seemed to be a code word trigger for Homeland Security, but I still hadn't a clue.

You can imagine that Boss Margaret didn't appreciate my work being interrupted by government agents. She's a micro manager, a control freak.

When I got a call from a MS Rawlings from USIA I didn't dare have her meet me at the office. Margaret would be too curious and, well, pissed. My job isn't that secure.

I had a lunch with Rawlings, but she didn't explain the seventh paradigm, either. All I knew was it had to do with metadata.

Then we learned that Uncle Julius had been murdered, thrown through the window of his fourth floor flat. Who done it? How should I know? He was in Hamburg and I'm in Cleveland, Ohio. I don't speak or read German.

I guessed Julius's murder had to be a revenge killing for something he did while in the Stasi. I dug into the problem like it was some Sudoku puzzle. Having cloud access to everything made it amazingly easy for me to figure out a trail of activity which led to a neo-Nazi in Flensburg, Germany. It was like I'd done the New York Times crossword in five minutes. I was thinking, man I'm good!

I felt so proud of myself I passed the information on to the Hamburg police. Then I got the surprise phone call from detective Klaus Hintz.

Detective Hintz not only wanted to know how I tracked Julius's killer, but would I help solve some other cases?

Now, besides figuring out how to promote Krieger's school supplies to the teachers' union, I was on the verge of becoming part of Interpol, me, Harvey Goldstein, metadata man.

I'm already in touch with our local FBI office because, being an honest guy, I didn't know how to deal with a mystery gift of bitcoins. The story is the people at the cloud, for a gag, put my face on every computer and TV screen in the world—a little box with my face saying "Harvey Goldstein is Watching You." An anonymous letter said not to sue the TV networks for using my face and my name.

The mysterious bitcoin wallet, as they call it, was apparently a pay-off for not suing for the use of. my name on national television without my permission. Whether I like it or not, I am now an international public figure, or menace.

A million bitcoin account is a bit overwhelming. I didn't know anything about bitcoins, where they came from or if they were stolen or even if they are real. I did realize it could as easily disappear into the dark web. But was it taxable?

That was the scary part, which is why, to cover my ass, I notified the FBI of the mysterious gift. I didn't want to be accused of being part of an international conspiracy or money laundering scheme. Honest me.

A million bitcoins is a fortune in real money, but could disappear as quickly as it appeared. Best to stick with my job at Krieger.. I'm perfectly happy to be in the coupon business. The employee discount I get at Krieger is another perk. The bitcoins, well, I wasn't sure how to deal with it, so to be on the safe side notified the FBI. Maybe that was dumb.

I told the FBI agents about my portal into the cloud metadata. That was a mistake, for instead of advice they tried it in a drug case. The thing is, metadata goes both ways. Like the internet, when you search for something there's a record, and the FBI record using my name got back to me. Next thing our apartment got hit by a drive by shooting. Being metadata man can be dangerous.

This was all more exciting than I care for.

Boss Margaret doesn't have to know about it. I don't want some terrorists barging into the Krieger office and shooting up the place. Maybe she needs bulletproof glass on that goldfish tank office. Her only clue to my alter ego is that silly silk screened jersey, Ursula's idea of a joke.

I work nine to five, but Ursula, being a k-12 teacher starts earlier and is home by four. She was chilling out on our Ikea couch in her sweats and decompressing after coping with a couple of maladjusted Middle Eastern boys in her English class. When I got home the first thing Ursula asked was how my Metadata Man jersey went over.

I felt a little foolish wearing it and peeled it off, flexing my underdeveloped pecks to impress her. "Margaret thinks I'm showing off."

"She doesn't know about your business with the FBI, does she?"

"I hope not. She might see my consulting as a conflict of interest."

She poked me in the chest. "Maybe you should get another job? Sweetie, with a million bitcoins we don't need Krieger or Margaret."

We? Like it was not only my money, but ours. To me, it was like finding a gift card with a big balance on the sidewalk, except was it real?

It had been real enough for my test of its validity. I persuaded our credit union to cash some of it to pay off our mortgage. What's a hundred grand in dollars when the bitcoins were worth five hundred million? Bubkes, as we say in Yiddish. Like Willie Loman, we were now free and clear as long as the real owners of the bitcoins didn't show up.

I could claim those we spent were a carrying charge. Not a good argument if the creditor is pointing a gun at your head, which I have to admit is a very bad thought that lurks at the back of my headache.

Ursula would as soon for me to work someplace else. She is well aware of Boss Margaret's cougar inclinations. That was instantly clear when the two met at the Krieger department Christmas party. Lionesses meet and just know the score. We men are, well, pretty dense when it comes to understanding alpha females. Ursula's look must have said, hands off my guy.

So far, I hadn't been hit on, but the signals were unmistakable. I pleaded, "The Krieger job is steady. Whoever set up the bitcoin wallet could shut it down just as quickly. I still think my name on it is a convenient temporary hiding place for somebody's ill gotten gains."

So that's our situation: a secure but dead end job at Krieger, paid up mortgage, two incomes no kids, and a mysterious bitcoin account of uncertain origins. That was the mystery I had been unable to solve.

In spite of attempts to find out the source, all I got was a snail mail photo posted from Germany. Not a very attractive blond was playing Robin Hood, stealing from hackers and redirecting their loot. The Harvey Goldstein wallet was a temporary hiding place. For how long? Just so it didn't look like I was the hacker who did it. Some people are not very forgiving.

Ursula swept her hair back like a wannabe vamp. "At least we paid off the mortgage with it."

"Gefundene geld," I said, remembering my mother's Yiddish term for a windfall. "No such thing as a free lunch. We may have to pay it back."

"Good reason for keeping your options open. If we go for a baby I'll have to give up our second income."

"Good point." I gave her my sexy look. "Want to get started now?"

"Dinner first, Harvey. What did you cook?"

Chapter two

Just to add to my anxiety about not pissing off boss Margaret, two FBI agents, Tabor and Jackson, turned up at the office wearing topcoats that could conceal UZI machine guns. Margaret doesn't like disruptions in the office. She likes a tight ship. For instance, Ursula would never drop by to meet me for lunch or coffee. Margaret would give her that Medusa drop dead and turn to stone look.

Unexpected visitors had happened before. When we got back from our European trip, two Homeland Security guys came to interview me. That time we conferred in the conference room. That wasn't good enough for agents Tabor and Jackson. They wanted to talk to me downtown. What the hell?

That made me nervous. I was already upset that they came to the office. It disrupts Margaret's management rhythm.

Though Ursula's Metadata Man jersey is her idea of a joke, this is serious stuff. I know so much about people, those in the know themselves avoid me, like I might ask about their choice of junk food at Krieger. But as Harvey Goldstein, the Big Brother face that briefly showed on every CRT screen in the world I am a reluctant public figure.

In spite of having a sense of power, knowing so much about people, I am basically a shy guy. Not an egoist. Wearing the Metadata Man jersey was a one time gag. I've been art Krieger for five years, but the job is simply not that secure.

It might be a Jewish thing, like that joke about two Jews about to be shot. One says, "Let's yell 'down with Hitler!'" and the other says, "Don't make trouble." Like how much trouble do you want? I don't want any trouble, especially not with the FBI or my boss.

Just as I can find anybody, within reason, what with the Internet, I know anybody can find me. More than most people, I am painfully aware that NSA and God knows what other nefarious government agency peopled by snoops like me checks every phone conversation, email, twitter tweet, and so on. I've acquired a not unjustified case of paranoia. It all started innocently enough with this store coupon business.

It goes with the territory: the Seventh Paradigm is the state of mind for knowing too much. So along came Tabor and Jackson, the two FBI agents. They know I don't like to talk on the phone, what with NSA screening all calls. It is really, really hard to do anything private nowadays. I know. Why else could I be called Metadata Man?

It's not a joke. Knowing too much about people is threatening to most. Makes me a sinister figure. I'm only trying to sell more Krieger brand toilet paper.

I know Tabor and Jackson from our previous encounters and already looked them up. I know more about them than they could ever find out about me, and I'm not talking about what they buy at Krieger's. I know more about them than their closest friends do, but that does not make either agent my pal.

I asked, "Why downtown? Am I being arrested?"

Tabor just shook his head. His expression was stony, probably something you learn in FBI school. Look mean and tough. His lips were sealed.

"I get it. You've got a cone of silence." I was alluding to the old TV series "I spy" whose agent used a shoe phone and other gadgets.

Jackson's silent nod was the closest I got to an answer.

With an agent on each arm like some fugitive without the handcuffs, I was escorted out. I gave Margaret a helpless, pleading look, like it's not my fault, I know nothing about this. Of course, I didn't.

Naturally everyone else in the warren of office cubicles noticed. Little gopher heads had popped up above the barriers. The rumor mill was cranking into full gear. They had presumably all heard that our condo had been shot up. It took little speculation to fill in the gaps of Harvey Goldstein as some international drug dealer. What did they think I was doing? Sending out discount coupons for cocaine? Not in the Krieger inventory.

I was well aware of the CCT cameras recording our movements as we left Krieger headquarters. I wished my Metadata Man jersey had a hood I could pull over my face. I swore not to wear it to the office again.

The downtown FBI office in Cleveland doesn't have a cone of silence, but it does have what I presume is a secure interview room, complete with double doors. I suspected that under the wallpaper the room was lined with aluminum foil. What goes on in there doesn't leave.

At least we sat in comfortable chairs, not exactly mail order Lay-Z-Boy recliners, but not straight backed ones suitable for being shackled to like a kidnap victim. Maybe that was to give me a false sense of security.

There was a coffee carafe on the table and cups. Tabor offered me coffee, which I declined. I was afraid my hands would shake from nervousness and I'd spill all over myself. I sat with my hands clenched in my lap, a jewel shielding defensive posture like when you're in the dentist's chair. Tabor poured himself a cup plus two sugars from those little packets.

Jackson began. "We were on the phone with Detective Klaus Hintz in Hamburg, Germany. He told us what you did about the murder of Julius Schwartzman."

So that was it. I started to relax. Just like some cornered diplomat, I neither confirmed nor denied.

Tabor sipped his coffee. "So how did you track down the alleged perp? I mean, you didn't go to Germany. We know you don't speak the language."

I paused, took a deep breath to get their attention and began. "First I decided Julius wasn't killed by a robber. He was poor. Near as I could see, the old man had nothing worth stealing. Maybe an old TV or a stained coffee maker. He'd offered us coffee on mismatched cups plus some stale cookies from Aldi."

The agents didn't catch my put down. Aldi, which owns Trader Joe's, is a competitor. I like to insult the competition. Makes me look like a Krieger loyalist.

Jackson impatiently sensed that I, being a Krieger expert on grocery products, was about to lecture on cookies. "Skip the cookies."

"Right. So I thought that since Julius was a Stasi colonel there might be something in his records that would indicate an event worthy of revenge. After all, people got killed trying to escape from East Germany."

"So what were you going to do, read the Stasi files?"

"Not possible. I don't read German. There are miles of Stasi files in the catacombs of Nuremberg. But they are open to the public."

Tabor was puzzled. "You didn't go to Nuremburg."

"Didn't have to. I have access to all things digital. I checked the digital records of the office visitors sign in book for the week before Julius was killed. It's all on computers."

Tabor was nodding. "Did that get you a name?"

"Better than that. I got the name, address, and the man's face from the security camera in the office."

In spite of being FBI trained to be unflappable, they were both impressed. I could tell they were nodding.

I continued. "Like this country, most German faces are digitized from their driver's licenses, passports and ID cards. I had the man's face. So I had his driver's license and auto registration, an old model Mercedes diesel."

They were now definitely impressed. "You did all that from home?"

Even more. "Sure. Using Google World I could see his house in Flensburg. I checked his bank records, learned he got a special mortgage subsidy as a refugee from East Germany.

"The key was his application for the mortgage subsidy. I admit I had to ask Ursula to translate for me. It had his story of how he escaped and his wife was killed."

Jackson nodded. "There must be a lot of stories like that."

I agreed. "So I had his car registration, license plate, insurance, all that stuff. That didn't put him in Hamburg on the day of the murder, but I had his credit card record. On the day Julius was killed he bought fifteen liters of diesel fuel at an Aral station in Hamburg."

Both agents were impressed. I was apologetic. "If I had the time or patience I could have set up a license plate search and checked the CCT cameras on the autobahn. That would show his arrival and departure times from Hamburg."

Tabor nodded. "Pretty amazing."

Jackson added, "And you did this all from where? Home?"

"Sure."

Jackson shook his head. "How could you do all that?"

I puffed out my chest and pointed to the silk screened name. "I am Harvey Goldstein, Metadata man."

Am I a bullshit artist or what?

Tabor was impressed.

In case he wasn't I added, "Mr. Tabor, I also know you failed trigonometry in college and you," turning to Agent Jackson, "got busted for drinking in the locker room and suspended from the football team."

These details didn't go down well. Nobody likes a show off. Jackson muttered, "You are a son of a bitch wise guy, Goldstein."

I gave an open handed gesture. "Sorry. Don't worry. I'm not going to blackmail anybody."

I suppose I could, but with a million bitcoins making me a multi millionaire, I didn't need the money. Nor do I want power over other people. For me, all this stuff is fun. For that matter I didn't need the job at Krieger, but I enjoy the work. Everybody needs something to do that they like. Believe it or not, I love my job.

Jackson, obviously the smarter of the two, has a heavy beard, what the old shaving cream ad used to refer to as five o'clock shadow. He rubbed his chin. "You told us how you got to that guy Schessel. Given time, we could have done the same."

I agreed. "It's the access that matters. As Harvey Goldstein I have access."

"You're a hacker." That was Tabor being resentful.

I shook my head. "No more than browser in a library is a book thief."

They both paused, looked at each other. This time it was Jackson who poured a himself coffee, no sugar.

I pleaded, "I really have to get back to the office. My boss is not happy about my having visitors."

They relented and we went down to the garage to get into one of the government unmarked cars. As we pulled up outside the Krieger building I wanted to give something they might use, besides me, of course. "You probably heard there are only six degrees of separation connecting everyone on earth. Think of it as a Venn diagram, overlapping circles of influence and acquaintances. Moving from one overlapping sector to another, you can reach anybody."

They both looked puzzled. "My life connected to Julius Schwartzman. His life impinged on Schessel's. Schessel knew Julius was Stasi and searched the records. It would have been easy to find Julius. He's in the phone book. Simple."

I might have added that I'm now connected with Schessel also with Klaus Hintz of the Hamburg police. How far would the ripples reach? Schessel had friends.

Would Schessel's neo nazi pals in Flensburg backtrack to me like the guys with the AK47 did outside our apartment? Those were overlapping circles, too.

When I returned to the office Margaret's curiosity had to be massaged. She was wearing one of her red, tight sheath dresses so short that if she didn't cross her legs she risked flashing her privates. She asked "What was that all about?"

I ignored her invitation to sit in the visitors chair. I didn't want this to be a long conversation. "The murder of Ursula's uncle in Germany."

"What about it?"

"I figured it out. Did it just for fun."

"For fun?"

"It was all in the metadata. Julius had betrayed a couple who were trying to escape from East Germany. She was killed. Her husband wanted revenge."

Her eyebrows went up a notch. "And you figured it out?"

"Yeh. Mostly. Ursula helped with the German part."

Margaret was impressed. "So now you and your wife are amateur detectives like Nick and Nora Charles?"

"You've been watching Turner Movie Classics."

"Is this going to interfere with your job here?"

"I hope not. I like this job."

She changed the subject. "Your IT friend Grabich said something about a bitcoin account. What's that about?"

I paused to hide my irritation. "He shouldn't have said anything about it." What should I say? How to begin? "You remember when the cloud merged suddenly my face showed up on screens everywhere. I didn't appreciate the invasion of my privacy, the use of my photo without permission. When I was being interviewed about on the Good Morning TV show I was ticked off and said I'd sue, like Hulk Hogan did for invasion of his privacy. Hundred and forty million dollars. That scared the TV people off. Didn't want me back."

"You didn't sue?"

I shook my head. "Not my style. Someone noticed and I got a letter saying I was not to sue, and here was a bitcoin account. Like I was being paid to be silent."

She was intrigued. "Who did that?"

"An anonymous hacker."

Fortunately, like most people, Margaret's curiosity had been satisfied. She did not pursue it. If she had asked me how many bitcoins I'd have had to be evasive or lie. My account in dollars would make me a multi millionaire, if it were real money.

Not sure that it was, I thought "What the hell? Why not?" We'd tested it and paid off the mortgage on our condo using bitcoins. It was a gamble that it wasn't real or that there might be consequences. You never know. I was still waiting, sometimes fearful. Who's money was it? Where did it come from? Would they want it back? If it was stolen, was

I a guilty co-conspirator? Would the aggrieved party send a hit man to kill me? All those possibilities give me a headache. Not knowing where it came from, I couldn't give it back, either.

It was like being given a white elephant that couldn't work but had to be fed. In this case, it was like someone handed me a ticking bomb that might go off any time.

The bitcoin wallet was real. At least now we are debt free. Still, I was regretful about dipping into the account. There might be strings attached. It was like a mysterious treasure chest with a warning: do not open. Contents may kill.

I went back to my cubicle. The little wooden Russian doll with its enigmatic smile Uncle Julius had given us was on the counter beside my monitor. I wondered what stories it could tell about the days before the wall came down, about people trying to escape and Julius after them with border guards and machine guns. Ironic that he ended up in a shabby post war apartment block in Hamburg on the west German dole. The doll sat there, in silence, a testimony to a dark East German past.

I thought my business with the FBI was settled and I wouldn't be bothered, but my troubles weren't over.

I hadn't seen my IT mentor Grabich in several days. I was peeved that he had told Margaret about the bitcoin account. I called and suggested we meet at Starbucks after work.

We had taken at a table for two in the back at Starbucks when a disheveled-looking man approached.

He asked, "Harvey Goldstein?"

When I said that was me, he handed me an envelope. "You've been served." He disappeared.

Confused, I opened the envelope. It was a subpoena.

Grabich asked, "What's that?"

I studied the formal layout. The State of Ohio versus…but I had no idea who the people were. "I'm supposed to be a witness at a trial."

This distracted me from my purpose to confront him about the bitcoins. That was supposed to be a secret. The names of the two defendants on the subpoena were not familiar. Then I remembered. "I think these are the two guys who shot up our condo."

Grabich scratched his bushy hair. "But you weren't home at the time. How could you be a witness?"

I explained that as Harvey Goldstein I tapped into the tapes of the CCT camera across the street, the one the FBI installed. I saw the drive by, noted the license plate of the stolen car, tracked the GPS of the cell phone one of the two shooters was carrying, saw the location on Google World where they torched the car and were picked up by a friend and driven to the Moosehead Bar and Mini-Brewery. I then got their faces off the bar's surveillance camera, sent my report to the Cleveland police. "I didn't look up their mug shots," I explained. "Those were already on file. Let the cops do some of the homework. Couple of gang bangers."

Grabich gave me an unaccustomed look of admiration. After all, he's the guy who has to explain things to me. "Then you are a witness."

I thought about having to reveal the secrets of Harvey Goldstein in court. Who would believe me? Not everyone lives in a morass of metadata like I do.

I changed the subject. "How's everything between you and your Iranian girl friend?"

I was referring to his hacking into the files of Immigration and fixing her with a Green Card. Illegal, but Grabich is an ex-hacker who got a legitimate job as Krieger's IT guy.

He was downcast. "She stayed with me long enough to save up for a damage deposit and a month's rent in advance, then split."

"Too bad." I remembered his cluttered basement apartment full of computer stuff and wire. I wouldn't have wanted to share with him, either,

"She got another boy friend."

"Sorry."

He shrugged it off but I could see he was disappointed. "She was too tidy for me. Always putting my stuff away so I couldn't find it."

I remembered Grabich's basement apartment and the mess of monitors and cables. Even a rat would get lost in there.

Neither of us had any experience with the courts. Grabich asked, "Do you get paid for being an expert witness?"

"That would be something else. I'm just a plain bystander."

"When's the trial?"

"In another week."

Grabich sensed my nervousness. "Maybe you should take Ursula along for moral support."

"Right. She's a victim, too. It's scary shit to have your condo shot up. The FBI has installed a bulletproof picture window, but we have to replace the curtains." I didn't mention my fish wall decoration that used to sing "Take me to the River" until a bullet silenced the mechanism.

"Why did the FBI do that? What about home owners insurance?"

"It was their fault. They used my portal to investigate a drug case, so it got back to me. You know everything is tracked."

Grabich nodded. "Yeh. I once Googled pretty Iranian girls and have been hounded ever since."

I laughed. "Serves you right. It's your metadata, Grabich. You're a marked man. Sure you didn't search for Japanese schoolgirls?"

He shook his hairy head. "If I did I'd be offered once worn girls' panties."

Chapter three

For Ursula to attend the trial as a spectator would require getting a substitute teacher to fill in for her. That might be OK for the English as a second language classes, but not for the German. It was bad enough for me to show up in Boss Margaret's fish bowl with the subpoena in hand and ask for a day off. She relented, but would dock me the day's wages.

Not that my wages meant anything when I harbored five hundred million bucks in illicit bitcoins. Still, money earned at Krieger was real. In my mind, like hairs of fear standing up at the back of my neck, was the anxiety that whoever's loot had been parked in my bitcoin wallet for convenience might not be happy about it. A hacker did not have to hire a couple of gang bangers to shoot up my apartment. A hacker can destroy your identity.

I'd already been deleted once, left stranded in Utah with no money, credit cards or identity. I was rebooted thanks to Grabich and a system restore. Suddenly being a non person was something I did not want to repeat.

I knew enough to understand that a murderous hacker could break into my doctor's records and change my prescription to something fatal, all without leaving his Rumanian or Bulgarian attic room. If I were a hacker I could do the same, but I am not a hacker or a murderer.

If anything I'm just a snoop, a sort of internet professional peeping Tom. Uncle Julius thought that was great, but he was Secret Police. That was his job. At Krieger it's my job, too, sort of. I do have occasional pangs of conscience. One can know too much. I was beginning to have trepidations about that.

It was with serious trepidation that I packed my laptop in its carrier, put on my sport coat and my one actual necktie, and drove to the court house for the trial. Security was tight. My bag was inspected and I was wanded by the nervous guards. I even had to take off my shoes, grateful that my socks had no holes. At least I'd remembered to wear clean underwear in case security got that personal.

Who knew? I might have been a terrorist or an irate parolee bent on revenge.

Once in the courtroom, I thought that maybe I could sit in the back, but I was spotted by the assistant prosecutor, a young guy who looked like the print on his law school diploma might not yet be dry.

He was followed by an older lawyer in a rumpled, gray suit and hard expression. He was for the defense. He did not look like a pro-bono public defender, but someone the two shooters could not afford. Whoever hired them must have promised to cover their asses if they were caught. There was serious money behind this. Was the assistant prosecutor out of his depth? Out gunned? Ooo, bad pun.

Was I the shuttlecock?

Near as I could see, there were no other witnesses. If that was the situation, the whole trial depended on my testimony.

I had my own resources. After all, I am Harvey Goldstein. I just have a burner track phone, but I borrowed Ursula's I-phone and used it to photograph both lawyers. Transferred the photos to my laptop.

The prosecutor was Charles Wallace and while I pretended to be playing a computer game got his dossier and Facebook profile. Wallace was married, had a two year old daughter, wife also a lawyer. He was a plain vanilla guy, no criminal record, and to my disappointment not a Krieger customer. If he was I'd know his favorite candy bars.

The defense attorney, Morris Cohen, didn't like my taking his picture. I pretended to be a jerk, took a selfie for Facebook pages. He hated it.

Cohen had a hard look even a mother could hardly love. I Googled him. His law degree was from some small college in Nebraska, but he had moved to Chicago where he hooked up with the City of Chicago insiders. The Chicago machine was full of feather bedders and scoundrels. The Sun-Times reported Cohen had defended a city elevator inspector who never inspected an elevator but took a bribe from everyone who had an elevator until one failed. An old apartment house elevator had dropped, killing a mother and two kids. Cohen successfully defended the so-called inspector who was moved to the street department, a ghost job that paid well for not showing up.

Cohen had a police record. An accusation of jury tampering had put Cohen in the hot seat. He was now working in Ohio. Cohen was not a nice guy. He was also divorced, remarried to Patricia. I found out she was a real estate agent who had moved up from being a night club hostess. These were not my kind of people.

When I got to the courtroom the jury had already been selected the day before. I took a group picture. I ran their faces individually though the facial recognition program. They all had drivers licenses and were therefore in the data base. I knew where they lived, if they were registered to vote, color of eyes, racial identity which in some cases was "other." That's also a gender designation. The world changes.

Now all I needed was the scoop on the two defendants, the gang bangers who shot up our condo and killed my singing fish wall decoration.

Finding an African African-American is this country only happens if the African actually came from Africa, like Kenya or one of the other forty countries on that continent. My two guys were of mixed race, chocolate Americans with maybe Native American blood besides whatever got mixed in from the old plantation owners. If a slave cost a thousand dollars and you could make babies with her for free, it was profit.

Except when they came into the Moosehead bar and showed up on the security camera, I hadn't seen their faces. They both had rap sheets. The tall, frizzy one was Wayne, the shorter with a jar head hair cut was Leroy. They both had no fathers to speak of and been raised by granny until they got in trouble and spent some time in juvie. This was sadly typical.

I'm no sociologist. I just collect metadata. Neither Wayne nor Leroy were Krieger customers. There was no Krieger store in their neighborhood, no place to buy fresh fruit or vegetables. There was a gun store, a payday loan shark, a 7-11, and fast food joints.

Why would Cohen be assigned their defense? Maybe he'd been demoted.

The judge came in, a gray haired woman with a tired face. I'd heard judges were overworked and had full dockets which explained why the constitutionally mandated speedy trial was a sad joke. If you couldn't make bail you could languish in jail for years before being found not guilty. By then you'd have lost your job and be homeless. Justice in America.

The bailiff told us all to rise, which we did.

While the judge went through the preliminaries I was absorbed in my research of the jury and didn't pay attention until I was called to the stand.

The first one to call me was the prosecutor and I swore to tell the truth, the whole truth, and nothing but the truth which could turn out to be a whole lot more than they bargained for or I was willing to reveal.

I affirmed that I was, indeed Harvey Goldstein and lived at our address. I was asked where I was on the day of the drive by shooting. "My wife and I had been out to dinner."

That was what the prosecutor wanted to hear for it led into his next question: "So how could you witness the shooting?"

"I saw it on the CCT camera recordings across the street."

"How do you have access to those recordings?"

"I am Harvey Goldstein. I have access to all data everywhere." I then went through my step by step reconstruction of the crime. I ended my narrative with identifying the two defendants from their pictures in the bar. "The police can confirm all that information."

I was then turned over to Morris Cohen, the defense lawyer.

He took a deep breath to be sure he had the undivided attention of the jury, then turned to me. "Just what do you do for a living, Mr. Goldstein?"

"I do grocery coupons for Krieger."

"Just how do you do that?"

"We identify all the purchases by all our customers individually. I then issue them coupons for products they usually buy and some our data indicates they might buy in the future."

"So you manipulate data."

"Metadata," I corrected.

"Just what is metadata?"

"It's all the information about everybody anywhere."

"And you have access to all of this?"

I nodded.

"Is that a 'yes', Mr. Goldstein?"

"Yes."

"Can that data be altered?"

I could see what he was driving at. He wanted to cast doubt on the veracity of my data. "Data is data."

He nodded. "They say that figures don't lie, but liars figure."

I wasn't going to be caught in that one. "Once the data is there it doesn't go away. For instance, your request that the record of your being disbarred from practicing law in Illinois being sealed was approved, but is still in the record, which is where I found it."

Cohen was visibly shocked and had to control his anger. "You found that?"

"There's also a public record: a news story in the files at the Chicago Sun Times. Anybody can Google that." I sat at attention.

Cohen was obviously feeling a bit exposed. "But the court records are sealed. That's not in Google, is it?"

"I am Harvey Goldstein. I can find out everything about everybody. It's my job."

"At Krieger? Is Krieger in the business of snooping? Or is it just you, Mr. Know it all?"

At that the prosecutor objected that Cohen was trying to disparage my character. Sustained.

I explained, "Some of the information we know about our customers' buying habits is personal and confidential."

"But accessing the FBIs CCT cameras is not part of your job."

"No."

"Are you a hacker, Mr. Goldstein?"

He was trying to make my name something sinister, like Mark Anthony twisting the meaning of Brutus being "an honorable man" in Shakespeare's play.

"I'm not a hacker. I wouldn't know the first thing about it. Just looking at data doesn't change it."

"Then how did you access the surveillance tape at the Moosehead bar?"

I had to admit. "I don't know. It just comes to me."

"You imagine this?" Now he was trying to make me out to be a nut case. I suppose in the minds of some people he'd be right.

"No. Since the merging of the clouds I have access to all data, everything, even NSA's record of your two phone calls to Jurist Number 9." I indicated a light skinned African-American in the jury box. "She's Leroy's aunt. She's never going to say he's guilty." I turned to the judge. "You're going to have a hung jury, your honor. Mr. Cohen promised the lady $500 to vote not-guilty."

I thought Cohen would have an apoplectic seizure.

There was turmoil in the courtroom, all faces toward juror number nine.

I couldn't resist addressing Morris Cohen. "You were convicted of jury tampering in Illinois. Now you're at it again in Ohio."

Down came the Judge's gavel. "The jury will ignore the witness's remarks." To the two lawyers, "I will see you in my chambers. We will break for one hour."

I realized from the evil look on Cohen's face that for being a smartass I had now acquired an enemy a lot more dangerous than Wayne and Leroy.

I was released from the witness box and returned to my seat and my laptop. Why couldn't I keep my mouth shut?

I stewed for an hour in the courtroom. Eventually the judge came out and recalled the jury. Number nine was excused with a warning. An alternate filled in for her.

The trial resumed.

The prosecutor produced police reports that corroborated my story. It was clear that the two gang bangers were guilty. Stealing the car and setting it on fire was the only crime that had any weight. Shooting up my house was a misdemeanor violation for firing a weapon in the city limits. Possession of a firearm by a couple of felons was serious. They would get some jail time, but nothing they weren't already used to.

Morris Cohen, however, wanted revenge.

As I was putting away my laptop and getting ready to leave he threatened me though clenched teeth. "You were lucky you weren't at home, Goldstein when they shot up your place. Next time maybe not."

I clutched my laptop in its case in front of me like a shield. "Like I said, Mr. Cohen, I am not a hacker. I can find data, but I cannot change it. But I do know a hacker. A hacker can close all your bank and credit card accounts, empty your savings and checking accounts, foreclose on your mortgage, shut off all your utilities, get into your prescription records and change your meds for something fatal." I knew that because I'd been turned into a non person myself.

I let all the information sink in. Just to dot the I's I added, "NSA has all your phone calls. Every office copier has copies of your documents on its hard drive. You have no secrets from me, Mr. Cohen. I'm not interested in making any trouble for you. You already have enough. Just don't make any for me. Don't be a schmuck."

Morris Cohen was obviously what we call a co-religionist, a member of the tribe, but not all are good guys. I could think of a few Yiddish curses that might be appropriate, but I'd already made my point.

Cohen was clearly intimidated. He tucked his chin into his thick neck. "You're a dangerous man, Goldstein."

I shrugged, my nebbish pose. "Who me? I'm just a coupon clerk at Krieger." I'm not looking for fame. I admit I'm just a step above a nobody; just don't mess with me.

Even if I were a hacker, there was no point in stripping Morris Cohen of his identity. We are all vulnerable. Many Americans are one pay check away from homelessness. We walk a narrow line guided only by the hope that nothing will go wrong. All too often it does.

I didn't notice if there was a reporter in the courtroom. My wise ass exposure of Morris Cohen could have been managed in a more discreet manner. Now all my words were in the transcript, the public record. "I am Harvey Goldstein!" What a schmuck.

This was all giving me a headache. I couldn't handle the mental strain. It took intense concentration to bore in on the facial recognition programs for all the jurors. Though I could penetrate NSA's phone records, and find the conversations Cohen had with the kid's aunt, I felt weak. There was a price to pay for being Harvey Goldstein, Metadata Man. I just hadn't yet realized how serious it was.

Chapter four

I had a headache when I got back to the Krieger offices. Boss Margaret was surprised to see me. I guess she thought I'd take the whole day off.

She was plainly curious and maybe apprehensive. If I missed too much work she would have to find someone else to do the job. It wasn't that she particularly liked me. I was expendable. Recruiting a new person would be a hassle. She looked around the glass door of her office and asked, "How was the trial?"

"The defense lawyer tried to make me out to be some kind of a kook."

"You weren't wearing your Metadata Man shirt, were you?" It was her way of teasing me for looking like a star wars or some other teenaged fan.

"Jacket and tie." I slipped off the tie as too formal for the office. I looked around, felt disoriented. "Do you have any aspirin?"

She rummaged in her copious purse, came up with a small bottle of Tylenol. "Try one of these."

I carried the pill to the water cooler and chugged it down. Dizzy, I made my way to my cubicle with its monitor and the Russian doll. The enigmatic smile on that Russian doll's face looked like it knew something I didn't.

I sat down, felt nauseous, put my head down on the keyboard and...

...woke up in the hospital.

I was in a very white room. When I moved my right arm I discovered a tube was plugged into the back of my wrist. I was on some sort of a drip.

It took some time for me to focus on Ursula's face as she sat close to me. Her worry was contagious. My mouth was dry and I had trouble forming words. "What happened?"

"You passed out at the office. The EMTs thought you might have had a stroke."

"I'm too young for a stroke."

"A seizure, maybe. As soon as you're stabilized you're going to have an MRI."

I hadn't been a hospital patient before and certainly hadn't had an MRI. I was asked if I had any metal in my body. None, except for a couple of fillings in my teeth.

I felt confused and helpless as the staff shifted me onto a gurney and wheeled me through a maze of hallways and elevators, finally reaching a room dominated by a huge putty colored machine.

They stabilized my head so I could not move. I hardly heard their questions. Was I claustrophobic? Would I need a sedative in case I panicked? I didn't think so.

They lined me up and warned me it would be noisy. That was an understatement. It sounded like someone was pounding on the outside of a steel garbage can with me inside it. Bang, bang. I closed my eyes and held my breath.

When I was about to lose it, I was pulled back out of the machine. On a big screen I could just make out a display of sectional x-rays of my brain, like it had been sliced like a baked ham. None of it made any sense to me. Was this what my brain looked like?

I asked, "What did you find out?"

Of course, they can't tell you. They just take the pictures. It's up to the doctors to interpret them.

One thing I did notice. Everything around me looked sharper, like I'd just got a new prescription for eye glasses, sharper but maybe a little distorted, like I had astigmatism. The light flickered like some laser show, so bright that it hurt, even when I closed my eyes.

I tried to focus on the nurse who was taking my vitals. She was wearing a hospital ID name tag around her neck, first name only for the sake of privacy. Funny first name, Oona. The only Oona I'd ever heard of was Oona O'Neil, daughter of Eugene O'Neill who married Charlie Chaplain when she was barely of legal age and then had about six kids.

"Oona Kaplan," I said, like I was reading off a chart. . "Graduated from nursing school five years ago with honors." Then it all came to me, like some mathematician who visualizes the formula for the secret of the universe.

Nurse Kaplan was surprised. "How do you know that?"

I covered my eyes with my left hand, the one without the IV attached. I sighed like someone resigned to a life sentence in the court I had just left. I realized I had crossed the threshold. Somehow I had become an extension of the cloud, not just someone with access to it, but absorbed by it, like an amoeba surrounds and absorbs the food it eats, except I was the one being eaten. "I am Harvey Goldstein," I said, my voice choked. God help me. "I know everything."

No surprise: she didn't understand.

Almost against my will, I rattled off her home address, her phone number, the names of her two children, a boy four and a girl two and a half. With an effort, I stopped myself. "I could tell you the numbers of your credit cards, how much student loan you still owe, and your medical history. I can even recite you recent telephone call to your brother in the army."

She drew back, like I was someone dangerous, a wizard, a witch, or the devil himself. "How?"

"I don't know," I said weakly, shocked and overwhelmed by the realization. "It's overload. I think I passed out because I blew a fuse in my brain. Too much information."

She left, or had she fled?

I closed my eyes, hoping the realization would all go away. I wasn't wired for this. I don't know what the capacity of a brain is. I do know there are people with total recall, what they ate for breakfast on March fifth, 2014. Were they savants, who could add up the numbers of passing boxcars, like in the movie Rain Man but couldn't make change for a dollar? Was I doomed to know everything but be incapable of anything else?

They say be careful what you wish for. I wanted all the data. It was greed. I always wanted more information, more metadata. It was fun for doing the coupons for Boss Margaret, but this was too much. I didn't need to know that Oona Kaplan's second child was born by C-section, that she had suffered from post partum depression. I didn't want to know everything, but I did.

When she brought in the doctor, Doctor Weiss, Ira, graduate of Indiana University medical school, neurologist, married to another Jewish doctor, and so on and so on. I couldn't turn it off.

He was troubled, standing there in his white coat and name tag, but Oona Kaplan had briefed him, so he wasn't totally surprised. "This is outside my area of expertise," he admitted. "You'll need to see a psychiatrist."

I protested. "I don't need a psychiatrist. I know what's happened. I don't know how I crossed the threshold, but I did." I told him about the merging of the clouds, how I'd been able to track down Uncle Julius's killer in Hamburg without leaving my desk.

With Julius that was just an expert search, except no expert without specials access could have tapped into the digital record of the surveillance camera in the visitor's office in Nuremburg. That was me penetrating all the firewalls and passwords of the cloud.

Finally I speculated. "I think I've tuned into a wi-fi receiver. Everything about us is electrical. Our muscles are activated by electrical impulses. Even plants have an electrical aura. I've just become a universal receptor."

Ursula had brought in a bouquet of flowers which now stood by the window, Chrysanthemums. I pointed to them. "Those flowers are aware of my concern for their trauma."

Was it just my imagination, my being empathetic to a flower?

I thought about that for a minute. "Reminds me that we are all part of the universe. We are all interconnected."

Dr. Weiss just stared at me, like I was some raving lunatic.

I continued,. "We are all connected by only six degrees of separation. That's us, connected to other people. But what if we are connected to all living things as well?

I realized we are, except for me. I was like a radio that got all the stations at once, a babble of white noise. Somehow I would have to learn how to tune in to a specific signal. If not I could go mad.

The doctors had a consultation.

Ursula asked me to return her iPhone. "What happened at the trial? Did that have something to do with this?"

I told her about Morris Cohen and how I had threatened to have a hacker destroy his identity if he gave me any trouble.

She gave me a look that said she didn't know I could be that vindictive. Even though we've been married five years, we still discover things about each other, not all of them pleasant. We all have our quirks. That's what makes life interesting, proving you are tolerant.

Love forgives. My love for Ursula overcame any little potential irritation, like did she put the cap back on the toothpaste? So what? If you love someone, such picky stuff doesn't count.

Ursula has her ways, little habits I'd never have guessed before we were married, but so what? I found getting to know her a pleasant adventure. I guess that's because I love her. If she bit her toenails I wouldn't mind.

I can hardly touch my toes, much less bite the nails. I'd have to be a contortionist.

But could she tolerate a Harvey Goldstein whose personality had changed so drastically? Had I become a stranger to her? A freak? I hoped not. In my new situation I needed her support more than ever. This could be a test for our marriage.

Two doctors came back to the room. One I knew at once was Samuel Halal, Samuel being an Anglicization of an Arab name. He was originally Muhammad and from Syria. I blanked out the other details. Didn't want to show off. I didn't want to know.

Dr. Halal was a pediatrician, specializing in premies, those tiny infants weighing as little as seven hundred grams.

He looked at my eyes. Tried to get me follow his finger but I could not focus.

"Mr. Goldstein, you are like one of my newborns. Their brains are not developed enough to cope with the stimuli. Their eyes are not ready to see everything and their ears not ready to hear all that goes on around them. They need time to mature."

He explained that was the curse of being born before full term. Lungs, brain, eyes were not fully developed.

Full of apprehension I asked, "So what do I do? You're not going to put me in an incubator."

Dr. Halal didn't laugh. He was dead serious. "You should stay in a darkened room and wear a blindfold. Absolute rest and quiet, and bland food."

"How long?"

He was not certain. "A month. You need to gradually be exposed to outside stimuli."

Doctor Weiss agreed. "Your brain scan is normal. No tumors or strokes. You can go home now, but you're not to drive."

Though the prescribed conditions might reduce outside stimuli, what about what was going on inside my head, all the time? Would it ever stop?

Weiss continued. "The human brain is constantly bombarded by stimuli. Thousands of commercials, for instance. To cope we learn to blot out, to compartmentalize, to filter everything. It's a coping mechanism."

I understood. We generalize about people, categorize them, probably unfairly. We see someone as black, or a Democrat, and stop there. It's too much trouble to know everyone well. Except in my altered state, I kept finding the metadata. I couldn't stop. What I wasn't certain of was whether I could cope.

Chapter five

Ursula drove me home from the hospital. The doctors had already blindfolded me and wrapped a bandage around my head as if I'd suffered a concussion. Even so, I felt every bump, heard every muffled sound. I felt like Munck's famous painting of the scream, except the scream was me.

Ursula helped me out of the car and held onto me to guide me up the steps to our front door.

I could sense that she was not ready to care for an invalid. She had bargained to be a wife, not a caregiver. I was like someone suddenly blind and handicapped. How long would this condition last? Would she stick it out, or walk away like so many spouses have when faced with this sort of problem? It would be an adjustment for both of us.

The doctor said a month. Would I have adjusted by then? Or would I simply go mad? End up in an institution, a raving lunatic?

Ursula gently led me to what I recognized was our recliner chair and sat me down.

Through the bandages I heard her say I'd been given a sedative, something to calm me down, relax me. I should sleep, if I could.

I felt like an insomniac who tosses and turns all night, brain fired up with intrusive thoughts. Eventually I relaxed. I still visualized a kaleidoscope of colors, information, data. Like membership lists scrolling across a computer screen I could read the names and data of the Teamsters Union, what personal vehicles they drove, what Krieger products might be of interest to them, what coupons I might send, their addresses, and on and on before shifting to the Teachers Union and their data, all this while the faces of the jurors and their background information flashed past in a jumble.

What had the jury's verdict been? Could I remember to ask Ursula when I woke up, or would everything in my mind disappear like a bad dream?

Eventually I did sleep, but didn't know what time or day it was when I stirred, seeing faint light through the blindfold. I needed to pee and tried to get up from the chair, did stand, then, irresolute, stood helpless and called out to Ursula.

Ashamed for having to ask, I said "Get me to the toilet. I need to pee."

I realized it was the middle of the night and I had waked her up, if she was able to sleep at all what with my tossing and turning. I guess there are advantages to twin beds, though I prefer the cuddles of a queen size. She guided me. For the sake of sanitation she sat me down on the toilet in case I'd pee all over the place. If you sit you don't have to aim.

I tried to remember the layout of the bathroom, so I could feel my way around the place. She patiently led me to the kitchen, sat me down on one of our Goodwill chairs and lifted the blindfold a bit. The sudden light was blinding, gave me a headache.

"Coffee?"

"Thanks. What time is it?"

"Four-thirty."

It made me feel ashamed, depriving Ursula of her sleep. She had to get to school in a few hours. My being incapacitated was hard on her.

I tried to organize my thoughts and recent memories. "What happened in the court?"

"You had a call from the prosecutor. I told him you were ill. I have his number. Do you think you can handle the phone?"

"Maybe later."

She got me to our bed and tried to get back to sleep but the alarm went off like two minutes later, even though it wasn't.

I peeked out from under the blindfold to see Ursula give me a worried look as she finished her breakfast, toast and a fried egg, orange juice and coffee. "You going to be OK?"

I lifted the blindfold and squinted at her. "I think so. Just so I don't make any sudden movements. I might pass out."

She left. Sometimes she jogs to school. It's only a mile, but this time she took the Toyota. I heard it drive off, a good excuse for me to hide behind the blindfold until offices opened.

I remembered the prosecutor's name and particulars. I had his direct line and he answered. I tried to make the call friendly and personal. "Mr. Wallace. How's that two year old daughter? Is she talking yet?"

He was surprised. "She says Mama but I haven't got her to say Daddy yet."

"What happened at the trial after I left?"

He didn't answer at first. "What did you tell Morris Cohen? I saw you talking with him."

I searched my memory. It was coming back. "I told him I was not a hacker. I can find information but I can't alter it."

"Meaning?"

"I told him if he gave me any trouble I knew someone who could destroy his identity."

"How so?"

"Closes all his accounts, delete him from the records, shut off his utilities, all those things that can be done if a hacker is malicious enough."

Wallace was silent for a moment. "I think you made your point. The judge was pretty mad about Juror Number Nine. Cohen persuaded the defendants to change their plea to guilty."

"Was that his ploy to avoid accusations of jury tampering?"

"Maybe."

Those two kids were bad asses. If we'd been home when they drove by with that AK47 we might be dead. I'd have liked to see them locked up. No such luck.

Wallace explained. "Stealing the RV and burning it were felonies, but since nobody was injured when they shot up your place, she gave them three years probation, a thousand hours of community service, and of course restitution for the cost of the vehicle and damage to your apartment."

"I can't imagine those kids coming up with what? Thirty thousand or more for the car?"

"It's hard to get restitution. Just because it is awarded doesn't mean it gets paid."

I pondered that. I was pissed that the FBI had used my Harvey Goldstein portal to the clouds in their own investigation. I hoped there wouldn't be others after me for some mysterious revenge. Certainly someone might want their million bitcoins back. That was serious.

"Your wife says you've been in the hospital."

"Yes. You could call it information overload. Someone else might call it a nervous breakdown."

"What do they do for that?"

"Tranquilizers. A month of isolation, blindfold, darkened room, like a kid with measles or mumps."

I thought about it. A month with Ursula having to nurse me. She might qualify for sick leave from her school, but I was afraid Margaret would simply fire me. She had been looking for an excuse. All my unexpected visitors had upset the rhythm of her management routine. Whether I caused it or not, it was a disruption. Any disruption meant she wasn't in control.

Just so Wallace, the FBI, and that German detective Klaus Hintz didn't come at me wanting the services of Harvey Goldstein, metadata man who knows all except he has to wear a blindfold and sit in a darkened room like some mental case, which I had to admit I was.

My whole life was uncertain. In the meantime, my brain was being bombarded with a roar of intercepted phone conversations from NSA, data about everything and everybody, and never any respite. With a sedative I had slept, but would I be kept up all night by confused thoughts and images? I felt like the guy whose tooth fillings worked like a crystal set and he heard the radio all night, except for me it wasn't just one station. It was everything. Maybe that's why people took drugs, just to escape.

I thanked Wallace for his information. I sat in the darkened room, tried to think of nothing, but it as impossible.

Was this what it was like to be a tiny premie baby? Of course, babies sleep a lot. Sensory deprivation was what they needed and so did I.

Like a man suddenly struck blind, I felt a sudden panic at being left alone. I felt helpless.

Maybe I could distract myself by trying to focus on one simple mental exercise, like counting backwards through the alphabet or counting down from a hundred, simple diversions from the roar in my head and the confusion of images. It would take concentration. No wonder insomniacs try counting sheep.

Chapter six

I tried to find a new rhythm to my secluded existence. We used the answering machine to screen my phone calls, which Ursula checked. She also reviewed my email, which was considerable, some weirdoes still responding to my query when I had tried to find out who my benefactor was. It was, of course, the German girl of uncertain age who had sent me her photo by snail mail, no message or return address.

She called herself Angel. I had suggested she was a modern Robin Hood who stole from the hacker thieves and redistributed their loot. Maybe someone who had hacked the Russian bank for two million rubles, which in real money is still a lot. Had she intercepted it and found other places to hide it? Did she convert rubles to bitcoins? Where had my million bitcoins actually come from? The bank in Panama where rich American stashed their trillions of surplus wealth?

If, for instance, my bitcoins had been part of the Bangladesh heist and they tracked the money through the maze of the dark web back to me, was I liable, like prison?

Did I dare backtrack it myself and not reveal who I was and where? Best to leave it alone and see what happened.

Then Ursula said I had an email from Angel. It was garbled German and English. She read it out to me and had to repeat herself several times. It was not coherent. If she was trying to be cryptic, she succeeded, for I couldn't understand the message.

Angel's mail, like my own, was routed through the TOR network that fragmented messages and sent them through various computers to be reassembled only at the destination. The only thing I did think I understood was that she was in trouble. Considering what she was up to, that wouldn't be a surprise.

Angel was a hacker with a sense of social responsibility. Not that she returned any stolen money she intercepted. She might not know the original source. What do you do? Put up an ad saying, "Are you missing a million dollars? If so contact…"?

She just diverted it from the other hackers. In a sense she was like the people who provided Wikileaks with stolen documents, like the Russian hackers had when they got hold of emails for the Democratic

Party before the Trump election. It was mischief, whistle blowers, people with a sense of self importance that justified their illegal means. Power corrupts.

I hoped that my powers as Harvey Goldstein wouldn't turn me into a monster. It's easy to fall into the trap, like when I brag "I am Harvey Goldstein, metadata man." Was I in danger of that kind of corruption?

Angel had power, too. Except with Angel it was money, not information.

Her message to me was that she was in trouble. Someone very angry was trying to find her. She was afraid.

Grabich had been a hacker once and had used his skills to get a green card for his Iranian girl friend. He knew that hackers were a kind of dark web fraternity, all using code names and exchanging tips and methods.

It didn't strike me as secure. All the FBI, KGB, or Interpol needed was a mole that could find out all their identities. That might explain why Angel came to me and not to others.

Some hackers did it just for fun, to prove they could penetrate a bank's records. Others sold the identities of customers and made money that way. Angel wasn't doing her thing for fun or for her own profit, near as I could tell. She was being her own internet cop.

She must have seen the TV broadcast when I was interviewed and my photo showed on everyone's screen, "Harvey Goldstein is Watching You.". That's when I threatened to sue for a hundred and forty million like Hulk Hogan had when his X-rated video got broadcast to the world without his permission. She sent me the bitcoins so I wouldn't have to sue, or so she said.

As Harvey Goldstein, metadata man, I might have an advantage. I had her photograph.

I took a chance and peeked out from under my blindfold to search in my desk drawer for the selfie photograph she had sent. It showed a not very attractive female of uncertain age with hair dyed blonde, bad skin, and an oddly twisted mouth. No wonder she retreated into the dark web.

I turned on my laptop and scanned her photo into a 300 dpi jpg. As Harvey Goldstein I knew how to access the visual recognition database. I queried, "Who is this?" and waited.

My laptop is not top of the line. Slow. The power saving feature blanked the screen. I woke it up again. Finally a result: the picture of

Angel identified as Liselottte Kraus. OK. That was easy. Next would be to get the address and her entire life history.

But wait… there was another person with the same face: Asa Kornblat. Liselotte was in Berlin. Asa was in Heidelberg. Made sense that she might change her name and move around if she were on the run. Trouble was, you can't change your face. She could dye her hair, put on makeup, even a mustache, but the data was the same telltale. Maybe she had a twin sister. Maybe the database wasn't accurate. I knew it was still not perfect.

I thought I was done: Asa Kornblat, Liselotte Kraus. OK. But before I could dig further, there was another name to the same face, Martha Blumenthal in Munich. Either the data was faulty or she was getting around a lot.

What they did have in common was the approximate age. She must have several different passports or drivers licenses. That was a possibility. If Grabich could get his girl a green card, Angel could get multiple identities.

I had heard that people, to take on an alias, sometimes use the same initials or variations of the same first name to avoid confusion. Angel didn't do that. Each name was unique. It would be better if she called herself something ordinary like, in the United States, Mary Jones. How many of those were there?

I still wanted to believe that the people I had found were the same person.

Well, maybe I should send each an email with a code word only Angel, the real angel--if she was real--would know.

The search was still on. More picture, more identities. Even a Polish or maybe Russian name, just to throw searchers like me off the track.

She reminded me of Salander, the Girl with the Dragon Tattoo, who raided her enemy's accounts and gave herself lots of travel money. With a couple of million DMarks, Euros or Bitcoins, who needed a job? Except there was nothing glamorous or sexy about Angel. Salander was tough. Angel was no Salander.

Being constantly on the run had to be incredibly stressful. How could she cope? The best tactic was to be invisible, so innocuous that nobody ever noticed you. That would be easy in Cleveland where most people are just looking at their cell phones all the time and don't even look up to avoid being hit by a bus or fall into a ditch.

What those people didn't know was they were being watched, not by other people, but by CCT cameras and computers set to look for a specific face like in an Amber alert. That's what I had done with Angel's face.

The stress of all this was getting to me. I was trying to formulate an appropriate email or twitter message but I was getting a headache again. I had to retreat.

My brain whirled with distracting images and thoughts. I bundled all those names for Angel into a file on a flash drive before shutting down and fumbling my way back to bed. The bedroom blinds were drawn, the lights out. I hid under the covers like some kid afraid of the bogy man.

I was shaking all over like some alcoholic with the DTs. If I could blot everything out maybe I could hold myself together until Ursula came home from school. Ursula was my rock, my anchor of sensibility in my world of chaos. She could rescue me. I hoped.

Chapter seven

"Are you all right?"

It was Ursula, back from school. I heard the thump as she dropped her backpack and came to the bedroom, uncertain of what she would find under the blanket.

I peeked out, blinking at the light. "I was looking for Angel."

"Under the covers? You're supposed to be resting."

I propped up against the pillow and stroked my chin. I hadn't shaved, in how long? "Turns out there is more than one Angel."

"That's not an impossible name. Many people could be named Angel. Then there's guardian angel, the angel of death..."

"Let's skip the angel of death. I was just searching the facial recognition databases. Several came up, different names, but the same face. I think she's running around Germany, using different aliases."

"Her email sounded frantic."

"If there was only one identity to track it would be easy. I got stressed out."

"I'll make you some warm cocoa. Then you get out of bed, shower and eat something. Did you eat anything?"

I hadn't.

She kept the kitchen dark and quiet, no TV or radio, as if a quiet environment would blot out some of the stimuli still whirling around in my head. I heard the loud crack as she cracked three eggs and scrambled them. All sounds were magnified. Frying eggs sound like a forest fire.

"Your boss wants to know when you can come back to work."

Boss Margaret. Memories of her tight, short skirts and worried look. "I guess it better be soon. Anything else?"

She was evasive. "We'll talk about it later."

Anything else might be, well, anything. The FBI might want to hire me to be a consultant. That German detective in Hamburg might have his own ideas. Harvey Goldstein, metadata man, was now a super hero in their minds, someone who could find out anything about anyone on short notice, anywhere. Except Harvey Goldstein was having, I had to admit, a nervous breakdown.

The judge whose trial I disrupted might want to talk to me, too. I didn't think I'd be bothered by Morris Cohen, the defense lawyer. I'd made my point with him. You didn't have to put his feet in a bucket of concrete and dump him in the Chicago River. All you had to do was destroy his identity. Make him a homeless street bum.

I was more worried about the potential back trackers who knew I'd been snooping the dark web. That could be anybody. It was enough to rob my eggs of all flavor.

It's not like I was on Facebook inviting any manner of death threats from crazy people. People on Facebook tended to shoot off messages without thinking, make threats, tell people FOAD, as in Fuck Off and Die. No wonder bullied kids sometimes actually killed themselves.

I'd been through that before and was glad the furor had died down.

Except it hadn't quite. When Ursula thought I might be feeling a little more relaxed she broke it to me. "A reporter from the Plain Dealer has been trying to get hold of you."

One thing I did not want was more publicity. I'd hoped my brief notoriety of having my face on everyone's screen had died down, been forgotten along with last week's earthquake, tornado, or other catastrophe. The public has short memories ands is easily distracted by the next so-called breaking news. The media seemed to want to keep viewers and readers at a fever pitch, except soon nothing is exciting any more. I waned no part of it. "Why did he want?"

"She."

"Alright, what did she want?"

Ursula sat close to me, took my hand to soothe me. "They sent an intern to cover the trial. Didn't suspect that Harvey Goldstein, Metadata Man would put on a show."

"I didn't put on a show."

Ursula laughed. "Your show of modesty doesn't convince me. You pulled a stunt."

"I did not. I just did my homework."

"And found out the jury was rigged."

I admit I thought I was pretty cool, but I didn't want to be in the newspapers. "If she calls again, tell her it was a stunt, a conjurer's trick. Something more exciting will come up. I've had my five minutes of fame."

The message Ursula sent the Plain Dealer was congressional: no comment."

I didn't think an intern would have the experience or the smarts to pursue the story. What did an intern at the newspaper earn? Free coffee and a stale donut? If lucky, a byline on a three inch story.

Discovering that my hands were shaking, I put down my fork, took a last sip of cocoa--more soothing than a caffeine kick I didn't need--and dared ask "Was there anything else"

"The FBI wants permission to use your portal."

"Tell them no. They used it as a test and we ended up with bullet holes in our picture window. Let them take their own risks." I could just imagine all the public enemies on their list after whoever was trying to catch up with them. Using my portal made it look like it was me. No thanks.

Ursula agreed. "At least they replaced the window."

"But not the drapes or my singing fish. Anybody else?"

"There's a letter from the IRS. They're auditing."

"Cute. Does the Treasury Department deal in bitcoins?"

She didn't know. I guessed that imaginary or simulated currency didn't fit into the revenue code. Of course, we had cashed in enough to pay our mortgage. It was just a test to see if bitcoins could be real. That must have shown up as suspicious. The government watches deposits over 10k.

"What am I supposed to do? Drop in at the local IRS office?"

She was troubled. "We haven't done anything wrong. Haven't lied on our tax return."

"Then we have nothing to worry about. If there's a tax on the bitcoin account, we can pay out of it." After all, I thought, it's other people's money, whoever they might be. Is there a tax on gefundene geld? Found money? I don't declare pennies I find on the street either. What does the IRS say about that?

I put my dish, cup, and tableware in the dishwasher. I winced at the sound of the door closing. Every sound and stimulus was magnified. I was not going to worry about the IRS.

"What should we do about Angel and her many identities?" I explained all the places and aliases where she had turned up.

"Maybe she should get out of Germany."

"What, and visit us?" We had already provided a safe house for Grabich's Iranian girl friend while he sorted her green card. I didn't want any more strange women sharing our single bathroom. "I don't think any place is safe unless maybe if you're off the grid, have no phone, no Internet, no connection with the rest of the world."

Ursula already knew better. "That's pretty drastic."

I speculated. "Maybe if you're dead people stop looking."

Ursula had put the coffee maker on. It made gurgling sounds and a trickle of coffee started flowing into her cup. She shook her head. "Remember what happens if you reject junk mail and mark it 'deceased.' Social Security cancels your pension."

"If Angel has stashed enough stolen loot, why would she need a pension?"

Ursula had a point.

"If you went to a strictly cash situation, no credit cards, no checks, if you have no phone that could be tracked or tapped, maybe you could disappear."

Ursula disagreed. "As long as you were never seen by a CCT camera. She'd have to go around in a burka, even eyes veiled."

"When I got out of the hospital they had my head all bandaged, blindfold. She could look like a burn victim."

It sounded pretty hopeless. Disappearing in our society with all that surveillance was pretty impossible. Like DNA we leave trails everywhere.

You couldn't walk around with a million in cash. With the watchers checking bank deposits, you'd have to stash your nest egg someplace, like several safety deposit boxes in various places. I vaguely recalled the Illinois Secretary of State who had collected so much in bribes and kickbacks he had shoe boxes full of cash under the bed, so many fake names on deposit boxes they never found it all when he went to prison.

I wasn't going to cash in the bitcoins and carry millions in cash. "You know, honey, we should divide the bitcoin account and create one in your name, just in case."

She gave me a wide-eyed look. "Ursula Goldstein, millionaire? You sure I wouldn't take the money and run off with some personal trainer?"

That kind of suggestion is a sure path to marital crisis. I didn't want to go there. "Maybe a joint account. Two signatures."

She laughed. "So much for trust."

That was dangerous territory. I gave her a loving look. "Just for your protection in case."

"In case of what?"

"In case the person those bitcoins belong to bumps me off."

Her eyes opened wide. "You're trying to scare me."

"I just have to think of all the possibilities.."

She shook her head. "Harvey, you think too much."

"No. I worry too much. " My overloaded brain was already working overtime.

187

I had to figure out a way to contact Angel in one or all of her false identities. I was confident that no one else was using her face. An alias was pretty useless when every CCT camera could check out your face in the database.

Mine, of course, was well known, having been displayed without my permission on every CRT screen in the world. That was the folks at the cloud being cute. Fortunately I'd been glowering at the time. It was a face you didn't want to look at. Considering most people with I-phones were playing Pokeman Go or some other nonsense, there was little risk that they would look up and recognize me. How to hide in plain sight?

Come to think of it, Angel's face was not that attractive. Who would give her a second look?

I suggested, "So you think she should leave the country?"

Ursula made a face at me. "Just don't invite her here. We already had Mia."

Mia, Grabich's girl friend. I remembered girl stuff drying in the shower. I was glad when Grabich got her a green card and she no longer had to fear deportation. She didn't stick with him, either. She moved on.

"There has to be a way to communicate safely with Angel, but how? She has so many aliases."

"Try the most recent one."

That was logical. I was always straight forward. I had no experience at being a fugitive. Anybody could find me. "Unless she moves from one to another."

Ursula always has ideas. I always feel she's the brains of our family even though she is not a metadata person. "Send her a coded message. Something nobody else would understand."

I thought about it. "If I refer to the First Commandment and tell her to deposit one bit coin to our account, that would be like using two passwords."

"Why not?" I plugged in the USB flash drive with the list of aliases, found email addresses associated with each one, and sent a query, ending with "If you are my Angel, call me." Using TOR I didn't have to reveal where my message was coming from. Slick.

Then we waited. The FBI, the IRS, the reporter... It was too much. By then I had another headache and had to go back to bed.

Chapter eight

Using facial recognition files, I found several possible identities for Angel: Liselottte Kraus. Asa Kornblat and Martha Blumenthal. I suspected there would be more, as the computer search was still plowing on through millions of files. I sent the same message to all three.

Before I got a reply Ursula poked me under the blanket where I was hiding. "You've got a phone call."

I peeked out, blinking at the light. "Who is it this time? The FBI?"

"Germany."

I almost jumped out of bed. I hoped it was Angel. It wasn't. Blinded by the light, I staggered to the phone. It was Klaus Hintz, the police inspector from Hamburg.

He didn't waste any time getting to the point.. "Mr. Goldstein," He pronounced it Goldschtein.

"Yes."

You are looking for ein Asa Kornblat."

It wasn't a question. "How do you know that?"

"We have our resources, too, Mr. Goldschtein. "

I don't lie but I can try to be evasive. "I thought she might be a friend of mine." I mean, if someone gives you a million bitcoins that's a friendly act, right?

"I regret to inform you that Asa Kornblat is dead."

"Oh." I let that answer hang in the air. What should I say next? Ask for lurid details, like was she murdered?

"You also tried to reach Liselotte Kraus."

Hintz certainly had done his homework. I was not as anonymous or smart as I thought I could be. "Yes."

"She is also tot, dead."

"Dead? How?"

"A reported suicide, but we have not recovered a body. What have you to do with these two deaths?"

"Nothing. I know nothing about them."

"How is it you know these two people and when you look for them they turn out to be dead?"

"I have no idea. What about Martha Blumenthal?"

Hintz made a little noise like he was surprised. "Blumenthal also?"

"She would be next."

"I do not understand. Do you have a hit list, Mr. Goldschtein?"

"No. I'm just looking for a specific face."

"And people with that face end up dead?"

I took a deep breath. "How do you know they are dead?"

"We have reports."

I got it. I didn't believe Angel was dead. Angel was covering her tracks, hacking into police records, creating false reports of her false identities. I cautioned. "Don't believe those reports. It's a smoke screen."

Now Hintz was confused or being sarcastic. "Are you part of an international conspiracy zat contracts for murders?"

"I hope not. I am metadata man who knows too much about everything. It gives me a headache. All I can say, Inspector Hintz, is that the people you are looking for are not real and the reports of the deaths are false."

"I find zat hard to believe."

"We live in a complicated world, Inspector. I believe I am looking for a real person. I don't know how you found out about my search. If the person I am looking for isn't real it is all an exercise in fantasy." It made my head hurt.

Hintz wasn't buying that. Being a German policeman he was tied to the public record. Facts were what he was after, not fantasy. "Are you real, Mr. Goldschtein?"

"Sometimes I'm not so sure myself. I've been confused lately. How do I know you are really Inspector Hintz or someone pretending to be?"

Hintz sighed. "We are watching you, Mr. Goldschtein."

"So is everybody else. Join the club." Exasperated and angry, I hung up.

I must be getting sloppy, or maybe just overwhelmed. After all, the searches I usually made were for who bought what products at Krieger, not anybody's faces. This was unfamiliar territory, like I'd been given a box of special tools I didn't know how to use. I had not looked long enough for the aliases Angel was using to discover that they were reported dead, if they actually were people with the same face or a close match.

I returned to German sources, even though I can't read the language. I had to depend on Ursula for that, even though she reminds me that she teaches beginning German, sort of like the middle school math teacher who doesn't need to know trigonometry. Limited though her German was, it was miles above my "Ein Bier, bitte."

Ursula teases me about not knowing a foreign language. She's offered to teach me German, says with the few words I know of Yiddish I'd have a start. She can teach me German and I can share my rudimentary Yiddish. I don't mind the idea of being her student. If I make a dumb mistake we can both laugh about it. She's never cruel or vindictive. That's not how you treat someone you love. Being called a schlemiel isn't cruel as long as it's said with affection.

Feeling very much the schlemiel, I searched. Any time your name appears anywhere, Google lists it. The names I found for Angel were, indeed in newspapers in sections called *Todsfall*, which Ursula explained meant deaths. See, I'm learning already.

I also knew that Bugsy Siegel, the infamous Jewish gangster in California who collected a million bucks for arms for Israel, stole the money and had a friend plant a story in the LA Times that said the ship had been sunk, a two line story on a back page to back up his lie.

There were other Jewish gangsters like Mayer Lansky. We Jews keep track of such things, what movie stars were Jewish, etc, like Heady Lamar and Lauren Bacall. It's part of being members of the tribe. We pay attention. We care.

When someone like Bernie Madof steals millions and goes to prison we are all embarrassed and ashamed.

As for the German newspaper obituaries, Will Rogers said all he knew was what he read in the newspapers, but the newspapers were unreliable. So were police reports.

Fake news makes all news suspect. So who do you trust?

Ursula had the right idea: if you are dead people might stop looking. Angel was ahead of me. Was she real?

One thing I was sure of: the bitcoin account, however it might be cooked up using some mathematical formulas, was real enough for us to pay off the mortgage. Then again, it might be no more valid than Monopoly money. Who knew?

If I tell you a piece of paper is worth a million and you believe it, then maybe it is. That's what stock brokers do all the time. Then there's the Federal Reserve…

It's all based on trust. Without trust, what's left?

It was enough to make me want to go back to bed.

I still didn't know where or who Angel was or even if the picture she sent me was genuine. A fake picture might cover her ass. Or his. Angel could be a guy.

Chapter Nine

Focusing on a specific problem helped clear my head. I was learning to blot out extraneous sounds and references. I was feeling better. I took off the blindfold and opened the drapes. It was still disconcerting, but my filter was starting to work. I didn't have to see and hear everything. I could be more selective.

"I should get back to the office."

Ursula was uncertain. She had taken sick leave to be with me, one of those rare perks the teachers' union had negotiated. "You shouldn't be driving yet."

She was right. Getting behind the wheel of a car is one of the most dangerous things we do. Too much is always happening even without crazy road rage drivers who might shoot you if you wait to long for a green light. So I let her drive, with me in the back seat with my blindfold on.

When she stopped outside Krieger headquarters and I got out she rolled down her window so I could kiss her goodbye. She was plainly worried. She was not used to being a caregiver. "Sure you'll be alright?"

"I hope so."

She drove off, leaving me standing there, wondering for a moment which way was what.

I felt uncomfortable suddenly being on my own. She could pick me up after work, but what if I couldn't hold out that long? I didn't want to end up in the hospital again like some cringing drunk with the DTs or a catatonic insane person.

When I got up to the marketing office Boss Margaret was waiting. She was wearing a black leather outfit and a belt that dangled, a hint of an invitation to S&M. I might have asked her if she also had handcuffs, but that would be courting disaster. What if she did?

"Glad you are back, Metadata Man," she said with more than a hint of sarcasm.

"I hope so." I entered my cubicle, my little sanctuary with its monitor, two drawer file cabinet, and a shelf with Ursula's picture and the little Russian doll Uncle Julius had given us when we visited him in Hamburg.

It took the doll and absently fiddled with the wooden figure. The paint was old and chipped and the sections rather stiff. I knew the really elaborate ones might have as many as six or seven nesting dolls. This had only three levels and the smallest one was, indeed, a wooden egg.

It was heavier than I'd have expected. The geometrical design painted on it was a bit dazzling, intended to confuse the eyes, which in my case needed little prodding. Squinting, I thought I detected a crack along one of the lines of the pattern and twisted. Like a Chinese puzzle, it opened.

Inside was a miniature electronic something. I muttered, "Julius, you son of a bitch." It had to be one of those old Soviet bugs, the kind that need no batteries but are activated by powerful microwaves. The transmissions weren't there to harm people, just to activate the bugs. I'd heard that the US embassy in Moscow was riddled with them and they had to put aluminum shutters on all the windows to protect employees from the microwave transmissions aimed at the building in case they turned the building into a microwave oven.

Julius's antique must have been one of his own sentimental souvenirs. Of course, that was long ago, before the Wall came down. Nobody would be activating this baby now. Or would they? Unlikely.

Just to be on the safe side I took it to the break room where we can heat up sandwiches brought from home. I put the wooden egg in the microwave and gave it a one minute exposure.

Sparks flew. The egg started to smoke and I quickly opened the door. "Well, that's one bug that won't be sending signals any more."

How different the Russian doll was compared with today. How old fashioned. Now unless I put tape over the camera on my laptop for privacy I might be observed by malware, no need to engineer a Russian doll. Just sneak in the right software tacked onto an innocuous program upgrade.

Of course, now I was the watcher. I was watching everybody, not only every Krieger customer, but whoever or wherever I cared to probe, being Harvey Goldschtein, as Inspector Hintz called me.

Did I feel any pangs of conscience, being able to peer into other people's lives? Not as long as I was trying to push the latest Krieger store special. I was marketing, not eavesdropping. At least, that's what I told myself. There's a fine line between being able to do something unethical and to actually do it.

It's that knowledge edge. No wonder insider traders are tempted to cross the line and deal to advantage.

Was I feeling pangs of conscience? Was this an unanticipated consequence of my new found ability? If Superman can see through walls, does he peek into the shower of the girl who lives next door?

Back to work.

Logging on, I detected a slower speed. The system was what? Clogged with interfering programs? Malware? I ran our anti-virus program. All seemed OK, but there are devious Trojan horses that elude filters. Maybe Grabich, my IT guru, would have an idea.

I didn't even get that far. I looked up to see Margaret looking down over the top of my partition. Made me wish I had a real office with opaque walls, not a fishbowl like hers. "What's up?"

"What do you know about encryption?"

"Not much. If the computer screen shows a little padlock it's supposed to be encrypted."

"That's only a 128 algorithm."

I didn't understand algorithms. Math is not my strong point. I just sort stuff. "What's that mean?"

"It's weak."

"OK, so it's weak." I should have understood, but ever since I'd become Harvey Goldstein the bogy man who is watching everybody, lots of things that might be private were clear to me, not that I wanted to see it all. My skeleton key presence got me past firewalls and protocols. It was like being the fire truck or ambulance driver who can control the traffic lights by remote control.

"I got a call from your friend at the FBI office."

That gave me a belly cramp. First the Hamburg policeman and now the FBI. I didn't want the FBI upsetting Margaret's routines. "He's not my friend." I apologized. "I asked them not to call here."

"There's an investigation. Naturally, he didn't explain, but it has something international to do with bitcoins."

I tried to feign total ignorance. "Oh?" Like I didn't know a bitcoin from Hanukah geld.

"I just want to make sure you're not using your job here for personal business."

"You mean like writing personal letters on company letterhead?"

She shook her head. "You know what I mean."

"Actually, I don't. If I have personal business I do it at home on my own time."

"Bitcoins?"

I shook my head. "Nothing to do with Krieger."

"There's something you're not telling me, Harvey."

I leaned back in my ergonomic chair. "I think Grabich told you I have a bitcoin account. It's nothing to do with Krieger."

She was obviously burning with curiosity. Gossip is the fuel that fires office energy.

"The old FBI advice is whether something is a need to know. Best not to know what you don't need to know. People misconstrue, misinterpret, jump to wrong conclusions. "

She demurred. "Silence is golden."

As she turned to leave she had another comment. "What happened to your hair?" Women are always distracted by their hair, the color, the curl, or whatever.

"My hair?"

"It's turned white."

I had noticed, of course. It was the shock of knowing too much, of being Metadata Man, I mean for real, not as Ursula's joke.

"Worry," I explained and tried to smile. "Stress. Too many police asking questions."

Her last words were "You must have a guilty conscience."

Fact is, she was right. Some people always need to have the last word. I was glad she left, but sure that wasn't the end of it. I would have to call the FBI myself and find out what the hell was going on. Something else to worry about.

That German detective Hintz said they were watching me. Like what was I? Public enemy number one? Just because I looked for Angel and didn't find her, or him? Looking isn't against the law.

Trouble is, just looking can draw suspicion, like the kid who visits too many ISIS sites on the Internet. Stuff like that can get you on a watch list.

Obviously I was being watched. I wondered if those jokers at the Cloud outside Salt Lake City were playing more games with me. Maybe their boss, Mrs. Post, was up to something. Someone once wrote that female CEOs can be tough, having had to be ruthless to break the glass ceiling. Nothing like having a dominatrix to crack the whip over a bunch of male flunky subordinates like me.

With all those distractions I simply could not focus. I couldn't concentrate on the next Krieger job. We had acquired a line of cosmetics aimed at an ethnic category of customers. It wasn't hard to tell the system, like a game of Go Fish, "give me all your Hispanics between fifteen and thirty."

196

My risk was I'd advertise hair straightened to Nordics. Some people, are easily offended. One wrong move in Marketing and you lose a customer or even your job. There is a tyranny in being forever politically correct. The world is full of whiners as in "He hurt my feelings." Tough shit, kid, suck it up.

My head was buzzing again and I could hardly wait for Ursula to pick me up after work.

It was nearly five o'clock when Margaret came back to my cubicle looking stressed. "That FBI man, Agent Walker, called. Says you're to meet him in our parking garage. Top level."

I looked up from my keyboard. "Did he say why?"

She shook her head.

"You sure it was him?"

"Said he was agent Walker."

"Did he give a password?"

She wrinkled her forehead in disbelief. "What?"

"Mention the name of his dog or his kid?"

"Certainly not." She shook her head like she thought I was being crazy, which I have to admit, I was feeling.

I had not arranged any passwords for dealing with the FBI. I was just joking with Margaret. Of course, if I did have an actual conversation with someone who claimed to be Walker I knew enough about him to trick any imposter. It was like the Grandpa scam phone call. Ask the caller what's my dog's name, something like that.

What if it wasn't Walker? Why do I keep worrying about this stuff? Well, for one, parking garages are perfect places for ambushes. Happens in the movies all the time, probably because the film crew can clear the place of rubberneckers.

Even if I weren't Metadata Man I would still be aware that even a phone call is not secure. If someone had listened in to Walker's call, they could beat him to the garage and pop us both. Now what?

That's the trouble with being paranoid. You become suspicious of everything and everyone. If internet searches were anonymous it would be different. As it was, there was a record of every search. By looking for Angel's real identity I had tripped someone's alarm bell, notably Detective Hintz in Hamburg, but who else? I was certain others were looking for her, too. Or him.

My job in metadata was strictly for marketing purposes. I sold Kreiger groceries. But I was keenly aware of the political implications, like Uncle Julius had said, I was lucky compared to his job in the Stasi secret police when you might be on an all night stakeout standing in a rainy doorway in the cold needing to take a leak. If Uncle Julius had been metadata man, no one could have made it over the wall into west Berlin. No one could escape. They'd all be dead. Shudder.

What if that happened to us here in America? It was frightening.

I knew. Hadn't I freaked out the Homeland Security agents by revealing what I knew about them just from their Krieger purchases?

That we were all walking around like we were free was an illusion. All that was lacking was for someone like Uncle Julius to slam the cell door and turn the key. We were prisoners in our own metadata, not anonymous, living in an illusion of anonymity. And I was part of the insidious system. I am Metadata Man. Be afraid.

I had used the data for my own purposes, or tried. So far the search for Angel had yielded nothing substantial. Anybody watching my activity could come to their own conclusions.

Then there was that bitcoin business. A million bitcoins was worth five hundred million in real money, if money itself was real. After all, the Federal Reserve just prints it on demand, limited, I guess, by the supply of paper and ink. Only the government can legally print money, but whoever created the bitcoins is in a world unto themselves.

Though I was afraid of meeting Walker or anybody else in the Krieger parking garage, I did have an advantage. I could log onto to the security cameras and see everything that went on. No surprises, I hoped. The disadvantage was that at five o'clock there was lots of activity as people headed home after work.

I watched and waited.

As the traffic thinned out, the top level was almost deserted. Only one person was hanging around. I thought I recognized him, Walker. He stood beside a parked SUV with dark, tinted windows.

The license plate wasn't in the field of view of the CCT system or I would have checked the registration. Was it a government vehicle?

OK. I put on my jacket with my blindfold in the pocket like an infant's pacifier. As if I could just put it on and the world would go away. Fat chance.

Unless I moved my head slowly, I tended to get dizzy, all those new images and impressions. Nervous about being trapped in the elevator, I took the stairs.

Chapter ten

Reaching the top floor of the parking garage I hesitated. Parking garages spook me. I guess I've seen too many movies where somebody is bumped off, etc. in those deserted places. Most of the cars were already gone. I could hear someone driving off from the next level down.

I spotted Walker. He was wearing a team jacket so he looked like a Cleveland Indians fan, complete with a baseball cap. Maybe this was his under cover outfit for stadium crowds.

I walked up to him, trying not to look nervous. "What's up?"

He motioned to the passenger door of the SUV. "Get in."

"Why couldn't you just meet me outside on the street? Ursula's supposed to pick me up."

He didn't answer. Just got in the driver's side and buckled up.

"I was going to call her to say you were meeting me, but phones aren't secure."

"One of the team is waiting for her outside, so you're covered."

So how did he know that? "What's this all about?" I didn't know if he was in touch with that German detective Hintz or not. The search for Angel was, I thought, my own business."

Walker started the engine and began the spiral down through the garage to the street exit. "It's about your bitcoin account."

"I told you about that. Didn't want you to think I was hiding something, laundering money, or like that."

Walker gave me a sideways glance. "You didn't tell me how much it was."

"You didn't need to know that." I was being coy, throwing back that need to know stuff.

"I appreciate your honesty. You've been cooperative. I apologized for the incident with the drive by shooting. Won't happen again."

"You were using my portal."

"Only once."

I shook my head. "Like the girl who gets pregnant because she only did it once. You could have got us killed."

199

"Sorry we blew your cover."

I sighed. "Hell, as Harvey Goldstein I have no cover. Everybody in the world knows who I am. I could as well have a big billboard on the lawn "Harvey Goldstein lives here.""

"Most people have already forgotten that business of your face on every TV screen. If they haven't they probably think it was a prank."

"Which it was."

He agreed. "Since you've been honest with us and cooperative, we owe you one."

"How so?"

Walker had driven to the waterfront and parked. "It's an inter agency thing. You know, the federal government has a lot of fiefdoms that don't necessarily cooperate with each other. There are grey areas and ambiguities in the protocols."

I waited for the explanation.

"And disputes."

Walker raised his eyebrows. "Understatement. Harvey, I don't want to see the SEC and the IRS fighting over your corpse."

I didn't like that choice of words. My right hand drifted to my pocket where I had my blindfold. I swallowed, wished I was wearing it to blot out all the outside world and give me a moment of respite. "Just those two?"

Walker shook his head. "Well there's the international banking people and Interpol. You're turning into a popular guy, Harvey."

I shook my head in denial. "They must be grasping at straws if I'm their only lead. I'm not a hacker. Not a thief, either. International hacking and money laundering? That's not my game. I'm a nobody."

"Don't underestimate yourself, Metadata Man.".

He must have heard about the shirt. I leaned toward him. "I bet they all smell money and want a piece of the action."

Walker was puzzled. "How much are you talking about, the bitcoin thing, I mean."

"My guess is five hundred million in real money, whatever that is."

Walker almost choked.

I hurried to dispel his suspicions. "That's my guess. It's not my doing. I don't know where it came from and am no longer sure of who set it up. Near as I can figure, putting the money in an account with my name on it was a way to hide it from someone else."

"Who would that be?"

"I'm guessing the original thieves. If you pay attention, there are hackers all over the world. Stealing identities is penny ante stuff. The big guys are plundering the treasuries of countries with weak security. Bangladesh got ripped off for sixty million. The Russian bank got hacked for two million rubles."

Walker shook his head. "And we chase drug dealers."

"I thought that was the DEA."

"Entrepreneurs don't stick to only one line of crime."

"I'll stick with grocery coupons."

"You sure?" He obviously wasn't. In his job you always had to be suspicious.

"It's a dark world out there, Agent Walker."

"Like I didn't alread6y know? I just wanted to give you a heads up."

I was ready put on that blindfold and hide in my bed again. "You're scaring me."

"Don't be. Just be your honest self and you have nothing to worry about."

"Yeh, sure. And innocent people don't get sent up on life sentences."

Our conversation had run its course. Walker started the engine again. "Look, if worse comes to worst, all you have to do is give the money back."

How could I give it back if I didn't know where it came from? I wondered if he knew we'd spent a chunk of it on our mortgage. I stayed silent.

Walker took a deep breath. "I think I can help you."

"How's that?"

"If you're working for us the others looking for you would have to go through channels."

That was interesting. I was beginning to understand. Walker was using the bitcoin business as leverage to force me to work for him. "What do you want me for? A consultant? Like a paid informant? I don't know anything."

Walker shook his head. "I thought you knew everything, Goldstein."

So, now it was Goldstein again. Harvey when he wanted to be chummy, Goldstein when tough. Walker was good cop bad cop all in one package. I shrugged. "I can find out stuff. So can the FBI."

"You'll have to sign the official secrets act."

That would make me part of God knew what secret establishment. With what implications? "I'll think about it."

He started the engine. "I'll drop you at your apartment."

Chapter eleven

Ursula was already home when I got there, watching from our bulletproof picture window for me to arrive. Before I reached the front door she opened it, greeted me with a hug. I guess I looked like I needed one.

I melted into her arms. She was my island of refuge. I didn't want to let go.

She was worried. I could tell by the way she gnawed her lower lip. "Are you all right? What happened? I thought you were arrested when that FBI guy came up to me outside the building."

"I got waylaid by that FBI agent, Walker."

"Did you tell him the window is replaced but the walls haven't been hardened."

"I forgot." They were supposed to reinforce our walls to make them bullet resistant. Some sort of compressed plastic fibers, Kevlar or something. I guessed the work order was tied up in red tape, like whose budget was this supposed to come out of? And while they wait we get dead.

"So?"

"He wanted to give me a heads up. I guess even the FBI is afraid they are being watched so we had a conversation inside a car."

Ursula shook her head. "I don't think those men are normal."

Normal? I sure wasn't. I took the blindfold out of my pocket and thought about putting it on. Everything was too bright. "I don't even know what normal is any more. Walker says our bitcoin account has attracted the attention of numerous agencies, like the IRS, Interpol and what not."

"What do they want you to do? Pay taxes on it?"

I grinned. It was not a happy grin. "That wouldn't be a problem. Even if they wanted thirty percent, we'd have plenty left over. I think receiving stolen property is more worrisome, like jail time."

I suppose that would depend on whose jail, like Russia if it was stolen from the Moscow bank, or maybe North Korea. Norway might be OK. I heard they have nice prisons.

We moved into the kitchen. Ursula still hadn't let me get back into my routine of making dinner. Eating out with all the stimuli of strange places and faces and the lights was too stressful. I was like a combat vet with PTSD. If a wait person came up I'd automatically just know all their metadata like some reflex. I personally didn't care what size underpants or bra cup a waitress wore. Unless she got them at Krieger. I just couldn't help it. Force of habit.

"If you returned it, maybe there' a finder's fee."

I laughed. "Or at least a commission. Or a reward, you think?"

She rooted around in our packed freezer. "Depends on who it belonged to."

"You mean if we dug up a pot of gold in the back yard. Then the archeologists would claim it was historical and belonged to the government."

She'd found a couple of frozen pork chops, unwrapped them and put them in the microwave for a quick thaw. We don't keep kosher and are not even vegetarian.

She wasn't going to speculate on an imaginary pot of gold bitcoins. She was into the task of cooking dinner. "How about string beans?"

I started setting the kitchen table. I could at least do that much. "If I could only locate Angel, whoever she or he is."

"That German detective said the leads you had were all dead ended."

"Allegedly dead."

"He might come up with something. He has connections."

I had to admit that my blunt force searches were not sophisticated. There were too many possibilities. Police had their own procedures. I had exhausted the facial recognition approach. The term "Angel" was too big a category, like guardian angel or the angel of death. Made me shudder.

At least at Krieger I had lots of metadata in the form of previous store purchases. For instance, I could find everybody who bought Killer bread, or search for a product that was recalled for salmonella and who bought it.. With Angel all I had was a photograph that might not be genuine.

Ursula was cutting up an onion to fry along with the chops. "What can you do? Put an ad in every German newspaper? "Will Angel please call me?"

"The dark web internet would be better."

"Maybe she or he has a blog."

"The hackers are a kind of international secret club. They exchange ideas and tips."

"Then try that."

"I'm not a member."

She rapped the frying pan with her spatula and waved it in my face. "Come on, Metadata Man. You are Harvey Goldstein. I thought you could do everything."

I sighed. I wasn't feeling myself. I didn't even know who myself was. I was having a crisis of identity. I had already seen it reflected in the face of my friend Grabich. Maybe it was my suddenly white hair. He had a different definition of me, expecting me to do things I didn't know I could myself. I think he still thought I was personally responsible for the anonymous installation of a Porsche engine in his old Carmen Gia. The risk was he might want me to materialize a Lambardini for him, wave my magic wand and ta-dah! A sports car.

Not that I couldn't afford it with a million bitcoins in the account. The risk was I'd end up like people who win the power ball lottery. Leeches, con artists and greedy relatives gang up on them and they end up broke.

I finally relented. "I'll try the dark web." I stared at my plate, afraid to look up. The dark web? That was a mystery to me.

Ursula smiled, but it was a different smile than I'd seen before. She was smiling at a stranger, like a condescending token of sympathy for a homeless person. It gave me a shiver of anxiety, like all this was straining our marriage. She'd been happy enough as Mrs. Goldstein, but maybe not Harvey Goldstein in all caps, Celebrity Spouse. For how long?

Chapter twelve

As if to complicate things even further, the next day there was a lawyer letter from a firm called Lye, Cheet and Steele. The signatory, Mr. Steele, offered services and suggested we meet for dinner. I was surprised at how rapidly this stuff was closing in on me. No sooner had Agent Walker told me all those agencies were interested in me, for their own purposes, than some law firm got wind of it and smelled money, billable hours and fees.

From what I'd seen of Morris Cohen, the lawyer for those two gang bangers, I wanted nothing to do with them. If I'd won the lottery, people with wild investment schemes would descend. Here was a lawyer who allegedly wanted to protect my interests. My interests? Or a piece of the million bitcoins? That, if real, was more than any lottery.

I had sensed that Morris Cohen would want revenge for my exposing his past during the trial. I had warned him not to mess with me, but maybe that wasn't enough. Now I took the time to look him up more thoroughly. Though Cohen's office was now in Cleveland, before he left Chicago in disgrace he had been, sure enough, associated with what was then Lye, Cheet, and Cohen. Steele must be a new partner.

All I had to do was respectfully decline the offer.

I could have pursued it further, like who paid Cohen to defend the two thugs who shot up our apartment? I could get into his checking account and see what checks were deposited to it, then backtrack to whoever's ox was being gored by that FBI probe that set off the whole business in the first place. Of course, Cohen night have been paid in cash and stashed the payments in a shoe box under his bed.

On second thought I did not want my digital fingerprint on the FBI's business. Harvey Goldstein could break into the bank records, but the FBI would need a warrant. I could see why they might be interested in my extra-legal access.

No surprise that the government might do something underhanded like hire Harvey Goldstein to snoop for them. A judge might throw out evidence illegally obtained, but case histories were full of suppressed evidence and prosecutorial mischief. Ambition was known to interfere with professional ethics. Best not to dig too deeply into Morris Cohen's associates, at least not now.

What about my own ethics? Knowing metadata was my job. I didn't do research for personal gain. Krieger wanted me to sell more house brand toilet paper. I didn't alter personal records. My steadfast alibi was I am not a hacker. I don't pillage country's financial holdings. I just look.

I wondered just what it was Walker wanted me for. He said my being associated with the FBI and, incidentally a signee to the Official Secrets Act, might give me a hiding place from other agencies. It was the old government dodge, "That information is classified." Yah. "Harvey Goldstein? We don't talk about him." Sure.

I didn't trust Walker. He probably wanted me to do something extra legal. Why bother to ask a judge for a search warrant if Metadata Man can snoop right away? Saves time. As Metadata Man I could snoop everybody and anybody, but there was something called invasion of privacy. Privacy was an illusion, fiction.

I remembered Hulk Hogan and his hundred and forty million settlement that had set off my own bitcoin business. Could I be sued, and Krieger for that matter, for knowing too much personal stuff from our customers purchases? They had a legitimate gripe. Target had been sued for their metadata program because they knew before family members if a customer was pregnant, like maybe a fifteen year old daughter.

The FBI had used my portal for their case using my identity as their cover. Their use backtracked to me. Somebody had been awfully vindictive to take revenge using a couple of thugs to intimidate me when I had nothing to do with the business at all. Nasty people.

I decided to respond to Mr. Steele as ambiguously as possible. I sent him a snail mail note thanking him kindly for his concern for my welfare but also that I had other arrangements. In other words, go away.

It was another issue for my hand written CYA file. I also wrote a report to Agent Walker explaining Steele's offer and that I had found out Morris Cohen's connection to the Chicago law firm.

It made me feel a bit old fashioned to be writing snail mail letters, like a character in some pre-Victorian English epistolary novel. I didn't trust the phone or the electronic communications. Just for fun, I classified my note to Walker as BBR, Burn Before Reading. No cell phone texts. Nothing digital.

Ursula was bothered by my response to Steele. "What's this about other arrangements?"

"Agent Walker wants me as a consultant."

"A consultant?"

"He says if I'm working for the FBI he can be a buffer against other agencies that want a piece of me."

":Like who?"

I sighed. "Maybe Interpol, the Securities Exchange Commission, NSA, what do I know?" The maze of government agencies eluded me.

Then I added, "Oh, and he wants me to sign the Official Secrets Act."

"What? Are you getting a security clearance?"

I shook my head. "Beats me."

Now Ursula was concerned. "What's Walker want? To make you into a spy?"

"I don't know. Anyway, I haven't signed anything."

Put another way, I was already an informant.

Ursula didn't appreciate the stress of all this. A siege mentality is hard to shake off. After all, we did have our place shot up. How must those people in black Chicago feel with random drive by shootings, kids with guns and anger? It would be terrifying. I couldn't imagine the long term trauma for those school kids afraid to play outside. Or maybe inside. Bullets go through walls.

Ursula hadn't replaced the shot-up drapes. She inspected the damage:. a lot of holes. "Spies get killed."

How close we'd come and we hadn't done anything.

I resolved to let things lie. Walker had the ball.

To our joint surprise we got a call from the hospital, a follow-up on my examination from Doctor Halal, the specialist who dealt with underdeveloped babies. How did I feel? Did the isolation and sensory deprivation help?

Yes, I was feeling better. I just didn't like surprises.

 He wanted to examine me further.

I suspected he had plans for an article in a medical journal. "I don't want any publicity."

He was defensive. "Is just an examination."

"If you have thoughts of a medical journal article, I have to be anonymous."

He assured me. "No problem,".

I knew, being Harvey Goldstein, that Dr. Halal's digital notes could be extracted from his computer or even from the hard drive of his office copy machine. In my world there was no such thing as anonymous.

Security? Forget it. The only files I knew that were secure were my own hand written CYA memos to myself locked in my desk drawer.

At Krieger, given a short list of items purchased I could narrow the digital field to just a few prospects. Like Go Fish I could say "gimme all your people who bought oranges, organic pineapple, Simple Truth ground beef, and croissants and I can name the customer." Out of millions. It was that simple.

Except when it came to someone called Angel.

So for Dr. Halal, if he published an article about me, how many adults were there who suffered from sensory overload and became wi-fi interceptors? Me, party of one.

Nevertheless, I was curious. Halal might have some insight I wasn't aware of. I agreed to an examination providing Boss Margaret would give me a few hours off. Her patience was already tried.

Would I be able to drive myself?

If not, I'd take a taxi or Uber or Halal could fetch me himself.

Chapter thirteen

Since this was a medical issue, Boss Margaret reluctantly let me have the morning off. She was not happy. I had already missed several days after my seizure. Then there were those official visitors. I was supposed to be just another invisible computer jockey, plugging away at my job. I had disrupted the office routines.

Krieger can't afford to stand still. If we don't keep tweaking the customers they might be lured away by competitors like Safeway or Publix. Retail is a dog eat dog world. I was just another dog in Margaret's kennel. If I didn't produce there were others who would happily take over my cubicle.

I had seen people who were fired, their stuff in a cardboard box as they were frog marched out of the building. Would that be me?

Was it time to move on? To what? Secret metadata man agent of the FBI?

My Krieger job was not dangerous. If I sent someone a coupon offer that offended them, the most we'd get would be a phoned complaint. What Walker wanted might get us killed.

What was I, chopped liver? Just another expendable soldier of misfortune? I'd opt for my nice safe cubicle, thank you very much, and don't forget the benefits and the pension plan.

I didn't owe Walker anything. His oblique offer of protection under the FBI umbrella, something he could not guarantee, was just a means of getting leverage, to force me to do something I'd rather avoid.

My only tangible vulnerability was those bitcoins, where they had come from, and whose money, real or digital, was it anyway? Not knowing who it belonged to, I couldn't even give it back. You can't confess to something you don't know.

Just to make it more difficult I couldn't locate Angel or whoever that really was.

Then I realized another vulnerability. Dr. Halal might want me institutionalized as some kind of freak. I would be on my guard. That was what was going through my mind when I drove to the hospital for the mysterious tests.

Dr. Halal shared an office in the pediatrics department. Had it been his own I'd have expected to see his diplomas on the wall. There were none. He sat me down in an uncomfortable plastic visitor's chair and handed me a clipboard with lots of fine print. I was supposed to just sign.

I insisted on reading everything. It was a consent form with legal implications, like in case of a dispute would I accept arbitration? I'd been warned about that. It gave up my rights to a jury trial if there was a malpractice suit.

There are too many lawyers in the United States. This is such a litigious society hungry lawyers are always hoping for a suit that will pay their office rent or maybe their student loans.

I struck out that paragraph. No arbitration.

"What about this paragraph on use of humans in experiments? What experiments?"

Halal's smile was phony. "It is just a formality."

I thought 'Yeh, and the car you're selling me has no guarantee on the power train.' Maybe he should have been in the mortgage loan business with balloon jump up interest.

My metadata awareness was ringing alarm bells in my head. I had a vision of a brain operation followed by a cretin state. The cure for an information overload was a lobotomy like in One Flew Over the Cuckoo's Nest. No thanks. "I'm not taking part in any experiments. No injections. No operations. No shock therapy."

By now I had scratched out half of the document I was supposed to sign. Finally I refused and handed back the clip board. "Why don't you just ask me questions? I'll try to answer."

I did let him shine a light at my face and ask me to look left and right. I let him put ear phones on me and play different things in each ear. I was supposed to sort them out. It was irritating, but not a bother.

When he offered to have me take some sort of pill I balked. No psychedelic drugs, please. I had to be able to drive, not fly myself home in some hallucinated state..

He wanted a case history, like when did I first acquire this ability to know so much about everybody. I told him there was a seventh paradigm, but I only took him to about the third, the level where you had a lot of marketing sales information and could sort it. I didn't want to go into the cloud merger and that prank that put my face on every screen as Harvey Goldstein the bogey man watching you.

That this had led to my threat of a law suit against the TV network and the mysterious bitcoin wallet was none of Halal's business. My own metadata was already out there. If Halal wanted more he could Google me.

I'd clearly tested Dr. Halal's patience. I was an uncooperative subject. While he tried to persuade me my overactive brain found metadata about a scientific paper he had co-authored but was disputed later. One commentator called Halal a quack. Professional jealousy, I suspected. There must be lots of hard feelings about who was listed as a co-researcher and who was left out.

I wanted no part of it. It was not my world.

I wasn't sure just what my world was now that I was Metadata Man but it wasn't medical research.

I escaped. I just hoped that would be the end of it.

Back at the office Boss Margaret met me with a worried expression and called me into her office. She even shut the glass door and closed the blinds.

Apprehensive, I sat down in the visitor's chair. Now what?

She paused while I got my bearings. "You've come a long way since I hired you, Harvey."

"It's a swell job."

"Not challenging enough. Not since you talked to the cloud people in Utah."

I shrugged. "Well, I saw more possibilities." I would have gone on about the Teamsters and teachers union as our extended marketing audience, but she cut me off.

"The fact is, Harvey, you're over qualified for your job."

I swallowed. It had been a stressful day. Maybe if Halal had offered to pay me as a subject I might have an out if Margaret fired me. I didn't really have a plan B. "Am I being fired?"

"Promoted, Mr. Metadata Man." She was referring to the gag shirt Ursula had made for me in the art lab at her school. "They want you upstairs for long range planning."

I didn't know what that meant. "Is there a job description?" I'd read that everyone rises to his level of incompetence. The smart worker knows when he has reached his level of competence and doesn't accept a promotion into a position where he will fail. Sometimes promoting someone beyond their level of competence is a trick to make them fail so they quit or are fired.

She was non committal about the job description. "It's new. You're one of a kind, Harvey."

"Starting when?"

"As soon as you can train up your replacement."

I had been afraid I'd be fired for being too disruptive of Margaret's routines. I hadn't thought of being promoted for being overqualified. That was an excuse for not hiring people with advanced college degrees even if they were desperate enough to ask to be janitors. Over qualified people went looking for better jobs and didn't stick around.

I felt Margaret and I had a good working understanding. I didn't respond to her cougar signals and she accepted that I was unavailable. We could get on with the work. No complications. They say better the devil you know instead of the devil you don't. Long range planning? Who was in charge of that?

I was still getting over my unpleasantness with Dr. Halal. My heart wasn't ready to think about changing jobs..

She caught my hesitancy. "I hear you are some kind of a bitcoin millionaire. You still want to keep on working? I mean, you and Ursula could retire, travel." She sounded envious.

Our trip to Europe had had unexpected consequences, that business with Uncle Julius and the Seventh Paradigm, the visit from Homeland Security afterwards. As for the bitcoin account, that had come out of thin air and could disappear as quickly, leaving us with what? A mystery.

"Does this job involve travel?" My last business trip to Utah had left me stranded with no identity and almost no cash. If I had to be out of town and Ursula came home from school to find more bullet holes… I wouldn't want her left alone.

Margaret claimed she didn't know. Was she being deliberately vague? Hiding something? I never trusted her. I guess she had risen to her own level of competence and looked no further. Smart.

"I'll talk it over with my wife," I said. "We're a team."

Sometimes it's not good to have too many choices. You don't know which way to jump. FBI Agent Walker had made a vague proposal. Krieger had its own plans. I'd told Dr. Halal and that crooked lawyer basically to piss off. Or, as Margaret suggested, I could chuck it all and retire on bitcoins.

I was at a crossroads. It looked like I could not go back to mere cubicle life and the coupon business. What was this "move upstairs"? Real or fantasy?

Then there was still the search for Angel, dead or alive. And Inspector Hintz of the Hamburg police. He had ideas, too.

There was the possibility that the real owners of the bitcoins would want their money back even if it wasn't theirs to begin with. Bangladesh had lost sixty million dollars. What did they do, just write it off? Print more money? Or seek revenge?

Whatever Ursula and I decided, there might be no turning back. Things are always changing.

Chapter fourteen

At first I thought Margaret wanted a procedures manual, but that was already spelled out in my job description. What she explained was she wanted a step by step diagram of what I actually did, decision moments, choices, and reasons for the decisions, something like the IRS flow diagram for who should file and on what form.

I stuck it out for the afternoon, putting together a process diagram. Some of what I did was routine to me, but would not be intuitive to someone else. Should I leave instructions for how to use the cloud connections? Or were those available only to me, Harvey Goldstein, Metadata Man?

Instructing a replacement would be like teaching a new language, not possible if you didn't know the words and grammar yourself. Ursula teaches German because she has the training. I had no training in how to introduce our computer system to a newcomer who might not even know how to use a keyboard.

I was reminded of my own beginnings. I'd watch as a lightning fingered technician blew through routines intuitively. Doesn't work if you have no intuition.

Ursula could give me advice. I saved my draft of a decisions diagram to a flash drive to take home and puzzle over.

I was still preoccupied with my own issues when I got home to find Ursula crying. She hadn't changed into her usual track suit but just plopped down on the couch with her briefcase on the floor beside her.

"What's wrong?"

She wiped her eyes. "*Sheisse.*"

That much German I knew: shit.

I decided not to tell her about my job but to listen first.

When she settled down she explained. "The school is dropping German. You know they already dropped music and art. The only reason I could make you that Metadata Man shirt was because the art lab isn't being used for lack of funds for a teacher. Foreign languages are next, except for Spanish. Half the kids already know Spanish."

"So what happens now?"

215

She was in despair. "I'm left with bonehead English for immigrants. Only half time."

I sat down beside her and gave her a hug and kiss. "Maybe it's baby time for us."

She sniffled. "You're trying to distract me."

"Why not?" Having a baby was something we'd thought about, but not seriously. We'd needed two full time jobs. That was before we paid off the mortgage, before the bitcoins.

What with Margaret's suggestion that we just retire and Ursula's loss of job security, the baby alternative was nearly thrust upon us.

For a minute or two I had this fantasy of being a stay at home Dad while we lived off the bitcoin account, providing it didn't disappear under the fingers of some hacker. Angel might have second thoughts and shut it down.

To cover my indecision while I tried to focus, I got up to put on the coffee pot. I took a Sam Adams from the fridge and popped the top before I broke my own news. "Margaret says I'm over qualified. I think its an excuse to get me out of her department."

"She firing you?"

"Supposedly promoted. Maybe a sideways move within Krieger."

"If you're promoted and make more money, my being half time wouldn't be so bad."

Neither of us really took the bitcoin account seriously. It still wasn't real. It wasn't like a bundle of hundred dollar bills you could hold in your hand or hide in a box under the bed. Even a check made out as a hundred million dollars was just a piece of paper and the number just a lot of zeros. We didn't think of ourselves as millionaires.

The only time the bitcoin wallet account seemed real was when the credit union guy accepted bitcoins to pay off our mortgage. It was like I'd found Monopoly money on the street and it turned out to have value. Wow! Until then it was just a number on my computer screen. Thanks to the mysterious Angel we had passed Go and collected.

Making decisions is the hardest human endeavor. I have to admit to a certain amount of paralysis. Faced with an elaborate restaurant menu with too many choices I'm likely just to take the day's special.

But sometimes choices are thrust jupon us.

I poured Ursula a cup of coffee and sipped my Sam Adams while we sat at the kitchen table. She'd stopped crying and was focused again. "You know, Harvey, maybe your boss is doing you a favor. You've been too comfortable in that job."

I had to admit much of the challenge had gone out of coupons. Even though Krieger had millions of actual customers and stores across most of the country, I'd set up the mailings so they practically did themselves. Only the addition of the cloud connections had kept me interested.

Concentrating on who might have murdered Uncle Julius had been something new for me. Solving that puzzle was actually fun. I mean, I did it all at my computer. I hadn't had to do as Uncle Julius had said, stand in a cold rainy doorway all night on a stakeout. I hadn't been in on the arrest of the alleged killer, either. I wasn't going to appear in any German court as an expert witness. It was absorbing, but more like a puzzle at the back of the Plain Dealer. You don't get a chill of fear doing the New York Times crossword. It was all safe.

In a computer game you might encounter monsters, but none of it was real. It was a fantasy. Maybe it was too safe. If things went wrong, all you had to do was log off.

Nobody was going to shoot holes in your window.

Whatever the FBI had done when using my portal the consequence for us was we might have been killed. Real bullets had torn up our picture window, killed the microwave and my silly singing fish. I did not want a repetition.

I hadn't found Angel, but whoever she had hacked would want their money back. The trail led to Harvey Goldstein. Whoever they were, they were real.

I had to be Angel's idea of a diversion. If they followed the money, it would lead them to me, not to her.

Bitcoins might not seem real to me, but changing jobs and Ursula's possibly losing hers was real.

Maybe Walker could help. He was using the bitcoin situation as leverage to persuade me to work with him in some capacity as Metadata Man. I realized that finding information out there in the world was not enough.

I needed some technical assistance.

Breaking my routine of fear of phones I called Walker. I actually got through. He was not standing in some doorway in the rain needing to take a leak. He asked, "Have you considered my proposition?"

I dodged. "I'm not sure what your proposition is. What I'd like is to trade some information."

"Trade?"

"I think you're as curious as I am about the bitcoin deal, like where it came from and whose was it. I'm sure it has connections with international crime."

"So?"

"So I tried to find the person called Angel on the internet and in German records but found only dead identities."

"So what you want from me?"

"I still have the envelopes and the photo that came from Germany. What I can't get on my own is a DNA sample from the envelopes. People leave their DNA when they lick a stamp or seal an envelope. Analysis of the paper can pin down its source. This is stuff I can't do while sitting by my computer."

"You want me to look for DNA for you? What good will that do?"

It was my turn. "Get me the DNA off that mail and I'll have the ancestry of the person. If it is thorough enough I can sort the world for someone who is a match."

He was interested. "How does that help our own investigations?"

"It's a thread that may lead to the hackers who are the source of currency Angel converted to bitcoins."

He agreed. "Could happen."

"As I see it," I suggested, "Hackers are like a secret club. They may not be organized as part of some government like the Russians going after our political parties, but if they connect with some other hackers for advice or insights, we can follow the leads."

"You think you can do that with a DNA sample?"

"I am Metadata Man." It was a boast and a bluff. Maybe I couldn't, but it was worth a try.

I delivered the envelopes sealed in a plastic bag to avoid even further contamination.

What I needed was a better understanding of bitcoins and how they worked.

Chapter Fifteen

The only person I knew who was informed about this stuff was Grabich, our IT guy at Krieger. He'd hacked the US Immigration system to get his Iranian girl friend a green card. She'd overstayed her student visa and risked deportation. Ursula and I had even provided her with a safehouse until Grabich did his thing. Then, once she was legal, she split, but that's his heartache.

I snagged Grabich in all his hairy splendor at the water cooler. "Margaret wants me out of her department."

His eyes, almost invisible under that main of wild hair, were evasive. He had something else on his mind, something he wasn't telling me. After a hesitation he suggested, "Why don't you give her what she wants?" and made an obscene gesture.

I took a deep breath. "I think she's like that Russian nymphomaniac Alexandra the Great. I'd never satisfy her and be dumped." Not that I'd even consider cheating on Ursula. We've got a contract: 'til death do us part,

"So what's your alternative?"

"It's my bitcoin wallet. I'm afraid it could disappear as quickly as it showed up."

Grabich nodded. "I get it. What do you want to do? Convert it to cash?"

"I don't know."

Grabich smiled, showing crooked top teeth. "I should have your problem. Let me explain this stuff. Let's sit down in the break room."

We retreated. I sat down on one of the well worn chairs that had trickled down to our level when worn out at higher altitudes of administration.

Grabich stroked his chin like maybe he had a resident hitchhiker in all that beard. "Look at it this way: bitcoins are part of a mathematical chain. It's all anonymous. Nobody who has bitcoins knows what you have. You can hide your bitcoins from the world and from the tax man That's why the banks and governments hate it."

I was puzzled. "So nobody else knows what's in my wallet?"

"Yes. Banks are different. They are controlled by the government and regulations. You know if you made a deposit of over ten grand, the IRS is notified. I think that whoever created your bitcoin account did so by converting some real currency or credit to bitcoins to escape government scrutiny."

"So as long as I keep it in bitcoins nobody else knows,"

Grabich cocked his head back and forth like a ruminating rooster. "If you cashed in your bitcoins for dollars, the banks and the IRS would know about it. All that stuff about your confidentiality is bullshit. "

As Metadata Man I knew that.

I had discovered that the value of a bitcoin floated. Major sudden withdrawals affected the pool.

Grabich wasn't finished. "If you try to cash it in your sudden supply of dollars or whatever will attract the attention of government regulators like the SEC or the IRS or whatever."

Thinking out loud I said, "Then when we paid off our mortgage, which was over way over ten thousand, the IRS would want to know where we got the money."

"They haven't notified you yet?"

I shook my head.

Grabich smiled. "Just wait. You'll get one of those threatening letters."

I sighed. This money business was over my head.

"If I were you," Grabich suggested, "I'd spend those bitcoins a little at a time to not attract anybody's alarm or attention. "

I was beginning to understand. The original source of our bitcoin wallet had to have been in real currency hacked from some big treasury or foreign bank. When that was wired to the hackers' accounts or their friends or whatever, Angel had intervened and converted the stolen currency to bitcoins. The currency had then disappeared off regulators' radar. It was gone.

Except I had some of it.

Best thing I could do was nothing.

I thanked Grabich for his advice.

He winked at me from under bushy eyebrows and suggested if I had any surplus, he'd be glad to hold onto it for me.

Through this entire conversation I sensed he was holding something back. Grabich can be a cagey fellow. I decided it was something I didn't need to know or shouldn't yet.

My only recourse was to go back to my search for Angel.

Chapter sixteen

Before Grabich left me to go back to his warren of cables and monitors he had an idea. "Did you see that bit in the Wall Street Journal?"

Margaret leaves WSJ in the break room for our edification. "What bit? I only read it when there's something about Israel or boycotts and anti-Semitism."

Grabich had his own preferences. "I read it for the fraud stories. Wall street is a gang of thieves and fraudsters."

"You mean like Volkswagen cheating on the emissions controls for its diesel vehicles?"

"Yes, but I look for hacking stories. It wasn't only Bangladesh or the Russians that got hacked. It was the Chinese."

I hadn't heard about that.

"Somebody ripped off the communist bank of China for a billion dollars in huan. Officials have been arrested. Heads will roll."

If the Chinese government shot a corrupt official, that didn't worry me. "Could be worse. Somewhere I read about Shanghai. When it was one of the most sinful cities in the world there were foreign enclaves and gambling dens. The penalties for people who didn't pay their gambling debts were severe. There was the death of a thousand cuts. Worse, the victim would have all his tendons cut."

"You mean like escaped slaves sometimes had their Achilles tendons cut so they could no longer run away."

"Yep. But the Chinese cut every tendon. The victim was dumped in the gutter unable to move any part of his body, a living blob."

Grabich shuddered. "I wouldn't want to be one of those who hacked the Chinese Central Bank."

I could imagine that the Chinese secret police would track down the hackers and torture them to find out where the billion went. What was the old torture? Pulling out fingernails?

"I'll have to watch for information about that hack job." If what I had was stolen from the Chinese, someone might be after me with snips.

Grabich doesn't have a personal coffee cup in the break room. He tossed his disposable cup in the trash. He gave me a sly look. "What if the money you got from Angel was part of that heist? Those Chinese agents are going to follow the money. First the hackers, then Angel who diverted the stolen money, and then you, old buddy."

I suddenly had dry mouth. "You're scaring me."

"Be scared, Harvey."

If Angel had diverted funds stolen from China, her life wouldn't be worth a huan. But so far as I understood, she or he wasn't the thief. She had stolen from the thieves themselves. She hadn't stolen from the Chinese, but I didn't know.

Of course, this was all speculation, another what if story. I didn't know who had stolen the billion from China or if the hackers had been killed. There was so much thievery going on, so much crookedness.

Some of the Volkswagen officials might actually go to jail. I didn't think they risked having all their tendons cut. What about the Japanese airbag company? Did their CEO have to commit hari-kari? Or was paying a billion dollar fine enough punishment for knowingly selling airbags that could explode and kill people?

Grabich hadn't said when the Chinese case happened. The news might not have gotten out until much later. Did the dates connect with the delivery of my bitcoin wallet?

I'd have to search. Too bad I don't know Chinese. There must be an auto-translate feature in Windows for Chinese to English.

This was definitely a job for Metadata Man. If my bitcoin wallet contained Chinese loot, Angel would be in danger, even if she laid a false trail of dead identities. To follow the money might lead Chinese assassins to Harvey Goldstein. Oh, goody!

What I didn't realize was that Grabich had deliberately diverted me with the Chinese huan story. He was up to something I didn't know about.

Chapter seventeen

Ignoring my instinct not to use the phone, I called Walker at his FBI office. Now it was even more important to extract DNA or fingerprints from the envelops I'd received from Germany. I had to find Angel and learn where she got the money she (or he) put into my bitcoin wallet. "Do you think you can get any DNA off the envelopes I gave you? Or finger prints off the letter?"

He sounded like I was being a pest. "The labs are backed up for several months. You have to be patient."

The wheels of government grind exceeding slowly. I knew that rape kits languished in police labs for years without ever being tested. That must be a gamble the rapist took. By the time the evidence was checked he'd be in an old people's home or in jail for something else. So why would anybody be in a hurry to extract some DNA from a letter that wasn't necessarily connected with a crime at all?

"Identifying the sender of those letters is vital. Angel could be murdered. If you can't get the DNA extracted quickly, I need those items back."

"I don't have them."

"What do you mean?"

"Passed them on. They're in the pipeline."

My frustration was growing fast. "Then get them back."

"You know, Goldstein, you're getting to be a pain in the ass."

"Are you asking me to check your emails and the contents of the hard drive of your office copier so I can track them myself?"

He hesitated. "You could do that?"

I was ready to put down the hammer. On his head. "I am Harvey Goldstein. Get it?"

I don't think he believed me. I can get anything digital.

He didn't like the FBI being threatened. "Watch it Goldstein. Don't make trouble for yourself."

"If the hackers who stole that money are pursued by assassins, the paper trail will lead to the bitcoin purchases and to me. So I am in trouble already."

Walker waffled.

I insisted. "I need those envelopes by tomorrow. If they've gone out of town, have them brought to me by courier. I will get them to a private DNA lab myself."

"That'll cost you."

"Not as much as my life." Whatever the cash costs might be, the bitcoin wallet would cover it. Why did I turn to Walker in the first place? He was acting like another flunky bound up in government red tape.

I tried another angle. "Maybe you don't get it, Agent Walker. I hear there was a major hack of the Chinese central bank. A billion in huan. Know anything about that?"

If l had a Skype phone I could have seen him shaking his head. "We have enough on our plate dealing with people trying to get into our own data. Besides, that's not even my department. I leave that to the teckies."

"Sorry I asked." I hoped my sarcasm was obvious.

Finding Angel was not going to be easy. I already had several false leads. At least three hits on the facial recognition had turned up as reported dead. The recognition program was only 70% accurate, so could I rely on it?

I was convinced Angel was setting up false leads for her pursuers. If I could find her I could ask if it was hacked Chinese loot she had redirected. Then I could warn her, or him.

Who handled this stuff? Since Angel was apparently in Germany, it wasn't an FBI job. Their territory was domestic. Foreign intelligence was for the CIA.

I wasn't ready to contact the CIA. Better do my homework first, like Google and all sources open to my expanded consciousness.

I was beginning to realize the Harvey Goldstein did not have access to everything. I don't know Chinese or anything but English. Navigating foreign web sites was tough. I might be able to access all the clouds here; that wasn't international enough. It was basically an American phenomenon. Not everyone in the world has a computer or a cell phone. I didn't have an iPhone myself though 90% of Americans did. It was probably more than had bath tubs or television sets.

Trouble was, this was giving me a headache. I was afraid to push the envelope too far and end up hiding under a blanket sucking my thumb like a sick baby.

I felt like a marathon runner whose toenails are coming off and everything ached, but I had to press on. I realized that it obviously wasn't only hacks that broke into the treasuries of foreign countries. Their own officials did. The outgoing president of Rwanda left with the contents of the treasury tucked away in various banks and among friends. My bitcoin wallet could contain tainted wealth from any number of places. China? Not necessarily. Could be Rwanda or Yemen, or Panama.

I didn't think Kentucky. American officials are more subtle. Being an insider trader would never reap as much as a billion huan. At least I didn't think so.

If a hacker got into a central bank, resources would be applied to track him down. What would be smarter would be to steal from the ex president's stash. Who could he complain to?

That expanded the field for searching enormously, considering the amount of massive corruption in the world. Still, a million bitcoins was significant. It was not like tracking down some petty crook who bought social security numbers and tried to get IRS refunds before the real taxpayer filed. You don't get a hundred million dollars that way. Let Walker go after those small crooks.

I bet many of them were already in prison. Robbing tax refunds was sort of a cottage industry.

Considering the multitude of possible sources, I reasoned that my task was not so different from my coupon job at Krieger. I just had to sort known currency thefts, starting at, say, ten million dollars. It was like Go Fish: gimme all your thefts over ten million. Please.

In Go Fish you had to say please and thank you. That was the purpose of the kids card game.

I could increase the threshold amount until I got to the value of a million bitcoins.

That would cut down the list significantly. It also gave me approximate dates and locations. They were all foreign. Even overpaid American CEOs who got remunerations of ten million a year hardly qualified. Those millions were allegedly legit until the shareholders revolted.

Now I had evidence, but knowing about a theft was not enough. I had to find out who did it and what happened to the thief or thieves.

Who to turn to? What database should I probe? For Metadata Man to start probing the CIA was a bit more dangerous than snooping the Teamster's mailing list. My last resort would be to make an overt query, like write an actual letter. Emails can be filtered as spam or deleted by the touch of a key.

Before writing the CIA I considered an alternate route. Grabich said that all bitcoin purchases were anonymous. Their value depended on market activity, like the value of gold. Buying a million bitcoins had to affect their value.

How could I trace my bitcoin wallet back to its origins?

I had one remaining lead. It was Liselotte Kraus, one of the names that turned up when I looked for a face that matched the photo, except Kraus was allegedly dead, along with the other names that turned up.

Had Liselotte Kraus been real at all, or just a fake, a pseudonym? There might be a German record. I could look up birth certificates, drivers licenses, and so on just as I'd tracked Uncle Julius's killer. Kraus had to have had an address, neighbors. She might have disappeared into thin air, but not without leaving behind her DNA in the form of signed documents, and so on. Once data is in the system you can't delete all of it. It gets replicated. Something always remains. Someplace.

Angel might have been able to assume various aliases, but somewhere on that list of allegedly dead faces there might be a diploma. Better yet, a school transcript or an employment record. I suspected Angel had worked in computers even if was no more than take a technical course.

People who might go into hiding were also likely to get jobs in what they knew, like carpentry, or buy tickets to certain concerts, games, or events that followed their interests. It was not so different from my Krieger data sorting job.

I realized I'd been sitting with my eyes closed and my hands over my ears to blot out external stimuli. My head hurt again. I opened my eyes, looked at my watch. I had been sitting for what? An hour?

"Are you all right?"

It was Margaret looking down over the top of my cubicle.

I uncovered my ears. "I'm not feeling well. Stressed out."

"Ever considered Valium?" She looked like she was familiar with the drug.

"I think I'd better go home and rest awhile."

"Want me to call your doctor? I have the number for a doctor Halal."

That gave me a stomach twinge. "No. Not him. I'll be OK. Just got to take a break for maybe a couple of hours."

"Want to lie down on my office sofa?"

It was Margaret's suede leather casting couch, as Grabich and I called it. No way. I just shook my head.

"How's your procedures graphic coming?"

So far I'd done only a rough outline. "It's coming."

"I need it."

She sounded urgent, like the pressure was coming at her from upstairs. That should have sounded my intuitive alarm bells. Maybe someone had been paying attention to all the work I had missed. If I missed too much time I'd be fired.

Getting behind the wheel of my car was so confusing I was scared. Was this what people experienced with early Alzheimer's? No longer remembering how to get home?

Nothing looked familiar. I was tempted to get out the GPS and ask it for directions to my own condo. Maybe this was how it was when you were drunk or buzzed on marijuana.

I made it, dizzy and disoriented. When I got home I just went to bed and hid under the covers like a sick kid. I had a headache. I was confounded by a kaleidoscope of thoughts, images, and ideas.

Ursula came home from school and was surprised to find me hiding. At least I wasn't under the bed with the dust bunnies.

"What's happening, Harvey? Are you losing it again?"

I peeked out, blinked at the light. "I think I'm having a nervous breakdown."

She crawled into the bed beside me. There's nothing like a cuddle. She's my teddy bear. "You want to see a shrink?"

"No. Call Grabich. I need his advice."

Ursula called him and he showed up, looking bleary-eyed under all that hair like he'd been glued to a computer screen for too long.

I sat up in bed and pleaded with hi. "Grabich, I'm stuck. How good are you at navigating the dark web?"

He was non-committal. "You gonna read me my rights? Like anything I say maybe used in a court of law?"

"I'm not a cop I just need your help. I need to find out about the person called Angel who set up my bitcoin wallet account."

"I thought you said she was dead."

I didn't want to repeat my conversation with detective Hintz of the police. "Supposedly. I think records of the death are faked, planted like Winston Smith did when rewriting history."

Grabich didn't remember Winston Smith, the protagonist in Orwell's 1984.

I didn't bother to explain. "Even dead she or he has a history. I got to find her…him…whatever."

Why should Grabich have any better luck than I did? If my so-called benefactor was German, at least I had Ursula for translations and

227

her own insights. But I wasn't familiar with bitcoin operations. There I was at a disadvantage. The transactions were supposed to be anonymous, but who used their own names? Anybody?

I should have gone to him in the first place. My fault for being egotistical enough as Metadata Man to think I could do everything myself.

We moved from the bedroom into the living room where I had my desk and laptop. "Best you use my computer. If anybody backtracks the searches you do they should come back to me. No need to expose you.:"

He gave me a sideways look. "You think it's that dangerous?"

I nodded. I glanced at our bullet riddled curtains.

I entered the access code to my portal and let him have at it. "You'll be Harvey Goldstein. It's for your own protection."

Ursula watched over our shoulders. She didn't work in the same areas of computing that I did, but she knew her way around. She didn't bother with her Facebook or Twitter accounts, finding those diversions a waste of time. To her mind that social networking is teen-aged stuff. She had enough work to do with school paperwork.

At best Facebook was a diversion from endless repetitions correcting basic *der die das* grammar.

While Grabich and I were both hunched over my laptop she brought us each a Sam Adams. "Thanks."

Grabich asked, "Got some tape?"

"Desk drawer."

He found it and stuck a piece over the laptop's camera. "We don't need anybody watching this and circulating my picture."

Then he got to it. Grabich was so quick on the keyboard that I couldn't follow him.

The dark web was a mystery to me. It was where hackers and crooks pursued their nefarious activities. It was where the Silk Road internet market for illegal drugs had flourished until its founder made the mistake of sending a single email that was traceable back to him. He's in prison now, claiming someone else had taken over the Silk Road. The judge didn't buy the argument, gave him a life sentence.

Most hackers when Grabich was at it were kids under twenty four who had time on their hands, sometimes teenagers after school, pecking away at their keyboards with parents unaware of what was going on. Then most of them graduated, got jobs, and moved on, though some made it into NSA or other government agencies. Grabich still had one or two contacts among the survivors.

One was called Fox and used Snapchat for messages that would disappear in seconds after being read to avoid leaving a record.

Grabich entered "Looking for a hacker called Angel."

This flashed on the screen: "Angel is gone."

"Where? Dead?"

"Gone to Never Never Land."

"What's that."

"Fourth dimension."

I had a pull on my Sam Adams. I had made it to the Seventh Paradigm, but had no idea about the fourth dimension.

Grabich entered a string of question marks. "?????"

"A web beneath the dark web."

How many layers could there be? Theoretical mathematicians claim there are many dimensions.

That was beyond Grabich. He'd been out of that world for some time now that he worked for Krieger and was legitimate. He looked up at me. "Now what?"

"Tell Fox Angel's been redirecting money hackers have robbed from places like Bangladesh or even China. Does he know anything about that?"

Grabich asked.

Fox said he'd look.

That was that. We would have to wait.

Grabich logged off and sat facing me for my attention. "Harvey, I think you're in this too deep."

"Like Margaret says, it's above my pay grade?"

He nodded. "Harvey, you are way out of your depth. The Internet, the clouds, the dark web, it's like the deep sea ocean. It's full of sharks and deep sea monsters."

I reluctantly agreed.

He asked, "What do you want to get out of all this?"

My answer was lame, almost infantile. "I'm just doing the coupon thing."

"No you're not. You are a data hoarder, Harvey. You can't get enough data and now it's overwhelmed you."

I had to admit he was right, but I wasn't finished. "There must be bitcoin wallet records. Who bought the million bitcoins? Using what currency? When?"

"Let it rest, Harvey old buddy. Why don't you and Ursula here just forget all this shit happened. You don't need it. Let it go."

I wasn't ready yet. Was I simply obsessed, like someone stuck in a puzzle with no solution?

Grabich read the pitiful expression on my face. "Harvey, you are not going to find that Angel person, if she even ever existed. It's a fake."

I pleaded, "You're not much of a help."

He gave me a gap toothed smile, all that hairy face and beady eyes. "Give it a rest."

Ursula had her arms around me in a comforting, motherly hug. "He's right."

Grabich got up to leave. He still had one swig left of his Sam Adams. Putting town the empty bottle he said, "You aren't going to find anybody, Metadata Man. If they want to find you, they will."

Feebly, "That's what I'm afraid off. A million bicoins is a lot in any currency. Someone will want it back."

Grabich sighed. "Look a it this way: your bitcoin wallet is a convenience for someone who stole from the hackers. The original victims will get the hackers, but not you. As for a million bit coins, so what? There's more where that came from. The dark web is churning with people making deals. They move on to other deals. I think you will be forgotten."

I blinked at him.

He gave me a look that said his mind was on something else. "Stick to your Krieger job. Don't jeopardize it."

Did he know something I didn't?

Chapter eighteen

When I returned to the office the next morning the shit hit the fan.
Margaret called me into her goldfish bowl office and put on a grim
expression. "You aren't training a replacement."

That could be taken in many ways, like the whole deal was off, no
replacement needed. Or why didn't I get the job done as she requested?
Didn't she like what I had prepared? What was this, some kind of a test
of my efficiency? Or something worse? "Is my job being outsourced to
India? Costa Rica?" like maybe I hoped it was a joke.

"It's being automated. Your method of dealing with the data can be
done by AI, artificial intelligence."

My stomach clutched. "I'm being replaced by a robot?"

She nodded. "You and millions of other American workers."

It was a familiar situation. Trouble for the economy was robots
don't buy the stuff those factories produce. Consumer commerce drives
80% of the economy. If nobody was working or making more than
minimum wage, who would buy? Corporations were cutting costs and
cutting off the purchasing power of their own workers who were
potential customers.

Who would hire the workers laid off by automation? Who would
hire me?

Henry Ford paid his workers five dollars a day so they could buy
the cars they were making. If the factory was staffed by robots, who
would buy the cars?

Of course, if the car itself was a self-driving robot who needed a
driver? What would we all be doing? Sitting at home watching Netflix?

My product, if you could call it that, was coupons. My trouble was,
the coupons I created were for food. Everybody had to eat, but an AI
program could issue those coupons probably better than I could, and
faster. If I was replaced by a computer program, would I have the cash
to spend those coupons myself?

I saw that Margaret's serious look wasn't only in sympathy for my
predicament. I wasn't the only victim of progress. "What about the
department?"

I was referring to the other wage slaves in the other cubicles that made up this office space.

Boss Margaret, the office cougar, suddenly had the look of someone who had been somebody but wasn't any more. . "They're going to rip out all the work stations and use this space as a work out gym for top management."

In this country you are asked two questions: what church do you go to and what do you do? If you don't do, you ain't. I don't go to any church and without this job, what was I? A goofy guy with a silly Metadata Man jersey and no job.

I shook my head. I could just see it. The work stations were flexible, easily assembled into new configurations or simply removed entirely leaving a few marks on the floor.

I was suddenly feeling sorry for Margaret. She was at that transition age when a woman is easily replaced by someone prettier and cheaper. Once you hit fifty jobs were scarce. "What'll you do?"

Her thin smile showed she was trying not to cry. "Maybe someone out there in cyber space will give me a fat bitcoin account."

I didn't answer. I just nodded.

With me out of a job and Ursula only half time, how could we manage? With the bitcoin wallet, of course, providing it was real. Bitcoins seemed to me to be a conjuring trick. I knew the system was mathematical, like string theory or something scrawled in chalk on a blackboard proving multi dimensions of commerce, but real?

I turned to leave. "When does all this happen?"

"We have a week for the transition to AI."

I could only offer "Sorry."

She was right. Ursula might be half time at the k-12 school and I would be out of a job, but we did have the mysterious bitcoin wallet. Trouble was, it was like a hologram, an image of something that wasn't real. It was like I was walking around in a virtual reality with one of those gadgets over my face. Following that simulated world you could fall off a cliff.

Nothing like being fired to put things into sharp focus.

Now it was more important than ever to find Angel or whoever that was.

And split the bitcoin balance into separate accounts, just in case someone wanted it back. Before it was like a fantasy, a game of Monopoly, the money not real. Now I grasped it like a bit of flotsam after your ship sinks.

I remembered a story of a World War II veteran who came upon a wrecked German train full of money. Only American dollars were real to him, so a handful of German bank notes in his helmet could serve as toilet paper. That is until he actually tried to spend it in a German shop and found out it was real.

I went to visit Grabich in his IT office with the monitors and cables all over the place. He was uncomfortable when I confronted him.

"You knew about this, didn't you?"

He didn't need me to explain what "this" was. He nodded, looking guilty. "It was top secret."

"Thanks a lot."

"It wouldn't have made any difference if I told you. It was a done deal."

"What about your job?"

He leaned back in his ergo metric chair. "There are always intruders trying to break into our system, steal all the customer metadata. Nowadays metadata is like gold."

I tried to look macho. "Then Metadata Man must be rich."

"Depends on what you do with it. Money in the mattress doesn't earn any interest." He was referring to the billions stashed in foreign banks. So much for the trickle down theory. Stashed money doesn't create jobs. He changed the subject. "Any luck in your search for Angel?"

"I think a DNA sample would give me a lead."

"Then you better get on with it." He turned back to this monitors. "Krieger isn't awarding any severance pay."

Thanks a lot. I'd forgotten to ask Margaret about those dirty details, like what happens to our health insurance?

That was the hard reality of our situation. It shoved dealings with Walker and the FBI and the German detective to the bottom of the stack of the to do list. Or maybe to the top. I needed a plan B.

I hadn't vacated my cubicle yet. The only personal item in it was a framed photo of Ursula taken on our honeymoon. The Russian doll was back in our condo. "Screw it," I mumbled, and used the company phone for a personal call to Walker at the FBI. I had his direct number.

When he answered I asked about the envelope from Germany.

To my surprise he said he'd rescued it from the pipeline and would see that I got it ASAP.

He was true to his word. When I got back to our condo there it was, sealed in an evidence bag inside an express envelope. No note of explanation needed.

I surfed the net for DNA labs. Cost wasn't an issue. Time was.

I cooked up a story that Krieger was doing more metadata research. It wasn't very convincing. What I asked for was DNA from under the postage stamps and the flap of the envelope. When you lick a stamp or envelope you leave a DNA trail. Lots of people had handled it, but only one person would have licked the stamp or sealed the envelope. There was tape on it, too, and inevitably something would be on the sticky side. That should be no more difficult than catching the burglar who drank from a soda bottle before leaving the scene.

Then the issue would be if that DNA turned up in a registry anyplace. Did the Germans take DNA samples of everyone arrested for anything?

I asked how long would this take?

The answer was ambiguous. It would depend on this, that, or the other.

Ursula was glum when she got home from school. I hardly needed to ask. She said, "You know the old story. Budget cuts. Foreign languages other than Spanish are luxury courses. Arts and music went. Now all that matters is teaching to the tests."

"No wonder kids drop out."

Her face was grim. "They didn't cut football."

"Naturally. All Americans really care about is sports. Listen, I think we should go out to dinner. We can celebrate, if that's what you could call it, my being laid off and your cut in salary." It was like the last meal before the electrocution.

She was startled and troubled. "Laid off? You took too many sick days?"

Too many sick days or not, she knows that you can be laid off for no cause. That's America.

I sighed. "I've been outsourced by an AI robot. The whole department. Margaret's canned, too."

"What about your buddy Grabich?"

"He's IT, another department."

We both understood that Margaret would have a more difficult time to find a new job than I would. When you are middle management and change jobs it generally means a pay cut.

234

What about me? I'd been at Krieger five years, long enough for it to almost feel like a rut until I expanded into the cloud sources. Even so, I'm not a programmer like Grabich. I'm marketing in a dog eat dog world except in my case the dog that ate me was a computer program. How many guys were like me, bumped from their jobs by technology?

Lost in our own thoughts Ursula and I both dressed up for the occasion. We decided on Al's Steak House, for us a real splurge.

Al's is an upscale place. You make a reservation and wait until the hostess takes you to your table, table cloths and the nice table settings, wine glasses and cloth napkins, none of that plastic stuff rolled in a paper napkin.

An older waiter, not a kid just learning the job, brought the menus. For once I tried to ignore the prices. Al's was one of those places where the prices were all in whole dollars. It was not one of those eateries where you ask for a doggie bag and take home the uneaten rolls.

We ordered filet mignon and a red wine.

The waiter made a show of the ritual in which he poured a little wine for me to sniff, taste, and approve. Aside from Manischevitz Passover wine, my alcohol of choice is Sam Adams beer. This was not our world.

Ursula was uncomfortable. She looked around the place to see who else was there and was surprised. "Is that your FBI guy, Walker over there?"

It was. He was wearing a dark, pinstriped suit and accompanied by an older man who might have been his boss.

I got a good look at Walker's companion and tried not to think about it, but my Metadata Man brain kicked in. Facial recognition. By the set of his eyes and nose, it was Albert Speerson, a government official with a long history of agency hopping. I forced my Metadata Man brain to stop before I got to the man's personal data, like did he have Cheerios for breakfast and keep a mistress?

Walker saw that I was staring and came over to our table. He knew we normally didn't eat fancy and asked, "Celebrating?"

"If you can call it that. More like a wake. Krieger has outsourced my job to an AI computer and Ursula here's been cut to half time at school. Seems the German language is a luxury the Cleveland school system can't afford."

Walker seemed genuinely sympathetic.

"So you're dining with Albert Speerson," I said. "You must be on per diem. Your salary doesn't justify Al's steak house." I knew it made him uncomfortable that I knew his GS rating and salary scale.

He was duly impressed. "Speerson isn't a public figure. How did you recognize him?"

I gave an insincere apologetic grin. "Facial recognition."

Walker shook his head with admiration only an FBI man might acknowledge. "How do you do that?"

"I don't know myself, but I learned that all the information in the entire world can be stored as DNA code in a space as small as a sugar cube."

"And I thought the human brain can hold only so much memory. It's time you worked for us."

If only I understood it myself. If I tried to think about it I'd start blowing my own fuses again. I didn't want to hide, sucking my thumb under my blanket.

Our dinner wasn't the time for accepting the job offer, whatever it might be. I wasn't ready. "What's the occasion of his visit? Speerson isn't FBI."

"As you know, Harvey, the FBI deals with domestic crime. You fall into a different category."

"Me?" Now he was calling me a criminal, not right out, but I got the drift. It was enough to make my twice-baked potato stick in my throat. "What crime?"

"International money laundering. I'm thinking of your bitcoin account."

Now I was really on my guard. Was this Speerson an enforcer? ":What about it?"

He didn't answer. "Got any report on your DNA sample?"

"Not yet."

"Stop by the office tomorrow. Speerson will want to talk to you."

OK. With my job terminated, maybe this was Plan B opening up. We had to do something for real income in genuine currency. I didn't dare freeload on a bitcoin account that might disappear any moment. The people it was stolen from might be vindictive. It's hard to plead innocence when you're standing at the end of a pier with your feet .in a bucket of fresh cement

Walker returned to his table. I saw him talking with Speerson and gesticulating. Speerson looked over at us and, smiling, gave me an index finger salute, which could mean anything. At least it wasn't the middle finger.

Ursula was too stuffed to order dessert, but was willing to share a piece of New York cheesecake.

By then, I was getting edgy again so she did the driving back home while I kept looking back to see if we were being followed. It was silly, of course. If the FBI were doing their job, they'd have planted a GPS tracking device in the car. They would know where we were at all times. Goes with living in a police state, I guess.

I wondered what Speerson wanted.

Chapter nineteen

The next morning I parked our car in a pay lot close to FBI headquarters. I'd been there several times already, but if the security guards recognized me they still treated me with all the suspicion due to a bomb-wearing, armed terrorist. I did the airplane thing, arms outstretched while I was wanded. They even made me take off my shoes. Maybe next time I'd have a bona fide ID badge. Those guys don't have much sense of humor, but I guess in that job you are scared all the time.

The office gatekeeper expected me. This time I didn't go into the sound proof interview room but joined Walker and Speerson in an office, no window, not like Margaret's.

In a police interrogation room there might at least be coffee and a stale donut to break the ice. No donut at the FBI and I skipped the coffee. I got right to it: "Tell me why I'm here."

Speerson introduced himself, which was unnecessary because by this time as Metadata Man I had his whole life and even his bank accounts in my history. "Agent Walker says you're the recipient of stolen goods."

Walker added, "He's talking about the bitcoin wallet."

So that was it. They were trying to intimidate me. "I don't know if it's stolen or not or who it's from. So far as I know, it's gift to keep me from suing the TV network for using my face and my name without my permission." Did they remember that incident when my face was on screens all over the world?

They were both silent, waiting for me to talk myself into some sort of a confession leading to an indictment or conviction.

I continued with "If I found it buried in my back yard, It'd be mine to keep. Possession is nine tenths of the law. Right?"

Speerson backed off. "I'm not concerned about your having the bitcoin account. It's just a small piece of a much larger picture. Finding out who gave it to you is more important. Agent Walker says it was someone called Angel. This Angel is either a major international internet thief or knows who they are."

Walker knew something about it. "There are about a dozen unidentified channels used to divert stolen assets to places like the Cayman Islands, the Bahamas, Panama, and other countries where bankers ask no questions."

Speerson nodded, "We're talking about some two hundred trillion dollars. Your bitcoins are chump change."

He might say so, but Speerson sounded like he wouldn't mind having a whack at some of that loot. I'd seen his metadata. He was making sixty thousand a year, which made me suspicious. With that much floating around, temptation would be great to get in on the action. Were both of these men honest?

Whitey Bolger, that Boston murderer, had a bent FBI man on his payroll. Considering what I saw in the Wall Street Journal copies Margaret left it the break room at Krieger, the world was full of thieves in high places.

Having our apartment shot up by street thugs was a hiccup compared to what Ursula and I might be getting into if Agent Walker and Speerson were a couple of goniffs who might be tempted. Could I trust them? There was so much corruption, I could just see them using me to get into the dark web schemers for their own benefit.

"Where's the two hundred trillion come from?"

"Different countries. Money that should go for food programs and earth quake relief, for instance."

I remembered the sixty million hacked out of the Bangladesh account at the Federal Reserve. I leaned back in the chair and shook my head. "You don't think I'm superman, do you? Savior of the world, feeder of all those starving millions, rebuilder of fallen cities?"

Walker chucked. "It takes more than a Metadata Man shirt to do that."

His sarcasm wasn't wasted on me, but I agreed. "And I take it we're not dealing with a single villain like the Joker in Batman. God knows how many corrupt officials and bankers there are around the world. That's reality, not comic book fiction."

"As fast as we can unmask one of those networks, others crop up."

I was relieved. They didn't expect me to save the world. All I had to do was find Angel and learn where she had got the money for my bitcoin wallet. I offered, "As soon as I can find Angel, you might get somewhere." You and not we or me. OK I was game for that much.

Walker seemed satisfied. "International corruption is a bit outside the FBI venue. Speerson here will be your guy."

Each agency had its own bailiwick, which was why lack of communication between them failed to stop the 9/11 attack. I was being handed off like a basketball star in a trade.

Speerson: "I'll have some documents prepared."

Was I to sign the Official Secrets Act? As far as I knew this wasn't the CIA or NSA. Speerson's current job description was for an agency whose cooked up name I didn't recognize and might mean anything, like James Bond's Import-Export cover. "Am I being hired? If so, on what terms?" Being newly fired, I was sensitive to the loss of details like health insurance, like if Ursula and I were having that long discussed baby.

Speerson gave me a thin smile. "We don't have a pension plan."

I nodded. "You mean nobody lives that long in your job." It was another reason to steal to create a little retirement cushion.

Speerson gave me a stony look. "You people drive a hard bargain."

I got it. "You people" was a euphemism for you Jews. I bristled at the anti-Semitism. "That's why we survive," I said, giving back an equally hostile look. This was not going to go well. It doesn't take more than a word to screw up a relationship big time. At least I would be on my guard. This was a man who wouldn't hesitate to throw me to the wolves as in "Harvey Goldstein? Never heard of him. Not one of ours."

Speerson took a deep breath and let it out slowly. "You understand, you are not exactly being hired. You won't be an employee. You'll be a private contractor, no benefits, and responsible for the self-employment tax on anything you're paid."

I got it. I would be like Gary Powers whose U2 plane was shot down over Russia and the CIA claimed they didn't know him. Must have stolen the plane. Yeh, right.

"What about expenses?"

Speerson conceded, "Sure."

"Per diem?" I was thinking about the restaurant where we spotted the two of them. Our steak dinner cost more than our weekly grocery bill, and I get a Krieger employee discount. Used to get.

Speerson nodded reluctantly. "Within reason.'

I was already planning ahead. "Angel is probably in Germany. Can I hire a translator?" I was thinking of Ursula, of course. In Hamburg I'd needed her help to give the Arab cab driver directions to Uncle Julius's.

Walker interrupted. "Don't press your luck, Goldstein."

So now it was Goldstein again and not buddy-buddy Harvey.

Speerson was non committal. But he didn't outright say no.

I didn't feel comfortable if hunting down Angel meant traveling alone in Germany. When we were in Hamburg except for ordering a beer in a restaurant I was dependent on Ursula's language skills. Not everyone speaks English. When they do, you get better rapport with people when you speak their language, even if poorly. It shows you care and have respect, not like those American tourists who simply talk louder if not immediately understood.

Speerson got down to business. "Contact me when you've got the DNA report. If you have a plan, write it up. Let's see if Metadata Man is the real stuff and not just a shirt." He gave me his business card.

The guy could be sarcastic besides being a closet anti-Semite. I bit my tongue.

Now I had to break the news to Ursula.

She had problems of her own. When she came home she threw down her briefcase and surprised me by getting a Sam Adams out of the fridge. Stewing, she sat on the couch and explained. "My afternoon German class has been cancelled."

"You can finish the term, can't you?"

"It's not just that," she said after taking a swig of beer and making a face. She normally doesn't drink beer. "It's a first semester class. To count for graduation they need a full year to satisfy their language requirement for toward graduation. One term of a foreign language is almost useless."

I had taken Spanish in high school and forgot all of it after the last exam. So much for my own language skills, and now she wanted to teach me German.

"They can still graduate, can't they?"

"I don't think the school board cares. Our school has no better than a 70% graduation rate. I think the school boards have already given up trying."

"What about the teachers' union?"

She shook her head. "No clout."

"What about the PTA?"

"Not many parents care a rats ass for German. If you cut football there'd be a howl, demonstrations, stuff like that. Not for a foreign language class."

"Maybe you should just quit."

"You have any other suggestions?"

"I've been offered a contract with the government, guy named Speerson. He wants me to pursue the bitcoin thing."

She was angry about her job and I'd lost mine. Even though cashing in the bitcoins could easily buy us our own plane with a pilot to fly to Germany or anywhere, I didn't think in those terms. Mentally I was still just Harvey Goldstein, a wage slave who worked in a cubicle at Krieger. Used to.

The risk was that I might be like the power ball winner who went nuts over the sudden wealth and blew it all, ending up broke. People used to wealth know how to live with it. Not me. To me, even though we'd used some to pay off the mortgage, the million bitcoins were still not real. It was all numbers on a computer screen.

I still had fears that some scary people would show up with guns demanding their bitcoins back.

As for the money, I'm not a shopper. I don't need to own stuff. I'm content with one sport coat and one tie for dress up. Best not to speculate about it. It would be too distracting from my real task. That was finding "Angel."

Chapter twenty

Ursula was wide-eyed and intrigued when I told her about the encounter with Speerson. She liked teaching but was mad at the school board and the principal for cutting her German class. She enjoyed German, but teaching English for foreigners was tough. Not everyone had the finesse, diplomacy and understanding it took to manage a classroom of immigrants from various countries who could not pronounce "the". There were students from at least six different countries in her bonehead English class, some of them sworn enemies not long from the killing fields. If she quit, who would take over?

When I asked her, she had already made up her mind. "Screw it. You think we have to go back to Germany?"

"Finding Angel is not going to be as easy as me sitting at my computer and making a virtual visit to the Nuremburg archives to find Uncle Julius's killer. Somehow we're going to have to meet Angel or whoever that is face to face."

My conventional searches and facial recognition queries had led to several possibles but Klaus Hintz, the German police detective in Hamburg, said those were all dead. Metadata Man had advantages but there were limits. I could only look; a hacker could alter files and corrupt sources. Angel could duck and cover her—or his—tracks.

"And the DNA? What will you do with the report?"

"If I'm lucky I'll find a match in the German records."

"You didn't do so well the facial recognition."

I hedged. "Facial recognition is only 70% accurate. There were several names that matched the face we had. Stolen or fake identities."

Ursula remembered the Hamburg detective's report. "And dead."

I nodded. "And dead."

"Maybe whoever she stole from already killed her."

I agreed.

"And they may be waiting for you."

"Now you're scaring me."

Ursula laughed. She was laughing at me for being a fool. It wasn't funny. "You sure you want to do this?"

I shrugged. "Why not? Plan B." It would be more exciting that confinement to a Krieger cubicle which was, no doubt, already dismantled, leaving no trace. My job and even where I had worked, was erased like someone hit the delete button.

Ursula was right, of course. She usually is. Since I have never seen the person called Angel in person, anybody could claim to be her and I'd be no wiser. It might be like the imposter who uses another face for an on line dating service and turns out to be Jack the Ripper. Or Jill.

The DNA report was slow in coming. I made myself the squeaky wheel demanding grease and called the lab every other day. I explained that I didn't just want one of those Twenty-three and me genealogy reports that say you are .05 percent Neanderthal. I wanted a complete genome, something that revealed genetic disorders, like a propensity for Alzheimer's or some other disease. A really thorough DNA genome taken from the envelope I provided might, for instance, even tell Angel's eye color.

Then all I'd have to do was compare it with sixty million Germans and God knows what immigrants, that is providing Germany had a library of residents' DNA.

We do DNA samples of all military recruits and people arrested for serious offenses. Might be good in wartime if all graves registration finds is a body part after an IED blast in Afghanistan, but did we really need it for the civilian population? It's all part of our police state take over. The data collection wasn't just for Krieger to sell house brand toilet paper.

This was a job for Metadata Man. Too bad the skill didn't come with the shirt. Well, if I failed, we'd at least have a trip to Germany and maybe stay in some five star hotels along the way at Speerson's expense. Nothing like hanging on the government's teat.

Ursula was intrigued at the prospect of change. She was glad I was no longer within the reach of Boss Margaret and her casting couch. Didn't Ursula have any confidence in me? Well, maybe she was right. We men are such simple creatures. Flash a bit of cleavage and the male brain shuts down.

Gambling that she might trigger my information sensory overload, Ursula, dear wife that she is, set me up with some simple German language lessons. Our now outdated DVD of the Encyclopedia Britannica had come with a language disk, tourist German, like "I need a round trip ticket to …" or a double room, etc. It even had me speaking to the laptop microphone to correct my pronunciation. Wouldn't help if the answers were complex, like "You'll need a reservation for express connections" and "do you need a couchette?" But it was a start. Once you got the hang of a simple sentence structure you can substitute words, like "I'd like to buy a…" and insert "meal" "overcoat" or whatever, just so you are understood.

I was on my way, Harvey Goldstein, linguist. At least I didn't need a dictionary. My brain was a virtual library if I could only extract what I needed without going catatonic.

I had read that scientists were using DNA codes to store information. Every cell in our bodies contains our complete genetic code. Applied to other data, DNA was so efficient that all the world's knowledge could be stored, so they claimed, in something the size of a sugar cube. Maybe that's what was happening to my brain.

So we waited for the DNA.

Chapter twenty-one

I made a last visit to Krieger. At the personnel office I learned my health insurance had a grace period that would soon lapse. As long as Ursula was teaching I was insured as her dependent. Krieger never had a pension plan, but I did have a 401k so that was portable. I hadn't thought much about retirement. I knew that most people like myself were often one paycheck away from homelessness. Fail to pay the rent or the mortgage and you were out on the street. Eviction or foreclosure.

Grabich's Iranian girl friend had been in illegal limbo until he engineered a clandestine green card for her by hacking into the system. She'd lived with him in his basement apartment but once she had that green card, no longer lived in fear of ICE, our equivalent of the Jew-hunting Gestapo, she felt secure. She saved up for a damage deposit and a month's rent in advance and split. That was the way of life in America.

I returned to the floor where my job had been. I was hoping to say goodbye to Boss Margaret, but she wasn't around. My cubicle and the whole warren of work stations was gone, dismantled and replaced by an open space now being furnished with exercise equipment. The only feature that remained was the glass office where Margaret had overseen her flock of computer jockeys. She would no doubt be replaced by a professional trainer who advised employees how to lift weights without wrecking their backs.

I left the place with a sense of loss and even nostalgia. It had been fun, especially when I hooked up with the cloud. I didn't look in on Grabich. He hadn't been made redundant by an AI program. For the time being, at least, his job was safe.

I realized that my relationship with Grabich had been superficial, built around chats in the break room. True, we had invited him for a cookout on our patio, and he had given me insights to the dark web. I was wary that he might ask for money from our bitcoin wallet. It was one of those relationships where people use one another without real friendship. With me out of my job at Krieger, I was no longer a potential asset.

I guess it was the reality that in America you are what you do and if you no longer do it, you are a nobody. My father is retired and said he was once asked "What were you when you were somebody?" So what was I? Unemployed.

At least, as long as the bitcoin wallet existed, I wasn't broke. What happened with that depended on my search for Angel.

When I got home a message on the answering machine. said the DNA genome was ready. I could download it.

I would have preferred getting the report on a disk or flash drive. In spite of firewalls and encryption, anything that was transmitted was not secure.

While the genome was being downloaded, I phoned Hamburg. Hamburg was six hours later than Cleveland, but Inspector Hintz was still in his office, working late.

It took him a moment to switch to English. "Ah, Herr Goldschtein. How are you?"

"*Gut*," I said, practicing my alleged German. "I have a DNA genome report taken from the envelope I was sent by Angel. Now I need to compare it with German records and look for a match."

Hintz was hesitant, apologetic. "Our DNA records are not so *gross*." He told me how to access the German data base, but being Metadata Man I already knew that. I was just trying to keep Hintz up to date. I wanted to be in his good graces. You never knew when you needed a friend with the police.

"My wife and I will probably go to Germany."

"Do you zink zat is necessary?"

He did not sound welcoming. My presence might be an infringement on his territory. Maybe he saw me as an uninvited guest, a foreign meddler in his business..

"I am working with a US Government agency," I explained, hoping my official status would satisfy him.

He was tactful enough not to ask which agency. Just as well; I wasn't so sure myself. Speerson had worked for a number of agencies. He had enough contacts and access to pull many strings, a man of many hats..

"When I locate the person I believe is Angel can I count on you to help?" I was gambling that Hintz, being a Hamburg cop, had so many criminal cases and potential terrorism suspects he might welcome a change to international money laundering.

I must be dreaming. Hamburg's Reperbahn red light district with prostitution and drugs would be more exciting than the tedium of trolling the dark web for suspicious numbers. That kind of work was more suitable for a computer jockey drudge like me.

"Depends on where your case goes," Hintz said, which wasn't an offer.

I got the point. Ursula and I would be on our own unless something in his area of urgent interest came up.

He wasn't finished. "It was helpful you led us to your uncle's killer. You are a person of interest, Herr Goldschtein."

Did I misunderstand him? Did he mean an interesting person? A person of interest could mean I was a suspect. Thanks a lot.

"So I should warn you," he added. "We are not the only ones watching you."

And I thought Harvey Goldstein was watching everybody. Yeh, right. What goes around comes around. The watcher is watched.

I hung up and turned to Ursula who was listening on the speaker phone. "I think we are not the only ones looking for Angel. Someone must be letting me do the work for them."

Everything on the internet was so transparent. What was clear was we had to get to Angel first. I might search the German DNA archives from home, but there was no substitute for a face to face encounter.

It reminded me of Uncle Julius. He'd said I was so lucky, keeping tabs on people from my work station, but in the end, there was no substitute for standing in the rain in a trench coat and floppy fedora, as he said, needing to take a piss..

I was stressed out again. Just so I didn't relapse. Dr. Halal would want to get his hooks into me. I started shaking, held my hands over my ears.

Ursula diagnosed me immediately. "Take it easy, honey. Here." She took my hand away from my face and pressed it against her breast.

It was a distraction. "What?"

She grinned, a wicked salacious grin. "See that? A man doesn't have enough blood to operate both brain and penis at the same time. Any time you get overstressed by all those conflicting stimuli, think of sex."

I kissed her, one of those long, deep smooches that lead to other territory. "You are my medicine. Dr. Halal, eat our heart out." I sure wasn't going to smooch him.

"Stick with me, liebchen, and you will be OK."

Liebchen. I would have to add that to my rudimentary German vocabulary.

Chapter twenty-two

Just as I was capable of shadowing someone on the internet, others had the same capability to shadow me. People who live in glass houses shouldn't run around naked. I knew privacy was an archaic concept. How could anyone keep a secret what with NSA snooping phone calls and emails and CCT cameras almost everywhere? You could switch off your cell phone and remove the battery to avoid being tracked, at least for now. There were rumors that we would soon all be chipped with GPS locators.

Granted, it required massive computing power to keep tabs on everyone but computers were more powerful than ever and cloud storage of the information was infinite. I saw my own metadata powers, such as they were, as obsolete.

I could hope that the systems could be overloaded. Maybe I should track sun spots for the possible disruption of the satellites. Could create a window for me to get ahead of whoever might be following us. Then again if sunspots blocked someone else, they would block me, too. Nothing accomplished.

I got down to business to run a comparison of the genome extracted from the DNA left on the licked flap of the envelope Angel sent. My computer is no Cray. I handed over the genome and the German files to the cloud for faster computing.

Germans were known to be filophiliacs, obsessed with files. That's how we knew they'd murdered six million Jews, all those prisoners with tattooed numbers on their arms, all duly noted in the books now stored in Nuremberg. How many DNA samples did the Germans have on file?

I set the search in motion and we went to bed, letting the cloud do its thing. I lay beside Ursula, unable to sleep. I speculated. "I don't think the genomes the lab extracts are complete. There are fragments."

Ursula cuddled close to me, a deliberate distraction. She knows my hot buttons. "Go to sleep."

I awoke to a grey dawn. It was raining. I had covered the outdoor grill and the heavy drops made a reassuring sound. There was a world out there. I was not entirely lost in a stream of data.

I took a shower to wash the sleep out of my system and stood in the kitchen by the coffee machine, impatient as my cup filled. Then I took it to my desk where the computer had gone to sleep thanks to the power saver. One click and it woke up.

So did I.

Ursula, still in her pajamas with the panda bear pattern, looked over my shoulder. "Any results?"

"Looks like six possibles, probably near relatives, and two probables. So far no exact matches."

"Can you get addresses? Names?"

"Depends on how recently the data was collected."

Ursula got her own coffee, added milk. "The facial recognition program got you how many? Three? All different names, and all supposedly dead."

"Not quite all." I selected two files and printed them out. "One is in Hamburg, or was. The other is in Stuttgart."

"Could they be the same person?"

"Unless there are identical twins."

"Do you think Angel has a twin?"

"We'll have to find out. Let's notify Detective Inspector Hintz and make a plane reservation."

"And your Mr. Speerson, too."

I didn't trust Speerson, but agreed. We were on our way.

Chapter twenty-three

Fortunately, our passports were still valid. The EU, in retaliation for the president's ban on people from certain countries, had threatened to reinstate the old visa system. When Ursula and I made our trip to Europe our American passports were good almost anywhere for up to a three month stay without a visa. Now it looked like every border crossing required paperwork, a visit to a consulate, an application, and God knows what interrogation.

The world was afraid of terrorists. As if you'd get a straight answer to, "Are you a terrorist?" from someone who really was one. It was almost enough to consider blowing up some rude consulate officer.

Once an American passport had been as good as gold. Now it was tainted. Maybe, as an American Jew, I should apply for dual citizenship and an Israeli passport. It would be good almost anywhere except Saudi Arabia. Would I have to make alyah, spend time picking oranges or feeding chickens at a kibbutz? Learn Hebrew?

Maybe I could use my Speerson connection to get some sort of free pass diplomatic authority to get around the visa requirements. I knew from his employment history and resume that the man had connections.

Ursula paid a visit to the school superintendent's office to ask for a leave of absence. They had already said her German class would be cancelled. If she came back after a long absence, her substitute might have inherited what was left of her job. At this point, reminding me that technically we were filthy rich on bitcoins, she no longer cared.

Ursula had made all the reservations for our previous vacation trip. Confident that our bitcoin account would not simply disappear, she booked one way tickets from Cleveland's Hopkins International airport to Hamburg. I'd read about some incredibly cheap fares, no leg room, plus extra fees for baggage, no meals. Even a bottle of water would cost five bucks.

Nuts to that. We would fly first class. No cheap charter flight this time, but who cared? Thanks to Angel we were millionaires—on paper. Just so we wouldn't be stranded in Germany if the wallet disappeared into the dark web.

I'd been stranded once in Utah without my identity, no credit card, almost no cash.. I didn't want to go through that again. I had hitched rides back to Cleveland on Krieger delivery trucks. No such trucks drove trans Atlantic. Anyway, I wasn't a Krieger employee any more.

It wasn't summer any more, either. This time we would have to pack warm clothes. How long would we be away? If she or he wasn't dead we might find Angel in a few days and be done with it. Then again, if she were elusive as the trail of reported dead women with the same face, who knew?

We were heading out into the unknown. The only address of any sort of relative we had in Europe had been for Uncle Julius, and he was dead. We knew nobody in Germany.

We were like people who go hiking in the woods. Best to leave a note on the dashboard saying where we were going and when we expected to return. As a safety precaution I called Agent Walker at the FBI office and Speerson, gave them our plane reservations, but no Hamburg address.

Speerson was cautious. "Before you go you'll need to be briefed. I'll come to your place with some useful information. When you do get to Europe check in at the nearest US Embassy or consulate so they know who you are and why you are there. Just in case."

"In case of what?"

There was a pause. "In case you disappear."

Disappear? I was scared already.

"Do you want to be chipped?"

"No thanks." He was talking about my having a GPS locator embedded somewhere in my body. This was no longer science fiction. I didn't want to be watched that closely, liked a felon wearing an ankle bracelet. It was more than enough that Ursula's cell phone was tracked. That was how Homeland Security found out we'd visited Uncle Julius, the old Stasi colonel.

This was all starting to look like some CIA black operation. Hell, I was only trying to locate Angel.

We were already packed and ready for our departure the next evening when Speerson showed up with a heavy briefcase. He was wearing a brown leather bomber jacket and slacks, not the suit I'd seen him in at the FBI office.

Speerson had not been in our condo before. He assessed the living room with its Ikea couch, coffee table, and flat screen TV. He viewed the television with suspicion. "You should locate the hidden camera in your TV and put some tape over it."

I didn't realize our TV might be watching us, shades of Winston Smith in 1984. "How do we do that?"

"Make the room dark and shine a bright light on the screen. It will show what's behind it."

I suddenly realized that I shouldn't walk around naked in front of the television. Ursula and I better not make out on the couch for fear of showing up on U-Tube. You never knew who might be watching or what they did with the pictures. I could hardly restrain myself from looking for that camera right away.

Ursula fetched a bath towel from the john and hung it over the TV.

"Let's go into the kitchen," I suggested. I wanted to escape the TV. Maybe it could listen, too.

I was already so skittish I was suspicious of the microwave. What about the kitchen radio? The refrigerator? I was afraid to ask. If my refrigerator was watching me, did it report to the dishwasher? Speerson might think I was goofy.

Speerson followed us into the kitchen and opened his briefcase. He took out a dark blue Vinyl folder and showed is a couple of pictures. "These are two known hackers. Krisha, the one on the left, is Russian, so you are not likely to run into him. The other one is Vladimir, a Bulgarian. With the open borders, he might turn in Germany. In any case, they have friends we don't know."

I didn't think hackers would be dangerous. They would be like Grabich, stay at home hermits glued to their monitors.

"It's not the hackers themselves I'd be worried about," I said. "It's the people they stole from. Angel in turn stole from them."

"Find her first. She'll lead you to the hackers."

Seemed reasonable.

Speerson wrote something on the back of his business card. "If you get in trouble, call this number."

He was reluctant to tell us any more.

Ursula watched him drive off in a black SUV. "I don't trust him."

"I don't, either."

So off we went, like Hansel and Gretel, into the European woods. Would we find the witch? Would someone else find us?

Chapter twenty-four

Even leaving the country on an international flight is getting to be more of a hassle. Ever since ISIS figured out how to make a laptop into a bomb, they can't be carried on. Checked computers have a tendency to disappear so I needed to back up my data. Ursula fixed me up with a new German password, allegedly more difficult to break than the common asdfjkl; or 12345678 but just to be on the safe side a bought a terabyte flash drive to carry in my pocket. It has all that DNA culled by the lab from Angel's envelope. If the laptop took a walk, I could buy another and load it with data from the flash drive.

We were wanded, groped, and ex-rayed before we could board the international flight. A few hours of fitful attempts to sleep. Arriving jet lagged and numb, at the other end we were interrogated. Did we look like terrorists? When we arrived in Europe clearing customs was more formal than it had been in the past. Then one was simply asked a routine question, had a chalk mark checked on our luggage and were waved through. That's what we'd experienced when we arrived at Schlipol in Holland last summer on the charter flight.

German customs was more formal. The official looked at the mostly blank pages of my passport, made sure my face matched the photograph, and said, "Welcome back, Mr. Goldstein." At least he got the pronunciation right.

I was almost out the door when I thought, 'Wait. Our passport wasn't stamped when we left Germany to catch our charter flight out of Holland, and not when we entered Germany on the train from Copenhagen. Maybe he recognized my face after all that "Harvey Goldstein is Watching You" nastiness, like I was some kind of celebrity or movie star. Or maybe he was forewarned by Detective Hintz. It was getting hard for me to be incognito.

On our first trip to Europe we did it the cheap way with a charter flight and rail pass, so traveled with back packs. This time we were First Class and rented a car from Hertz. It turned out to be a Volkswagen diesel, no doubt unfit for export to the USA without having the emissions controls updated to telling the truth.

We showed our driver's licenses and Visa card, signed the rental contract. Ursula handled all that, even though the clerk spoke fluent English. I said I was afraid I wouldn't be able to read German road signs for "bridge out." The truth was I was nervous about the inevitable flood of stimuli on my overworked brain. I was afraid I'd relapse into some kind of catatonic withdrawal, hiding in the back seat with my head under a towel. I let Ursula be the driver.

She didn't look like she was ready. The VW was unfamiliar. We had never driven in Hamburg and knew only the railway station and the building where we'd met Uncle Julius. I would never have puzzled out the GPS in German.

Ursula started the engine, entered the location of the hotel on the GPS and we were at the mercy of an electronic gadget.

I remembered Herbie, the self-driving car that had taken me from the Salt Lake City airport to the cloud company. One day we'd all be passengers and not drivers. I asked, "You ready for this, honey?"

"If it's too exciting for you, Metadata Man, just cover your eyes."

"Thanks a lot." But she was right. Jet lagged and dopy I wasn't ready for all those foreign stimuli.

We were off into the stream of Hamburg's busy traffic.

She had made a reservation at a Marriott because it provided parking but didn't realize how expensive parking was. It was enough to make me wish we were taking public transportation or even a taxi.

I had to keep reminding myself that we were bitcoin rich. Screw the parking fees. Old frugal habits die hard.

 I would have preferred a real German hotel or even a B&B run by a retired couple, but that took time to arrange. You don't see a foreign country by going to the American places like KFC and Burger King. I reminded myself that we were not tourists this time. We were sort of amateur detectives.

I instinctively looked for the CCT cameras and waved. I didn't give the CCT camera the middle finger salute for I didn't know who was watching the monitors.

The Marriott desk clerk instantly spotted us as Americans and addressed us in English. Insisting on speaking German Ursula checked us in, filled out the registration card, took charge of the two magnetic key cards.

The room was on the fourth floor, clean, decently furnished, and had a good bed. We fell into it. The room might have been in Cleveland, so American. What did I expect for two hundred euros a night?

Just to be on the safe side, following Speerson's advice, I took a guest towel from the bathroom and hung it over the TV screen. All we needed was a good bed to sleep off our jet lag. We'd been traveling all night

My brain, mercifully, switched off. I'd barely kicked off my shoes before I passed out.

A few hours later the phone rang.

Who knew we were there? Inspector Hintz, of course. I guessed he must have seen the hotel registration cards, was tipped off, or had been watching Ursula's messages to make the reservation.

We had drawn the heavy curtains to make the room dark. I didn't know what time it was. I'd forgotten to reset my watch for German time. "What time is it?"

Hintz replied, "It's Tuesday afternoon. Four o'clock. Did you have a good flight?"

I grunted an uh-huh.

Hintz got down to business. "What progress have you made?"

I sat up, rubbed my eyes and protested. "We just got here."

Ursula rolled over and tried to sit up, stiff. "Who is it?"

"The German police inspector."

Mumbling, "He sure doesn't waste any time," Ursula got up and headed for the toilet and a shower.

I remembered the Hamburg address we had for one of the possible DNA matches. My pronunciation wasn't very good, but Hintz figured it out. "It is near the botanical gardens. Before you go there, Herr Goldschtein, we should have a dinner to discuss your plans."

"I have to check in at an American consulate."

"Ah."

That could mean a lot of things, like "ah, so?" or "That confirms my suspicion."

"But maybe not until tomorrow," I suggested. "Dinner is OK." I realized I was hungry. We'd had breakfast on the plane, being First Class passengers. That was hours ago.

"I'll pick you and your wife up at your hotel in two hours. Does zat give you enough time?"

So he knew Ursula was with me. I was beginning to feel like my life was an open book.

I had the uncomfortable feeling that I was a person of interest and everything we did was on film someplace. I told myself to get used to it. Homeland Security via the German police had tracked us to Uncle Julius's address thanks to her cell phone call, conveniently recorded and, for all I knew, the GPS of the taxi that took us there. I was beginning to feel like a celebrity who can't scratch his ass without some paparazzi selling the photo to a gossip magazine.

I hung up and called to Ursula in the shower, "We're having a meal with Hintz. He'll pick us up."

I changed out of the clothes I had slept in on the plane, had a shower,. and got out the laptop to study the Google map of Hamburg.

There's no such thing as a free lunch. What did Hintz want?

Chapter twenty-five

We had hardly reached the entrance to the hotel and stood under its glass canopy when Detective Hintz arrived. It was raining and cold, a chill wind off the Elbe. Klaus Hintz picked us up in an unmarked, black SUV that might have been a personal, private car, except for the extra antennas on the roof and the computer monitor in the front seat.

I must have a guilt complex. Getting into the back of a police car gives me the willies. I checked the back seat to see if the windows had handles and if the doors could be opened from the inside. I didn't want to feel like I was a prisoner. At least this car didn't have a grating behind the driver in case whoever in the back seat had murderous impulses.

Mercifully Hintz didn't broach the subject until we had settled at the table of a mid-priced German restaurant. You can tell by the table setting what the prices might be. This one had paper place mats with photos of Hamburg sights, no water glass of course, this being Europe where people don't drink tap water. My assumption was that, unlike Speerson and Walker who had no doubt been enjoying government per diem for their meal when we ran into them at Al's Steak House, Germany was not as generous.

I had dry mouth, a sign of anxiety. If I wanted a drink of water I'd have to order a bottle of something fizzy at an inflated price.

Menus in a foreign language can be distressing for me. I'm afraid I'll order the manager with extra fries. Being Metadata Man is bad enough when your brain is so active that it absorbs everything and can't sort it out fast enough. Ursula translated the menu for me and I ordered something called a Rumpsteak with red cabbage and boiled potatoes. No salad. An American restaurant like the Olive Garden would have plied us with bread and a huge salad. I knew from past experience there would be no free refills on the coffee.

Ursula ordered some sort of fish that turned out to be herring. Hintz ordered something called a Belegtes brot, which turned out to be a stack of mixed cold meats. And beer, of course.

I was leery of the high octane German beer and ordered something lighter, a Danish Karlsberg green. I'd had that when we were in Copenhagen.

It was all getting to be too much for me. I sat with my hands over my eyes to blot out some of the external stimuli.

Hintz noticed. I heard him ask Ursula, "Does he always do that?"

Ursula explained. "Sensory overload. Harvey isn't autistic. He's just too receptive. It overwhelms him."

Klaus Hintz had not seen me before or observed my odd behavior. This revelation caused him to revise his original assessment of me. He had to reboot before getting to the point. "As I understand, Herr Goldschtein, you are still looking for someone called Angel."

It was still Herr Goldschtein. I would have preferred Harvey and Klaus, but I remembered Ursula had explained you did not use first names until you'd been "dusened" which was a formal custom. One was supposed to lock arms and drink a slug of beer together which put you on a first name buddy-buddy basis. That was the difference between Sie and Du, something we don't do in American English. We don't usually talk to each other in the third person, like "Does the Detective care to order?"

Did I have to address him as Detective Hintz? I uncovered my eyes and focused on the issue. "Yes. This time we have DNA analyzed from saliva used to seal an envelope mailed from Germany."

He was impressed.

Carefully choosing my words, I added, "Of course the DNA was fragmented, incomplete, but we have several possibles."

"Who did the analysis for you?"

"A private, commercial lab."

Hintz was puzzled. "Why are you doing this? It must be quite expensive."

That was a fair question, a question I had not really asked myself. I could say it was a lark, or that since I had just lost my job I needed something exciting to do, but those were not the real answers. I dodged with, "It's part of a wider investigation of international hackers."

"With what agency?"

Ursula broke in. "We're not at liberty to say." It was another way of saying we don't know or none of your beeswax.

Hintz didn't like that. He would have to speculate on his own. "That could be dangerous."

"That's why I called you," I said. "It helps to have a friend with the police."

He wasn't ready to accept my claim to his friendship. He cocked his head to one side and sipped his beer, daubed at his mouth with a paper napkin. "So you want our assistance but won't say who you are working with."

Ursula admitted. "It's not clear exactly what agency it is."

"CIA?"

I shrugged, not knowing. "The United States is a police state. You never know what branch you might be dealing with."

"Yet you have come to Germany anyway not even knowing who you are working for?" He laughed. "You are babes in the woods."

I was embarrassed. "We just want to locate the person called Angel. That's all."

"What will you do if you find this person? Arrest her? You are not police."

"We'll inform my sponsor," I said, not having a better answer. "This may be something bigger than a single hacker."

"You should be careful. You don't know what you may fall into."

I took a deep breath. My brain was starting to work overtime again. I needed to simplify. "I think this Angel is someone who works alone and discovered some other hacker who stole an awful lot of money. I don't think there's more to it than that." I hoped.

"Don't be so sure." Hintz shuffled in his chair and leaned closer across the table. "We are investigating much internet criminality. For example, the Russians who decided your last presidential election."

I caught the dig at our damaged Democracy's ability to elect a president without foreign help. "That's out of our league. We're just looking for one person."

Hintz shook his head. "You never know where these things lead."

That left me with a host of possibilities I didn't want to think about, like being kidnapped and held for ransom until we paid back the bitcoins, or simply killed. I wasn't James Bond with a toolkit of secret weapons or training in how to kill with one finger.. All I had was data. That's me, Metadata Man, for what it was worth.

You could be killed for data if you knew too much..

I turned to Ursula and whispered, "Let's pay the tab for the meal. I don't want to be beholden to this guy."

Detective Hintz was surprised when Ursula picked up the check. "What is your next step?"

"We have an address here in Hamburg and another in Stuttgart, what we had before. It's a start."

Hintz knitted his brows. He remembered. "I told you both of those were reported dead."

"If they were real. Could be stolen identities. Con artists check the graveyards and pick a name they impersonate."

Hintz knew the method. "Get the birth certificate of a child that died young and use that identity."

Ursula was skeptical. "That only gets you to a dead person."

"We have to pursue every lead."

Hintz doubted we would get anywhere, but suggested, "If you need back up, you have my number."

"And you have mine," Ursula held up her cell phone. "You always know where we are."

Being tracked by a cell phone's ping might be an invasion of privacy, but there were advantages.

Klaus Hintz returned us to the Marriot in the unmarked police car. We retired to our room to make plans for the next day. We had one address in Hamburg.

Chapter twenty-six

The next morning we found the American Consulate and I checked in, told the receptionist that we were to stay in Hamburg a couple of days at the most, were at the Marriott. Not many tourists bother to register unless it's in a dangerous country. Only when I said if there was any problem Speerson was to be informed. I provided his phone number. That got the receptionist's attention. There was a suspicious hesitation.

It looked like we might have to talk to someone more official, but we hurried out. Next stop, the alleged address of the alleged Angel.

I was nervous about navigating Hamburg, reading all those unfamiliar, German signs, and glad Ursula was driving. At least the VW had its own built-in GPS. She easily managed the instructions and entered the address.. I said, "It sure helps to have a smart wife. Where would I be without you?"

She game me a knowing smile. "Lost."

How true. At least Europe has international road signs, not like the United States. My German lessons were continuing. Ursula explained that "Einbahnstrasse" meant one way street. I had a lot to learn, was glad she was my navigator and guide. I might be Metadata Man, but she was the brains of our family. In my overstressed, over-stimulated state I was glad to let her take charge.

I could see that my Metadata Man skills could be a handicap. Often overwhelmed by data, at times I felt like an emotional cripple. I was dependent on Ursula to keep me on an even keel. Would she get impatient? Tire of being my baby sitter?

I began to regret that I had only my dumb track phone. Ursula's cell had a GPS app. With that we could never get lost. Otherwise I might have had to walk around with a folded street map, a compass, and a German-English dictionary.

For our search for Angel we had two clues in Hamburg, the one for the facial recognition program, allegedly for a dead person, and the genome, a possible match. We followed the German GPS voice to the address.

Even though I had been the Krieger watcher on all our customers, I still felt uncomfortable being followed myself. I knew that the VW GPS would record wherever we went. For all I knew, it would note if we broke a speed limit and would add a surcharge to the bill when we turned the car in.

I knew the GPS kept a continuous record of the car's location and speed. What I wondered about was whether it could be accessed by a third party. Just as a cell phone was constantly being tracked by the towers so calls could get through, some cars GPS systems could be used to locate the vehicle if stolen.

Harvey Goldstein could access those records. Could anybody else? Well, probably Detective Klaus Hintz or anybody else on the police force, but who else?

Were we being watched?

If we'd had time I would have preferred public transport. It was more innocuous, but in a world of CCT cameras, and GPS tracking, we could not avoid being traced and tracked. My face was well known.

Hamburg had been firebombed during the war. It had been an experiment: first wave of bombers dropped high explosives to blow out all the windows. Second wave dropped incendiaries. Had to be done during a high pressure weather pattern so the result was a firestorm that melted asphalt streets, sucked out all the oxygen, and suffocated people in the bomb shelters, precursor to the devastating raid on Dresden. Hamburg had since been rebuilt. Uncle Julius's apartment block had been an early replacement.

The address we had was, as Hintz had said, near the botanical gardens in what had once been a middle class neighborhood of four story apartment buildings with shops on the ground floor, no elevators. It had been rebuilt in the original architectural style with small balconies overlooking the quiet street.

I hesitated at the entrance, read the names beside the door. The entrance had a panel listing residents. You had to press a button and be buzzed in. None of the names looked like they might be the one we wanted.

I had a copy of Angel's photo on the gamble that whoever we met would be her. Ursula asked, "What will you say if she's here?"

I shrugged. "Might not have to say anything. She knows my face. The whole world knows Harvey Goldstein."

"Don't flatter yourself."

263

The only button to push without guessing was one marked Portwacht, which Ursula explained was the concierge.

We were buzzed in..

The concierge's office was right inside the entrance. I guessed that the job came with a small apartment. It was a system created by Napoleon who, at every entrance, put a watchman. The porter would keep tabs on who came and went. It was part of a national spy system, neighbors watching neighbors, precursor to the Stasi and Uncle Julius

Besides sacrificing the cream of French manhood in his disastrous campaign against Russia, Napoleon had achieved lots of social change. He not only introduced a nationwide secret police network of informants, he also demanded that everyone had a surname. Jews who had names like Nathan the son of Michael suddenly had to have a family name. Anti-Semitic officials made Jews take family names like Tannenbaum, Christmas tree. I don't know what country my ancestors in Europe came from, but at least we got the name Goldstein and not Dumbkopf.

We were greeted by an elderly women with neatly coiffed grey hair and a pink plastic flower over her right ear, an echo perhaps of more flirtatious days. She said something in German.

I don't know what Ursula told her but she nudged me and I took out the photo. "Have you seen someone who looks like this?"

She gave the picture a long look before turning to me and answering in halting English. "Are you *polizei?*"

'No."

"Family?"

"We owe her some money."

The woman made a face like she'd tasted something nasty. "She leave and not pay rent.. Maybe you pay her bill?"

"When did she leave?"

"Last August."

She did not know where Angel had gone. No forwarding address.

Ursula asked, "What name was she using?"

"Hilda Platzbecher. Is that who you look for?"

"We just need to find her."

"Sorry." At that moment the phone rang and she turned away. Before she disappeared, she added, "You are not the first to look for Fraulein Platzbecher. Two men here last week."

Before I could ask who they were, she was gone and the door closed.

I was not about to leave. We knocked at her door to get her back.

She returned, obviously losing patience. I told Ursula, "Ask her about the two men, description, ages, nationality."

She did and got a surprisingly detailed description. I guess if you are the concierge it is your job to be observant.

I was dying of suspense, not understanding what the old woman said. I remembered Klaus Hintz's warning.

Back on the street I stood beside the Volkswagen while Ursula unlocked it. "We better give Detective Hintz a heads up on this. We're not the only ones looking for Angel."

"And the others are ahead of us."

"Call him." She did and got his voice mail. "Two men were also looking for Angel. Foreign looking, spoke poor German with Slavic accents, possibly Polish. Maybe Russian. Wore overcoats. " She turned to me. "The old lady remembered the Gestapo dressed like that. Memories from her childhood."

"She told you all that?"

"Just a hint. Her parents had hidden Jews during the war and were arrested."

"Everybody has a story."

Ursula nodded. "I figured you could relate to that.".

I didn't need to be reminded. We are all Holocaust survivors. Jews have long memories. We remember the expulsions and the pogroms, the Inquisition. "Ask Hintz if he has anything on Hilda Platzbecher."

As soon as we got back to the hotel WiFi I'd see what I could learn myself.

Before we drove off I instinctively looked for a CCT camera. As Metadata Man I could access and review the records for the previous week. No camera. Shucks.

"We'd better get on the road to Stuttgart."

Chapter twenty-seven

We returned to the hotel and its free Wi-Fi connection. I booted up my laptop and searched for Platzbecher. Why was I not surprised when I found the girl by that name had died at the age of ten. This was another of Angel's false identities. There was no DNA record for that child. She'd died before the genomes had been discovered, another dead end.

I didn't find a national health record, either, and no bank accounts under that name. German DNA records were sparse and had not been cataloged, no cross references. What identity was she using now?

We did have her genome. She was of German-Scandinavian descent. Would have what Hitler had described as Nordic features, blond, blue-eyed. But she also had some genetic defect I wasn't certain of. Mutations occur by accident and may be recessive, not passed on to offspring. Angel might be a one-off, possibly Downs syndrome. I'm no geneticist and have no medical background. Number crunching does give you a limited view of the world. Just having a lot of data doesn't automatically provide wisdom or insight.

Was I like Rain Man in the movie, able to count cards in blackjack but not make change for a dollar? I hoped not.

We checked out, putting everything on the Visa card including that pricy parking fee. When the trip was over we'd cash in bitcoins to pay the bills. If I had enough chutzpah I'd give Speerson the receipts and see if we'd be reimbursed. Not for the first class air tickets, I was sure. The best his government agency might spring for would be business class. Or it might be for nothing. Like Mama always said, "If you don't ask you don't get."

Stuttgart is a helluva a long way south of Hamburg. Ursula entered the Stuttgart address in the VW's GPS and let the German voice guide us to the autobahn. It sent us west toward Holland until the highway split off for the south. Traffic was basically local until the turn off and then... well, fasten your sea belts, folks.

Turns out there's no speed limit on the autobahn. Hitler had it built to facilitate blitzkrieg. The super highway made it possible to move tanks and troops quickly. When Eisenhower saw the German autobahn during

World War II he was inspired to build our own Interstate highway system.

Driving a leisurely eighty five miles an hour, we had to stay out of the passing lane to make way for BMWs doing over a hundred. You think you are OK passing a truck at sixty but behind you comes a screaming speeder flashing lights. Get out of my way!

I was glad Ursula was driving. I may be Metadata Man but she has nerves of steel. I never suspected it. After all, in Cleveland if we did over forty it was a big deal.

I had to cover my eyes and didn't look until two hours later when we pulled off at a rest stop to refuel and decompress. In the past when Ursula and I traveled we packed stuff for sandwiches, but this trip hadn't had time to shop before leaving Hamburg.

Old habits die hard. I had to keep reminding myself that the prices in Germany were nothing to worry about. We were rich, thanks to Angel.

It was good to take a break, but I could not fully relax. Metadata Man kicked into gear. I started checking the license plates of other cars that had parked at the rest stop. Who owned that bright red Porsche, for instance?

Unable to restrain myself, I got my laptop out of our luggage and connected to the free wi-fi at the rest stop. Took only a minute to learn the Porsche was registered to a restaurant owner in Kassel, a Friedrich Schultz, who had to be the man in the sheepskin jacket sitting near the rest room. Figuring out that stuff gives me a sense of power and authority. I was tempted to go over and ask Mr. Schultz how he liked the Porsche, but that would be showing off. .

A small Mercedes SUV had pulled in right after us. A quick check of its registration told me it was a Hertz rental, same place where we got the Volkswagen in Hamburg. I suppose I could delve into the rental agency's data base. They would record the driver's name, license, home address and credit card number.

Ursula was impatient. "Why don't you cut that out? Eat your sandwich. You're snooping again."

I apologized. "Can't help it."

"You're getting obsessively compulsive."

"Sorry." I shut the laptop and went back to my sandwich and fizzy orange drink. I was hungry. That imitation of an American breakfast at the Marriott was long gone.

We tanked up with diesel, self-service with the Visa card, and we were off again, from the dead stop to a frantic ninety mph on the Autobahn speedway. It was starting to rain, making the spray from the trucks hazardous. I wished we had radar or maybe a Tesla with automatic braking.

At the next rest stop, this time for morning coffee and a pastry, Ursula noticed the Mercedes. It was traveling our same route. "Do you think they are following us?"

Again I got out the laptop. This time, between sticky bites of Bienenschtuck pastry, I connected to the Hertz car rental and the Mercedes. I gave Ursula a superior grin. "That car is rented by someone named Boris Gudenov."

"You're kidding. Boris Gudenov is the name of a Russian opera."

"Oh."

"Look him up, Harvey. You have his home address?"

I did. I went to Google World to find the address of the alleged Boris Gudenov, a street in a town that had been East Germany. "There's no such place."

Ursula scoffed. "Then I bet there's no real Boris Gudenov, either. What about his credit card?"

I checked. The Visa card was stolen.

"Whatever or whoever it is, it's not kosher."

That didn't mean the mysterious Boris was actually following us. The Mercedes was just part of the stream of south bound traffic. Maybe we should take another route just to find out.

"Let's got off the autobahn. Are we in such a hurry?" I was puzzling over her map. "Let's leave this madness and take the Rhine River highway. Should be scenic."

Ursula agreed. Belting along in the hundred mile an hour traffic was too white knuckled stressful. We left the Autobahn for the Rhine river highway.

This was an ancient water highway. The river was bustling with barge traffic. Unfortunately, the rain and mist along the river made it a rather dismal ride. I saw one of those Viking River Cruises long boats. Nobody sunbathing on deck at this time of year.

Every so often, if we could make it out without getting sore neck from looking up, we passed one of those castles that dominated the river traffic before Germany was unified. In the old days a river pilot had to run a gauntlet of castle toll collectors.

We passed the infamous Lorelei narrows but didn't see any Rhine maidens, just dancing channel buoys pressed over by the treacherous current.

When we stopped for lunch at a town I couldn't remember, there was the Mercedes again. Yes, we had company. Should I approach it? Tell "Boris" his cover was blown? Better not.

Instead I tried to get a good look at whoever was in the Mercedes. Actually they were two but when they got out of the car they weren't wearing sinister overcoats and floppy fedoras, just baseball caps and sport jackets like they were part of a soccer team.

Using Ursula's cell phone camera I took several shots of the two men, got passable facial pictures. Maybe they were in the facial recognition database.

"Boris" and his partner were subtle enough not to follow us into the restaurant where we had lunch. Unfortunately there was no wi-fi. I couldn't use my laptop to connect to the German national facial recognition data base. That might give me the real identities of the two, that is, if they were on record.

Uncle Julius, that old rascal, would be proud.

I'd have to learn how to use Ursula's smart phone. She could connect to cell phone tower signals; I was limited to wi-fi. Maybe It was time I got my own smart phone. I had resisted because I didn't want to be tracked. But of course, I was, we were, everybody was.

I told Ursula, "Call Hintz. Tell him what we've found out."

She was doubtful. "I don't think Detective Hintz will alert the Autobahnpolizei over a stolen credit card."

I'd seen one of those. The autobahn highway patrol had to drive souped up cars to be able to catch the speeders. At what speed? A hundred and fifty? I shuddered at the thought.

While we waited for our soup to be served, Ursula tried again to reach Detective Hintz.. Again voice mail. Maybe Hintz didn't want to be disturbed.

I would feel better if I knew Hintz was keeping track of our progress. Not that he could come to our rescue, as we drove farther and farther away from Hamburg. We were in a foreign country. We knew nobody.

I wasn't in my secure Krieger cubicle any more.

Chapter twenty-eight

I didn't mind that Ursula was doing the driving and making all our arrangements. I yielded to her language expertise and appreciated her taking the burden of dealing with all the details. She knew how fragile I was, how likely to break down from the overload of stimuli.

As she paid our lunch bill Ursula turned to me with a stern look. "Harvey."

I blinked, distracted by the restaurant's Teutonic décor. "What?"

"Do we really have to be doing this?"

"Doing what?"

She held my face between both hands. "Look at me. Do we really have to be hunting Angel? Why don't you just send her an email, ask her to meet us?"

"That would be too easy."

Now she was exasperated. "You're acing like Huckleberry Finn."

"How's that?"

"He wanted to take that raft all the way down the Mississippi so the slave Jim could be free when all he had to do was cross the river to Illinois. Illinois was a free state."

"Then he'd miss all that adventure."

"You're hopeless."

I admit I felt stupid. "It's a puzzle. You know how I like puzzles."

She shook her head. "No you don't. You don't do the crosswords or even sudoku."

She had me there.

"You just want to see if Metadata Man can track her down."

"I guess."

"That's an ego thing, Harvey."

I shrugged. "Harvey Goldstein is watching you." It was a lame excuse. "Humor me."

She sighed as we returned to the car. "Give me her email address. I'll send her a message myself."

I might had said it was cheating, but didn't want an argument. I was afraid if Angel knew we were closing in she'd disappear.

Driving through Germany on Speerson's dime was, well, fun. Stressful but, I hoped, it was exciting, playing cat and mouse with Boris whoever, just as long as we didn't meet face to face.

I had another idea. I didn't like being stalked by Boris I and Boris II. Maybe I should notify Hertz. I got out the rental agreement for the car for the Hertz number in Hamburg and used my track phone to call.

The clerk switched immediately to English when I said, "I think one of your rentals is stolen." I told her the license number and all the particulars of Boris. "The Visa card he used is stolen."

"How do you know that? Are you the polizei?"

"No. I am Harvey Goldstein."

She did not know Harvey Goldstein. Shucks. What good is being famous if nobody knows you?

"My wife Ursula rented the car we are driving. Ursula Goldstein."

That seemed to provide enough bona fides for the clerk who sounded pretty young, had learned American English, possibly in school. So what did we expect her to do?

"Can you track the Mercedes through its GPS?"

She could. Damn, everybody's watching everybody. Who needed Uncle Julius nowadays? Everybody could be his own detective.

It reminded me of the nanny dolls, those teddy bears with cameras that watched the family dog while everyone was at work, or the kid when parents thought a hidden camera was a substitute for a real baby sitter. Trouble was, nobody bothered to set a unique password for cell phone access to those nannies. Burglars could case a house without going inside.

When I was still at Krieger and reading Boss Margaret's Wall Street Journal in the break room, I'd read that in Germany the nanny dolls were considered spying and made illegal. Anyone with one could be fined, big time.

The Hertz clerk was almost convinced. After all, I had given her all that information, even the number of the stolen Visa card.

Maybe Hertz would notify the autobahn highway patrol to flag down Boris. Made me feel pretty smart.

Off we went, further south.

Ursula was improving her own Harvey Goldstein skills. I had located the Mercedes GPS tracker on my laptop. Now she connected using her cell phone. There on the screen was a German map and on it a little moving car that was the Mercedes with "Boris" and his buddy. We knew where they were, at least, we knew where their car was.

I just hoped that they didn't have the same skills we had. It was looking like a computer game of Packman, only we didn't know which would eat the other first.

I suppose in the near future the Mercedes would be self driving. If we hijacked the controls we could send them to Berlin.

That gave me an idea. Was Boris driving, or had he set his GPS to take him someplace? Could I, by remote control, change the destination?

Not likely. We had a Stuttgart address. If he had it he would be there already. If he could hack into our rental's GPS why follow us when our destination was already entered? Otherwise there was no point in tailing us. He could beat us there.

Maybe Boris wasn't after Angel, but after us. That sent a shiver down my neck. I told myself, no, they could have forced us off the autobahn, pulled up alongside at a rest stop, robbed and shot us both—if that was their intention.

All that speculation sent my brain into another tailspin. It wasn't healthy for me to think too much. It was the metadata curse.

I didn't mention all this to Ursula. She had her hands full just driving. Roaring down the Autobahn in hundred mile an hour traffic is stressful. I hardly dared to look. She was tired. In a rest stop souvenir shop I bought some very dark sun glasses, not to shut down the glare as there was no sun, but to dim the stimuli which threatened to send me over the edge.

While I was shopping for sun glasses Ursula was fiddling with her cell phone. She said she wasn't going to be hooked on games and apps like most people who are glued to those tiny screens and likely to walk in front of a bus, but I had my doubts. What was she up to? Candy Crush?

Out of the blue, she suggested, "You need a break. We might as well do something touristy," she suggested. "I'll book a hotel in Heidelberg. I heard that's a beautiful place. The autobahn goes right near it. You watch my cell phone and see whether Boris stops there, too."

"Yes, boss."

She didn't mind the sarcasm. As long as she was the driver, she was in charge. Fine with me. I certainly wasn't capable of driving at those speeds,

Some time later, namely two coffee and pit stops on the autobahn, the Mercedes stopped moving.

Had they given up? Been stopped by the police? Abandoned the car? If they realized they'd been spotted and switched cars we wouldn't know who might be following us. Maybe, like us, they were just taking a breather.

Unfortunately, I couldn't stop. At each rest stop I made a note of all the other license plates, even the long haul trucks pulling two trailers like a train. Who drove that Renault? What about that Volvo with an export license plate?

It gave me a sense of superiority, knowing all that stuff, even if was useless information. Why did I keep on doing this? My brain was working overtime again. It was time to switch off. I didn't want to be a passenger with a towel over my head.

We could stop in Heidelberg for the night. Decompress, or so I thought.

Chapter twenty-nine

According to Ursula's smart phone, Heidelberg has over a hundred hotels ranging from a backpacker's hostel to deluxe. The Marriott in Hamburg had been too, well, American, so Ursula booked us the hotel Zum Alte Brucke right downtown. Luckily, there was parking, at least for one night.

We checked in, Ursula taking over even though everybody seemed to speak English. She had a discussion with the clerk in German. Why? Did she just want to practice?

I hung back, always the observer, absorbing the stimuli. Arm in arm, we set out on a walk of the main street of the old town. I got the impression that Ursula was hanging onto me, leading me like I was a kid who might, distracted, wander off, or maybe someone handicapped.

That would have been a fair assessment, for I tended to get dizzy from all the unfamiliar sights, the shop windows, the restaurants. I couldn't help checking license plates of cars on the street. Was this becoming an obsession? Or was it something I did just because I could do it?

Heidelberg is a historic city on the Neckar river. Its famous castle overlooks the town. Its ancient university is the locale for The Student Prince operetta.

Heidelberg is also the headquarters for USARUR, all US Military forces in Europe. That we have so much of our army and air force still in Germany so long after World War II must be a vestige of the Cold War. We thought Russia would march in from East Germany at any time. The Cold War is supposedly over, but we are still there. When you hear about casualties being evacuated from Afghanistan, they go to Ramstein air base.

I expected to see GIs in uniform. Where were they? Maybe they showed up in the evening or on the weekend. What did I know about the military? Only that the military industrial complex had taken over the country. We had troops in a hundred and seventy eight places around the world, like the old Roman empire, spread thin everywhere.

I had missed the Vietnam war and wasn't foolish or patriotic or desperate enough to sign up for the National Guard and get sent to Iraq because I couldn't find a job. Posted casualties on PBS often identified the dead as from some rural town where there were few opportunities other than the military.

So what did small town enlistees do in Germany when not on duty? Rural kids were not tourists. The GIs probably hung out in bars looking for women or stayed on base in the service clubs. Gomer Pyle would have loved it. I could just imagine. German beer was a lot stronger than my favorite Sam Adams. Party time.

Heidelberg looked prosperous, congested, and, being historical, very Germanic. Hamburg had been rebuilt after the war, but Heidelberg, not bombed, was authentically old.

According to Ursula's cell phone app, she said we had to visit the castle and its gigantic wine barrel, so big it had a dance floor on top of it.

I wondered what about a big wine barrel appealed to Ursula. We're not wine snobs. I'd have preferred to sit along the river and watch the barge traffic, but I went along to humor her.

Until we took the little funicular car up to the castle I didn't suspect a thing. Then I noticed Ursula was paying attention to the time. Were we in a hurry?

We paid admission to the castle in Euros and waited. "What's going on?" I asked. "There's something you're not telling me."

She gave me an evasive look. "There may not be anything to tell."

At the edge of the wall overlooking the river valley and the town, I grabbed her arm. "What is it?"

"I sent Angel an email saying where we'd be."

"The only possible address we have is in Stuttgart. This isn't Stuttgart."

"I don't know where she really is. You don't, either."

She? Then the photo we were sent was authentic.

I guessed, "So are we meeting someone?" That's the wonderful thing about being married to Ursula. There are always surprises.

"Maybe. Let's check out the wine barrel." The enormous cask, remembrance of a time when the keeper of the castle commanded the accumulated crop of his vassals, was in a gloomy cellar. It smelled of old wine-soaked oak. I half expected to see torture instruments from the Inquisition.

Ursula checked her watch and we stood, me feeling foolish on the miniscule dance floor built on top of the huge wine cask. I'd have danced, but there was no music.

Someone was laboriously climbing the wooden flight of steps. It was a very short woman in a shabby trench coat, the belt hanging loose. She had a disproportionately large head, thick, black hair that might have been a wig, and a somewhat familiar face. She was not a dwarf, but somewhere in between. Could it be?"

"Harfey Goldschtein," she said in a thick accent. It wasn't a question. She knew who I was.

"That's me."

Her short arm reached out to shake my hand in a snappy, Teutonic manner, a quick, firm grip and then gone. Did I detect a semblance of a curtsey, like children might be taught in the old days for meetings with somebody important?

"I'm Ursula." Another handshake. "Glad you could come."

"You can call me Ludmilla. That is not my real name. It is enough for now."

The dance platform was getting crowded. Other tourists had come to see the barrel. We went out of doors to talk in private.

For a change, the overcast had eased. Some sunshine broke through. Except for the haze, we could almost see the Neckar river valley all the way to what? Mannheim? Frankfurt?

I studied the woman's face, tried to imagine her with blond hair. "You're not Angel."

"Angel is her internet name. Her real name is Gunilla. We call her Gulli. I'm her sister."

That explained the resemblance. By then the copy of Angel's photo I carried had been folded so many times it was in danger of falling apart. I showed it to Ludmilla. "Is this Gulli?"

She studied it. "It is not a good photo. She has changed her hair. It is now brown."

I had to revise my memory, but I also knew that facial recognition programs depended more on spacing of the eyes, measurements of the nose, and so on. Hair color could be changed, but not how far eyes are spaced apart. "Do you have a recent photo of Gulli?"

She did, it was a selfie on her phone. Ursula copied it.

My mind went back to the DNA analysis. Short of stature had to be a family trait, but I didn't know how to read a genome. What good was all that information if you didn't understand it?

"Why are you looking for her?"

Ursula explained. "We think she is in danger." She went on to describe the car that had been following us, "Boris" and his partner.

That put a cloud over Ludmilla's face. "It's true?"

"We don't know for sure," I explained. "I just know that there's a rented Mercedes driven by someone using a false name and a stolen credit card."

She wasn't surprised. "I do not understand. You think Gulli is in danger and you come all the way from America?" The way she said it it was clear she thought I was being stupid. Maybe I was.

"Harvey is obsessive," Ursula explained, as if to apologize for my irrational behavior. "When he has a problem he has to solve it, get to the end. It's because of his job."

"His job?"

"My ex-job," I explained. "Data management."

Ludmilla shook her head, clearly in sympathy for my dilemma. She must have thought anybody absorbed with data management had to be pitied. "You would get along well with Gulli. She spends her time on the computer. She thinks she is amateur detective."

"Does she work with the police? Interpol?"

Ludmilla pursed her lips. "Gulli is her own person. She does not like police."

"She created a bitcoin account for me. Do you know about that?"

Ludmilla laughed. "Yes. She said something about it. A joke. A trick on some hackers."

Thinking about Boris and his pal, I didn't think it was funny. Angel, or Gulli, if that was her real name, worked alone. At least at Krieger when I got stuck I had Grabich to fall back on. "Do you know what hackers?"

She cocked her head from side to side, Indian fashion. "Perhaps some Russians."

If they were Russians they would be beyond our reach. I definitely was not going into Putinland to look for a hacker. That was the origin of the damage done to our presidential election. The Russian secret police had a way of poisoning people they didn't like, or, like what happened to Uncle Julius, throwing them out of fourth story windows.

Should I tell Ludmilla that we were working with Speerson and Detective Hintz of the Hamburg police? Probably not. "Gulli's skills are very valuable," I suggested. "She could be a real asset in catching international criminal hackers."

Ludmilla looked up at me and studied my face. "Gulli is a woman."

The way she said it explained a lot. To be a woman, and, if as small as her diminutive sister, she would literally be looked down upon, not respected, not taken seriously.

Ursula nodded. We both knew how sexism hindered women's careers. No wonder Gulli worked alone.

Ursula asked, "Can we see her?"

"She does not stay long in one place. Uses internet cafes and public libraries." Ludmilla gave us a sly smile. "She looks for unsecured wi-fi service."

She had to be a moving target. Ursula and I were conspicuous. We were easy to follow, all those CCT cameras and tracking possibilities, the cell phone, my little track phone, the GPS in our rental car. We could hardly hide from anyone.

"I will give you an address, but she is never anywhere for long." She wrote an address on the back of a grocery receipt. No business card. We knew only her pseudonym.

It was not the address my internet search had turned up. That was for one of those facial recognition identities, one Hintz said was reported dead. But it was still Stuttgart.

She declined an offer for lunch but suggested a restaurant by the old bridge. It was close to our hotel. We left her at the castle, took the funicular car back down to the main street.

Not far away Ursula spotted a bar. She had done her homework, wanted to see it. "That would be the Zum Zeppel," she said. "It's an old student hangout."

It was another of her surprises. The Zum Zeppel was a small place that had obviously not changed in hundreds of years. The wooden tables were carved with names that might have included Goethe. Overhead the place was decorated with stolen signs, like "Vorsicht bissiger hund" which Ursula translated as "Danger biting dog," and others that translated like "Don't spit on the floor," and so on. The place reeked with atmosphere and old student mischief. It also smelled of stale beer.

At that time of day we were almost the only customers. We got a table by the window overlooking the main street.

I ordered a Cola and Ursula, who seldom drinks beer, took a chance on a light beer, a Hellas. I didn't want alcohol making my brain any less focused. "I think I understand what Gulli was up to, arranging that bitcoin account."

"How's that?"

"The theft of high sums of money like the hacked Russian bank or Bangladesh attracts a lot of attention. Gulli doesn't steal it herself, but redirects it from the hackers' destinations. When my picture, Harvey Goldstein is watching you, showed up everywhere, that made me an easy target, a diversion. She wasn't just being generous to a fellow computer jock. She made me look like a hacker."

"You think that's why they're after you?"

"Sure. I'm a link. Find me and find whoever set up the bitcoin wallet. It's not going to be the original thieves. Gulli will know who they are."

Ursula thanked the waitress in a black apron that concealed a coin purse. We would pay when we left. In the meantime, our cardboard coasters got a pencil mark to keep track of what we ordered.

"What happens if Boris and his partner catch up with us?"

I tried to feel safe. "We're innocent. We don't know who stole the money in the first place." I gave her a feeble grin. "We don't know anything."

"Gulli does."

"Then they'll be after the original crooks."

"Not if they think Gulli is the hacker."

I sipped my Fanta cola. It was warm, sweet, and would have been better if it were beer. "There will be a lot of people after our bitcoins. The country they were stolen from. The hackers who lost it to Gulli. "

"And Speerson and Klaus Hintz. They are interested parties, too."

I was worried. "They want us to do the work for them." That gave us a lot to mull over.

Just then we were joined by a very drunk student with a bandage on the top of his head.

Not being partial to drunks, I would have avoided him, but Ursula was curious. She said something in German and his answer was a surprise. She explained, "He's been in a duel. They use swords called schlagers. If you duck you lose. He obviously lost."

"I thought dueling went out in the Middle Ages."

"Apparently not. This is Heidelberg."

The student wandered off. Presumably the winner was with pals. The loser drank alone in disgrace.

Once he was gone Ursula fiddled with her cell phone and reported, "In the olden days the duelists got a choice of a leather collar or goggles. The goggles avoided blindness and the leather collar a slit throat." She showed me a drawing.

279

I cringed. "Some blood sport. Let's check out Ludmilla's suggestion for dinner. Then a good night's sleep before we head for Stuttgart. Get an early start."

Chapter thirty

Ludmilla's was a good choice, a little restaurant called The Goldene Hecht, which Ursula explained meant the Golden Pike, table cloths, wine glasses and menus in German, of course.

"Here's something authentic for you. Wildschweinkotletter."

"What's that?"

"Wild boar chops. I guess they're hunted in the Black Forest."

I quipped, "Complete with tusks?" I had a brief image of a wild boar's head on a platter with tusks and an apple in its mouth. Fierce.

"No, Harvey, and not kosher, either, in case you're feeling Orthodox."

The tuxedo-clad elderly waiter was a pro, not one of those surly teen-agers on his first job. He was obviously proud of his skills and fussed over us, made us feel like his most important customers ever. What a treat!

We both ordered a red wine.

While we waited for our order I asked Ursula to check her cell phone. "See if the Mercedes is moving again."

She found it. "'Boris' and his partner are parked in the newer part of Heidelberg at the Holiday Inn Express hotel." She suggested, "When we've finished dinner, why not drive over there and see what they're up to? They've followed us. We can follow them."

"What? And just walk up and talk to them?"

"Be cool, Harvey. We can make up some excuse to introduce ourselves. Of course, Harvey Goldschtein Metadata Man doesn't need an introduction. The whole world knows you."

My gutsy wife! That made me more nervous than ever.

We paid the bill, noted that the tip was included, and fetched our rental car from the hotel space. Then it was over to the Holiday Inn Express.

I was glad Ursula had got us into a centrally located older hotel. The Holiday Inn Express was a white, sterile looking boxy building furnished in American minimalist. It had all the ambiance of a MacDonald's joint. A hospital might have been more inviting.

The GPS made it easy to locate the parked Mercedes, but the license plate had been changed. The car now had a Hamburg plate. "It's HH," Ursula noticed. "It's a Hamburg joke, Hummel-Hummel, moos-moos."

Not knowing the language always made me feel inadequate. "What's that mean?"

Ursula laughed. "It means kiss my ass."

"Not kush mir am tuchas?"

"German, not Yiddish."

The Holiday Inn Express wi-fi signal could be picked up in the parking lot. I got out my laptop and logged on. Took only a minute to identify the license plate. "The Hamburg license plate is stolen from a car that belongs to a Doctor Shultz. I wonder if he knows his plate is missing."

"Maybe Hertz called the highway patrol in response to your report. Boris switched plates. He could do that in a minute or two at a rest stop."

"Maybe we should play catch up," I suggested. "Let's check out the registration desk."

Unsure of what I was up to, Ursula tagged along as I approached the registration. I asked, "Do you have a Boris Gudenov staying here? He would be driving a rental Mercedes from Hertz."

The clerk, a blond kid whose hair threatened to hang over his eyes and a beginner's pale mustache, wasn't eager to give out any information about the guests. "Do you have some identification? Passport?"

"You must recognize me. I'm Harvey Goldstein. My face was on every screen: Harvey Goldstein is watching you?"

He didn't remember, which I have to admit was a little disappointing. I felt like a celebrity who had not been noticed. What did I expect? Paparazzi asking for autographs?

"Never mind me," I apologized. "The two men in the Mercedes are traveling under false names and using a stolen credit card. The number is," and I rattled off the stolen credit card number.

It was like a magic password. The kid was impressed.

"You can call Detective Klaus Hintz of the Hamburg police. Mention my name. He will confirm it." I gave the kid Hintz's number.

I turned to Ursula. "Let me see your cell phone."

She handed it over and after I asked for help got to the photos I had taken of the two men when they were at the rest stop. I showed the screen to the clerk. "Do you recognize these two men?"

To my relief, he did, but didn't remember their names.

"Show me on your hotel register."

It was not Boris Gudenov, but something Turkish and for me not pronounceable. To be on the safe side, I photographed the ledger. I didn't want to hang around the narrow lobby. As we left, I cautioned the clerk not to mention our visit, just call Hintz in Hamburg to give him a heads up,

The clerk didn't know what a heads up meant. Ursula explained it was a notice, a warning.

We retreated to the car and I got out my laptop, was able to connect with the hotel wi-fi signal. Sure enough. The faces were included in the German facial recognition database. It sure helps to be Metadata Man if you're not actually freaking out.

It was not Boris, of course. I showed Ursula the entry. "These guys are both small time criminals." Their rap sheets listed theft, burglary, stolen firearms, but—to my relief—no murders or fatal assaults. "They're first generation Turks. One is Burak and the other Ahmed. They're brothers. " I also had their birth dates and last known addresses from their arrest records. It made me feel really smart.

Ursula explained. "That means they can't be German citizens. Just being born here doesn't make you a citizen if your parents are foreign, especially Turkish."

If I was willing to wait around in the wi-fi range I could find out more. I was getting nervous. "Now we've poisoned their well. Let's get out of here."

I packed up the laptop and Ursula started the car. As we pulled away I noticed we were being observed. It was one of the Turks. He had recognized the car.

Back at our hotel room, I phoned Detective Klaus Hintz in Hamburg. This time I found him in. "We're being followed by a couple of Turks, small time criminals," I reported. "Burak and Ahmed. I got their rap sheets."

Hintz was impressed. "How did you get that?"

"I'm Harvey Goldstein." Like, isn't that explanation enough?

Hintz paused. I could almost hear him thinking, like tumblers in a combination lock, click, click. It was his keyboard. What he was doing was checking his own records. "Those two have been suspects as autobahn bandits. They probably spotted you at the Hamburg airport when you leased your car and followed you."

That reminded me of a Florida case. Crooks on the Miami freeway would spot rental cars by their stickers, bump them, which got people to stop, and then hold them up. As a result, the car rentals no longer put ID stickers on their cars.

"You say they're at the Holiday Inn Express in Heidelberg?"

"Yes."

"Well, unless they actually do anything we have little reason to pick them up. A stolen credit card is hardly worth our pursing them at this stage. We have more important people to watch, Herr Goldschtein. We have our hands full from terrorists."

"I suppose if Barak and Ahmed rob us you'll have grounds to go after them." I hoped he heard my sarcasm.

He didn't admit it, but I could tell it was true. Thanks a lot. Maybe if they kidnapped or killed us Hintz would get more serious. To him Ursula and I were just a couple of amateurs who would be better off taking pictures of churches and castles.

I could continue my research. Hintz might be right. Why did I, in my paranoia, always fear the worst? It could be a coincidence. Barak and Ahmed might just be joyriding in a stolen car and having a vacation on someone else's credit card. As for being spotted, well, tit for tat. They had followed us. Now they knew we were following them. Did they suspect they were dealing with Metadata Man? They couldn't know Ursula and I could track their car's GPS on her phone.

First things first. It was best to get on with the business of finding Gulli and learning where she got the money for the bitcoin wallet.

As for Barak and Ahmed, my uncontrolled metadata curiosity might turn up any number of shady characters along the way. I just couldn't help it.

Chapter thirty-one

I slept pretty well. I briefly felt like a tourist instead of an amateur detective. The bridge hotel had a view of the Neckar river and the barge traffic. The old bridge looked like it might go back to Roman times. Certainly it wasn't wide enough for trucks. Those used a modern bridge downstream. This part of Heidelberg was the old town, narrow streets, walk up apartments with shuttered windows.

We were up early, loaded up at the breakfast buffet, and saved a couple of apples for later. I would have liked to find a grocery store like Aldi before we left town. Aldi owns Trader Joes, a Krieger competitor in the States. I would have liked to check the prices and product lines, old habits from my ex-job. I wondered what they charged for Nutella. Did they use coupons?

The motorway runs close to Heidelberg. Leaving the leisurely old town traffic and entering the speedway took my breath away. We were off. Zoom. At those speeds we should be in Stuttgart in a couple of hours.

I admire Ursula. She has nerve at those Autobahn race car speeds. I wore the dark sunglasses. I would have preferred to hide in the back seat under a blanket, but she needed me to watch the road signs. She explained that Ausfahrt meant exit. At least in Europe with all those languages, the international signs were easy to understand. I was beginning to translate the kilometer signs to miles. A fifty kilometer speed limit meant thirty miles. The scale was printed on the odometer, something I had never paid attention to on our old Toyota dashboard.

We pulled off before entering Stuttgart. Ursula sent Gulli an email saying we were on our way, had met Ludmilla, and were coming. She entered Gulli's address in the GPS. Should be easy.

Just in case, I asked Ursula to check her cell phone GPS to see if the two Turks were still on the screen. They weren't. At least she didn't find them. There's nothing like doubt to rattle you, like did you remember to turn off the stove? Lock the front door? Obsessive compulsive disorder. Was that me?

Though the roar of the traffic, engine and pavement sounds had lulled me, getting to the city pricked my excitement. We were finally going to meet my bitcoin benefactor.

Stuttgart is a spectacular city situated on seven hills, like Rome, which means a lot of up and down grades. Mist or smoke down below turned the hilltops into islands. Following the German instructions on the car GPS, we homed in on the address.

Gulli lived in a neighborhood of grand old Victorian houses where the original builders had emulated castles, houses with round towers. The house we were led to by the GPS (the German equivalent of "you have arrived.") was brick.

The villa might be old, but I spotted a security camera. Sometimes I hated them for watching me. Other times, like when our condo got shot up, they were helpful.

There were several names beside the door which told us the house had been broken up into apartments or several people shared. It was typical of places where property taxes made it too expensive for edifices built for large families to house couples or single moms. I wondered how many single parents made up the German population, or didn't people have children at all? Statistics said Germany had an aging population. ZPG had been passed. Without immigrants, Germany, like Italy, would fade into a massive old folks home.

I guess they need those Turkish guest workers. But what about the Arab refugees? A population in flux invited conflicts. Did Germany permit burkas?

Gulli's name was not on the house list. Ursula pushed buttons until someone responded over the intercom. Did a small woman named Gunilla or Gulli live there? She did, up in the tower.

It was a four story climb up creaking, narrow, wooden stairs to her tiny space. Ursula knocked.

Having met Ludmilla, we were not surprised that Gulli was also small. She was ungainly, like she had one shorter leg, or possibly a club foot or painful hip. Certainly, for someone in her twenties she had the body of an older person. Perhaps she had been in an accident that broke a lot of bones. She met us bundled up in a heavy, wool sweater and skirt over black tights. She wore warm slippers. Whatever pain she suffered, she had a twisted, welcoming smile when she recognized me. "Harvey Goldstein."

"My wife Ursula."

Gulli' head bobbed as she welcomed us inside. "Bitte."

The small tower room had windows on three sides, single pane. It was chilly. Being in a tower, it didn't have a fireplace or even a cast iron radiator. It had one of those electric oil filled heaters of decent size but not adequate for the space. I could imagine that when the wind blew she would not need a refrigerator for perishable food.

It was about as basic a living space as you could get. She had a desk and a neatly made cot with a heavy, folded blanket at the foot end, one chair, a free standing clothes cupboard, a child-sized bureau, and a couple of suitcases that looked ready for a quick departure.

Ursula and I sat on the cot while Gulli found a couple of cups in a desk drawer. She poured us coffee from a electric pot that stood on the corner of the desk. Fortunately we didn't ask for sugar, for she had none. I did see a bottle of powdered creamer.

We sat, feeling uncomfortable and not sure how to begin. We had been looking for her for a long time and suddenly were tongue tied.

I joked "You must feel like Brunhilda up here in this tower."

She plucked at her dyed hair. "I have not the braids for it."

"And maybe no prince to rescue you," Ursula added.

So much for levity.

"So," Gulli began with a twisted smile. "How do you like to be a millionaire?"

I shook my head. "I don't think about it."

"He's worried that the people whose money it is will come after him."

Gulli cocked her head to one side, her thinking pose. "Kein gefahr. Honey bear has been shut down."

"Honey bear?"

"A Russian hacker. He was in Putin's gang to make Trump your president."

That already explained a lot, but not enough. "I thought Putin just wanted to own our president."

Gulli nodded. "He does, but *shade*, it not going as he pleased."

I wasn't so sure of that.

Gulli sipped her coffee, made a face like it was too bitter. "It is gefarlig, dangerous to give a dishonest person tools to steal. Honey bear was what you call a rogue."

"How's that?"

"The malware the Russians used to get into your American political parties is also a window for planting ransomeware. Honey bear planted ransomeware all over the world. Now, if he is alive, he is so rich he does not know what to do with all the money. Your bitcoins are a drop in the ocean."

"Did our bitcoins come from Honey Bear?"

She shook her head. "At first."

I was puzzled. "I don't understand."

"Even bed bugs have fleas," Gulli explained. "The robbers get robbed. Then I take from the robber that robbed the robber." She laughed.

"Do you know who he is?"

She shook her head. "Only his computer name."

"So how did you get bitcoins for my wallet?"

She smiled slyly. "I follow him. He has so much money he loses control."

Losing control. That was something I could relate to. "You mean he doesn't remember where he stashes it?"

She nodded. "Possibly. He must also hide. One mistake and poof. He is dead."

I got that much. She could be dead, too, good reason to stay on the move. "The world's police must be after him."

Gulli laughed. "You do not hack two million Euros out of the Russian state bank without someone be angry."

Ursula and I could see that. I was upset enough when my talking fish got shot. That was obviously by accident.

Gulli would have refilled her cup, but her pot was empty. She returned to her only chair. "For my amateur robber it is a game."

Ursula suggested, "Like playing cops and robbers?"

"I do not know cops and robbers. Perhaps your cowboys and Indians."

I sniffed. "So for that hacker it's a sport, stealing large sums of money, blackmailing people."

"What else?" Gulli asked. "You have a million bitcoins. What do you do with so much?"

I had to admit it was numbers on a piece of paper. The difference between a check for one dollar and a million is a bunch of zeros. It's not real until you spend it.

This got me to my real reason for finding Gulli. "Who do I give the million bitcoins back to?"

"No one. There is more where that came from and it cannot be traced."

It began to sound like our own Federal Reserve bank. If you needed more money, turn on the printing press.

So how to you thank someone who has given you something you can never reciprocate?

Ursula gave me an ear-to-ear grin. "Satisfied?"

I was flustered. Before I could answer, there was the sound of heavy steps on those wooden stairs and a pounding on the door. "Aufmachen! Politzei!"

We'd been followed after all.

Chapter Thirty-two

Gulli shrank in fear. She had been small before. Now she cowered like she wanted to disappear into the woodwork, except there was no place to hide in that small space.

Ursula stood in front of her, like a shield. I opened the door.

There were two men, not the two Turks I had identified. Polizei? Their only uniform consisted of stern expressions. No badges. No thrusting of an ID in our faces.

At least, they weren't brandishing guns

In the narrow space at the head of the steep stairs, one stood in front, the other close behind.

I put out a hand to restrain him.

He did not look to me like a policeman. A cop would be clean shaven like Klaus Hintz in Hamburg. In spite of a tendency of some men to affect an unshaven macho look, these men simply looked unkempt.

Weren't secret police supposed to wear long overcoats and sinister fedoras? In the States it would be helmets with face shields, body armor and full swat team gear. The leader was bare headed, needed a haircut. He also needed a shower or at least a deodorant. The guy behind him had a fake fur hat that looked Russian. I figured them to be phonies.

I wanted to stall them, defuse the energy of their excitement. Anyway, they were both winded from hurrying up the four flights of stairs. I demanded, "Let's see some ID."

Ursula translated. "Ausweiss bitte."

Clearly they had not expected to encounter three people and resistance. Their bluff had failed.

Some fumbling for an inside pocket and something, anything we might believe was valid ID.

While he fumbled, I called to Ursula. "They're not cops. Call the police!! How do you call 911 in Germany?"

The leader fumbled with what he had taken from his pocket, dropped it, bent to pick it up. I gave him a push. "Piss off!"

He was off balance. Down they went like a couple of bowling pins..

It was a long way down four flights, but they tangled after the first one.

I slammed the door, saw it had double locks, and on the floor—lucky break. The jerk had dropped a passport or some sort of ID.

Gulli had recovered her initial fear. Now, breathless, she was phoning.

"Tell them we stopped two robbers."

Ursula was concerned. She had never seen me do anything violent, especially not pushing people down a flight of stairs. "They might be injured."

What was I supposed to do, administer first aid? I just hoped they weren't dead. "Copy this photo," I said, holding up the document. "I can't read the name. It's in Cyrillic. The whole document looks like Russian. Maybe Chechnian." My lack of foreign languages was showing again. At least I was sure it wasn't Chinese or Japanese. "Send it to Detective Hintz."

Wonders what those I-phones can do. Made my burner phone look like a toy even if it is 21st century.

I heard moaning on the stairs below and a commotion. The tumble had attracted the neighbors.

Holding our breaths, we waited.

In a few minutes we heard the claxon of an emergency vehicle on the street below. I looked down from the window, turned to Gulli. "An Ambulance. Didn't you call the police?"

"No police."

I remembered: she didn't like police. No surprise since she was a hacker and no doubt wanted by her vengeful victims. International hackers are fair game for anybody.

I watched as one of the men was taken our on a gurney and the other was helped into the ambulance. Looked like he had a broken arm. I was sure the police would follow. "Is there a back way out of here?"

Yes, there was.

"Let's get in the car and drive somewhere there's free wi-fi. I want to check that CCT camera once we're at a safe distance.

Gulli was querulous. "You can do that?"

"I may not read Cyrillic, but I am Harvey Goldstein!" Like, I am superman and can see through walls. Well, not quite.

Gulli hesitated. She was looking indecisively at those suitcases. Should she split, gamble that the men who came were just a coincidence? Or assume rightly or wrongly that they had come after her and not us?

Whichever it was, I didn't want to hang around

"Is there a way out of here? A back exit?"

There was. We hesitatingly crept down the stairs, saw blood on the first landing. Not until the second floor could we cross to the back of the villa and go out a servant's exit.

The back garden was not well kept. A potting shed, green, plastic garbage cans. Being on a hill, there was no back alley. We went out a gate, found a path behind the next house, and got down to the street a safe distance from the entrance to the villa.

Of course, our car was parked just outside. The ambulance was already gone We heard another claxon horn. Probably the real police.

I wasn't ready for that.

Before I could compose my rattled brain, the police arrived and stopped right in front of our car.

Shouting to Ursula and Gulli to wait next door I got into our rental and backed.

This was the first time I had driven the Volkswagen and nearly put it in drive instead of reverse. Bumping the police car would have been, well, embarrassing.

Two uniforms were getting out and giving me curious looks. Before they could approach me, I gave them a friendly wave and backed up.

When I got to the next corner and stopped looking backward I turned to face the front. Then I saw it, a black Toyota Camry parked on the other side of the street. It had a German plate, but there was a sticker, CD.

Our rental had a D sticker for Deutschland. I knew GB stood for Great Britain, and F for France. As I got out of the driver's seat so Ursula could take over, I asked, "What's CD stand for."

She was busy getting Gulli buckled up in front. Turning her head, she said, "I thought you knew everything. CD stands for Corps Diplomatique."

I pointed to the Camry. "You mean that's an embassy car?"

Oh, shit.

Our victim's ID document on the seat beside me, I sat in the back with my laptop while I searched for an unsecured wi-fi signal.

Gulli had regained her composure. She was such a little thing she could hardly see over the dash board. She knew a nearby hotel where we could pick up a guest wi-fi signal.. I started searching the German facial recognition programs for the picture on the intruder's ID.

Ursula took a photo of the Cyrillic text, sent it to my laptop so I could run it through the translation program.

Gotcha!

While she drove, Ursula explained, "I sent a signal to Detective Hintz that we escaped from a couple of would be kidnappers."

"That was premature, honey. I'm afraid we've set off an international incident. The guy I pushed down the stairs is a cop after all. Sort of. He's someone from Romanian state security. He's going to want his ID back."

Gulli was not surprised. She had been expecting an intervention. She just didn't know who would find her first.

I could not help thinking we had led them to her. We were tracked. So why didn't the Romanian involve the German police? Or was searching for Gulli so sensitive and maybe embarrassing that it had to be a secret operation like our CIA guys who kidnapped an Italian for which, by the way, several went to prison?

Gulli directed us to a parking lot and Ursula turned off the engine. She turned to me with her accusative schoolmarm tone. "So now you've assaulted a foreign diplomat?"

I protested. "How was I to know? He looked like a thug. I couldn't read his ID."

"Maybe Romanian diplomats all look like thugs."

We had parked outside a hotel where we could capture free wi-fi. I could look up the registration of the Camry and the biography of the men I'd pushed down the stairs.

Ursula asked, "What should we do now?"

"Just wait. If Hintz is worth his salary he'll alert the Stuttgart police and they'll pick us up. They'll know where we are. No point in hiding."

Gulli had another reason to panic. She was trembling. "Please, not the polizei."

"They're not after you," I explained. "They'll be after me."

Gulli unsnapped her seat belt. "I must go."

"No you don't. We've looked for you for too long, You'll just hide someplace else."

Gulli was fearful and tearful. "What do you want from me?"

I remembered Speerson. I pleaded with her. "Since you claim we don't have to worry about returning the bitcoins, and you didn't steal them from the original hacker, all we need is his name. Who is it?"

Chapter thirty-three

At first Gulli didn't know his real name. He was Honey Bear. That was the same name used by the team of government-sponsored Russian hackers who interfered with the US presidential election. It wasn't like the name was trade marked. Anybody could call themselves Honey Bear.

There had to be more to it than that.

I was sure, or hoped, that the Russian team would not engage in robbing their own state bank of two million dollars. Putin didn't need hackers to do that. He could just help himself. Russia was a cleptocracy. They were all thieves.

"I'll bet it's someone using the Honey Bear hacking tools for his own benefit." That made sense, but who? The whole world was full of wannabe hackers and mischief makers. With the internet it was like why bother to lock your front door? Just put out a welcome sign: help yourself.

I suggested, "You must know who you stole the bitcoins from."

Looking at the problem from that angle, she did. It wasn't The Honey Bear crew. It was someone disguised as one of them, an imposter.

Gulli's expression clouded. Her forehead wrinkled. Her eyes were focused someplace else. "He made a mistake. Accidentally sent an email without encryption."

That was what broke the case of the Silk Road dark web drug mail order outfit. One careless email.

After much thought, all the while looking over her shoulder to see if the police were following us, Gulli finally came out with it. It was one of those eastern European names, all consonants that I couldn't spell or pronounce. She couldn't pronounce it, either.

I handed her my laptop. She changed the display language, something I had never done. It was now one of those scores of foreign language alphabets built into the operating system. Amazing.

What remained was to Google that name. Harvey Goldstein was on the trail. Hi Ho Silver!

It took only minutes to put together a complete dossier of the hacker. Turned out it was a kid, sixteen years old, who lived with his grandmother. I wasn't surprised. Google World showed me the house, decrepit-looking with a tile roof needing repair, chickens in the back yard. Poverty.

What was he going to do with all those bitcoins? Buy a tropical island? Maybe he couldn't even get a visa. Money doesn't buy everything.

Maybe what was important was the game itself. That would be the challenge. For a sixteen year old sitting in an attic bedroom hacking must be like a computer war game, breaking into imaginary banks, moving imaginary money to distant off-shore countries, converting the loot to imaginary money called bitcoins. It didn't have to seem real to him. But it was.

Maybe it was like a game in virtual reality, like Pokemon Go. Except it was real. Sometimes it's hard to tell the difference.

Most hackers are young folks under age twenty-five with nothing better to do than make internet mischief. But this kid, well, stealing millions from central banks and stashing it wherever was big time stuff. It was a lot heavier than breaking into your school's grade records and changing your D to an A minus. It was more exciting.

And dangerous. One thing about people under age twenty-five: their brains have not developed to the point where they are aware of consequences. That's why car insurance rates for them are higher. People over twenty-five are less likely to play chicken on the highway.

He was sixteen, a juvenile. If caught, would he go to an adult prison? Or just be given a slap on the wrist and his toys taken away? The trouble is, consequences of big time hacking could be prison or worse.

I turned to Gulli. "Your place will be a crime scene. Do you have somewhere else to hang out for a few days?"

She was used to running and hiding. She would not take a taxi and we could not drive her anywhere, being tracked. Off she went on foot, no forwarding address, a small, innocuous woman. I noticed she wore orthopedic shoes to compensate for one short leg. No one would notice her. We watched her disappear in the crowd, wondered what next.

We had searched for her and now she was disappearing again like a wraith, a ghost, gone. I felt a wrenching sense of loss.

I had to collect myself, to recover. Finally I suggested, "For now, the best we can do is to find the hospital where the Romanian diplomat is and return the ID document. We can also hand over the information on the hacker. That is, I'm sure, what they are really after. Gulli is only an ancillary person. "

"You hope."

"Yeh, I hope. If I give them everything they want to know, maybe they'll be satisfied. I know Speerson will."

"Speerson or Hintz will want to hire her. She's a valuable source."

I shook my head. "She won't do it."

"Then it's up to you Metadata Man. You're responsible for her now. If you do your part they won't care about Gulli. If they catch the hacker, she'll be home free."

"Maybe." Then I wondered, what if she fabricated the kid hacker? She was adept at deception. He could be a skillful construct, a fall back position if she was cornered, like some sort of internet hologram, but not real.

If the kid was real and innocent, would he be kidnapped? Jailed? Murdered? If you steal millions from somebody, they might get a bit perturbed. Would it be on my head for taking part in Gulli's ruse? I didn't want to think about it.

That was dangerous territory. My mind started to take off in several directions at once. The strain was getting to me again. I took a deep breath, tried to focus. "It'll be more interesting than Krieger coupons."

That, too.

Ursula leaned over the back of the driver's seat. She gave me a wicked smile. "And you can keep the bitcoins. They may not seem real, but they paid off the mortgage."

Chapter thirty-four

It was easy to locate the hospital where the men had been taken. I just walked up to the reception desk and handed over the passport, saying I'd found it. Then I retreated to the hospital parking lot and the wi-fi there.

To my relief, nobody followed us or noticed.

I put together a complete report of the hacker's identity, address, and so on. Sent it to Detective Hintz and Speerson. I could only speculate what they would do with the information. After all, the kid, if he was real, was in a foreign country beyond their reach.

We didn't know where the kid had stolen money from. If not from an American bank or corporation, it wasn't our business. We couldn't have him arrested for stealing something abroad. Even if we could, what about extradition? If there's no extradition treaty, felons far away can't be touched.

What bonanza for criminals! Grabbing someone's purse was risky, done in front of CCT cameras. Sitting in your bedroom and hacking a foreign bank was safe. Was I in the wrong business? Wage slave in a cubicle for Krieger?

Ah, but I am not, as Nixon said, a crook. I'm just a professional snoop marketing house brand toilet paper. Was. Lost that job to artificial intelligence.

But I am also the recipient of stolen bitcoins, a cousin of a hacker once removed.

I knew there were watchers screening the email—NSA, probably Russian intelligence, and God knows who else. Nothing is private any more. It wasn't quite as open as putting the story on the cover of the New York Times. Some smart investigative reporter might find it and think she had a scoop.

When I hit the send button I turned to Ursula with a weak smile. "I guess that's it. Mission accomplished."

It was almost a shock. All that suspense and suddenly it was over.

It was also the end of other things for us. I had lost my job to a computer program. Ursula had lost half of hers to a budget cut. We needed a new beginning.

"What now?" she asked, giving me a suggestive cuddle.

"That, too."

"Whatever we do, I don't want to be watched."

I suggested we return the GPS trackable car to Hertz. We hadn't seen much of Europe on our two week vacation, just Amsterdam, Copenhagen, and that quick change in Hamburg with Uncle Julius. "How about a second honeymoon in the Swiss alps?"

Why not?

Not long after, just for curiosity's sake, I checked the Internet records for the boy hacker. There was no sign of him. He had disappeared, or been expunged. If Gulli had fabricated him, he was erased, deleted, shut off like a virtual reality hologram when the switch has been pulled.

Where was Gulli? No telling. She was adept at assuming different identities, living in the shadows, a small, innocuous woman no one would ever notice.

Book three

INTERNET COP

Chapter one: Home again

Ursula and I returned from our holiday in Switzerland where we celebrated our independence as surprise multi-millionaires thanks to a mysterious million bitcoin wallet, me from being fired from my job at the Krieger grocery chain where I collected metadata on all our customers, and Ursula from her teaching job in Cleveland where the curriculum was cut, taking away her German classes and leaving only bonehead English for immigrants. We were starting a new life, or so we thought.

We had a souvenir: After five yeas of marriage Ursula was pregnant. Our new chapter had begun, except we were haunted by the past.

The reality is, wherever or whenever you go, you carry with you baggage of old memories, conflicts, and obligations. That struck me the moment we entered our condo. It had the look of a bad memory, as if the tenants had fled in a hurry, which we had, in our sudden dash for Europe and the hunt for the mysterious "Angel."

We had washed the dishes, but there were spoiled things in the fridge, like milk that had gone bad and something mysterious and moldy in the back. My no-longer talking fish was still on the wall where it had been shot in the drive by shooting. That seemed very long ago.

In our absence someone had taken down the bullet-ridden drapes over the picture window and left them folded on the floor in the corner. It looked like the FBI had finally lived up to agent Walker's promise to armor the wall panels, but now the window sill and frame would need paint.

Though our key fit the lock, the front door was new. I suspected it was also bullet proof. I had no plans to test it, not owning a fire arm. If I did, I would look pretty stupid shooting at my front door.

We had hardly put down our new luggage when the phone rang. Naturally, it was FBI Agent Walker. "You're back."

I was not surprised. "You've been watching the CCT camera across the street."

"That, too. We never sleep."

"Yeh, you and Pinkerton. So what is it?"

"We've got a problem. Rather, Harvey, you have a problem." When he calls me Harvey he's playing Good Cop. When he's being tough it's Goldstein. I doubt if he's even aware of it. So far as I'm concerned it's always Agent Walker, or sometimes just Walker.

Of course, I do know his first name, his address, his medical and bank records even what he eats. That's what I get for being Metadata Man. Too much information.

"Something you've been saving up for Metadata Man?"

"That, too."

"Something else?"

"We'll talk about it tomorrow. I'll let you unpack, first."

"Thanks a lot." He was teasing me. I shook my head in frustration. Being a real cop, Walker is tenacious and manipulative.

Ursula was being sick again, one of those side effects from being pregnant. Her whole body had gone through a transformation. I heard the toilet flush and the water run in the sink. When she came out of the bathroom, still wiping her face with a towel, she asked, "What's Walker up to now?"

"Didn't say. Maybe it's the IRS."

She sank into our IKEA couch and pulled off her shoes. to massage her swollen feet. It had been a long flight.

We were both tired. Overnight from Zurich with a change in New York Kennedy... Too much sitting.

"I thought he promised you some protection from the IRS, top secret mission, need to know, all that stuff."

"That was Speerson the hacker hunter. We're done with him."

I never liked Speerson ever sine I detected he was a closet Anti-Semite. Walker was all right. The FBI was domestic. Speerson was something international, like the CIA or some agency that tracked cartels, hunted off shore accounts, hidden money, ill-gotten gains, like our million bitcoin wallet. Unfortunately I suspected Speerson was the kind of guy who would actually believe the Protocols of Zion, that fake document cooked up by the Czar's secret police. The Protocols claimed the world was run by a committee of three hundred Jews. It wasn't the Jews, of course, but the Russian Mafia.

We were done with Speerson. He was so devious he might think that the Russian Mafia were Jews and that Harvey Goldstein, being Jewish, albeit secular, wouldn't expose a Jewish Mafia or might even be a closet member of the three hundred. It's a mistake to prejudge something based on your own prejudices.

The difference between the old Mafia, some of whom like Meier Lansky actually were Jewish, and the Russian Mafia is that the Russian Mafia ARE the government. The Italians might bend a few cops, but they had to lie low. The Russians, being a cleptocracy, a government of thieves, could do it all in the open without being challenged. Anyone who did went to prison and a convenient death.

I wanted no part of that scene. I just wanted to be a daddy.

Turned out it was the IRS after all.

Chapter two: The Pitch

Walker lost no time in picking up where we left off months ago when he handed me over to Speerson like a football lateral.

At least he waited until the next morning, giving me a chance to shower and have breakfast, even though, not needing to go to work anyplace I was still in my tighty-whities and a Tee shirt. I had thawed two slices of the bread we'd stuffed in the freezer at the last minute when we left. It was a bit desiccated, but the toast was OK.

Ursula wasn't having any. The sight of food set her off. At least she hadn't wakened me in the middle of the night demanding a kosher dill pickle.

We had a ton of mail that had accumulated on the floor under the slot. I'd sorted out the junk, set the bills to one side of the kitchen table, and saved the official looking envelope from Internal Revenue for dessert. They wanted an audit. Ah, well.

There were a lot of ways to look at our fortune in bitcoins. A gift? That incurred a gift tax. My idea was it wasn't my money, that I am just a custodian, like a trustee, and anything I spend of it is either a commission, a fee, or simply embezzlement. If embezzlement, who would sue? We didn't know where or who it was stolen from. Then again, receiver of stolen goods is also a crime. Maybe I should hire a tax lawyer.

I was mulling over it when Walker showed up at our door.

When I let him in he inspected the door, shifted it, closed, opened, and appeared satisfied with the job.

Ursula rushed into the bedroom when she heard the bell. Walker had not made an appointment, which I thought suspicious. In the past our meetings were at the FBI office or even in the Krieger parking garage. I knew this wasn't a social call and if it were, like, an arrest he wouldn't come alone. So what was it?

I apologized for meeting him in my underwear. I indicated he could take our recliner chair. I took the couch. "If I'd known you were coming I'd have baked a cake or at least put on some pants."

"You're funny, Goldstein."

Goldstein, so it was business, not pleasure. "You were right about the IRS." I indicated the official letter. "They lost no time. I thought Speerson was shielding me."

Walker shook his head like he was ducking a fly. "That later. First, let me congratulate you on your mission to Germany."

"I can't say I found the hacker. I did find the woman who called herself Angel, if that's what you mean."

"No problem so far as the FBI is concerned. You proved yourself."

"You mean, like it was a test?"

He was non committal. "How do you feel about your country?"

It was an odd question. "What are you asking? You want me to be an under cover daredevil?"

"No. Nothing like that. What are your politics?"

"Conservative liberal." That was about as innocuous as I could put it.

"Red or blue?"

I could see those were euphemisms. The FBI is supposed to be non-committal, not political. To him saying Republican or Democrat must be like swearing. "I'm in favor of the Constitution."

He did like that. "Fair enough. We swear to defend the constitution against all enemies, foreign and domestic. Were you ever in the service?"

"You know that already."

He was having trouble getting to the point. "Harvey," he began.

Ah, it was Harvey again. I waited.

"Harvey you have certain talents that can be useful to us."

"How's that?"

"You have access to information we cannot get without a court order. You can get through all the firewalls, dig into all digital records, even read sealed files."

Now I got it, why this was not an official visit. This was something so secret they wouldn't even talk about it at the office. "You're asking me to be a snoop."

Walker laughed. "You already are. You used to do all those grocery coupons for personal stuff people bought at Krieger. It's called Big Data. Of course you're a snoop."

"So what don't you know already?"

Walker sighed. I could see this was painful for him. "It's about our elections. You know the president wanted to know all the voting records of every citizen. The cover story was he wanted to prevent fraud."

I couldn't see what that had to do with me. "Everybody with any sense knows that's a lie. Actual voting fraud is extremely rare, maybe a dozen votes out of millions."

"If you were going to rig an election, Harvey how would you do it?"

"I wouldn't add bogus names or vote as dead people, if that's what you mean. This is Cleveland, not Chicago."

He nodded. "So what would you do?"

"I'd delete the names of people I didn't want to vote. Something more subtle than demanding photo ID or proof of citizenship. Those tactics are obvious. People get pissed off."

"So what would you do?"

I sat back, wishing Ursula would emerge from the bedroom. It was taking too long for her to get dressed. "Delete individual names. We already have metadata on everyone. We don't know exactly how someone in the privacy of the voting booth actually casts a ballot, but we can be pretty sure."

Now Walker was interested. He leaned forward, intense. "So how do you control that?"

"Lose his ballot."

"What? After the vote? Get into the ballot box and throw out votes for the candidate you want to lose?"

I shook my head. "A lot of places have mail in ballots so people who can't get to the polling place can still vote. Don't send them a ballot in the first place. Purge the mailing list."

"Who would do that?"

"Anybody. The Russians, the reds, the blues, even the greens and yellows if there's a yellow party."

"Exactly. Harvey, our democracy is at risk. The states can refuse to provide the White House from getting all the lists. Secretaries of the individual states are jealous of their integrity and privacy. The FBI has no access to that information without individual court orders we can never get, and if we could it would take so long the elections would be over."

Now I was curious. "So how did the Russians do it?

"Instead of deleting names, they made slight alterations in the names and addresses of known Democrats. When people went in to vote the records didn't match and they were turned down."

I could see then how important the party rolls were. They knew who was a registered Republican, who a Democrat, who an

Independent. It was all there. Simple. Our data was working against our democracy.

I figured it out. "Compare the current rolls with the previous undoctored one and correct. I could do it. I Metadata Man." I'm the super hero who knows too much. I quickly added, "But that would be up to the individual secretaries of state as a check of all rolls against previous correct ones. The backup files, if you will. It's their responsibility."

Walker nodded. "It's illegal for you do it , of course."

"That kind of tampering, yes. Which is why you're talking to me here and not at the FBI office. You're asking me to break the law."

That made him cringe. "That's why I can't hire you as an official FBI employee."

"What then?"

"As a private consultant. An informer, if you will. We do pay informants even if they get tips illegally that we can't use in court."

I got it. He was offering me some sort of job. I knew that, being fired from Krieger, I qualified for unemployment compensation. Ursula didn't. She'd quit. Unemployment compensation would hardly cover our expenses, certainly not health insurance.

I also realized that comparing files with past records or backups could be done with a computer program, which is how I lost my job.

I'd already been outsourced by an artificial intelligence program. Jobs like mine were evaporating. What could I do? Data entry? That was dumb stuff for high school drop outs, maybe paying minimum wage plus coffee from a machine in the break room.

I also knew our sole real assets were the paid up condo and our old Toyota. The bitcoin wallet might be worth millions, but it could disappear any time into the dark web. "You offering a salary?"

Walker nodded. "Within reason."

"Health insurance? Ursula's expecting."

Haggling made Walker nervous. Setting salaries was probably above his job description.

I glanced at the letter from Internal Revenue. "What about my problem with the IRS?"

He didn't know. "Not my department."

"If I understand you correctly, you're asking me to break into confidential voter registration records, like FBI-gate."

He accepted there was some risk to that.

I was afraid to ask how much jail time you got for internet burglary. I'm not a hacker, just a snoop. I don't steal anything. I'm not in the business of selling credit card numbers or personal ID. I could, of course. I knew some companies shared their mailing lists. Others sold tem. So what was the difference? Marketing wasn't exactly identify theft.

He saw I was hesitant. I also saw he had no leverage that could force me to do his dirty deeds. His only option was to appeal to my patriotism.

I didn't really relish the idea of going through thousands of precinct records for thousands of counties and towns and fixing the errors. People did move. People married and changed their names. It would take an army, an army with access.

While I was busy being evasive, Ursula came in. Her body was changing. She was wearing her sweats with the expanding waist. Her breasts has swelled, possibly in anticipation of nursing. Her loose blouse covered the waistline. Her pregnancy was not so far advanced that it was obvious.

They exchanged perfunctory pleasantries. Ursula parked herself on the couch and put her arm around me, an act of protective possession. "Why are you here, Agent Walker?"

"I need Harvey's help. I need yours, too."

"How's that?"

Walker was apologetic. He absently fiddled with the lever that controls the recliner chair, thought the better of it. "I know your husband has had bouts, occasional bouts, of information overload."

That pissed me off. "You've seen Dr. Halal's reports. They're supposed to be confidential."

Walker raised his eyebrows. "I couldn't be here if I didn't do my homework." He turned to Ursula. "I know you have been able to intervene when he has his, er, spells. If he does decide to help us out, can I count on your support?"

Ursula's eyes narrowed. "I support my husband. I don't know about you."

Walker shook his head. "This is not about me. It's about our democracy. Somebody or someone, or maybe more than one, is messing with our elections at all levels. Any help Harvey here can help us with may be vital."

That gave us pause.

Walker made a last pitch. "I know your bitcoins make you wealthy enough to go any place any time. You can bail out, live anywhere, and drop out. I don't see you doing that."

I felt myself smirking. Sitting in my underwear was hardly a conventional scene for a job interview. Nor did it give me a psychological advantage. Walker was right. We could split any time, providing the bitcoins didn't disappear into the dark web where they came from, leaving us with no jobs and an uncertain future.

"What you're suggesting is a huge task," I began as I took a first mental assessment of the problem. "Voters don't vote in a block. If you want to swing an election you have to do it precinct by precinct. The difference between 49 and 51 percent may be only a few votes."

Walker understood. "You'll have help."

"Think of it: George W. Bush was selected over Al Gore as president because of under four hundred disputed votes in Florida, four hundred out of millions. It was that small and it changed the course of history. If Gore had been elected we wouldn't have invaded Iraq and the world wouldn't be flooded by refugees whose homes and families were destroyed."

"Then you understand. We're looking to find whoever might change a few hundred borderline votes."

"In fifty-one states? For a national election that's plus Samoa, Puerto, Guam, and other colonies in the American empire? The Guamian vote could swing an election."

"You don't have to go to Samoa or Guam."

"I don't have to go anywhere. I can work from home on this stuff."

"Would you want to do that?"

I could see him imagining me at my computer in my underwear. No necktie required. But I remembered that any internet activity, and most email could be tracked, which is how our place got shot up. What if it was the Russians? The North Koreans? They could find us.

"This is going to take a team of computer experts. I don't feel qualified."

"You have anyone in mind?"

The only one I know of was Grabich. His IT job at Krieger had not been outsourced. I couldn't see him in an FBI office with his beard and Bigfoot haircut. And of course, he had hacked into the immigration and naturalization files to create a green card for his now ex girl friend. Being inside the FBI offices might make him nervous. "Give us a few days to think about it." Since Ursula was part of the deal I wasn't going to decide for her.

Ursula saw Walker out. I didn't want to stand in the open doorway in full view of the CCT camera across the street. When we'd come home I also forgot to cover the TV with a towel in case it was watching us, too. Those internet Big Data marketing snoops might check the label on my underwear and offer me a deal on some Fruit of the Loom. I hadn't used that TV network when I was doing coupons for Krieger, but I could have. Watch people snacking while watching sports and offer a deal on Freetos.

Ursula suggested, "You'd better get dressed in case someone else drops in."

"Or looks in our picture window. It may be bullet proof, but it is see through. Time we got some new drapes."

I got back to unpacking. In Zurich I'd bought a ski jacket and hung it up, wondering when I'd ever go skiing. Cleveland isn't exactly alpine. Once baby came we would not be doing much outdoor sports except maybe stroller races.

I offered Ursula some breakfast, but wasn't sure what she could keep down. She settled for coffee and plain toast then asked, "What do you think of Walker's proposition?"

"I think it's impossible. It's easier to notice if someone is added to the voter list than it is to see if someone is missing."

"Harvey, you don't have to check every list. The way things really are both major parties know who their faithful are. They have to go after the undecided or the unsure. In a close election its that narrow margin that decides it."

"The one percent you mean."

She looked across her cup at me. "But it's not just the reds and the blues who are also after that small margin. It's foreign governments that can benefit by picking our elected leaders."

"You mean like North Korea."

She agreed. "And anybody else."

I couldn't imagine any candidate the North Koreans would want. I countered with "What about the Poles? Would they want a Polish candidate? Everybody had their own agenda. Too many people were one issue voters, like the right to lifers. If all competing parties could purge the voting lists of people who didn't vote their way, nobody would be left."

Ursula laughed. "There's your problem, Metadata Man."

I shook my head. "I can't do it."

"You mean without Metadata Man our democracy is doomed?"

"Couldn't I just save the planet single handed? That's comic book super hero stuff."

We both laughed. It was ridiculous.

When we stopped laughing, I wondered just how serious Walker was. It would take a task force to find a way to protect our election process. Congress was so splintered and disorganized and factious and ineffective they couldn't decide on anything except pay raises for themselves. God save the Republic.

Chapter three

"I think Walker is going at this the wrong way."

Ursula was cuddling with me on the couch as we ruminated. "How's that?"

"First, you got to follow the money. Who benefits from an election? Special interest groups like the NRA gun lovers or the oil companies who want deregulation."

"That's only two."

"Trouble is, what Walker does is police work. Before you can solve a crime, the crime had to take place. We don't throw people in jail on the chance that they'll do something illegal but haven't yet. It's called preventive detention reserved for countries like Russia."

"And if we wait until after an election, it's too late."

I agreed. "He doesn't need me. He needs a statistician, someone who studies past performance and detects changes outside a standard deviation."

"You mean party wonks."

I'd hadn't anything to do with any political party. All I did was my duty to vote which was more than about half the country, the people who didn't care or who had given up, lost faith in the process. If people didn't vote, our democracy was in peril. "I don't see how I can be any help to the FBI on this. I think it's a job for cyber security. Not my line."

Having been out sourced by an IT program, I felt pretty dumb, like the old phone switchboard operators who plugged in phone calls in the days when phones were hard wired. Obsolete. Even at Krieger with their massive data base, you didn't have to be a rocket scientist. If there was a recall on Goober Peanut Butter it was a simple task to locate everybody who had bought some and send them a warning. It was like the kids card game "Fish." "Please give me all your Goober customers." The computer could do that, no benefits program needed and no overtime pay, either. Reminded me that now we were back from Switzerland I had to check with Cobra on Ursula's health insurance. Pregnancy wasn't a disease.

I decided to tell Walker I wasn't qualified for his job. Instead I'd see what deal I could make with the IRS. They might give me a big bill, but I reasoned that it wasn't my money. It was somebody else's bitcoins.

Nobody publishes phone books any more. The assumption is that everybody has access to a computer or a smart phone. I had resisted buying a smart phone because I didn't want to be trapped into an addictive Candy Crush game and walk into a bus.

I found the local IRS office was on ninth street in the maze of downtown freeways made obsolete when Cleveland ceased to be a major city. It was beginning to look like Detroit, abandoned malls, empty store fronts. Why go shopping when you can get everything on line?

I called the IRS office and made an appointment. What was it about? An audit, I think.

I suggested, "I think we better go together, in case I freak out again." When I come to a strange place with all those faces I can't help but recognize I'm like some marine combat vet with PTSD, except I wasn't afraid all those people wanted to kill me. Of course, some might if they knew what I know about them, being Metadata Man, God help me. As in, "Hello, Mrs. Jones, how's your hemorrhoids?" which I would know if I was still at Krieger and saw she had bought Preparation H.

So Ursula drove us downtown to the IRS office. We were directed to a waiting room and took a number among all the other worry warts and tax evaders. I didn't bring my old tax return. It hadn't included the mysterious bitcoin wallet. So who knew I had it? Had the FBI ratted me out to the IRS?

When our number came up we were let into a cubicle. Two visitor's chairs.

The clerk had no name plate or tag, but I knew who he was. Clark Conrad looked like he had heard every lame excuse and plea for pity in the book. This gave him a tired expression that mixed boredom with a worn, practiced vindictive hostility, no doubt part of his job description. I knew Clark Conrad drove a tired 2002 Chevy pickup truck, was married to Suzy Baby, his childhood sweetheart who was a member of Alcoholics Anonymous--not as anonymous as she thought. They had four kids, the youngest, rebellious one who had done some dumb stuff and spent time in Juvie but was reformed now if she could only get her record purged. I knew she couldn't. Too many people had access and long memories. Once you're marked as a loser you're done. I had the whole family situation and felt sorry for Mr. Conrad. He had been with the IRS for twenty years and had heard it all.

Except my story.

"It's about my bitcoin wallet," I explained.

Conrad wasn't that familiar with bitcoin. "What's its value?"

I took a deep breath and let it out slowly. "It fluctuates. Bitcoins are fluid. I haven't checked since we got back from Switzerland, but it's in the neighborhood of, well, five hundred million in dollars."

That got his attention. Conrad's household income, with his wife working, was about forty-five thousand a year, according to his last 1040. I don't think he had many multi millionaires in his clutches.

While he recovered from the shock, I explained. "It's not my money."

"How's that?"

"The wallet was created by a German hacker who diverted the bitcoin from an internet thief."

Conrad was curious and searching for an answer that fit the IRS regulations. "So where was it stolen from?"

"I have no idea. Ursula and I went to Germany to track down the person who created the bitcoin wallet account in my name."

"Then it was a gift? Like someone gives you millions of dollars in digital currency?"

I knew the gift tax kicked in when you hit about thirteen thousand dollars per person per year. That wouldn't cover five hundred million. What was the tax? Thirty percent? If I paid it and the so-called giver wanted it back, would I get a refund? "I think the account was created as a front, like a shell corporation."

I was reminded of the myriad of phony shell corporations created to hide deals like buying Trump properties with laundered Russian money.

"You're claiming the bitcoin wallet is not yours?"

Ursula joined in. "Right."

Conrad had another card in his deck. He'd found something on his computer. "You made a payment in bitcoin of over a hundred thousand to clear your mortgage."

I had to admit I did. "I wasn't sure if bitcoin was real or not. It was a test."

A skeptical "uh huh."

"I also had no idea whether the person who opened the bitcoin account would close it without warning."

"So you helped yourself." Conrad was looking like bad cop.

I admitted, "I suppose you could call it embezzlement."

Conrad nodded, like he thought he had me.

"But the source is unknown," I explained. I remembered the-- what was it? Rumanian sixteen year old who had seen the whole business as a computer game? I wasn't even sure he existed. Certainly I had no idea where he'd stolen it. The loot had been intercepted and passed on to me by the woman who told us her name was Gulli. I even doubted that. "If it's embezzlement, it would be up to the victim to sue me. I've no idea who that is."

Conrad wasn't buying it. "You'll have to report what the bitcoin account was worth when you got it and what it is worth today. The difference we regard as a capital gain or loss, just like a stock investment."

"And if it's a loss?"

Conrad was back in familiar territory. "You can claim only $3000 a year and carry over $3000 to the next year."

"But if I claim it, then I'll admit that it's mine." Paying the tax was one way to admit ownership.

Conrad smiled like the cat that swallowed the canary. "Unless the person it was stolen from comes after you."

That, of course, was the unanswered question, the source of anxiety I didn't want to think about. As long as I did not claim ownership, I could plead innocence. Except for the mortgage payoff, of course.

I dodged. "I think it's up to the IRS to determine the real ownership of the bitcoin wallet."

"Your name is on it. That's enough for us."

I hadn't pursued that part of it. "What if there are other names claiming co-ownership?" Maybe Gulli had her fingerprint on the bitcoin, a string attached so she could draw it back any time..

"You'll have to work that out with your partners, Mr. Goldstein."

Now my head started spinning again.

Conrad had another suggestion. "If you claim you are just a custodian, like a trustee, the mortgage payment you made might be construed as your fee. Then you can pay the tax on that as income and the bitcoin are not actually your property."

That sounded reasonable. "So how do I declare it?"

"As income."

I figured if I paid the tax out of the bitcoin stash it was still free money. I got up to leave. "Thanks, Mr. Conrad. You've been very helpful. By the way, how long has Suzy been in AA?"

He had not identified himself and was shocked. "What do you know about that?"

I gave him my Metadata Man grin. "I am Harvey Goldstein." Let him puzzle that one out.

We left. On the way out Ursula admonished me, "You're showing off, Harvey. You shouldn't do that."

"I couldn't resist."

"I thought members of AA were anonymous."

"Nobody's anonymous any more." As we left the government building I waved at the CCT camera. Just waved. No middle finger.

Chapter four

With our mission to Germany for Speerson over, we wanted to decompress, take a real holiday. We had been gone for more than three months, as long as we could stay in Switzerland without attracting the attention of the Swiss police. Three months was all a visitor was allowed.

In the meantime I had no contact with anyone in the States except some post cards mailed to our folks. We dropped out of sight of Speerson and the Hamburg Police Detective Hintz, remaining as low key as was possible in a world of CCT cameras and facial recognition. Of course, I knew we could not disappear entirely.

The local Swiss knew we were there by our hotel registrations but no one bothered us. If anyone remembered my brief exposure on every computer screen and phone in the world, my fame was short-lived. Nobody noticed. Ursula and I just wanted to be an innocuous Mr. and Mrs. Goldstein.

Now we were back in Cleveland, land of deserted shopping malls as everyone was shopping on line. Before phoning Agent Walker I decided it might be helpful if I got hold of my IT office pal Grabich. Now that we were back I wondered how things were going at my old job at Krieger.

"Harvey, old man. You're back!" was his happy response when he saw my caller ID and heard my voice.

"Yep. Back from Europe."

"Tell me about it."

"Not over the phone. How about a cookout on our mini-patio tonight?"

It was short notice. I would have to get some groceries for our depleted larder. Ursula and I had a brief discussion about who should do the shopping. She was afraid I would make some remarks to total strangers about their personal lives, like I had with Mr. Conrad at the IRS.

I relented and went out on the patio to resurrect the grill. The plastic cover had blown off and tore. There were leaves to be swept up.

The plastic chairs were grimy as was the table. I made a quick job of it and was done when she returned with steaks.

It reminded me of the last time Grabich was there. Then it was with his Iranian girl friend Mia who ended up as our brief house guest while he engineered a green card so she could be legal. How much had changed in our lives since.

I the meantime I phoned Walker and left a voice mail. I told him I didn't feel that my so-called talent fit into his plan to rescue our democracy from election fraud. I was polite and civil, didn't tell him to piss off.

I heard Grabich drive up in the Carmen Gia, now with a purring Porsche engine, thanks, I was sure, to Gulli's intervention.

If anything, Grabich was hairier than before. At least he had a man bun now, the hair bundled up at the back of his neck. I suspected he kept his wild appearance to avoid being promoted to a more conspicuous job. It is a wise employee who knows not to rise above his level of competence.

We gathered, three somewhat distant friends. Time apart does that to you. I asked, "Did boss Margaret find another job?"

The reference invoked memories of tight, very short leather outfits worn commando style.

"Somewhere upstairs in Middle Management. I think she's being transferred to Kansas City." Cleveland had become a dead town. She could do worse.

Kansas City was where one of the Krieger truckers had passed me off to another Krieger truck when I was hitching my way back to Cleveland after the wags at the Cloud erased my identity.

"What about you, Harvey? You left in a hurry after you were laid off."

"It was what the Brits call hush-hush. I had to sign a security oath. Some guy named Speerson sent me off to find some hacker. You wouldn't believe the amount of money being stolen and stashed around the world."

Grabich would. He lived on the edge of the dark web. "So did you find the hacker?"

"We did," Ursula passed a big salad bowl. Ursula had bought some prepared salad at our local Krieger store and some fresh dressings, an assortment. Grabich chose French, not my favorite.

The steaks-- she had splurged on top grade sirloins-- were sizzling on the grill.

"So who was it?"

I needed to protect Gulli's identity and made an excuse. "Turned out to be an odd woman who has a hobby of raiding stolen loot and diverting it. Where she gets it I we couldn't prove. She keeps changing her identity to avoid the police."

"We don't know her real name," Ursula added, backing me up.

Grabich didn't ask further. Tell somebody you're a CEO and they might not ask what company. If you told them the name of the company, like IDEVCO, they wouldn't bother to ask what that was or what the products were. So much for curiosity. "So what happens now? You looking for another job?"

"I'm not…" I began.

"We're having a baby," Ursula said, both shy and proud.

You never know how bachelors take to that subject, like didn't Grabich know where babies come from? Or how they get started. He said, "Great. Congratulations? Boy or girl?"

"We don't know yet. Going for the surprise."

"As for a job," I began, "I think I have a lead for you if you aren't afraid of the FBI."

Grabich was cutting into his steak and looked up with hesitancy, suspicion, and apprehension. "FBI?" The agency obviously made him nervous.

"Agent Walker was over here. He wants to find out how or who rigged the last election. I told him it was over my head. Should I recommend you?"

Grabich concentrated on his chewing, finally swallowed and said, "Depends."

I didn't know what that meant. "You mean, salary wise?"

"Could be. Would I have to get a haircut?"

That made us both laugh. Grabich's coiffure was apparently his own expression of his persona. If he had it cut, what person would emerge? What face hid under all that hair?

I compromised. "I'll mention your name and it will be up to you."

We changed the subject.

"How was Switzerland? Where did you stay? What did you do?"

Ursula laughed. "We made a baby." She made it sound like it was a major, time consuming project, like building a yacht in your back yard.

Grabich was embarrassed. End of the Q and A.

We had a nice visit, but being away from the Krieger scene, all the changes at the office meant that we no longer had the place or the job in common. When we said our goodbyes I had the feeling that we were not likely to see much of him again.

When I followed up with a call to Walker the next day he was not happy. You don't say no to the FBI even if what he proposed was not exactly legal. There were still a few guarantees of privacy, like bank records, which required court orders for official investigations, information I as Metadata Man could access.

If I were a crook, my access to personal data could be a ticket to identity theft, blackmail, and God knows what, but to quote President Nixon, I am not a crook.

I should have realized that Walker's plan had leaked, some word of mouth chain that marked me as a resource. The FBI might not be unwilling to go sub-rosa for information, but they were not the only party with nefarious intent.

With my IRS issue apparently solved for the time being I figured I no longer needed the dodge of saying my situation was classified, need to know and all that. Like Pinocchio, I had no strings attached. Metadata Man was a real boy. Ursula and I could concentrate on fun stuff, like internet shopping for baby buggies, cribs, and the like. I was becoming an authority on car seats.

Then I got a call from a private detective, or at least someone who claimed to be a detective.

Chapter five. A new job

The call came while Ursula and I were studying the layout of the guest bedroom which she had been using for her office before the teaching job ended. What wallpaper was suitable for a baby? Did it make a difference for boys or girls? Or were there gender free designs so as not to confuse potential gender switchers? That a wallpaper might be politically incorrect was a stretch.

Ursula borrowed a couple of heavy books of wallpaper samples from the paint store. I had never done wallpapering. For me a roller and bucket of white paint would be enough, but Ursula didn't want the nursery to look like a sterile hospital.

There were too many choices. Everything from old fashioned little pink flowers to metallic stripes. I thought zoo animals might be fun, instructive, too. This was getting stressful.

The phone call gave me an escape. "Hello."

"Is this Harvey Goldstein? Metadata Man?"

"My notoriety precedes me," I said with some chagrin. "Who's this?"

"J. C. Kohen with a K. People call me Jaycee."

Jaycee was identifying herself not only as a co-religionist but as a cohane, a member of the priestly caste of the ancient Hebrews. The family names often start with a K.

I fired back with some rudimentary Yiddish, "So vas macht a yid?" Translation: What's a Jew doing?

"Private detective."

"If you're looking for me, you found me. What's this about?" I had apprehension of someone wanting their bitcoin back.

"I understand from the grapevine that you are able to get information quicker than even the Hamburg Police."

If she was that kind of detective, she was trying to impress me. She'd succeeded. "You tracking Holocaust survivors or hidden ex-Nazis?"

"Whatever. Can you come to my office, or would you rather I come to you?"

Harley L. Sachs

She was on speaker phone, so Ursula interrupted. "Have her come here. I don't want you driving around town by yourself."

She was referring to my tendency to get distracted by an overload of inadvertent information. I agreed.

So it was set. She'd come by our place about three o'clock. That would give me time to tidy up. Got to do my duty as house husband and future daddy.

Jaycee Kohen turned out to be a short woman, just over five feet tall, wearing a long skirt like she might be Orthodox or had bad knees. Her mannish jacket was suitable for concealing a shoulder holster. Her business card done by Instaprint had her picture.

I didn't recognize the face at once, had to search my mental database. I invited her in, placed her on the same recliner Walker had sat in while I fetched my new android pad. I admit I was using it as a crutch but it's easier for me to focus on a screen instead of the jumble of data that fills my head. I compared the face on her business card with what I found and it came together in a rush.

She was J.C. Kohn, graduate of the University of Chicago, grew up in the same Hyde Park neighborhood when it was turning black. Graduated cum laude, only daughter of a couple of lefties who got caught up in the McCarthy scare. Jaycee had a scholarship, no student debt, practiced law for awhile but found the field overloaded with ambitious graduates unable to find lawyerly jobs, especially if they were women. Being a detective who was also a lawyer was more interesting than clerking.

I saw by her bank records, which I quickly found, that her income was sporadic. Occasional big fees were down, the deposits followed by periods of regular withdrawals. Detecting had its ups and downs. I suspected that one of the downs was why she was coming to me. I was a short cut for her otherwise tedious research.

After my long pause I looked up. "Sorry. I was just checking."

She wrinkled her forehead, fumbled with her briefcase which might have contained the remainder of her lunch. "What, my credit rating?"

"No, your First National bank account. No savings to speak of, and the last big deposit was two months ago."

Some people might resent the intrusions, but she didn't. She smiled. "That's what I wanted to see you about."

"What? Your bank deposits?"

"No. Your access to that sort of information. I have a client…"

"Ah."

Ursula came in carrying the book of wallpaper samples. I introduced her. "This is Ursula, my keeper."

"Keeper?"

I explained. "She tries to keep me out of trouble when I go off the deep end. Being Metadata Man has its hazards. So tell me your problem."

Jaycee was troubled. "I have a client who does not seem to be who he says he is."

"Oh?"

She had minimal information. Rudy Wayne Williamson. She had his home address, phone number and complaint. Said he was a victim of rumor and innuendo. He had been shamed on the internet because he looked like a notorious white supremacist. That would be a tough nut for a detective. Viral condemnations were anonymous, the scourge of social media. She did have his picture.

His face was in the database for Illinois drivers licenses. Rudy Wayne Williamson didn't look like a skinhead or Nazi. He had hair and no obvious tattoos, but he was white if that means anything "How detailed do you want this? You want a full dossier? Complete criminal history? Old parking tickets?"

Jaycee hesitated. "What's your fee?"\

I didn't need the money, so I said, "I'll do it and you tell me what it's worth to you." I imagined she charged two hundred an hour, standard lawyer's billable time. Unless she was corporate. In that case the sky was the limit. Big corporations have deep pockets lawyers love. Williams didn't have deep pockets.

I got the impression that she needed some fees fast to pay the rent on her one bedroom apartment.

Didn't take long. Williams had a DUI from California where he'd been on a business trip. He drove a leased Lincoln for show. He was married to Sylvia, had a son by a previous marriage who played football in college.

Williams also had gambling debts, had dealings with a Chicago loan shark, suffered from high blood pressure and drank enough to have liver problems. This didn't fit the profile of a white supremacist, but who knew?

I recited all this and advised, "He has unpaid parking tickets. I wouldn't lend him any money. He also might not be able to pay your fees."

She was impressed.

"You want to know if he's paid his dog license? Vet bills? Got it all."

For me it was just an exercise. I could also tell her what he ate for breakfast and he preferred Jack Daniels whiskey. His wife shopped at Krieger and Macy's. It was all there, except it didn't say where Williams worked or what he did for a living. Not everything showed up in his tax return.

I asked, "What does Mr. Williams do for a living?"

Jaycee hesitated. "He says he's a consultant."

"A consultant to what?"

"It's one of those descriptions that can mean anything."

I shrugged. "You could say I'm a consultant, too."

She was taking notes.

I waited. Finally, she looked up, expecting more information.

"What do you need Williams's information for?"

"I can't say. Lawyer client confidentiality."

"Does he want to sue Google for being shamed?"

No answer.

"Suit yourself."

"What about your fee? You needed only five minutes for this."

"Send me a check," I said, leaving it up to her. If she sent me ten bucks there would be no repeat performance. Not that being Metadata Man is a profession. What I do isn't a profession. It's not even a hobby. I just do it.

In fact, I can't help myself. It's become a compulsion worthy of a psychiatrist's bench. Ursula would testify to that.

Jaycee left leaving me with her business card. Ursula was puzzled. "What was that all about?"

"She has a client and wanted a quick dossier."

"She going to pay you?"

I just shrugged.

We returned to the wallpaper task for the nursery. We thought about a pattern of bunny rabbits or one of zoo animals. Zoo animals might give a kid nightmares of gorillas under the bed. I thought Winnie the Pooh would be good but there was no paper of that pattern. Bunnies won.

In the next few days I wondered if Jaycee would send me a check. None came, but there was a follow-up to Jaycee's visit. She phoned to say her client was getting death threats, dirty Nazi, stuff like that.

I suggested she track down the real nasty person he was mistaken for and see if she could get him to issue a public denial. Williams wasn't a bad guy. He was just a drinker who'd missed a couple of parking tickets and loved his wife. As for his gambling debts, there was no digital record.

Trouble was, the viral shaming had attracted a couple of investigative reporters who wanted to use Williams as an example of internet victimhood. The more journalists dig, the more they find out. Williams' gambling debt led them to some shady characters in organized crime. The spotlight aimed at Williams was also shining on people who like to stay in the dark.

Williams, as I saw it, was just another victim of compulsive gambling, not a main player. If anything he was an almost innocent bystander, but sometimes bystanders get caught in a crossfire.

"What am I supposed to do about it?" I asked.

I was deeply grateful that my "Harvey Goldstein is watching you" event didn't precipitate a flood of nasty mail. A few thought I was a twenty-first century Orwellian Big Brother but the furor faded quickly. People are fickle. A major earthquake holds interest only for a few days, though it may take many years for the victims to rebuild and recover. The Plain Dealer reporter who contacted me went on to bigger stories. Williams was not so lucky.

"Find the white supremacist who looks like Williams."

That was more like it. That was the kind of search I was used to. At Krieger I could sort the data and identify who among millions of customers bought toxic Goober peanut butter and send them a coupon for a free replacement of some other brand.

What databases had the pictures of known Nazis, white supremacists, America firsters, and other fringe kooks? Should that include the Bandidos, Hells Angels, and motorcycle gangs? The circles were growing wider and deeper. A link to the drug trade would be like a trap door leading to unknown, dangerous depths.

Not all of those organizations kept records that could be snooped. Some were at hoc. Not all the faces seen in the crowds of demonstrators were identified, what with bandanas and masks. This really was a job for Metadata Man.

What I hoped was the shaming would fade away and the journalists who wanted to exploit Williamson as a scapegoat would find better stories to follow. The intern at the Plain Dealer hadn't bothered with me.

"I'll see what I can find out," I said. It was a feeble promise. If I'd been paid up front it would be more serious, but I had no contract with Jaycee. I hadn't sent her a bill, either, had no idea what to charge.

I could just say I couldn't find anything and walk away. As for non-payment for my first investigation, I didn't want to push it. I could let it ride and bring it up later if I needed leverage.

Then I got a call back from FBI agent Walker.

Chapter Six

I guess a real cop has to be tenacious and persistent. I didn't think Walker's theory about manipulating elections and how to prevent it was feasible, but that wasn't what he was calling about.

"Goldstein," he began, so I knew is was serious stuff. If he was being good cop he called me Harvey. "What the hell are you up to?"

"Who me?" as in Mad Magazine's "What, me worry?"

"Your footprints are all over the place."

I feigned ignorance. In fact, it didn't take much feigning. I had no idea what he was talking about.

"You checked up on the dog license for Rudy Wayne Williamson."

"So?"

"And his unpaid parking tickets."

I laughed. "When you do a search you find all kinds of stuff, much of it of no importance."

"Who you doing this for?"

"I got a visit from a private detective. Williamson is her client."

I could hear that Walker felt put upon. I apparently was inadvertently treading on his turf. "You also were poking around Hells Angels, the Bandidos, and neo Nazis."

That was it. I knew that any time I did a search I left a footprint. I could be traced. Now maybe the animal control people in Chicago wanted to know who was interested in Williamson's dog license. Go figure.

I told myself it couldn't be that. "Williamson is being shamed. He resembles some neo Nazi or skinhead. It's a case of mistaken identity. Some people on social media are hysterics, vindictive, and mean. They'll say things on the internet they would never say to anyone's face. The anonymity of Twitter brings out the worst."

"You lecturing me, Goldstein? I know all about social media."

I admit I was talking down to him. If he wants to be bad cop, screw him. "Then apparently you've got a watch on my activity. Why's that? I'm no terrorist. Not looking at bomb making sites."

I heard him take a deep breath and let it out slowly. Must be advice from his doctor to keep his blood pressure down. I've seen his medical records.

"You're a dangerous man, Harvey."

So it was Harvey again. "I'm just a data junky who sometimes wears a silly Metadata Man shirt."

"OK. Just be careful. We're not the only ones watching you."

"What am I? A data porn star? Maybe I should wear a mask."

That cracked him up. When he stopped laughing he cautioned, "I'd like to be in the loop when you work with that detective."

"If she pays me a fee, will you match it?" Can you charge a kibitzer for looking?

"You being Jewish again?

I have a low tolerance for remarks like that. "No. Republican."

"It's not in our budget. Just as a professional courtesy."

Professional? It sounded like I'd been upgraded in the pay scale. I had signed the secrets act for Speerson, but that job was over. "If something comes up that belongs in your purview," I promised, "I'll let you know."

But I knew very well that if he had me on a watch list everything was already in his purview, trivial or not. Let him look.

I wasn't checking files of floor plans for a bank or anything like that, but I didn't know where Jaycee's search would lead.

I decided to call her. I knew all my calls were screened by the NSA, but you get used to it. It's a little like not bothering to draw the curtain when you take a shower. Somebody might look? So what? You never saw a naked person before? Just don't take pictures and put them on Face book. I'll leave selfies like that to Wiener.

I'm counting on the reality that ultimately nudity is boring. That's why bikinis are more sexy than nakedness. Face it, I'm no Adonis. My potential as a male pinup has long since faded. As long as Ursula is satisfied, that's enough for me.

Jaycee was surprised to hear from me and sounded like she might be embarrassed for not having sent a check. I wasn't calling to collect. "What progress have you made with your Mr. Williamson the alleged neo-Nazi?"

"He's got a few death threats. Someone sent him a package of feces."

"Better find the real Nazi quick and get him to send out a disclaimer."

"What about you?" she asked. "You're the expert at facial recognition."

"I'll see if there are faces on file that resemble him. Almost everybody has a driver's license and those are in the data base. That may give you too many choices."

Feces in the mail had to be a violation of the postal code. Last time I mailed a package they asked me if it contained explosives, ammo, or flammable liquids. Didn't mention poop.

I told Jaycee I'd try, then, as a kind of hint, asked "What do you think this is worth? You can just add it to Williamson's bill." I wondered what she got an hour.

"Depends on how long it takes."

"Fair enough." I hung up.

I'd check on it later. Ursula and I were going to Target to look at baby clothes. That sounded like more fun. Little sleepers with baby bunny ears, stuff like that. Jeeze, the baby wasn't due for months. By then the nursery would be crammed with baby junk. Money wasn't the object. Space was.

When I got back from shopping my laptop was signaling that I had email. My Googling had results.

Google is available to anyone. My advantage was as Metadata Man I could shortcut searches that might otherwise need a warrant or payment. It was a thin advantage. Hadn't my job at Krieger been made redundant by a computer program?

There were half a dozen faces that looked pretty much like Williamson. When a face is digitized there are about a hundred and thirty characteristics that are measured, like space between the eyes, height of the nose, width of the mouth, whether the mouth is crooked or not. None of our faces are exactly symmetrical. It they were we'd look like robots with faces printed by a machine.

The number of possible variations is huge, which is why facial recognition works. Maybe identical twins aren't distinguishable, but I doubt it. Our lives change our appearance. I no longer resemble my baby pictures or even how I looked ten years ago. Comparing old passport photos of myself was chilling.

Well, I had some possibles. Now I had to check the dossiers of each of them. So much of our metadata is out there we are unique. There are several Harvey Goldsteins, but I'm the only one with a wife named Ursula. In the case of the potential person who looked like Williamson but really was a thug, all I had to do was pick the one whose politics were extremist and nasty. Nobody can be anonymous in my world of big data.

I narrowed the short list down to one. It was a neo-Nazi, Larry Cooper, ex-Hell's Angels, had a Harley Hog registered in his name but sold. There are two kinds of bikers: those who have fallen and those who haven't fallen yet. Cooper had fallen. His German style Wehrmacht helmet hadn't protected him from a serious head injury. His leathers had shredded and left part of his right thigh on a highway in California. Now he was reduced to a cane and a diet of hate.

Cooper had been busted in a drug raid, did some time in Folsom, was high in the pecking order of the prison skinhead gang. It was all in his prison records. Recently he was out doing demonstrations and brawls which may be what caught the attention of the left.

You can't go anywhere without having your picture taken. Preserving Civil War monuments to slavery was a sideline. Mostly he was a Jew hater. I wanted nothing to do with that kind of scum.

I told Jaycee, "Your best bet is a scumbag named Larry Cooper.". I gave her his address and phone numbers. "I won't touch a creep like that. I'm sending you his dossier by email."

She quickly saw the resemblance. Cooper had grown his hair back, no longer had that prison look, though he had a tattoo of a swastika on his neck.

"What I suggest," I told her, "is to appeal to his ego. Cooper likes publicity. He'll resent the fact that Williamson has been mistaken for him. Cooper would be delighted to be shamed instead. He's beyond shame."

Jaycee was impressed that I'd accessed so many of Cooper's data. Just for fun I added that he likes Twinkies. That was in his Krieger file of past grocery purchases. "Maybe you could mail him a dozen Twinkies as an entree. Just don't mention my name. Take all the credit yourself. He'll be impressed, think you are a fan and a great detective. He wants to be famous."

"Thanks, Mr. Goldstein."

"And don't forget to send your check. You can add the cost of the Twinkies to Williamson's bill. Just don't mention me. I don't need to be hearing from Cooper and his cronies."

She said she would, but I was afraid I wouldn't be paid until she was paid. I'd be last on the list after her phone bill.

Ah, but in this business, I couldn't be invisible. A trustee at Folsum saw that I'd been snooping the files. The lunatic Right had their own grapevine. I was bound to hear from them sooner or later.

Chapter Seven

The first sign of my visibility was a trickle, then a flood of white supremacist junk mail. I was offered replicas of Nazi flags, swastika arm bands, Tee shirts emblazoned with anti-Semitic slogans, the whole bit. I knew there was no way to turn it off. Just so nobody called in an order for a dozen pizzas with anchovies. Such nasty tricks may be kid stuff, but they are annoying.

What I was sure of was whoever was watching my mail would notice. Naturally, that was FBI Agent Walker. He called. "What are you up to, Harvey? Have you joined the far right movement?"

At least he called me Harvey. "If you poke around in an outhouse pit you are bound to get some of that shit on your hands."

"And acquire a smell."

I had to admit that. "It's been an education. I was just doing some research for Jaycee, that detective. Her client was shamed as an alleged Nazi and I had to find out which one."

"Uh, huh."

"Put another way, I suppose if you searched the net for pedophiles you'd be identified as one yourself."

He agreed. "With us it's ISIS sites."

"So are you getting sermons in favor of Jihad?"

"Goes with the territory. So what about your Nazi contacts?"

"I never identified myself at any site, but as you know every hit is trackable. As long as I don't buy any racist Tee shirts they won't think I'm a serious follower."

"Don't be surprised if you get an invitation to a meeting."

"You want me to go under cover? I suspect I look Jewish."

Did Jesus? Reminded me of all those crucifixes of Jesus. None of them look Jewish. Funny. Jesus had to be a little, dark skinned Mediterranean guy. In some black churches the images of Jesus look African-American or maybe Ethiopian. It was up to the artist's own interpretation or imagination, not like the depictions of Roman emperors. Those were standard. At a neo-Nazi KKK meeting Jesus would definitely be out of place.

"I don't want to find your body buried in an earthen dam."

He was referring to those three civil rights workers who were murdered by the KKK. Not for me. I'd say above the Mason-Dixon line. "I identified the creep Jaycee is looking for as an ex-con named Cooper. He's not my problem. Jaycee has the ball now. I'm out of it."

"You think."

"I hope."

I tried to put the whole business out of my mind as little more than a brief search, hardly a challenge for Metadata Man, God help me. Instead, I focused on Ursula and the baby to come. She decided to get an ultra sound scan.

It was pretty cool, non invasive. They just grease up your belly--not mine--so the scanner can slide all over, then using ultrasound see what's inside. There it was on the computer screen, a shadowing little figure moving around in the amniotic fluid. We could see the little heart beating. Wonderful!

The technician, Suzanne Stevenson, local nursing school graduate, married, no kids of her own, and so on. I had to restrain my Metadata instinct not to explore her bank accounts and medical records. She announced, "It's a girl."

I couldn't tell by the little moving shadows if it was a baby or a puppy but I was sure it was a little person being formed in there.

A girl. Ursula was thrilled. I was happy. I'm not into little boy stuff, like baseball and football. I like girls. I didn't think I could handle the testosterone of a boy kid. They run around and do crazy stuff, all because of one chromosome.

We came away with a little black and white print of the scanned image. Ursula made copies to sent to our proud grandparents to be. Now the wallpaper choice was simplified. As for pinks versus blues, I had read that it was a psychological mistake to impose male/female stereotypes on an infant. Zoo animals might be scary. What about little birds? Angels?

Then there were baby books, titles like "Your First Baby." At least there wasn't one called "How to Make a Baby." We figured that one out, no handbook needed. But then a new selection of scary tomes about gender identification. It was a new round of political interference in people's lives. Theory was that you might have a choice of genders.

First there was this battle over right to life. Now we had a fringe group demanding no interference in an unborn infant's right to choose genders, gay, straight or trans. It was maddening. She's just a baby, right? And she's not even born yet.

At least this wasn't New York where the waiting list for admission to preschool was six years deep.

There was, or course, more to adding a new face to the Goldstein household. It was a new responsibility in a world where someone might drive by with an AK47 and blast your novelty talking fish. Suddenly I had a new round of worries, like kidnappers.

I wasn't worried about Lilith, the evil spirit of Adam's first wife alleged to steal babies. That was old world Jewish folklore. In that world of superstition a baby could not be left alone for fear of the evil eye. It went back to the commandment, Thou Shalt Not Covet, which translates as envy. Envy is one of those emotions that eats your guts, like jealousy, anger, and hatred. No thanks.

Ursula was gradually getting over that morning sickness. When baby started moving around, I got to feel it, but a mother has the advantage there. Fatherhood pales by comparison.

I read that there was a nurse-in at Target, nursing mothers protesting the ban on feeding their babies in public. What could be more natural and beautiful? That's what boobs are for: feeding babies.

I sensed a pending touch of envy. No father can bond to an infant the way a nursing mother does. I guess I was feeling some sort of husband jealousy. Baby gets all the attention and Dad feels ignored. Imagine, competing with an infant for your wife's attention. The kid wasn't even born yet.

Jaycee called me back. She was sending a check, amount not disclosed, but was not finished with Williamson and the social media shaming. She had made a pitch to Larry Cooper, that nasty Nazi scum bag. Cooper, as I expected, was miffed that Williamson was getting all the credit for being a neo-Nazi. Yes, he would notify all his contacts and the world that people should lay off Williamson. Social media, Twitter, Instagram and whatever would all be mobilized to get the heat off Williamson. Cooper demanded all the credit for the hatred. Williamson could rest easy, renew his dog's license and pay his old parking tickets.

Jaycee thought Williamson's problems might be over, but the gambling debts were catching up. Ten percent interest compounded every week adds up fast. It was worse than the payday loan business, which is also a racket preying on the poor. She asked me, "How can I get the heat off my client?"

"Pay it."

"He can't pay it."

"Then he shouldn't gamble."

She explained, "It's an addiction. Don't you understand addiction?"

I have to admit I do. I'm addicted to data. Can't get enough. Knowing too much about everybody is a curse. "First pay it," I suggested. "Then send him to gamblers Anonymous."

She was worried. "If he doesn't pay they threaten to cut off his fingers."

"Must be Japanese," I thought. If it was Italians he'd go swimming with his feet in a bucket of concrete.

Her long pause told me she had run out of ideas.

"Counterattack," I said. "If your Rudy Wayne Williamson has any guts he can go to the police. I happen to know an FBI man who could use a few tips."

"If Mr. Rudy Williamson goes to the police he won't need a detective."

That would kill what might be her cash cow, and I knew Jaycee needed the money. "But you're a lawyer, too."

"I think what he really needs is a bodyguard."

"Count me out. If he becomes an FBI witness against loan sharks he may need a new identity." It reminded me of Gulli, the hacker in Germany who made me the repository of stolen bitcoin. She changed identities quicker than the seasons. I bet if Gulli needed a real job instead of being Miss Robin Hood she could be a consultant to WITSEC.

"Did you reach Cooper?" I'd given her the address and his phone number.

"Cooper is in trouble with the police after that last demonstration. He's been arrested for assault."

"Not for defending his first amendment rights?"

"For doing it with a baseball bat."

Nice guy. I suggested, "Maybe he should claim the police got the wrong guy. Say it was a look alike named Rudy Williamson."

She actually laughed. "Williamson has an alibi. Cooper is in all the CNN videos, swastika tattoo and all."

I didn't want any part of it. "Let me know how it works out."

She changed the subject. "You know anything about a loan shark named Fat Eddie?"

"That's another search. I haven't got my check for the first one yet." I wrote the name down. "Tell me about it."

"Rudy Williamson is vague on the details."

"At least find out Fat Eddie's real name. Maybe he'll sell you a debt he can't collect, like the credit card companies that give up and sell debt to the so-called paper boys who hound people forever. Getting ten percent is less risky than being arrested for cutting off Williamson's fingers."

I'd read that in cases of stolen identity people could be hounded with threatening phone calls from collection agencies about bills they didn't owe. If they paid anything at all they were hooked. If they failed to show up in court to defend themselves, they could be smacked with a judgment. Nasty business, like people reduced to digging at the meanest, lowest level to make a buck.

I guess there are different levels of money grubbing. The guy who grabs your wallet off the grocery store checkout counter is just stupid. Does it in front of a camera. The money is in stolen identities, as long as you don't exceed the thirty grand threshold where the police find it cost effective to pursue the perp. Trouble is, people get greedy and careless.

Gulli knew the score: catch the major bank hackers when they move their loot around and snatch it herself. As long as nobody caught up with her she was sort of safe. A hacker in Kazakhstan isn't likely to turn up on her doorstep, if he can find her in Germany. My last sight of her slouching along like a derelict old lady in Stuttgart wasn't very appealing either. She was afraid. What good is having unlimited funds if you live in fear and can't spend them? Sometimes being a poor nobody can be a good thing. Nobody cares; nobody envies, nobody notices. That was her cover.

As for Fat Eddie, I needed a real name to Google. I'd ask Agent Walker. I phoned him to bring him up to date on Cooper.

Just for fun I teased him a little. "Agent Walker," I began. "I see you bought a new car. You had a Camry before."

He was surprised. "Yes. Thought I'd go for a Ford Volt, all electric."

"Yes, I noticed the VIN on the registration."

"You've been snooping again."

"Me? Goes with the territory of you're Metadata Man."

"You still wearing that silly jersey?"

"It's in the closet. By the way, I saw your refresher course in shooting. Good score."

He was impressed. "You saw that?"

"Nothing escapes me except for one thing."

That there was something I didn't know pleased him. He wanted me to be vulnerable. "What's that?"

"Ever hear of a loan shark named Fat Eddie? I need a real name."

"What's that about?"

"Jaycee's client, the one who was shamed for being mistaken for a Nazi. He owes money."

"Some people have all the luck."

"Seriously. Ever heard of a Fat Eddie?"

Walker knew. "He's one of your boys. Original family name Abromovich. Eastern Europe ancestors. Changed it to Abramson and finally Abrams. Did time for car theft and moved up."

I'd heard of a car thief who got five hundred for a stolen car sold to a chop shop and six months probation, went back and did it again. Skillful but dumb. Stealing is easy. Getting away with it is hard.

"Thanks. I'll find him."

"Then what?"

"Don't know yet. Maybe I'll read him the Ten Commandments. Though shalt not steal."

"Don't forget the seventh one. Thou shalt not murder."

"You've been doing your homework."

He laughed. "Went to Sunday school."

Walker had a good memory.

Swell, I had a clue to this Fat Eddie. Wondered how fat he was. His face would be in the database but probably not his waistline.

Chapter eight: Fat Eddie

Once I had a real name and Googled Fat Eddie I had to sort through all the other fat eddies. There had been a Fat Eddie's pancake joint in Los Angeles. There were plenty of fats and eddies. But using other search words I got it down to the loan shark and definitely nasty person.

Fortunately, nobody is all white or all black. Fat Eddie had half a dozen credit cards, mostly used by his wife. She shopped. She shopped big time, buying junk bargains from the TV shopping channel, usually late at night when resistance is low. I got the impression that Dolly Abrams not only shopped but filled the basement with stuff. She was a hoarder. It would be enough to drive her husband to crime to pay it all off.

She also had an expensive white miniature poodle with a big vet bill. It was all there in the records I, as Metadata Man, could read.

As for Fat Eddie Abrams himself and the problem with Williamsons gambling debts, I had an idea. Against Ursula's better judgment, I called him up.

I told Ursula, "It's just a phone call. What could go wrong?"

I got his secretary. I tried to get her name. It was Flo. But Flo what? "I'd like to speak with Fat Eddie."

"What about?"

"One of his customers. Wayne Williamson. Owes money on a gambling debt."

"I'll see if he's in. Who's calling?"

"Harvey." I didn't want to give my whole name. Hell, she probably had caller ID anyway.

While she was asking him if he'd talk to me I checked Fat Eddie's tax return, his business records, and his payroll. Got Flo's name. Florence Reilly. Got her picture. Social security number. Home address. Medical records. She'd had an abortion. From the high hair and name I had a clue.

Hidden in the company files was the rental on an apartment. Clearly Fat Eddie' secretary was his part time schtup, and a shicksa to boot. His wife was too busy shopping to tumble to it. She would not be amused.

Amazing how much you can find out about people if you're Metadata Man. Smart me.

By the time I got Fat Eddie on the line I had it figured out. He was suspicious. "Who's this?"

"I'm a consultant for a detective trying to sort out the affairs of one of your customers. A Mr. Wayne Williamson."

"Williamson. That Nazi."

I could sense a motivation for being tough on Williamson. "He's not a Nazi. The Nazi is a creep named Cooper who looks like him. We've got that straightened out. Williamson is just your ordinary schmuck. Drinks too much and gambles."

"He owes me ten large. Plus interest."

"I have a proposition for you."

"What's that?"

"Sell me his debt."

"What?"

This was something he had never heard of. "I'll collect it myself. Buy his debt from you for ten cents on the dollar on condition that you don't let him gamble."

"You nuts? What's your name again?"

"Harvey. I'm a consultant."

Consultant can mean anything, like what brand of toilet paper should I buy? That I knew from Krieger. "What do you consult?"

"Sometimes I consult with the FBI. I do research."

Now he was nervous. FBI is not a good outfit to mention with people like that. My mistake. "Let me put it this way. I have access to everyone's private information. I know you're keeping Flo as your mistress and your wife is so busy shopping she doesn't know."

I let that sink in. While he was thinking about it I added. "I know you're a diabetic with a heart condition. One thing about diabetes it kills the circulation in your dick. If you don't take care of it even Viagra won't help."

He was reduced to an astonished exclamation. "Shit."

"Or go blind," I added. "So take some of the stress out of your life and sell me Williamson's debt. Ten cents on the dollar. Lower your blood pressure. Oh, and lay off the chocolate éclairs you've been buying. Think of your health Mr. Abrams."

"You know about my pastries?"

"And your shicksa schtup."

"You Jewish, Harvey?"

"Not since my Bar Mitzvah. I know a little Yiddish."

"I'll have to think about it. Since you're a member of the tribe…"

I let him think. There's nothing like an MOT connection. It's like a Mason's secret handshake.

Finally he spoke, still suspicious. "Why are you doing this?"

"Let's say I feel sorry for Mr. Williamson being shamed as a Nazi which he is not. Besides, it's a mitzvah."

"A thousand dollar mitzvah? You rich, Harvey?"

For a guy with a million bitcoin, current value five thousand dollars apiece, I could afford it. "It's not my money."

Spending other people's money was something Fat Eddie Abrams could relate to.

I was feeling sorry for the guy. "May I make a suggestion?"

He was game. "What?"

"You make good money with the three Laundromats. Cancel your wife's credit card and make nice. Take some of the stress out of your life. Diabetes doesn't have to be a death sentence. I don't want to see you blind in a wheel chair without your legs."

I sent him the particulars. He should mail me a transfer of debt document at General Delivery in Cleveland.

Before we hung up I asked to talk to Flo.

I was sure she'd heard it all on her phone and was pretty shaken by what I knew about her relationship.

I felt sorry for Fat Eddie Abrams. He was a troubled, sick man even if he was a criminal. Flo was a diversion.

She was very cautious, talking to me.

I asked, "Is he off the line?"

"Yeh."

"Do yourself a favor, Miss. If you want him to be your meal ticket, make him watch his diet. And if you'll excuse the expression, don't fuck him to death."

"Got it."

Mission accomplished. I turned to Ursula who had been watching the whole thing while turning pages in the Ikea catalog. Baby cribs. "You've got a foul mouth, Harvey."

I excused myself. "You adapt your language to the audience."

"I'd like to se what that Flo looks like."

I smiled. I had seen her driver's license photo. High hair. "She buys her stuff at Victoria's Secret. Bra cup side D. On his credit card."

"You know that, too?"

I laughed. "It's one of those perks if you're Metadata Man."

She gave me a smile and a wink. "You're a letch, Harvey."

No comment. Ursula isn't that chesty, but coming motherhood has filled her out a bit. Looks good.

She was interested. "I'll check their on line catalog."

"See if they sell maternity crotchless underpants."

Not bloody likely.

I phoned Jaycee. "I've taken care of Williamson's debt."

She was surprised. "How did you manage that?"

"I told him I'd buy the debt for ten cents on the dollar."

"You serious? Why should he sell the debt?"

I hesitated. "It's complicated. He hates Nazis. I assured him that Williamson is not a Nazi after all. And it would not be good if Eddie's wife found out he was screwing his secretary. I think divorce would kill him along with his diabetes. His wife would break him and without his money his mistress would drop him. Not a good outcome."

"So you're buying Williamson's debt?"

"Ten cents on the dollar. A thousand bucks. If you want, you can add it to Williamson's bill."

"Williamson doesn't have a thousand dollars."

"I'll pay it. If you like, you can fatten my check. Anyway, it's not my money."

"Who's is it?"

I laughed. "God knows." I don't think even Gulli knows where the hackers got it. She just liberated it.

Jaycee 's voice told me she was making a value judgment. "You're a bit nefarious, Harvey Goldstein."

I had to admit there were ethical considerations. It was a gray area at Krieger, knowing what ordinarily would be considered private information, like what personal hygiene products people bought in the store and using that in drawing profiles and estimating future purchase tendencies. We rationalized it, saying it was all marketing, but surely did we need to know if a customer had herpes or multiple sex partners? Or was pregnant at fifteen?

Nothing was private any more.

"I'll think over that you said, Jaycee. I guess whether or not I am nefarious depends on whether I use the information to benefit myself."

She was beginning to understand me. "It's an ego thing."

"I don't think so."

"You want to be the White Knight."

"Not that, either. I'm just Metadata Man. Ta-dah! Oh, and remember to send the check."

The White Knight? There's an idea. Would I have to wear armor and ride a horse?

I hung up. This had been fun. I wonder what Agent Walker would say about my deal with Fat Eddie.

The difference was Walker wanted to put people in jail. I just wanted to help them. Jail was expensive and didn't do people any good. It just took them out of circulation.

Chapter nine

I called Walker to bring him up to speed on the Fat Eddie business. Gave him a précis of the case file, leaving out Flo's bra cup size. Didn't want to appeal to any FBI prurient interest. What I did emphasize was I didn't think Fat Eddie Abrams would be a good prisoner if convicted. Diabetes is expensive, especially if he lost his feet.. He'd just run up the medical costs of an overstressed penal system. Dumping him on the street without medical insurance would be worse. He wasn't old enough for Medicare. No city needed another homeless cripple.

Time we had a single payer health system for people like that.

"I wouldn't pursue Mr. Abrams," I suggested. "I think I persuaded him to stick with his Laundromat business."

"That's not for you to decide, Goldstein."

So it was Goldstein again. I'd treaded on his territory. I changed the subject. "Got anything else interesting on your plate? I mean, besides taking on the KGB election crooks."

"You really interested?"

"Fat Eddie Abrams was a fun case. I could almost see him squirm when he found out I knew about his schtup."

Walker didn't know from schtup. He's a WASP.

I explained, "It wasn't blackmail. Just a tease, gentle reminder."

"Was he mad?"

"Embarrassed. Vulnerable. Anyway, he agreed."

"You got to be careful, Harvey."

I admit there was a risk if Abrams was vindictive, an angry, mean guy. I saw him as seriously ill.

"If I come up with something I'll let you know."

I returned to Ursula and the baby crib catalog pages. They also had some cute toys, little mobiles, stuff for babies to practice their manual dexterity as they discover the world and their own little bodies.

True to his word, Walker did have an idea. I think it's because he saw me as a potential asset to be taken advantage of. He called back and skipped the preliminaries. "What did you find out about that Angel person?"

Angel, Gulli's pseudonym. I recalled my last sight of her, limping on her short leg into the anonymity of the streets of Stuttgart, a pitiful looking character no one would give a second look, which is how she wanted it. "I told Sheerson to forget about her. She may be a hacker, but she's more like a scavenging vulture who cleans up someone else's killing."

"Would she work for Speerson?"

"Never. She hates police." If she didn't want to deal with Detective Inspector Klaus Hintz in Hamburg, why would she work with an American? Speerson is not FBI. He's in some other shadowy agency probably with some abbreviated alphabetical designation.

Walker should be minding his own business, sticking to FBI cases. Except when it comes to Russians, international hackers are not his bailiwick. "I'm getting some rumors."

I'm suspicious of rumors. There was fake news planted by Russian mischief makers, and there were tidbits that slipped out in conversations over too much wine. Some people can't keep a secret, and others like to brag because it gives them a sense of power because they think they are insiders. A word dropped here and a hint somewhere else. If you put them together you might get something. "So what is it?"

I could almost see Walker scratching his head. "Seems like there's a campaign to track down big time hackers and kill them."

I thought of the kid Gulli had tracked down, a teenager who thought hacking into big banks was a computer game, not real, and then when it was real, didn't know how to hide his loot. What do you do with sixty million stolen dollars? I had a memory of an East European house with a bad roof, chickens in the yard and a kid Gulli might have conjured up with her own skills into a believable virtual reality of a person that might not exist. Virtual reality and real reality were, well, grey.

I knew well enough about personal data to create a life history and background out of whole cloth. The risk was I might believe it myself.

"So who's getting killed?"

Walker wasn't sure. "What I think comes together is the hackers the KGB used on our election were using their skills and access to rob the Russian state bank."

I'd heard about the two million. "Putin would be pissed."

Walker chuckled. "You don't want to piss off Putin."

"So what were they? Poisoned with polonium, shot dead on the street outside the Kremlin? Tossed out a window." Those seemed to be known methods.

"One was hung from a bridge."

I thought hung or hanged? If you were well hung you had a big penis; if you were well hanged you were like a dead rabbit. If it was you from a bridge the difference was moot.

I had seen some news photos. "I think Svengali was poisoned, shot, and his throat cut. Very durable guy. Must have been the beard."

"Maybe you should grow a beard, Harvey."

"What, me? I'm no hacker. Metadata Man just looks, doesn't touch."

"They don't know that. Remember the Munich massacre of the Jewish wrestling term?"

I did. It was one of those events Jews remember along with the Crusades, the expulsions, the pogroms, and the Holocaust. Never forget.

"The Mossad put together an assassination team and killed most of the perps."

I had heard that, came out as a book called "Vengeance.".

"So now there's at least one assassination team out there killing off the hackers."

I thought of Gulli, but not of myself.

Walker was worried. "I think you're on their list, Harvey. Better ask Speerson."

That put another light on it. As recipient of a million purloined bitcoin, did it make any difference to the killers if I had stolen it myself or just happened to have it in my wallet? How to you plead innocent when they pour the concrete over your feet while you stand in the bucket?

I didn't like Speerson or his remarks about Jews. To him I was just another expendable resource. I did not want to be a throw away low level agent. The man had no loyalty.

I did not want Ursula to know about this. Let her concentrate on her mama to be status. Growing a healthy fetus was her sole occupation. Protecting her was my job.

Knowing what I did about privacy, there was no way in the world that we could disappear. If anyone wanted to find us, the CCT camera across the street, the NSA access to all phone calls and the internet use made us an easy target. Our cell phones are constantly tracked. There was no such thing as privacy or confidential records that could not be accessed. Hell, if they still printed it, we were in the phone book.

Chapter ten

Against my instinct, I got out Speerson's private number and called him.

He was cautious. If he was making a call he was confident. Then he was in control. If I called, he wasn't. To him I was a loose cannon who resisted all ties and encumbrances. He asked, "What is it you want, Goldstein?"

At least it wasn't Goldschtein, that Germanification of my name. "FBI Agent Walker tells me someone's out to kill the hackers."

"There's some indication."

"Anything firm?"

Speerson was warming to the task as long as I didn't hit on anything classified. "Ever hear of Honey Bear?"

I thought I did. "Russian hacker that fiddled with our election. Gave us your boy Trump."

He didn't like that. "Trump is not my boy. He's the president."

"I forgot. You're not political."

"I serve the Constitution."

I could see it. Speerson, great defender of the Constitution would say it was nothing personal when he stood you up for the firing squad. "So what about Honey Bear?"

Speerson sighed. "Arrested for hacking the Russian state bank out of two million."

"Some people can't keep their hands out of the cookie jar. So what then? Ten years in the Gulag?"

"I think they first wanted the money back. Tortured him for the links. Promised clemency."

"Uh huh."

"Then they beat him to death in his cell."

"Promises, promises." Never trust a KGB operative. I fervently wished that the Russian two million hadn't been diverted by Gulli into my bitcoin wallet. I hoped she stayed away from Russians. If they showed up I had no confidence that I could push their agents down some steep stairs in Stuttgart.

"Any others?"

Speerson was uncertain.

"Just what agency do you work for anyway, Mr. Speerson?"

"Can't say."

For a moment I thought these guys were so devious they didn't tell their mothers their own phone numbers. "Should I ask the CIA?"

"I doubt if you'd get past the gatekeepers."

"Not even Metadata Man?"

Speerson scoffed. "Metadata Man is bullshit."

Well, that was insulting. Here I'd been all pumped up, even had a Metadata Man jersey to prove it. So much for egotism. I did need a reliable source I could trust and that wasn't Speerson. "How about a phone number? Code word?"

Reluctantly he gave me a number I could call. Not use his name. Say it was about Hatchet Job. Goody, made me feel conspiratorial.

I hated begging Speerson for information, but if Gulli and I were both targets, I had to do something. She was all on her own, except possibly for her sister. We could both use some backup.

Could I rely on the German police? Detective Klaus Hintz? He waited until a crime was committed, then set about to solve it. If the crime was my being dead, it wouldn't do me any good. Walker was FBI, US domestic. I was sure that the hackers were all international. They were the sinister big boys, not kids trying to diddle the government web sites. But what did I know?

Every kid with skills, a computer, and time to waste could get into hacking. It must be a national sport.

Stealing millions was not. Stealing identities and opening fake credit card accounts was small stuff. The FBI didn't even bother until someone stole more than thirty thousand dollars. That's not in the international million ruble range that invites murder. That's the playing field Gulli was into.

Was everybody a crook? From what I'd seen in the Krieger break room and Boss Margaret's recycled Wall Street Journals, I'd say yes.

I thanked Speerson and rung off. I hoped the NSA listeners didn't care. Had to be a computer program anyway. If real people had to listen in the entire world would have to be listening in on itself.

Before calling the alleged CIA number I needed advice from Grabich. He still had his job at Krieger and I found him in. "Grabich, old buddy. I have a problem."

He'd obviously been busy with something else and had to adjust his brain for this conversation. "Harvey. How's life?"

"Hoping to preserve it. The word in the back alleys of the FBI is there's an assassination team or teams out there finding hackers and killing them."

That caught his breath. He fell back on his old excuse. "I'm not a hacker."

"I know, not any more. I need your advice. How can I be anonymous, invisible?"

"You using TOR for emails?"

TOR is a free US Government program that disassembles emails and reroutes them so they can't be traced. Its purpose was to protect police informants and undercover agents, but it was open source. The risk is your own computer is part of the network when it is on. I leave mine off. "Yes. I do that."

"Do you use encryption?"

"I know nothing about encryption."

Grabich gave me instructions which I dutifully wrote down on the back of an envelope. "What else?"

"Make your web surfing anonymous. There's a couple of cheap services that will redirect your activity to some dummy servers." He gave me that information, too.

That was a lot of homework. With TOR, encryption, and redirection I'd fit right in with the CIA, maybe. Of course, all those steps would make communication a bit cumbersome. At least I wasn't sending messages on microdots pasted under a spy's postage stamp. I could do it all from my laptop keyboard. Ah, technology.

No more tiny writing packed into a canister and tied to a homing pigeon's leg.

It was Grabich's turn to ask questions. "What's this about assassins?"

"A Russian hacker got caught, murdered. I don't think it's a safe profession."

"Nothing is safe."

"I just hope they killers don't decide I'm one of the hackers who stole their money."

I could sense a touch of envy in Grabich's voice. "That's what you get for having a million bitcoin."

"Shh, don't tell." I hung up.

Then it was the CIA number and the code word Hatchet Job.

Calling the CIA turned out to be a bit confusing. Instead of someone answering in an official voice, "Central Intelligence Agency," I got a simple female "Hello?"

Did I have someone's home number? Did I get a day care center by mistake? "This is Harvey Goldstein. I'm trying to reach the CIA. I'm supposed to say the secret word Hatchet Job."

She asked me to spell my name and asked for the last four of my social security number. Being Metadata Man I knew it was enough to trigger my entire life history on her computer screen. Took about thirty seconds. The magic word worked. "I'll connect you."

If she was that quick, what would they need me for?

After being on hold through half a concerto I got connected, this time to a man's voice. "Harvey Goldstein."

"Yes."

"Used to work for Krieger grocery?"

"Yes, in marketing, did coupons and metadata."

"What can we do for you?"

I paused and took a deep breath. "You probably know I worked for an agency in Germany to try to locate a woman code named Angel." I was hoping I sounded like an insider privy to all secret stuff.

To my disappointment the code name Angel didn't register. I guess he didn't need to know that. The world may be an open book to me but these people are so skittish they think everybody's going to be a Chelsie Manning leaker or whistle blower. Don't ask, don't tell, and if you know something be silent.

I felt like I'd have to start over. "I heard a Russian hacker named Honey Bear was arrested for stealing from the Russian bank and beaten to death in his cell. Part of a purge of internet thieves."

My listener neither confirmed not denied that one.

I pressed on. "I need to know if my name is on the list of targets."

"Why would it be?"

Obviously he thought I was a neurotic crank caller. "Because a large amount of hacked currency was redirected without my knowledge or consent to a bitcoin wallet in my name. So it may look like I stole it."

"I see. As Harvey Goldstein?"

"Yes."

"And you don't know where it came from?"

"No."

"Are you paying tax on it?"

This could give me a headache. Was the CIA also acting as proxy for the IRS? "We settled that."

Another pause.

Finally, "You still at the same Cleveland address?"

He didn't state my address. Maybe he was afraid the call was recorded. Good thing I didn't ask him what day it was. "Yes."

"You'll be hearing from us. We'll send someone around."

No indication of who or when.

At least it sounded like my call was taken seriously. Would this be someone like the two guys from Homeland Security that showed up at the Kreiger office? Or would a swat team bust in and arrest me for receiving stolen goods?

I felt like I knew even less than when I started. I'd follow Grabich's advice and then try to contact Gulli. Wherever she was, I was sure she was in danger, and Ursula and I were part of the chain.

Gulli. Such an unassuming almost pitiful person, always on the move, changing identities, fearing police and other adversaries. She was barely five feet tall, with a twisted face and a short leg. She must feel terribly vulnerable, but smart.

Chapter eleven

I sent Gulli the briefest of emails: "contact me," and hoped.

I didn't share this with Ursula. I wanted her to revel in the anticipation of baby to come leaving me to mull over the heavy stuff.

Our parents live on opposite coasts. My mother is in a retirement home in Los Angeles Fairfax neighborhood, street of kosher delis and bagel bakeries. She has a hard wired phone and an aversion to spending money on long distance calls. She'll complain that I never call, forgetting that phones are two way instruments.

Ursula's folks moved to Hollywood, Florida where they have a second floor condo. Her dad goes fishing every day at a public pier, so successfully that the neighbors hide when they see him coming back with fish. Maybe if he filleted them first they would graciously accept his gifts.

With our families on opposite coasts with Cleveland sort of in the middle, we don't see them. Typically American, I guess,

Ursula is more faithful about calling which gave me a twinge of conscience. My turn. In spite of my impatience about having to listen to a detailed report of the latest bingo game at the Golden Age club I called.

Instead of a bingo report I got "Hershele," (She always calls me Hershele like I still wear short pants.) "What are you doing with the FBI?"

"What?"

"I got a visit from the FBI while you were in Switzerland. Wanted to know what you were doing? Wanted to know if you were a communist."

"Ma, the McCarthy hearings were over years ago."

"Are you in trouble?"

"No. I was working with Agent Walker on a case. Is that all you were asked about? My politics?"

"He wanted to know what you do for a living. I told him you're in the grocery business clipping coupons."

Funny how people misconstrue things. "Not any more. I got outsourced by a computer program."

"So you're out of a job?" She was clearly worried.

"I'm doing some consulting work." I was confident that, like most people, she would be satisfied with that. No such luck.

"So what is this consulting?"

I sighed. My mother is a twentieth century woman who hasn't transitioned yet to the twenty-first. "It's about metadata."

Of course, she had no idea what metadata is. "It's about everything we know about everybody."

I let that sink in.

"Like what?"

"Like I know you have only six hundred and fifty three bucks in your checking account. That you get nine hundred and eighty bucks a month Social Security, and your blood pressure is 150 over 55."

"You know my blood pressure?"

"Last time it was taken."

"You should have gone to med school, Hershele. Coupons. Pfeh." I could almost hear her spitting three times against the evil eye.

I changed the subject. Yes, she got the copy of the ultrasound picture. When the baby came she knew a neighbor who could Skype. She was not going to fly to Cleveland for a face to face.

All of which may explain why I don't phone so often. What mattered was that the FBI was checking up on me. I wondered if they also showed up at the east coast Hollywood condo with similar questions. I'd ask Ursula. "Was that all they wanted to know? If I was a communist?" That seemed silly.

"There was another person who called. Couple of weeks ago."

"Who was that?"

"Just said he was a friend and wanted to get in touch."

Do I have any friends? That struck me as odd. "What did he want?"

"Your address."

"I'm on the Internet. Anybody can get that. It's in the White Pages."

"Maybe the caller didn't know from the internet."

"You didn't get the name?"

She blew me off. "If it was important, you'll hear from them."

So much for that.

Someone was looking. Could be anybody. Made me nervous, considering the possibility that it might be someone with evil intent.

I'd try Ursula. Turns out, her semi-pro sport fisherman Dad had a similar call from the FBI. He was told it was just routine. So when are calls from the FBI just routine? Not in my schedule.

I had to assume it was part of Speerson's security clearance. That's what I get for signing the Official Secrets Act which forbids me from talking in my sleep.

There had been no anonymous, mysterious email queries. Someone familiar with metadata would know everything about me, including my blood pressure, whatever it was.

Ursula wanted to talk longer, mother daughter talk about the baby stuff, but her father interrupted. They would miss the early bird discount dinner.

I had a fleeting image of doggie bag leftovers in their fridge and a supply of sugar packets liberated from the restaurant just in case they ran out at home. I hoped my budget would never be so pinched, but then it could happen if my bitcoin wallet was hacked and disappeared. I'd be applying for unemployment.

I told Ursula to ask her father to pay attention to any mysterious calls, but he had already hung up.

It occurred to me in a fit of paranoia that if I was a target of whoever was after the big time hackers, our families might be prey. This was not a pretty thought. "Hand over the million bitcoin or your father in law will fall off the fishing pier."

Once you start to worry, there's no end to it.

Gulli, where are you when we need you?

Chapter twelve, CIA visits

True to his word, the unnamed CIA person sent someone. There was nothing subtle or secretive about it, no casual meeting in Starbucks, with a folded copy of the New York Times as a recognition signal. Just a knock at the door.

I knew it wasn't a Mormon missionary because they come in pairs, wear white shirts and ties and carry a Book of Mormon.

He was probably about twenty six, nice hair cut, and dressed in a suit that fit, no schmate off the Ross discount rack. Without a word he held up an ID card that bore the Central Intelligence Agency seal and the name Gordon Moxon.

I asked to examine the ID card. Then before he could run away I popped open my little track phone and asked if we could take a selfies. He didn't like that.

I held onto his ID card. "Gordon Moxon? Come in."

I offered him the recliner chair and picked up my iPad, compared the selfie with my record.

I shook my head with feigned disappointment. "I don't like to start off on the wrong foot here, but you are not Gordon Moxon. You are Lars Liljefjiord, Norwegian extraction, graduate of the University of Pennsylvania law school, failed the bar exam, engaged to a Vietnamese-American girl, and you drive a Nissan. Want me to tell you the VIN?"

It got the right effect. He was shocked, embarrassed, like they say taken aback. CIA guys like to be invisible.

I reassured him. "I'm not angry. Disappointed, maybe. I knew you spooks like to be anonymous, but I can't work that way. I know everything about you, so don't bullshit me."

It was going to take him awhile to catch his breath.

Finally, he said his bit. "You're Metadata Man." Like he finally got it.

"It's my wife's joke," I explained. "How about a cup of coffee? Maybe we can talk better in the kitchen." I didn't want to ask Ursula to make coffee. She's not my step and fetch it.

We don't do donuts. Too fattening and they get stale. While I busied myself with a fresh pot of Folgers extra fine ground I explained our situation. "You might have been told that I'm the, er, custodian for a large sum of pilfered bitcoin. At least that's the way we've put it to the IRS. Saves being accused of being a receiver of stolen goods."

I assumed that his company had done enough homework and coordinated with the FBI so knew our situation, at least the raw summary of it. "I understand that Hatchet Job is the name of some sort of operation dealing with assassins who are going after the big time hackers."

Liliefjiord, AKA Moxon, nodded, his version of neither confirm or deny.

"What I need to know," I explained, "is who those assassins are. Would help if Ursula and I had some backup. You can imagine we're feeling a bit vulnerable."

He nodded.

I poured him a cup of coffee. Offered cream. He took two sugars Ursula had liberated from our last restaurant meal. Her mother's habits. The apple doesn't fall far from the tree.

He turned down a couple of double stuff Oreos.

Stirring the coffee gave him time to think. "What do you expect from us?"

"An open channel. I may be Metadata Man but I don't see everything. Your old college transcripts are just fluff. I need current, hard information."

He thought a moment. "Do you have any firearms?"

"I'm not into guns. If I did you'd know by the registrations." What did he want us to do? Take up shooting? I hate guns. Guns kill people.

I heard about the guy who peeked down the barrel of his shotgun to see how the shell came out. Blew him away.

Lilliefjiord admitted, "We don't know everything."

I apologized. "Sorry. Need to know. My trouble is I know a lot more than I ever need to. Goes with the territory."

After some thought Lillijefiord made an offer. "I'm just a messenger. I'll pass on your request. See what can be arranged."

I understood. My request might be deposited in what at Krieger we used to call the round file, the waste basket. I needed to make it worth his while. "Remember, my access to information is quick. Agent Walker at the FBI admits I can find out stuff that otherwise requires a court order and a warrant. That makes me an asset."

I guessed my quick identification of our visitor had sufficiently impressed him. Metadata Man might be bullshit to some people, but I did have some clout.

As a sort of peace offering, my visitor gave me his genuine business card, his real name. "Thanks for the coffee." He got up to leave.

"I assume I won't be seeing you again."

His suddenly shy smile suggested he'd had enough of Harvey Goldstein. He simply wanted to escape.

Before I let him out the door I asked, "Why Moxon? Don't you like Lillijefiord?"

His answer, probably not true but sufficient, was "Moxon's easier to spell."

I put his Norwegian name down the memory hole.

As I watched him go I told Ursula, "I guess I came on a bit too strong for him."

She put her arm around me. I discovered I was trembling. The meeting had been more stressful than I thought. You got to have chutzpah to intimidate the CIA, maybe more than I really have.

Chapter thirteen

Besides the erstwhile Honey Bear, now deceased, I wondered what others might have been snared in the assassins' net. Was there an organization? A squad? A couple of bounty hunter types freelancing for a fee? There was no telling.

Whoever or whatever they were, they could be just as anonymous and deceptive as I was trying to be. They were not going to pursue small fry, just as the FBI didn't pursue identity thieves who stole less than thirty grand. There being so many identity thieves out there, less than thirty grand wasn't cost effective. Only nasty vindictives like the California courts that would send a third time loser up for life for stealing a candy bar. There was no reward in that. I guess law enforcement has to be cost effective. The IRS isn't going to court over a hundred bucks or even one thousand. They need to recoup their expenses, too.

My guess was whoever was doing this would want a commission-- ten percent of what they recovered. Ten percent of five hundred million bucks was no chump change even if it's not real. To me it's just a number, granted, a very big number, but I rationalized that it's not my money, so what?

What I needed to search for were major thefts.

I found one. Alibaba, a Chinese mega-company, suddenly found its pension fund was looted, the whole frigging fund. That could be an inside job leading to death by a thousand cuts. In the olden days that would be the Tongs revenge. Nowadays the Communist Chinese government didn't hesitate to execute criminals. They even figured out how to shoot someone in the back of the head, keep him technically alive so they could sell his organs. No wasting.

If it were the Russians, besides having your oligarch's fortune confiscated and added to Putin's inventory, if you were lucky you could escape the country, broke but alive.

In Al Capone's day crooks stealing from crooks ended up in the St. Valentine's Day massacre.

I was betting Gulli would know how to identify the hackers.

Ursula was worried about the visit from the CIA messenger. "What was that about?"

The look on her face told me she was getting stressed. Not a good thing. I didn't want any early date contractions. Got to keep baby comfortable and content.

As it was, baby was taking up so much space there wasn't room for Ursula's bladder, which meant frequent potty breaks. Her back was also giving her trouble. What's a father to do? Come along on the pre-natal sessions and commiserate.

I confessed. "There are assassins taking revenge on the big time hackers. No idea who they are, or if there are several, depending on what country or bank got ripped off."

As soon as I said it I regretted. Ursula didn't need any more to worry about.

She didn't like the word 'revenge.' "What sort of revenge?"

"I suppose if they don't get the money back they kill people. Of course, if they kill someone, they won't get the money. It's not a good idea just to bump the hackers off unless it's to scare the rest of them."

"And there's no telling who they are?"

My own cup of coffee was getting cold. I'd rather have a Sam Adams, but we were out. "I just hope nobody thinks our million bitcoin makes us the thief."

Ursula doesn't need to be told twice. I could see she was getting scared. "So you're afraid someone will kill us for the bitcoins?"

I shook my head. "In some Cleveland neighborhoods you could be killed for your Wal-Mart wrist watch."

"You don't have a Wal-Mart watch."

"I'll try to explain that if the occasion occurs. But seriously, I think the person who is really in danger is Gulli. That's why I'm trying to reach her."

"She probably knows already."

"My impression was she was mostly afraid of the police." There was still coffee in the pot. I took down Ursula's favorite "I'm the Teacher" mug and poured some.

I continued. "Since Gulli doesn't like the police, thanks to her own dark web shenanigans, I think the smart thing for her to do would be to team up with the assassins."

"What? Are you crazy?"

"I've had my moments." Mostly it's been information overload.

"It sounds dangerous."

I tried to shake it off. "If you can't lick hem, join them. If she can find them first. One thing: Gulli is a champion hacker catcher. She detects who's stealing and then redirects their loot. Since a hacker is extra legal at best, better not for a hacker to chase Gulli. Just find another place to steal from. There are plenty."

Ursula understood. She was biting her lip, pensive. "Sounds pretty risky, teaming up with killers."

I nodded. The thought made the hair stand up at the back of my neck. I remembered the confrontation on the stairs in Stuttgart. "There is that matter of trust. How do you make a deal with the devil?"

"Gulli doesn't trust anyone."

I agreed. She wouldn't even stick with us for fear of being spotted. She just melted into the Stuttgart crowd. "She's such a little bit of a thing. All she has is her smarts."

"What could you do, Harvey? What could Metadata Man do?"

I'd have to think about it. Could I live p to my own dear wife's expectations? I'm Metadata Man, not Captain America Master of the Universe. I hoped I'd have an answer before someone came after us by mistake.

Chapter fourteen

The more I thought about it, the more I realized that the world is so full of thieves, schemers, crooked politicians, nefarious CEOs, bad cops, loan sharks, lying bankers, and greedy buggers that no white knight, not even Captain America, stood a chance at cleaning up the world. That's for Marvel Comics. Maybe our society was too far gone.

Human egotism, territorial imperatives, greed and short sightedness meant that all experiments at utopian states inevitably collapsed. The United States had been a breeding ground for utopian experiments. All failed.

Hippie communes did not grow out of a cross section of society, but out of a narrow rebellious age group. When people grew out of their naïve ideology, they moved on. The Shakers got old and died out. The House of David outlived their donkey baseball players. Nothing lasted.

At times I feared for our United States of America experiment. It was unique in the world, but eternal vigilance, as they say, is the price of liberty.

Technology had created transparency. As Metadata Man I had a short cut to everyone's personal information, but Agent Walker and Detective Klaus Hintz in Germany could do as well. It just took them a little longer. The CCT cameras on every corner, the NSA snoops, and the internet access to metadata changed crime. You were not likely to get mugged on the street for your Wal-Mart watch in front of a CCT camera.

True, you were vulnerable to identity theft. Even so, it was, as my mother might say, small potatoes. Considering the preponderance of crookedness, what chance did Gulli have as her own Sherwood Forest Robin Hood hero?

She had to limit her activity to the really big hackers. That was her specialty. She'd have no hope against the drug cartels or even big banks like Wells Fargo. They were all pages out of the same book.

Too bad those Ten Commandments got so little lip service: Thou Shalt not Lie, Envy, Murder or Steal. Those were the biggies. Adultery, not honoring the Sabbath day and not dishonoring your parents were also, technically, punishable by death if you read the fine print. Nobody did.

In Gulli's case, and ours, it was a matter of identifying what we could do and not trying to do everything. For us, it boiled down to a matter of self preservation. Avoid the avenging assassins. Find out who they were after. Gulli had a knack for that. My strength, such as it was, was to find out everything about whoever she fingered. That would be our partnership.

We could call ourselves Hacker Catchers, be a dot com and have a web site. Cool.

What Agent Walker, Speerson, the CIA, or the Hamburg police detective did with what we found out and handed over was up to them. Gulli and I were not official. We were not on anyone's payroll. We were free lancers.

I was not in it for any reward. Gulli did it for self satisfaction. I just wanted to save our skins. A million bitcoin attracts vultures. Even the dark web didn't guarantee anonymity. I was out there in plain sight.

If we did set up a Hacker Catcher partnership, who would be our first customer?

Equifax came to mind. Why did it take months before they realized they'd been hacked? Even when they knew, they kept it secret until after the top guns sold stock, knowing it will lose value of the secret was out. To my mind, they were as crooked as the hackers. It's called insider trading.

Though millions of personal files had been accessed, there was no proof yet that any advantage had been taken of it. No known sales of personal information to identity thieves. Like me, somebody might have just been looking. Look, don't touch.

The irony was that the president wanted the same detailed information from all the voters registrations, not to steal identities, but to prevent votes by opposing parties. It was supposed to prevent voter fraud. Nuts. If that file was hacked, the loss would be greater than the breach at Equifax.

Whatever happened to ethics?

I guess there wasn't any.

It was all about money. Money is fungible, has no loyalty, no nationality. It's just numbers.

Gulli had not responded to my email. Using TOR I tried again. I wrote: "I suggest a partnership. Hacker Catchers dot com. If they are after us, beat them to the punch. Hand them over to the authorities. It's our best defense. Want to build a web site?"

Maybe that would smoke her out of whatever hidey hole or faked persona she invented. Where would we start?

That was a good question. Do you go after the hackers who plundered the Bangladesh account at the US Federal Reserve bank? Honey Bear, the Russian who stole from the Russian state bank had been arrested and killed. Those were hack jobs.

What about the theft from an African country of the money from Bill Gates and the World Health Organization to fight Aids or Polio? Those weren't hacks. They were inside jobs. Corrupt politicians diverting funds. Did they count?

In countries so corrupt that bribery and theft were standard operating procedure and transparent, if someone cared and spoke up, they could be assassinated. A cleptocracy like Russia was beyond redemption.

I was stuck.

Chapter fifteen

Gulli did not respond to my emails, but Detective Klaus Hintz did. Our phone rang at five in the morning, waking me up from an uneasy sleep.

I groped for the receiver and nearly dropped it. My eyes weren't yet open. "Hello?"

"Herr Goldschtein?"

Goldschtein? Had to be that Hamburg detective. "Yes. Is this Klaus Hintz?"

"You recognize my voice?"

"No. How you pronounce my name." I tried to turn on what little German I knew. "Was ist los?"

I looked at my watch again. How many hours later was Hamburg? Six? Seven?

"The woman you call Angel is in Berlin. She was spotted by a CCT camera on Kurfurstendam. Same face, different name."

"Are you sure?"

"Now she is Gerda Schumacher. She was in the Deutsche Bank exchanging bitcoin."

That sounded right. Gulli lived below the radar of Euros and the German economy. She lived in the dark web. I guessed she dipped into her trove of bitcoin when she needed to redeem some cash. "Do you have an address?"

"Not yet. I wondered if you could help us. There's a case of a foreign diplomat assaulted in Stuttgart. You know something of that?"

"That was my fault. An accident, really."

"There is a complaint."

Ursula was waking up, wondering what the hell. She rolled over with some difficulty and got up to go to the toilet.

I asked Hintz, "What do you expect? I'm not flying to Germany."

"I think your Angel, or Miss Schumacher can help us."

"She doesn't like police."

"Zat is why I am calling you. You may persuade her."

"First I have to track her down. You say she is in Berlin? Was in the Deutsche Bank?"

Hintz could sense that Metadata Man was thinking. He'd given me enough clues for a start. The bank would have a record. Did she have an account? She could set up anything. I could get that if Ursula would translate. There were enough CCT cameras in Berlin to track someone street by street. Could be tedious, but at least I knew the face I was looking for.

I sat up and got a note pad out of the drawer beside the bed. "What do you want from her?"

"The Deutsche Bank."

That told me a lot. The Deutsche Bank had been in the news, fined for laundering Russian money. They had a three hundred million loan to President Trump, guaranteed by the Russian bank run by an ex KGB manager appointed by Putin. It was an unabashed shady business. The Russian cleptocracy was so brazen they could just challenge critics to dare speak out. Smart people were afraid and stayed silent. The risk was confiscation, imprisonment, exile, or death.

So what was Gulli doing in the Deutsche Bank? Did they take bitcoin?

"I'll see what I can find out," I promised. Not that I expected much results. I'd be satisfied if I got hold of Gulli in person.

I heard the toilet flush and Ursula same out, her nightgown barely able to cover her pregnancy. "What was that about?"

"Gulli's been spotted in Berlin. Changed her identity again."

Ursula was still too sleepy to focus. "So?"

"Something about the Deutsche Bank."

"Oh." She crawled back into bed.

I wasn't going to sleep after that, so got up to make some breakfast and catch a morning news broadcast. I checked my email, hoping to find something from Gulli. No luck.

At exactly eight o'clock the phone rang again. This time it was agent Walker. "Did I wake you?"

I was beginning to feel popular. "I was already on the phone to Hamburg."

Walker already knew. No point in pretending my phone wasn't tapped. It was like a bloody party line with all those snoops listening in. "Inspector Hintz. Right?"

"Yes. Something about the Deutsche Bank."

"What about Panama? Any mention of Panama?"

"Nope." I remembered the scandal about Americans stashing their loot in a Panamanian bank.

"Are you in touch with that Angel person you were looking for? The hacker?"

"Not yet."

"Did you get a letter from the IRS?"

Just the mention of the Internal Revenue Service gives most people the jeebees. "I thought we settled that." I couldn't imagine what else. We had a deal. I'd pay tax on the value of the bitcoin I spent and call it a management fee. I didn't want to explain that to Walker.

He wasn't finished. "You were in Switzerland, right?"

I gave him a cautious admission. "Yes."

"Zurich?"

"Uh huh." We had exchanged some bitcoin in Zurich for our expenses.

"Keep that in mind," Walker said, and rung off.

What the heck?

The Deutsche Bank? Panama? Zurich? Were those places hackers diverted stolen funds to? Or was this about something else?

I reviewed my own memory. There'd been a scandal about Americans stashing their loot in Panama, but nothing prevented people from moving their money elsewhere. The Bahamas, the Seychelles, any of the countries offered so-called flags of convenience to shippers who didn't want to pay taxes.

I vaguely remembered what Shell oil company did. They bought oil cheap in Saudi Arabia, sold it at a high price to their own tanker fleet which wasn't taxed, then charged their Swedish Shell outlets such a high price there was no profit in Sweden to pay tax on. The profits were all by the tanker fleet, registered under a flag of convenience. Those little countries charged a pittance to register a ship. For them it was free money. They didn't collect taxes.

The flags of convenience shippers also weren't subject to the labor standards and safety restrictions imposed by the United States. So the crews were poorly paid, badly fed and were dispensable. Who cared about a merchant seaman from Indonesia or some other poor country? If an old ship sinks, it's a tax write off and an insurance claim.

No surprise that the American merchant marine was history. Register the ship someplace else and skip the regulations.

Nobody wanted to pay taxes.

That must be what the IRS would call me about.

But Zurich?

Zurich, the so-called gnomes who lived in underground vaults full of money hidden behind numbered accounts.

I checked. Amazing what Google can find. For years the method was to have an anonymous, numbered Swiss account. Bank regs kept the secrets. The Swiss had been forced to reveal some otherwise confidential accounts--Americans who were avoiding US taxes. But now the IRS was going after them for big bucks.

What did all of this have to do with me or Gulli?

I didn't mind paying taxes. Taxes paid for schools, roads, airports, bridges, the whole infrastructure the country relied on. Government isn't a profit making business, it's a tax spending provider of services.

Were Gulli and I expected to become tax collectors?

Gulli didn't like hacker thieves. Maybe she wouldn't like tax cheats. I didn't know. Except maybe somewhere in Berlin, I didn't know where she was.

Chapter sixteen

I had to break off my search for Gulli while I went with Ursula to her prenatal motherhood class. I was learning enough, I hoped, in case she went into labor and I had to stand by for a home delivery. I hoped the stork knew our address. Learning how to pant between contractions made me dizzy, probably with the anxiety of what if this was for real?

I was the only guy in the room with nine mothers to be, a conspicuous male among all those baby bulges and sore backs, like maybe it was all my fault.

Ursula was proud of me, which was a relief. Other dads just opted out. Not fair, but then other dads had jobs.

Back to the search for Gulli.

She had been in the Deutsche Bank, as the bank's cameras revealed. In spite of my inadequate German, I got into the financial accounts. Schumacher was an ordinary German name, but easy to link to Gulli's face at the teller's window.

She'd been wearing a big hat that hid most of her face. Out of doors, she also carried an umbrella which helped with a disguise, but it took only a brief exposure at the teller's window to be detected by the facial recognition software.

Her transaction went into the bank's database. She had cashed fifty bitcoins. There'd been a run up in their value. The bitcoin had been as cheap as five hundred dollars. It had been driven up by speculators to eight thousand, then dropped again.

What was my wallet of bitcoin worth? I hadn't paid much attention. Like, it wasn't real money. Real money you could count out. You didn't put bitcoins in a piggy bank. It was all mathematical. Now I learned there were many digital currency outfits. Bitcoin was the biggest, and some smaller ones, hoping to cash in on the wave of speculators, had gone belly up. After all, none of this was real. It was like the old Dutch tulip mania.

Then I reminded myself that the value of money depends on faith. Once that faith was shattered you got hyper inflation, payrolls delivered in wheelbarrows and spent immediately.

So what was a bitcoin worth? Depended on how many loaves of bread you could exchange for it. Bread was real.

So Gulli had cashed in bitcoin for Euros. The nefarious Deutsche Bank had been a good choice. They were used to laundered money and shell company deals, no questions asked.

All this had happened ten days ago. What did she do with it all? Money has no meaning unless you do something with it.

Maybe as a MS Schumacher she was buying a condo. She didn't look like a yacht person to me. Almost anything would be an improvement over that cold turret tower in Stuttgart. Maybe she was tired of living frugal.

She did have to show an ID at the bank but I didn't believe it. The only thing on the ID the bank recorded that was real was her face. You couldn't change that. She was capable of manufacturing an identity like a short order cook dishing up burgers.

I was also confident that the Deutsche Bank, already notorious for money laundering, didn't care who they did business with.

I sent her another email. "Urgent. Contact me."

Then I set up a search in case her face turned up anywhere in Berlin. That's a lot of faces, but you can't escape the CCT cameras. My hope was the German data processing was not so slow that by the time she was identified she'd be long gone.

Gulli, where are you?

The money she'd cashed was not walking around daily pocket change. She had to be wanting to spend on something big. I was sure she didn't drive, not because she wasn't capable but because, as we had found out, vehicles were tracked almost as assiduously as cell phones. With a car, your location was known, at least the car's was.

You didn't have to follow an apartment. It was there even if you weren't. When we caught up with her in Stuttgart she was always on the move. What she needed was a safehouse, or maybe several. How many real estate agents were there in Berlin? They must have CCT cameras. Didn't everybody?

I asked Ursula for help. I didn't know what a real estate agent was called in German. How many would there be in the environs of Berlin? Plenty.

Ursula sat with me in her bathrobe and fluffy slippers in the kitchen when I turned my laptop over to her. As Harvey Goldstein I could access any portal, but it didn't help me much being ignorant of German other than really rudimentary stuff like ordering a cup of coffee in a restaurant. A Big Mac was a Big Mac.

"You think she's going to buy a condo, or maybe a house?"

"I think an apartment in a building with multiple exits would be safer for her than that old mansion in Stuttgart."

"A Safehouse."

"Yes, Mrs. Bond. Gulli may not be a secret agent, but she is a crook in her own way. She needs anonymity and escape routes."

Using a split screen, Ursula worked up a list. There were lots of web sites, addresses and phone numbers.

Which company would Gulli choose? Something small and discreet, or big enough to get lost in?

One thing was certain: she didn't need a mortgage or a bank loan. She'd said she gave me a million bitcoin diverted from the big hackers. She could do the same for herself big time. She could pay cash.

In her own way Gulli was like the Girl with the Dragon Tattoo who stole money from a crooked company and set herself up all over the world like millionaires who have houses everywhere. Gulli was totally nondescript and secretive, someone nobody would notice on the street.

I had another advantage, being Metadata Man. I could see what was on all those security cameras. Who came, who went. I just had to hope that Gulli's face turned up.

It did, at the office of Wohnung AG, according to their web site, a big property company specializing in high rise apartments. There was Gulli, dressed in a new outfit, carrying a shoulder bag I suspected was full of cash. In spite of her special shoes, she had that unmistakable limp. An orthopedic shoe can correct for some defect, but by the time she'd got those her hip had been damaged.

Unfortunately, according to the date stamp, the camera footage I finally latched onto was several days old. Maybe she'd been shopping and would return.

Her job done, Ursula dismissed me with a pat on the back and went into our living room to watch CNBC. We usually did that until the chit chat finally became an annoyance. They have to fill low news periods with interviews with experts. Talk, talk, talk.

If I had a command and control center in our condo, with lots of screens showing simultaneous locations, it would have been easier. I had decided on the Wohnung AG office to watch, but the time zones had me. Berlin was eight or nine hours later than Cleveland. Noon in Ohio was after closing time in Berlin.

I set up an alert. If Gulli came in the door of the Wohnung.AG, maybe the computer would wake me up.

Watching the 24 hour news cycle, we were distracted by the latest Washington scandal, fake news, and Whitehouse firings. I did dinner, gambling on fish and chips and hoping it agreed with Ursula's sensitive stomach.

The news was enough to put you off your food. We had lost confidence in what to believe. The Russian meddling with our election had planted so much fake news nothing was credible.

Ursula suddenly developed a hankering for pistachio ice cream.

We didn't have any. I relented, went out to find some and had to go to three locations until I found the elusive flavor. By the time I got back her craving had subsided. One taste and she made a face, apologized, and settled on the plain vanilla we already had in the freezer. At least it wasn't for kosher dill pickles in the middle of the night. Whatever she needed she would get. She was the one growing a baby, not me.

They say you are what you eat. If it was kosher pickles I wondered if you'd get a green baby smelling of garlic, like babies born of drug addicts who suffer withdrawal. Were kosher pickles addictive?

Tired, we went to bed.

At midnight or so something woke me up. I slipped out of bed, trying not to wake Ursula, and went to the computer. For a change, my CCT signal was in real time. It was Gulli, all right, coming in to make a deal.

I had all I needed about the real estate office, including the phone number. Maybe I could catch her. What was the international code?

I dialed. It was a very long number, the international code, the number for Germany, the number for Berlin, the number of the agency. On the second try, after a long wait, it rang.

A German voice answered. Confident that everyone there knows English, I said, "You have a customer there by the name of Schumacher. She is there now. Can I please speak to her?"

What was cool was the CCT camera was catching all of this, except without a sound track.

Gulli was surprised and not a little alarmed when the clerk, a smartly dressed. grey haired woman in her fifties, said something I assumed was "There is a telephone call for you," all pantomimed on the CCT.

I could see that Gulli had an impulse to simply flee. She must have thought it was the police. I said, "Gulli. It's Harvey Goldstein. I need to talk to you, so don't hang up or run away."

She was so shocked that I could catch up with her she could hardly speak. "How did you…?"

I didn't want to tell her the Hamburg police said she'd been spotted on Kurfurstendam.. That would freak her out totally.

I explained, "There are people tracking down the big hackers and killing them. Honey Bear, the Russian, was arrested and beaten to death in prison. We need to find out who is looking for the hackers and persuade them that you are not the one who is plundering the treasuries of the world."

Even with the limited clarity of the CCT camera I could see she was pale and afraid. "Where are you?"

"Cleveland. In America. I am watching you on the office surveillance camera. It is the middle of the night here. Call me back after your lunch." I gave her the number.

She handed the phone back to the puzzled agent. I watched it all on the CCT camera, but could not know what she said. Gulli looked up at the camera, nodded, and waved. Peek-a-boo, you see me.

A phone call was more secure than email. Email could be hacked and was not in real time. I was confident that only NSA was listening in to the international phone calls, but then, you never know. I didn't think Inspector Hintz was following me that closely. He had criminals to catch.

I went back to bed, too excited to sleep.

Chapter seventeen

While I waited for Gulli to call back I rehearsed what I would l say to her. My information was scant, but maybe Agent Walker would have more. I figured he would be in the FBI office at eight and just for fun tapped into the FBI's security camera to wait for him to arrive.

Walker came in at five past eight. I could see him, just taking off his coat and getting his first cup of coffee. He was wearing a god-awful necktie with a Cleveland Indians logo. I phoned his direct number.

He picked up. "Agent Walker."

"Nice tie, I said."

"What?"

"I'm watching you on your security camera."

This did not please him. Considering how in his job they set up surveillance cameras in hotel rooms and the like, why should he be surprised? He looked up at it and scowled. "Goldstein! What the hell?"

"Not to worry. Just having a little fun. I wanted to call to thank you for the tip about Berlin and say I located the woman called Angel."

"You were quick."

"Yeh, I caught up with her at a real estate office. You can bet she was surprised."

Walker had hardly sipped his coffee. He put down the cup and reached for a note pad. "What did she say?"

"It was middle of the night here. I asked her to call back, which may be any minute. I need to know more about the hacker assassins."

"Not much. I think they're after someone in Germany who did the Bangladesh heist from the Federal Reserve Bank in New York."

"You don't know who what is?"

"Nope. That's what we're counting on you for. Killing the hacker doesn't tell us how it was done."

"So you want my contact to get there first."

"Ideally."

"Any other people Interpol is looking for?"

Walker shook his head. "You'd be surprised how much. The drug cartels need to launder money."

"So do the Russians. Considering the plundering of the Russian economy I'm surprised there's anything left in the country."

"We don't go into Russia. The CIA might, but they have a poor track record. Did you contact them?"

"I did. Might be a dead end."

"Keep trying."

"Will do. Thanks." He stood under the security camera. "You really like this tie?"

It was ghastly, one of those sports booster gaudy gifts suitable only for Father's Day. "Not my style."

I hung up but kept watching. Walker definitely did not like the fact that the office surveillance camera could be tapped into. Normally nobody could, but I am Harvey Goldstein, Metadata Man who sees all knows all.

Frankly, it's not very interesting to snoop at someone working at a desk with a lot of paper work. It's like watching paint dry, or maybe those Norwegians who broadcast someone knitting all day long. If Walker was making out with a secretary, it might be entertaining, but he is not the type. Nobody is stupid enough to shag a secretary in front of a surveillance camera.

Finally Gulli called back

I cut to the chase as they say in the old cowboy movies. "I need to know how you track the hackers."

Her answer was a disappointment. "I don't. I watch for very large business. Then I break in."

"Can you trace the deals?"

She was hesitant. "Some. If they are very clever, not so."

They were probably using proxy servers like Grabich explained to me. "But everything can be traced. Everyone leaves a footprint somehow." That was how Google watched what we watched. It was, like we said at Krieger, all marketing. If Krieger could guarantee a percentage of positive hits, the advertising worked.

Gulli saw no benefit in it. "What if I find out who the hacker is?"

"Get me a name and a face and I will find out everything."

"Und then?"

"Maybe Interpol. Maybe the CIA. Depends on where they are. Hackers can be anywhere, even the North Pole."

She tool me literally. "Not the North Pole. No internet service."

"Whatever. South Pole maybe." For all I knew someone whiling away the long South Pole winter might be an international hacker. Anything was possible. "Whatever you find, just let me know."

"Why?"

I hadn't wanted to say this. "Because there are assassins after those hackers and they might think you are one."

That was Walker's story. Even as I repeated it, I wondered if it was true. Honey Bear was a Russian and it was the Russians who arrested him and murdered him in prison. Walker's assassin story was beginning to sound like fake news.

"Then you should find them instead."

I had no way to do that. They had to be detected and intercepted. That wasn't my job. Metadata Man was only good for data. The best I could do was finger the bad guys. I didn't put on a bullet proof vest, helmet, and kick in doorways.

Now, if Walker was right, Gulli had a different task, not just intercept stolen assets but find out who stole them. It was easier to spot a money transfer than track the deliberately anonymous culprits. She was watching the currency traffic.

This was my AHA! moment.

What did she do? Set her antennae for transactions over a million dollars? Could be legitimate. Where did she draw the line? Or was Gulli just a sophisticated crook herself? How was stealing from the crooks different from hijacking a major corporation's legit business deals?

Or was she watching the alleged six richest families who owned most of the world? At what point did simply rich become grotesquely wealthy?

I remembered reading about the dish washer who used public library computers to break into the accounts of the very wealthy on the theory that they never read their bank statements. Until they did and he was caught.

It suddenly occurred to me that I had never asked where exactly Gulli got the million bitcoin she put in my wallet. If it had been a million dollars, it could slip through the cracks of a really big account. I knew that accountants were satisfied if they came within 5% of accuracy. It's too expensive in time to search for the last nickel. If the account is a hundred million dollars, five percent is five million. That's like the politicians say, real money.

But a million bitcoin? Where had it come from? Or was it an accumulation of several heists? In my original confusion I hadn't asked because it didn't seem real.

How can such a big number be real? It's like the National Debt. Lots of zeros. You can relate to sixty-three cents in the coffee kitty at the office, but not to sixty-three million.

Maybe Gulli was using me as a patsy. Maybe Gulli was Super Hacker herself. Maybe the guy Walker, the CIA, and the alleged assassins were really looking for was Gulli, and I was the unwitting informant.

Would the police see me as Gulli's silent business partner, the invisible shell company manager who ends up taking the fall?

What with all the scandal about Russian hackers and the election, about the theft of NSA computer programs, of the Russian anti-virus software used as a back door into our government agencies, our detectives had enough on their plate. Gulli didn't hack the election. Gulli didn't buy ads on Facebook and Twitter. That was the Russians.

What Gulli was after wasn't political. My guess was she just wanted the money. I suddenly decided that Gulli playing Robin Hood was a ruse and I fell for it, Harvey Goldstein, Metadata Man, multimillionaire with stolen bitcoin, schmuck.

Now what?

Trouble is, you can get used to being rich. It was better than sitting in a Federal prison. If I ended up in the joint, as old felons called it, who would take care of Ursula and our future daughter?

I was trapped.

Chapter eighteen

I put it to Ursula. "Walker wants me to track down big time hackers before assassins get to them first. That's what he says. There's no way I can do that. Doesn't make sense."

Ursula switched off the twenty-four news cycle on TV. Enough was enough. "Gulli could."

"Why should she? If those hackers are stealing major money she wants to divert, it wouldn't be in her interests to stop them."

"What is?"

"Depends on her motive. Is she undoing the work of hackers, or getting rich herself? I think wealth is like a disease. You're never satisfied. You want more. Like King Midas."

Ursula disagreed. "We buy Newman's Own Dressing, don't we? The profits go to charity. Bill and Melinda Gates are using their wealth for good causes in Africa."

"I can't see Gulli setting up a foundation or a charity."

"Face it, Harvey. We don't know her." Ursula sounded bored with the whole business. Her main occupation was growing a nice baby. She was distracted by the occasional kicks.

"Then we have to find out."

We? That was my assumption. Ursula was preoccupied.

My thoughts went back to that confrontation in Stuttgart. We had seen Gulli as a nearly pitiful woman fearful of the police and whoever was after her. Was she just a small time hacker who got in too deep? Or was it all an act? Was she like the Sorcerer's apprentice who unleashed a whirlwind? Or as she infected by greed?

Gulli had called me back, but the number wasn't traceable. She probably used a burner phone, good for a couple of calls, then tossed.

If she bought a property through Wohnung AG, I could get that address but Gulli was adept at hiding. She had enough resources to buy properties anywhere under different names and had the ability to set up a shell company or shell companies to conceal the identity of the ownership.

If Ursula and I hadn't met Gulli's sister in Heidelberg and followed that up to the confrontation in Stuttgart, we would not be certain that she was real.

I was willing to bet that Walker and the CIA or whoever was just using me to find her. That business of assassins was bullshit.

Ordinarily, if there was trouble I could just walk away. Not this time. There was that little matter of a million bitcoins, purloined from whom? That made me a co-conspirator, Gulli's unwitting business partner, repository for stolen goods.

Being the sudden owner of a bitcoins wallet worth millions in dollars had been a shock. It was like winning a lottery but in Monopoly money. Converting Swiss Franks to dollars, we had looked at the foreign currency and wondered what prices were in real money. Until we made the calculations, it wasn't real.

I knew nothing about bitcoin, that anonymous mathematical manipulation of currency used by money launderers, Russian oligarchs, drug dealers and people who wanted to stay below the radar of banks and the IRS. That was not my world.

I'd let it be a mystery, hadn't asked questions. I guess I was like the kid who learns how to drive a car but has no clue to what's under the hood and doesn't care until the engine quits.

Ursula and I had gotten used to spending bitcoin. Had a swell holiday in Switzerland. Five hundred million dollars, even in bitcoin, was almost real money.

The old saw was not to look a gift horse in the mouth. It was time I did.

With Gulli in Berlin, if she was still there, and me in Cleveland, I couldn't confront her face to face. Skype might work, if she had access. Emails and phone calls couldn't survive if she simply didn't respond or hung up. I didn't have a snail mail address.

I fell back on an email and hoped. I asked a basic, non-judgmental question: "Where did the bitcoin in my wallet come from?"

I knew she used internet cafes and public libraries to protect her anonymity. She didn't sit by a screen all day long.

No reply.

I'd been fired by Krieger, bumped by a computer program. Gulli had created the bitcoin account. She could yank it any time. Without the bitcoin account I had no resources. I'd better apply for unemployment compensation and look for a job. I needed a Plan B.

The FBI would hire me as an informant, even if the information I got would normally require a court order. As Harvey Goldstein, Metadata Man, I could look up anything, but it wasn't technically legal. It would be like the CIA with Air America, moving arms but also drugs. Once you had access to a clandestine pipeline, everything was grey. That, I assumed, was how Honey Bear took advantage of official Russian hacking to do some for himself.

Work for Walker? The whole business creeped me out.

There was no call back from the CIA. I guess I spooked the guy who came to our apartment, Moxon or something Norwegian.

I didn't want to talk to Agent Walker, didn't trust him.

I logged into my bitcoin account to see what its current value was. The bitcoin world was changing rapidly. Speculators had created competing bitcoin companies. A couple had failed. Investors got stuck. After all, it was like investing in gold mine stock on the moon.

Bitcoin was the big player. The value of my wallet had dropped at one point, but now it showed a big deposit, another hundred thousand. Had to be Gulli. She had to be my silent partner. I was her shell company, Harvey Goldstein, invisible co-conspirator in whatever schemes she was in. I was like her banker in the Seychelles or Bahamas.

She could also close the account at any time, move the bitcoin somewhere else, speculate in drachmas or shekels like Soros, and cut me out. If she grew tired of me or lost trust, she would.

I couldn't share these thoughts with Ursula. Didn't want her to worry. She was in baby land. She'd bought more baby books from Amazon. First babies got lots of attention. I guessed by number six it was just another kid, like puppies. No way were we going to have such a huge family. Ursula's clock was running out. We were lucky enough to be expecting one.

I debated about shifting some of the bitcoin to another account as insurance. I could cash in ten thousand in dollars at a time without attracting attention. The IRS agent had accepted my proposal that any of the bitcoin I spent were part of my taxable commission as manager of other people's money. Taking big sums was embezzlement. So what? Would Gulli or the original sources of the bitcoin sue? Hardly.

I remembered a goofy story of a couple that stole luggage at the Portland, Oregon airport. The deal was they'd split fifty-fifty. When the guy reneged, his partner went to the police!. They were both arrested. How dumb can you get?

The world of international money laundering and crime Gulli operated in dealt with billions, even trillions. Back at the Krieger office I'd read in the Wall Street Journal that sixteen trillion had been stashed in various places around the world. Too bad money in banks doesn't create jobs. The trickle down theory doesn't work. No wonder the rest of us were poor.

How much could I divert as a so-called "Management fee"? Mandafort got sixteen million from the Ukraine for so-called consulting. The sky was the limit.

Our credit union had accepted bitcoin to pay off our mortgage. OK. In case Gulli closed my bitcoin wallet, I moved ten thousand dollars into our credit union account. I would do this every month. Call it insurance.

Like Nixon said, I am not a crook. Yeh, sure.

Metadata Man lives on the interface between legal and ethical. At Kreiger we called it marketing; others calls it invasion of privacy.

Then the CIA called back.

Chapter nineteen

This time it was a woman's voice. "Harvey Goldstein?"

"Yes."

"CIA. When can we meet?"

She didn't give her name, Was this going to be a repeat of that meeting I had with the woman from USIA when I hoped for steak but ended up at Red Lobster? We had danced around making evasive conversation until I mentioned the Seventh Paradigm. It was like I'd farted in church.

I wasn't going to say much over the phone. She could be an imposter. I wanted to see a face I could find in the database.

I agreed to meet her downtown at a sports bar.

I hoped we weren't going to have to watch a football game. Volley ball barefoot in bikinis might be all right.

I did tell Ursula someone from the CIA was going to meet me.

"You sure you want to go?"

"We're not meeting at the end of a dock at midnight." Like what could go wrong?

"If you don't come back in three hours who do I call? Agent Walker or the police?"

"I'll be back." I hoped it was the CIA and not some sort of trap. Agent Walker had spooked me about assassins wanting revenge.

I made sure my new tablet was charged. I put on my sport jacket and even the tie and went, not knowing if I was about to be arrested, spirited away, or simply put on a plane to some country where water boarding is allowed. "Mr. Goldstein, where did you get the million bitcoins?" Blub blub.

Turned out to be OK. Jakes Sports bar was quiet in the mid-afternoon. The wide screen TV over the bar was showing a golf game.

At first look, the woman who was waiting for me in a booth seemed younger than I expected, dark hair, easy on the makeup. I'd expected a senior government officer, then realized that though good looking, she was close to fifty. Those tell-tale lines around the mouth told of experience and disappointment. She frowned too much. As soon

380

as her facial expression showed recognition, I took her picture to run though the data files.

She didn't like that, being CIA and a spook. "Mr. Goldstein," she said, telegraphing disapproval.

"Mrs. Trenary," I acknowledged. "How's your daughter? Does she like Princeton?"

I was showing off, of course. I already knew in the time it took to cross from the door to Jake's Sports bar to where she was sitting, her whole story. The main thing was she was legit.

Mary Trenary was impressed. "You're quick."

I pretended modesty. "It's my job. I apologize. Didn't run the voice recognition file when you called. Amazing how quickly we recognize a voice over the phone." I was bluffing. To tell the truth, though about seventy percent of American faces are on file, voices are not collected. Not yet.

"We hadn't spoken before."

"No, but your face is in the database." I sat down without being invited. "So what did you want to see me about?"

"You wanted to see us."

"That's right." I recalled Walker's warning about assassins, a story I no longer believed. "Some sort of operation called Hatchet Job."

She was sitting with a cup of coffee and fiddled with the cup and saucer to win some time to think of her next remark. "What do you know about it?"

"FBI agent Walker said it was about assassins going after major hackers. He hinted that I might be a target. I think he was just trying to scare me. I'm not a hacker."

"What are you?"

"Metadata Man. Thanks to a fluke, a prank actually, the cloud people gave me access. I pass through all firewalls. That's how I know your driver's license number, your voting record, and VIN of your Prius." She was a registered Republican but I wasn't going to hold it against her. I have a couple of friends who are known Republicans. It's not like having been in the Communist Party.

"You could be an asset for us."

I wasn't so sure. "My only real advantage is I'm quick. I don't know anything that can't be dug out by your research staff if they are willing to take the time."

"You under estimate yourself."

I shook my head. "I thought my job at Krieger was safe but I got bumped by a computer program."

Mrs. Trenary sipped her coffee. "You and thousands of others. Do; you miss working at Krieger?"

She had done her homework. "It was fun at times, but it strained my sense of ethics, knowing too much about people."

"You seem to have got over that."

She was right. I didn't want to get into a philosophical discussion about the ethics of being a CIA snoop. "So what about this Hatchet Job? It is real? Or someone playing spy games?"

She took a deep breath. "Some people like conspiracy theories. The Illuminati, the Protocols of Zion. I think there are several groups working independently."

"That's out of my league." What did she expect me to be? A Dan Brown cryptographer, solver of riddles and puzzles?

"If I give you a face, what can you do with it?"

"I got yours, didn't I?"

She got her iPhone out of her purse which she had kept on the bench close to her right hand. She fingered the screen, swiped it a few times, settled on one frame. "Who is this?"

To my surprise, I recognized it at once. It was the diplomat I'd pushed down the stairs in Stuttgart. He'd broken an arm. I'd picked up his ID and delivered it to the hospital where he'd been taken. "That's easy. I know him already. We had a confrontation in Stuttgart and I pushed him down the stairs."

She nodded, had no comment.

"How did you get this?"

"The agency isn't entirely inept."

I couldn't see being hauled back to Germany on a charge of assault. "Maybe I could pay his medical bills."

She shook her head. "No need. Germany has National Health."

I sensed the connection was with Speerson, the man who send me and Ursula in search of "Angel." I didn't trust him, didn't like him. :If you need a reference, try Detective Inspector Klaus Hintz of the Hamburg police."

I figured that, being CIA, Mrs. Trenary would be trained not to show emotion, to have a dead poker face, but she was surprised. "What's your connection with the Hamburg police?"

I didn't want to go into the whole story of Uncle Julius being tossed through his fourth floor window. "I helped him solve a murder."

Harley L. Sachs

Her eyebrows went up. She would be a sucker at poker. When you get a straight flush your eyebrows better not go up. "You went to Hamburg?"

"Not until afterwards. I did everything from my home computer. I'm sure you know there are CCT cameras everywhere." I looked over my shoulder. The security camera for Jake's Sports Bar was behind the bartender's head. "We're being recorded now."

She instinctively ducked, would have hidden behind a menu if the waiter had delivered one. "And you can access that?"

I might have laughed if it wasn't so serious. "Don't worry. There isn't one in the ladies toilet."

She gave me a stern school teacher look. "If there were, would you watch?"

I shook my head. "I don't get off on someone taking a pee. Most of the time we are not worth watching."

She had taken out a little notebook and asked for the spelling of Detective Hintz's name.

I felt, frankly, pretty useless. Boss Margaret hadn't hesitated to fire me when my job was made redundant by a computer program. It was only a matter of time before some hot shot programmer/hacker created an app that did everything I did and made a ton of money on it.

It's already out there. If someone with a home Nanny doll can access the action from the office on an iPhone, so can anyone else.

As for my old job, it happens all the time. The milking machine put milk maids out of work. Saved them carpel tunnel syndrome from all that pulling on the teats. The automatic loom put the Scottish home weavers out of work. Metadata Man was, I had to admit, a fluke about as ephemeral as the winner of a hot dog eating contest. Of course, I didn't risk indigestion. Only indigence if the bitcoin wallet disappeared. Nobody needed a clerk who counted grocery coupons, not any more.

A job with the CIA, if they were offering one, would only tide me over until things were settled. "So are you offering me a job?"

She wasn't about to hand me a contract. "We have to run a background check, security clearance."

"I could do your background check in two minutes. I already signed the secrets act for Speerson."

She clearly felt at a disadvantage. Could be worse. When I come up with people's medical records and student loan debt they feel a bit naked. "We'll get back to you."

"I can be a consultant," I offered. Again I remembered Uncle Julius who recalled standing in a doorway in the rain all night needing to take a piss. It was an image that stuck with me. Every job has its hazards. Bus drivers suffer kidney disease. I guess secret police wet their pants. I wanted no job like that.

It was clear the job interview was over.

I said my polite goodbyes. She hadn't even offered me a cup of coffee or a beer. I did notice she sat with a view to the front door and assumed that purse beside her held a Glock or whatever heat female agents packed. Valerie Plame was said to have been able to take seven head shots in as many seconds. Not the world I wanted anything to do with.

Frankly, I was disappointed. What did I expect? I guessed that the Central Intelligence Agency was full of people suspicious of each other, wondering who in the office was a mole for the Nigerian Secret Police, or whatever. Maybe the Samoans had plants in government agencies. Who knew?

When I got back to our apartment Ursula was in the kitchen. She was on a baking kick. Must have been watching a Martha Stewart cooking show.

She wiped the flour off her hands on her Baby on Board apron and asked, "How did it go?"

"Nothing special. Met a Mrs. Trenary, grew up in Northern Michigan, got a daughter at Princeton, still has some left over student debt herself."

She cocked her head, held her stomach. "Maybe we should set up a college fund for our own little girl."

"Jeeze, Ursula, we haven't finished the nursery yet." I admitted she had a point. It wasn't too early to plan for a future. Who knew if our bitcoin account would still be there tomorrow? "She said she'll get in touch."

"Like don't call us, we'll call you."

Some alleged job interview. Which reminded me, I'd better not wait. I had upgraded to a top of the line laptop. I booted it up. If Hatchet Job had Gulli as a target, maybe I'd better follow her.

Chapter twenty

Again I ran Gulli's photo through the recognition program for Berlin. If she showed up on any CCT camera I would find her. She had been there when I caught up with her in the Wohnung AG real estate office, but now she was gone. Maybe she was hiding, or had left town.

She had made the purchase of a condo. I got that address. Using Google World I saw a satellite's eye view of the building and the neighborhood. There was a bus stop right outside the building so if she was quick she could wait out of sight of a camera and bolt for the bus when it stopped.

Unfortunately, she didn't show. Where was she?

The web site for Wohnung-AG had virtual tours of properties, what the apartments for sale looked like. You could shop without having to drive all over the city and waste hours. Just sit at a computer and get a feel for a place.

Of course, the virtual tours don't include noises from a neighbor that plays a trumpet at all hours or an all night dance locale downstairs.

Maybe Gulli had left town. I suspected she was setting up a string of safe houses she could retreat to using other identities. If she did that, since she didn't drive, I suspected she'd find a city on the rail line for easy access.

If what Agent Walker said was right, she had good reason to hide. So far as I knew, she only had a German passport, but with open borders she could go anywhere in the EU.

If I wanted to disappear somewhere in Europe, where would I go? Ursula and I had opted for a Swiss mountain village not usually visited by tourists, but we were limited to three months. After that the Swiss police would ask questions. It turned out that Swiss were pretty nosey people. An American couple staying for weeks became the subject of gossip. Buy a loaf of bread and the baker's grapevine is at work. Compare notes with the inn keeper and soon you're a public figure.

Fortunately, we were so far off the beaten path that nobody recognized me. My brief exposure on every TV and computer screen as

Harvey Goldstein is Watching You had been quickly forgotten, filtered out like we ignore commercials.

Switzerland would definitely not be suitable for Gulli. Amsterdam might. Amsterdam was a magnet for hippy types, pot smokers, and dropouts. If you decided to live there you had two years to learn Dutch. On our brief trip to Europe which ended with that visit to Uncle Julius in Hamburg, we had spent several days in Amsterdam. We saw the museums, the Ann Frank House, did the canal tour.

I also noticed, being a professional Krieger snoop, that people had rear view truck style mirrors mounted on their upper floor window frames. They could sit with their crocheting and watch who came and went. It predated the CCT cameras' 24/7 watch.

Metadata Man couldn't tap into the views in Amsterdam's window mirrors, but I could set up my own version of an all points bulletin for Gulli.

If she moved aboard a canal barge, she might avoid cameras. Then I'd be stuck.

Even my new laptop didn't have the power to continuously search every CCT camera in Europe for Gulli's face. There are limits.

It would be easier if she used a cell phone, not just a ten dollar burner she tossed after a couple of calls. If she had a car, it could be tracked, too.

She was adept at staying under the radar. A hoodie, a big hat, or an umbrella affectively hid her face from the street cameras. I'd have better luck tapping into private security cameras, like the one at the office of Wohnung AG.. or the one in the office of the Nuremberg records office, the one I used to find Julius's killer. Those were tougher.

Street CCT cameras were hooked into networks. Private ones in stores had to be checked singly. Her face might show up in a bakery, but by the time I got to it, she'd be gone.

This was giving me a stress headache.

Ursula tapped me on the shoulder. "Want a cookie?"

I looked up, dazed.

"Peanut butter. You'd better quit that computer stuff or you'll end up with another nervous breakdown."

She was reminding me of my initial stimulation overload. It put me under the blanket with a baby's pacifier in my mouth, or the equivalent.

Better to nibble a cookie than suck my thumb.

I took a break, ruminated over the problem. Gulli was adept at not showing herself. She could pay cash for everything, no credit cards, no checks. She would not leave a trail. It was hard to do in a surveillance state, but she had practice. Able to construct any identity, she could hide better than someone on the witness protection program.

If searched by the police, I wondered how many different ID cards she carried. They would think she was a spy. What she really was, I had to admit, was an international criminal. Just because she, as she insisted, stole only from the thieves, that didn't excuse her from being a thief herself.

And I was beholden to her. She was our benefactor. What did that make me? Whose money ended up in my bitcoin wallet?

What if I did find out where it came from? What then?

It would take more than a peanut butter cookie to calm me down.

Maybe if I could get the system to FIND GULLI and let it search she would turn up.

In the meantime I needed a nap.

I did. To my surprise I slept two hours. When I woke up it was late afternoon. I decided to phone Agent Walker to see if he had any news.

I didn't hook into his security camera. Last time he was irritated that I watched him on his own camera.

"What do you want, Harvey?"

"I heard that one of the Russian hackers was arrested, tortured, and beaten to death in his cell. Any word about other hackers?"

"Not my area. You're talking international. FBI is domestic. Did you check with CIA?"

"I did. Turned into a sort of job interview. You know, don't call us, we'll call you. What about NSA?"

"NSA is probably working on it. You won't get anything from them. They don't even talk to each other."

I ventured, "Maybe I could break into their files."

Walker didn't like that. "You do, Goldstein, and I'll be knocking at your door with a warrant for your arrest."

"Just wondered if you heard anything on the grapevine."

"What's your interest?"

I hesitated. "Well, you know I'm not a hacker, but some people might think I am because of that bitcoin thing."

"You should ask your friend Angel, or whatever she calls herself."

"Can't locate her. She was in Berlin, bought a condo, but now she's gone again."

"Give the German police a heads up."

"If she finds out I asked for police help she'll be pissed."

"Not my problem, Harvey. Now I have to go after some Opioid distributors before half of Cleveland dies of an overdose."

I sensed that he considered me a pest. The FBI was no help. Considering the difference in time zones, I'd take a chance and phone Hamburg after breakfast. Detective Hintz should be in his office then.

In the meantime maybe my computer search would turn up an alert.

On a wild hunch I asked Google for any murders of hackers.

The Google search engine can sweep up more than you want if you make the request too broad. When I google myself there's all the stuff about other Harvey Goldsteins. If I do narrow the search I get a hit on my high school graduation pictures.

"Murdered hackers" turned up murders and hackers, but not both, not at first. There was something, a kid in a previous Soviet state. Sounded like the one Gulli had tracked down, the kid who thought breaking into banks was a sort of computer game like the kid in the movie who thinks he's playing Thermonuclear War only it's not a simulation. It's real.

Sometimes someone will find what looks like a dead hand grenade until they pull the pin. Farmers in Belgium are still plowing up unexploded World War One ordinance. That can really mess up your potato crop.

I decided to go for "Missing Hackers" and there were two. An NSA employee on vacation had not returned. An IT contractor for Homeland Security had slipped out of the country.

Homeland Security focuses on keeping bad people out, but not keeping people in. Thousands cross into Canada and Mexico every day.

Were these two disappearances out of the ordinary? Husbands sneaking off on a flit? Or leakers carrying secrets to Wikileaks?

It's a big world out there and the internet traffic was more than even Metadata Man could handle. I needed an AI program faster than a binary system. The speed of light was too slow. Quantum computing looked like our next stage, faster than anything current. It takes years to learn to win at GO, but one such program taught itself to win at GO in only a month of reviewing every recorded past game.

If I had quantum capability maybe I'd find Gulli in minutes.

I was beginning to despair when my search program found her.

She was in Amsterdam. Ah!

Her face turned up in the melee of tourists at Amsterdam's main railway station. Other cameras followed her.

It was raining in Amsterdam. Hidden under an umbrella, I'd have lost her but I detected her characteristic limp. She couldn't disguise that.

She got on a streetcar, but then I lost her.

Too bad she didn't carry a cell phone. The ping would have caught her.

I'd have to reverse zoom and check the neighborhoods.

At least for now I knew she was in Amsterdam.

Gulli didn't speak Dutch. Ursula had tried her German when we were there, but even years after the war, German was not welcome. English was safer.

"She's in Amsterdam," I told Ursula with a sound of triumph in my voice.

Ursula no longer had clothes that fit comfortably over baby. Her bathrobe hardly closed over her. Time she checked the on line stores for maternity clothes. To her that was more interesting that my search for Gulli. My Googling was, to her, boring. "So what will you do now, Metadata Man?"

I ignored the sarcasm. "She'll probably go to an Internet café. Maybe I can intercept her if she goes on line."

"Your interest in that woman is making me jealous."

Jealous? Maybe Ursula felt neglected. Granted, being highly pregnant means she didn't have that svelte figure, but she was looking more like the Earth Mother, which is an ancient goddess. That's the power of fecundity.

As for Gulli, there was nothing attractive about her. What I wanted to know was where she got the million bitcoin, who I might have to beware of in case…

As soon as my search pinpointed her location in Amsterdam I'd contact her. Email worked only if she checked her account. I had no current mailing address. Since she changed names so often, the post office would not find her for forwarded mail. I had to admit, with some admiration and awe, that it actually was possible to drop off the earth even in these days of surveillance and tracking devices. Except when she actually bought that condo in Berlin she was leaving no paper trail. She might have created a shell company for the transaction.

Well, since she was in Holland, there was no point in calling Detective Hintz in Hamburg.

I got a hit. My alert system picked up Gulli in a grocery store. She was stocking up provisions, housekeeping stuff. Looked like she had found some new digs, at least for Holland.

From her grocery store I broadened my search of her neighborhood. Amsterdam was not as saturated with CCT cameras as London, but I had hopes.

Thanks to a camera outside the next address, I caught Gulli going into an apartment building, one of those narrow structures characteristic of Amsterdam where you might build a four story house on a ten foot lot. The security camera inside the door faced the entrance. That was it.

I set my system to record everyone who came in and left from the entrance. Sooner or later she would come out and I could track her. My hope was she'd stop at an internet café to check her email.

As it turned out, I was not the only one looking.

Chapter twenty-one

Holland is wet and windy. Much is below sea level, and the bottom land reclaimed. The incessant rain eventually washes the salt out of the rich soil. The wind powered the windmills that pumped the water out. It's a country where you need a good rain coat and waterproof shoes. Unless you're a drug dealer, it's no place to hang out on street corners.

I set up my system to save camera recordings of the apartment building entrance and the street outside. I could not read the names on the mailbox inside the entrance. Recorded in real time, the record would have to be played back in enhanced speed or I'd be stuck watching minute by minute for twenty-four hours. Fortunately, the camera was motion activated. If nobody came in the door for a long time, there was nothing recorded.

Would Gulli, like most of us, fall into a pattern? Go out every morning at the same time? That would make it easier.

I soon located a number of cameras watching her street, but there were gaps in the coverage.

I sent her an email to the one address I had and hoped she'd log on. Could be never.

While I waited for her to pick up her email I saw Gulli's pattern. She would leave about ten o'clock, take a tram, and disappear until I found the place where she regularly got off which was Dam, the square where buskers, beggars, and hippies of the world hung out.

I soon got to recognize the residents of the apartment house. There were four apartments stacked on top of each other. No elevator.

When Ursula and I stayed in Amsterdam we found the stairs at the cheap hotel steep, and the treads no more than four or five inches deep, so you climbed with your feet sideways or used just your toes, like a ladder.

This was worse than those German wooden stairs up to the tower digs she had in Stuttgart.

I saw that Gulli was the only resident likely to be home during the day. The other residents came and went like clockwork.

As for the street outside, this was not the best Amsterdam neighborhood. When Ursula and I were there it was obvious, early in the morning, that drug dealers took up their usual positions on their habitual street corners. That was probably one reason why you had to know the touch pad code to enter Gulli's building.

The weather was miserable. For the next couple of days I noted who came and went. One rough looking man hung around. At first I thought he might be a drug dealer, but nobody ever approached him. Remembering Uncle Julius's comment about being on a stakeout all night in the rain, I began to think the guy was watching the apartment entrance. Was he police? A detective? A burglar casing the joint?

I reasoned that if he was police, like any government employee, he'd be there in shifts, replaced every few hours by someone else.

At dinner time when people were returning from work, the watcher closed in and caught the door as it was about to close, then, after pausing until the resident disappeared up the stairs, he did something with the door jamb.

Gulli had gone out in the morning. Sure enough I saw on a security camera that she checked in at an internet café.

I immediately switched to my email server to wait for her response. It was simply "How are you?"

Afraid she'd disappear again, I got right to the point. "I need to know where you got my bitcoin wallet. Whose money was it?"

She didn't reply at once. I waited. Finally she sent "Do not look a gift horse in the mouth."

That didn't help at all. I thought I might warn her that someone was watching her building, but vigilance was her modus operandi.

During the time I was involved with the email, I didn't notice that a small, white delivery van parked across her street. The watcher got in. Now there were two and they didn't leave. Maybe there was a drug deal going down.

I would expect such a transaction to be quick. They just sat there watching the building.

I was getting nervous.

Gulli had only a short walk from the tram stop to her door. As she approached her entrance the two men left the van and crossed the street. As she entered the building the two men closed in.

I lost time while I switched to the security camera in the vestibule, watched in shock as one man threw a sack over her head.

Gulli is a small person, easy for a couple of guys to pick up. They carried her out and bundled her into the back of the van.

It took only second and she was gone.

Whoa! Hoping to get the license number, I tried switching to other cameras. Could I follow the progress of the van as it moved through Amsterdam? I felt like a juggler with all thumbs. Any hesitation and I'd lose the vehicle.

I caught up with it at a traffic light, but a cab pulled in behind it, blocking my view of the registration. All I could see was the sticker designating the country of origin. D. It was a German vehicle.

There was a dead spot in CCT coverage. I had to broaden my search and lost it. Too many crowded, small streets, too many cameras to switch to.

I was watching a kidnapping in real time, except I was in Cleveland, Ohio and she was in Amsterdam, many time zones away. How could I call the police in Amsterdam to tell them a kidnapping was in progress? How do you call 911 in Holland? Or is it like 999 in England? An internet search would get me to the Amsterdam web pages.

That web page was full of tourism stuff, links to hotels and restaurants, a city directory in Dutch which I don't read. It was frustrating. What is "police" in Dutch? Polizei? Polis?

"Ursula! Come here quick. Take a look at this."

She's a bit slow getting up from the couch. Being pregnant added about twenty pounds of awkward weight.

She came up behind me. Her back hurt. She leaned on my shoulder to look at the computer screen.

I replayed the surveillance tapes. Did it again slowly. Tried to make out the faces of the two men. If I got a good shot maybe I could compare it with the digital facial recognition record. How extensive was that program in Holland?

"Can you read the Amsterdam directory? I want to call the Dutch police."

She was skeptical. "Why would they believe you?"

I admitted, "I guess not everybody has heard of Metadata Man."

"I should never have made you that shirt."

Ursula had better luck with Dutch than I did. Dutch and German must be similar, but what do I know? I'm linguistically functionally illiterate.

We found what looked to be the Dutch equivalent of "contact us" and a number.

I had called Germany before, but did not know the country code for Holland. It took several tries before I got through to a robot answering machine. What was I supposed to do? Press one? What was Dutch for "emergency"?

My brain was hitting the wall. It's bad enough being overwhelmed with data I don't want. Now I couldn't extricate the data I did want.

"Let's try Detective Hintz in Hamburg. At least he speaks English."

This time I got through, except the time zones were against me. Ursula heard the message on speaker phone and understood that he was out of the office. "Leave a message."

Her back was giving out. She had to sit down.

"This is Harvey Goldstein," I began. "I've been tracking the woman we called Angel. She's in Amsterdam, but I just witnessed her being kidnapped. Two men took her away in a van with a German plate. Since she's probably wanted as a fugitive hacker, maybe Interpol would help find her. I hear there are assassins hunting the major hackers..." but then my message reached the limit to the voicemail recorder. I was disconnected.

I tried again. This time the message was unintelligible. I needed help from Ursula, my resident translator. I gambled and pressed zero. This time she was back and heard it. "Mail box is full." Nuts.

Hintz might not call back before tomorrow. Playing phone tag can be maddening. It was going to be up to me. Come on, Metadata Man. Do your stuff.

The faces of the two men were my next best bet. Then possibly the license plate of the van. The watcher who hung around must have shown his face. I was not entirely helpless even if I was thousands of miles away.

Tracking down the killer of Uncle Julius in Hamburg had not been in real time. I had visited the old Stasi files in Nuremberg and got the man's face off the security camera. That perp wasn't on the move. It was just a matter of passing the information on to Detective Hintz and sending someone to make the arrest. Gulli was on the move, might be crossing a border, might be anywhere.

The van she'd been taken in might be switched. Vans were pretty common. There were too many nearly identical vehicles in Holland. If I only had the license number!

I copied, cut and pasted incomplete shots of the faces of the two men. Maybe I could build a three dimensional mockup for identification purposes. An expert with photo shop could create anything, but I don't use that program.

In a kidnapping, every hour counts. If a child is taken by some pedophile if not found in three days it is likely dead. What about Gulli?

I did not think they would want revenge for Gulli's thefts. They would want their money back. Who would that be?

Could be anybody. She was capable of raiding offshore banks, shell companies, of intercepting money transfers and diversions. She no doubt had multiple enemies.

Was there a contract out for her murder?

By degrees, bits and pieces enhanced and assembled, two faces emerged from my cutting and pasting. I compared with the digital library of European faces.

I got a hit, two hits. Like the men who had followed Ursula and me on the autobahn in Germany, these were two brothers, in this case both Syrian refugees. They had been photographed after they landed in Greece on a rubber raft with a bunch of other victims of war. People arriving, shipwrecked, with no identification, had to be registered, fingerprinted, their photos taken , and some sort of papers issued. That was my best bet.

Refugees are running away from danger. But what do they run to? It's not easy to adapt to a new culture and a new language, to seek asylum where you aren't welcome and are at best the object of suspicion. How do you get a decent job if you don't know the language? How do you survive?

Some welfare state countries provide temporary housing and a stipend, at least for awhile. Then what? Maybe crime, drugs, burglaries, smuggling, whatever.

What I found from the registry of refugees was scanty, just the basics. They were Syrians, Johan and Lonan Mathullah. At least, that was who they claimed to be when processed among the refugees. They had asked to be relocated to Norway, were refused, also turned down by the Swedes. There'd been quotas in those countries. Scandinavians, like the rest of western Europe, had been saturated by millions of people fleeing from the Middle East wars and from Africa. How many could they absorb? There were more displaced persons than after World War II, an international tragedy.

My next best bet was the van. Parked across the street from Gulli's apartment house, the license plate was not in view. I backed up the recording of the CCT camera across the street looked for when the van arrived and when it left.

At last I got it. It was an oval export plate. If it had been a standard German plate, the first initials, like HH for Hamburg, would identify the city. For this one I'd have to find a directory of recent purchases and muddle through my language ignorance. Metadata Man might know everything, but when it came to foreign languages I was a dofus.

Translation programs were clunky. What emerged was not exactly English and lacked nuances. How do you translate a metaphor? Without cultural referents, what sometimes emerges is gibberish.

Ursula was not in the mood. This whole Metadata Man thing had become an irritant. My ability know everything about total strangers, to her was showing off.

She finally relented, took over my chair, and worked her way through the German bureaucracy. The van had been bought by a Danish businessman for eventual export. She even got the buyer's name and the Aarhus address.

Just when I was about to rejoice at her skill she had a PS: "It's been reported stolen."

Well, maybe the Dutch police could be put on the lookout.

In the meantime, what?

Chapter twenty-two

I thought I'd done pretty well, working out of Cleveland, Ohio on a kidnapping in progress in Amsterdam, Holland but I was dead ended. Detective Inspector Hintz had not called back. Nor had the CIA. I was like the job hunter waiting for a response to yet another dead end job application.

Ursula and I were the only ones who knew Gulli's real name, and not even her surname. She used so many fake IDs it was useless to look for people with those names. We had contacted her sister and had that meeting at the castle in Heidelberg. She should be told what we knew.

I sent her sister a cryptic email: "Your sister has been kidnapped. Please contact me for particulars. Harvey."

Then I returned to the scenes of the crime, so to speak. In search of the stolen van, I backtracked through CCT cameras. The wider the search, the lowest probability of finding it.

If I were doing the kidnapping, I'd ditch the vehicle, change to another, an older model without a GPS locator, and park in a garage or warehouse away from CCT cameras.

Ditch the vehicle was a good guess. Amsterdam is build on a circle of concentric, connected canals. When Ursula and I were there, I cringed at the sight of car parked beside a canal, no guard rail, not even a curb. A slight miscalculation, a foot slipped off the brake onto the accelerator, and splash.

I once saw a TV story of people taking lessons in Holland in how to escape from your vehicle if it goes into a canal. You can't open the doors until the vehicle is full of water. Then you have only seconds to release your seat belt, get the door open, or the window, and swim out, all this in murky water. The lessons were done in a swimming pool with a car that had to be fished out for every new lesson. Of course, when you know your car is going over the edge you have time to plan for it, get ready to undo the seat belt. It wasn't something I'd care to do even in practice with a scuba diver alongside.

But what about Gulli? If the kidnappers were disposing of the vehicle in a Dutch canal and her in it, she'd have no chance.

I looked for instances of canal-dunked vehicles.

The Dutch are prepared. They have teams at the ready. As soon as an alarm is sounded they head for the spot. By the time they arrive a diver is suited up and ready to go.

Sure enough. According to the time stamp on the CCT tape, an hour after the kidnapping the van I was looking for went into a canal. Not long after, a wrecker pulled it out, water streaming from an open door. There was no one inside.

Two divers stayed behind in case a corpse was down in the bottom of the canal.

No Gulli.

So where had they taken her?

What did she tell them?

Did she tell them about my wallet with a million bitcoin? A million bitcoin, depending on the wildly fluctuating value, had been worth five hundred million dollars. This was more than the Powerball lottery.

I could not even imagine five hundred million. A thousand dollars in currency is about my limited imagination. Five hundred million, to me, was just a number with a lot of zeros. For sure, it's not chump change. A small country's economy could rise or fall on that much.

So where had it come from? Venezuela? Brazil? Bangladesh? Would they want it back? If they did, what do you do, write a check?

Unless something came up, whether Gulli contacted me or showed up dead, I was clueless. Metadata Man, who knows all knows noting.

Then, in the middle of the night, from some insomniac or corresponding to some foreign time zone, I got the first phone call.

My caller ID showed only "unknown caller." I said, "Hello?" No answer. Nobody spoke. Not even heavy breathing. Then disconnected.

Was it just a wrong number.

I'd heard that if the caller asks if it is you not to answer yes because your voice can be recorded and the "yes" used to accept some offer over the phone. Latest scam. Just say something else, or nothing. .

A few minutes later, another call. No voice. This was on our hard wired land line. I unplugged it.

The phone had awakened Ursula. "It's two o'clock in the morning! Who was that?"

"Wrong number. Go back to sleep."

She couldn't. Growing a baby infringes on the bladder, which means frequent trips to the toilet. Ursula had to get up.

She had hardly got back in bed when her cell phone rang.

Nowadays everyone is totally wired. People can't take their eyes off their phones. Distracted, they walk into traffic. Millennials will check their I-phones eighty times an hour, interrupting conversations, work rhythms, and damaging the brain. I'm one of the small percentage that refuse to own one.

Ursula answered, her irritation obvious. "Hello? Who's calling?"

She handed me the phone. The lighted screen was like a little flashlight in the dark bedroom.

I realized I was being watched. There was my bleary-eyed face in a little box in the corner, and a masked face looking at me. A Skype call for God's sake. It was unnerving.

It was supposed to be.

The accented voice asked, "Harvey Goldstein?"

I wasn't going to say 'yes.' "Who wants to know?"

"Your friend." With that, the camera at the other end was moved and there was Gulli's face.

I recognized her in spite of a black eye and bruises.

Without a word, I showed the image to Ursula who was now wide awake.

Gulli said, "Entschuldigen."

My German is nix. "What's that?"

"She's apologizing."

"For what?"

"Probably for giving her kidnappers this phone number."

I took the phone. "What do you want?"

Gulli's faced was gone and the masked one was back. It was a scarf over the nose and mouth, only the eyes showing. "We want one million dollars."

"Ransom?"

"One million dollars or we will cut off her fingers one by one."

I stalled for time. "Who is this? Johan or Lonan?"

I knew that would rattle him.

"How you know?"

"I am Metadata Man. Harvey Goldstein knows all about you. You can cover your face, but not your eyes. Retina identification." It was a bluff, but a good guess. I was stalling for time while I traced the call. Of course, a cell phone call only gets you to the nearest cell tower, not the exact address, but at least that would be something and he would not know the difference "How do you want to be paid? In guilders, Euros, dollars, or maybe drachma?"

I'd once seen how much space a million dollars in hundreds took. It would load a pallet. A million in hundreds would not go by US Postal Service. Maybe UPS.

"We want bitcoin."

"I don't know how to do that." Our Credit Union accepted bitcoin as payment for our mortgage, but I didn't know how they did it. Since it's a digital currency. It's not something you carry around in a banker's courier bag.

"You have seventy two hours."

That much time would give me a chance to notify the Dutch police and close in on him. "Let me call you back. What's your number?"

A million dollars? Was that all? My bitcoin wallet was good for five hundred million. A million? Chump change if it saved Gulli's fingers or her neck.

I didn't know who sent Johan and Lonan to Gulli's address. They weren't very sophisticated. Most people don't even notice CCT cameras any more than lampposts. If they did, they'd hide.

The Chinese company that makes the cameras and undercut everyone else's prices claim they do not have a built in backdoor. That assurance isn't convincing enough for NSA and our most secretive agencies. The Chinese maker's name isn't on most of the cameras for they are sold by third party vendors.

Time for me to somehow contact the Amsterdam police.

Alright, Google: do your stuff. I booted up the computer and rubbed the sleepy dirt out of my eyes. Let's see what Amsterdam, Holland police gets me.

There it was: Politie Amsterdam-Amstgelland, Police Station, Amsterdam, Netherlands and the phone number +31 900 8844 and it even showed me what the building looks like. Ain't Google grand?

I dialed.

A long wait and some clicks and an answer, a woman's voice.

It was a gamble. Of course, the Amsterdam cops had to know English. "This is Harvey Goldstein in Cleveland, Ohio, USA. I've been tracking someone on the internet and witnessed her being kidnapped. I've identified the kidnappers as two Syrian refugees, brothers, Johan and Lonan Mathullah. They grabbed a woman I know only as Gulli from her apartment house and took her away in a van. The van has a German export plate, was stolen, and dumped in a canal."

I was speaking too fast, but then, I was stressed out and hadn't had my middle of the night coffee.

"How do you know this?"

"I'm Harvey Goldstein, Metadata Man."

That meant nothing to her, so I took myself to the security camera of the police station. "I see everything," I explained. "I see that you are wearing a dark blue blouse and a scarf. You have dangly silver earrings, and your bleached blond hair needs a touch up at the roots."

She was shocked. I saw her looking up at the camera and at me. I would have waved, but it's not a two way system.

"Good morning, or good afternoon, whatever it is in Amsterdam. It is two in the morning in Cleveland, Ohio. I do have the cell phone number of the kidnappers. I know you can find their location, roughly, but I can't tell from here unless they show themselves in front of a CCT camera."

"How do you do this?"

"I am Harvey Goldstein. Please, Gulli's life is in danger. They want a million dollars ransom or I am afraid they will kill her."

This was too much for the woman whose job was to answer the phone. She had to get someone else. I watched her stand up and go to the door and call something in Dutch.

In the meantime I had this feeling like I was bleeding to death waiting. What was happening to Gulli in the meantime? Had Johan and Lonan Mathullah got scared and ditched their phone? It was my only way to track them.

This time a uniformed cop showed up in range of the office camera. The woman pointed at the camera, and explained something, but she was no longer on the phone. I don't read lips, even in Dutch, but I got the idea.

The cop picked up the phone and watching the camera, asked me to tell my story. The Dutch accent was confusing but at least it was English.

I had to tell it again. The clock was ticking.

"If you need a reference, you can call Detective Inspector Klaus Hintz in Hamburg. I helped him solve a murder case awhile back."

This time he was taking notes.

"I also work with the FBI, agent Walker here in Cleveland, Ohio."

This was frustrating.

He consulted his little spiral bound notebook. "Who is this Gulli?"

I didn't want to tell him everything. He might simply arrest her for hacking. In some countries hacking is not a crime but was it in Holland?.

"She's an internet vigilante who intercepts money stolen by international thieves."

"And they want a ransom of one million dollars?"

"They want me to pay it."

"Can you pay a million dollars?"

Did I have to tell him everything? "Not in real money."

He was more interested in my ability to pay such a huge ransom than in rescuing Gulli. But then, Dutch cops can't be paid in such large sums. Nor were Krieger computer jerks. To most people a million dollars is a lot of money. As long as I didn't hold the cash in my hand it was theoretical, just a number.

I had to get him on track. "Look, I've given you the cell phone number. You should be able to track them better than I can in Cleveland. I don't know Amsterdam."

That's my problem, one of them. I can look, but I can't intervene. I can't reach out of a CCT camera and grab a villain like some plastic man super hero who travels through space. I'm no hero. I'm just some sort of keyhole peeper with great access.

The cop called another cop, this time a detective in mufti, and we went through it all over again. Their office was soon crowded with people staring at the surveillance camera.

Maybe now they knew what it was like when a nanny camera is hijacked by burglars casing your house. That's the trouble with surveillance cameras. They are always watching. They are not that private, certainly not when Metadata Man is watching.

My being able to watch them through their own camera was more upsetting to them than my urgent call for help to rescue Gulli. How much would it take to muster the Amsterdam police force to track down those Syrians before they started chopping off fingers?

"Look," I suggested. "I can put together the camera feeds and send them to your computers. See for yourself."

Of course, with today's technology you could seamlessly put the president's face on a monkey and nobody could tell the difference between what was real and what wasn't.

I don't have those skills, but I could show them the actual kidnapping and the video of the stolen van, even of it being pulled from the canal. They would know that part.

I had to hang up while I did that. What I needed was a bank of computers all watching different parts of the action. I had only my laptop.

It was now two thirty in the morning. Ursula, standing in the kitchen in her maternity pajamas and bunny slippers, was watching me. "You should send them Gulli's picture, too, so they know who they are rescuing."

"Right." I got to it, but it took a few minutes of precious time.

When I was done and sent the package to the Amsterdam police I went back to the cell phone location. The kidnappers were on the move.

That helped. If would have been easier if they were in a vehicle with tracking GPS, but they were in an older model car. Most cars look alike to me, especially seen from above, and I don't know foreign makes at all. As the pings from their cell phone moved from one tower to the next, I was getting a pretty good running update.

Then I got a break: the Amsterdam police were dong better than send a squad car through the traffic. They had launched a drone. Connecting to the drone's camera gave me a sense of super hero-ness. Metadata Man lives!

Viewed from altitude, the drone image looked like they were heading out of Amsterdam. Where to?

Ursula got into the spirit of it. She put on the coffee maker and pulled up a chair beside me to watch the action. "It's like a movie."

"Except it's for real." I would have switched to a succession of CCT cameras along the route, but when they reached the outskirts of the city into the suburbs there were fewer cameras. With the drone I didn't need to lose visual contact. Where were they headed?

I called the police station again. Anticipating the route of the Syrians they'd set up a road block.

I remembered the terrorist attack on the Glasgow airport. Two were killed, but their cell phone was recovered. The getaway car was driven by a third man who was surprised when, thanks to his cell phone track, he was caught on the highway bound for London.

If you have a cell phone, WE KNOW WHERE YOU ARE!

Unlike many American cities which are planned and laid out on a grid, European cities, having had longer histories, are full of narrow, winding streets.

Then, just to make things more difficult for me, the Amsterdam police shut off their office surveillance camera. Then the drone apparently ran out of gas or battery power. I was now blind. Nuts.

I had passed the ball to them. The most I could do was stand back and wait. Well, not entirely. I could call the kidnappers back, distract them in case they were aware they were being tracked. Negotiation could buy time for Gulli.

I called. No need to ask how the weather was or some such platitudes. I went right to it. "How do you want me to make the payment?"

I think the two Syrians were surprised that I was so willing to come up with a million dollars in ransom. They consulted with one another and returned to the conversation. "The million dollars?"

"Yes."

I think my quick agreement made them think they should have demanded more. Now they weren't sure.

"Normally, in a kidnapping, the payments are made in small denomination bills, not marked, and delivered in a suitcase at some drop point."

I let them think about that.

"I'm in Cleveland, Ohio, USA. Even if I could put together that much money at one time, I can't transport it out of the country. We have currency restrictions."

Hmm. They would have to think about that one.

"I can't get the ransom from one location." I remembered how the rich stashed their ill gotten tax evading money in Panama, the Seychelles, the Bahamas, and any one of many flags of convenience countries without extradition treaties and with banks that didn't ask questions. You don't put all your eggs in one basket, as the folks who did too much in Panama learned when the shit hit the fan there. The Swiss had knuckled under to IRS demands, too. It was getting a little harder to hide wealth.

Oh. The brothers were beginning to understand.

"A million dollars in hundreds is going to weigh a couple of hundred pounds."

They hadn't thought of that.

"Maybe I should write you a check." No body would be that dumb. How could anybody cash a check for a million dollars? And can I have it in dimes? Ha!

"No, no checks."

I thought about the Amsterdam police who, I hoped, were busy tracing this call. "Since I am not in Europe, perhaps I can arrange for a courier to make the payment and exchange the ransom for Gulli, unharmed, with all her fingers intact."

The logistics hadn't occurred to them. I suspected that whoever had hired those two to do the kidnapping as contractors did not understand the real situation. Did they think Cleveland was a suburb of Amsterdam?

I didn't mention bitcoin. Those dark internet transactions were done secretly. That was the beauty of it. Digital currency took up no space. You can't transmit a ton of bank notes, but you can transfer a billion with a few clicks if you know what you're doing. I don't..

The two would be kidnappers were beginning to sound like a Laurel and Hardy sketch, except for the cutting off of fingers part. Gulli had apparently convinced them that she had no money so they had to go to me. In reality, if my million bitcoins were any indication of her activity, she had trillions she could access, none of it her's, of course.

"Somebody hired you to do this," I concluded. "You've been conned."

They didn't understand 'conned.'

"If you don't get the ransom what happens to you?"

"We are just messengers," one of the brothers said. I didn't know which.

"If she dies, or if whoever hired you kills her, you are guilty, too, as accessories."

They didn't understand 'accessories.'

"I need to talk to whoever hired you."

"No. Then we lose commission." They were the middlemen and didn't want to be cut out.

It was becoming clearer now. If the party they were representing was in Bangladesh or Russia or whatever, these guys were just proxies. "What if I pay the million dollars and you just kill her and run away. How far do you think you'll get?"

They consulted.

While they were puzzling, I added, "The police know where you are and are on their way. If she is harmed, it will go poorly for you."

I couldn't come bursting in, guns blazing, to her rescue like some white knight, not from Cleveland. I didn't have a horse, armor, or even a gun.

Ah. I saw they were moving again. It was important to flush them out of wherever they had Gulli. Even without the police drone, once their phone was moving it was easier to locate them.

I phoned the police station again. Even though they had turned off their security camera, by now I recognized the woman's voice. "This is Harvey Goldstein again. Are the police tracking the kidnappers?"

405

She said the car was headed for Rotterdam on the motorway. They were waiting with a road block.

That was a relief.

Ursula and I sipped our middle of the night coffee, nibbled one of her peanut butter cookies, and watched my computer screen. For jobs like this I needed several monitors so I could switch between, but that would take too much space. It would convert our condo to a communication center.

The spare room was now the future nursery, complete with a crib and a butterfly mobile I'd hung from the ceiling. When baby came she could exercise her eyes watching the plastic butterflies as they moved.

I could see by the CCT camera that the Dutch police were ready at a motorway rest stop. The car they'd been tracking was pulled over by several police, one armed with an assault rifle.

I could plainly see two figures emerging hands up from the car. Two, not three. Where was Gulli? Had they dumped her someplace?

I could imagine those scoundrels tossing her off a bridge into a canal to drown.

Then a third person got out of the back seat of the car. I recognized her at once. It was Gulli, paused like the donkey who starves between two identical stacks of hay, trying to make up her mind which was worse: the kidnappers or the cops.

There was a moment of confusion. I couldn't hear any of this. The Syrians didn't speak Dutch, and their English was fractured. Lots of waving of hands and body language. Gulli was gesticulating to the police. She doesn't know Dutch, either. She pantomimed a need to use the rest stop toilet.

They let her go.

Whatever happened next was her problem. I had helped with her rescue. Her fingers were intact. She could probably talk her way out of it. How many fake passports did she carry? Would they arrest her as a spy? She was clever and looked like a harmless, handicapped little person, no danger to anyone.

It depended on what the two Syrians said about her.

They could claim she was a hitchhiker or a relative.

Too bad I couldn't be there to eavesdrop on the conversation. I was depending on the police believing the film clips I had sent.

If a Syrian immigrant kidnaps a handicapped German woman in Holland, who has jurisdiction? Do the Syrians get deported? What happens to Gulli if they find out she is somebody else who doesn't exist?

If anybody goes to trial will I be asked to testify? We could probably Skype an interview. No way was I going to Holland and leave Ursula expecting her baby.

Gulli didn't come out of the rest stop ladies bathroom. All the Dutch cops were men.

Traffic at the rest stop was busy. Cars and trucks came and went. There were plenty of opportunities for Gulli to disappear.

And she did.

When I realized that I had a moment of panic. She would not return to the Amsterdam address. I would have to start searching all over again. Where would she turn up next? In Italy? Spain? Switzerland? I still had not learned where she got my million bitcoin. If I had to return it, I needed to know to whom.

One thing I was sure of: those Syrian brothers were not coming to Cleveland to collect. The travel ban was in effect. Ursula and I were safe.

Chapter twenty-three

Or were we? The Syrians might not be able to come to Cleveland to hit me up for a million, but someone else might. Those two losers were just errand boys. Whoever hired them might find someone else to do the job, only this time go to me and skip Gulli. She was hard to find.

I was easy to find. I had called the Syrians on Ursula's phone, very traceable. I had never had a reason to hide and don't think like a fugitive. I don't change my identity, have multiple passports under different names, and many safe houses. I'm just me.

Gulli's kidnapping rekindled my paranoia. Up until then I had simply taped over the hidden camera of the TV to avoid being watched by Samsung. Now I could see the benefit of installing a motion activated home surveillance system as long as I could set a password so nobody else could access it. Too many people used nanny cameras without setting a good password.

It struck me as silly to use a nanny camera to keep an eye on Fido but unable from work to intervene if the dog decided to eat the furniture. Potential burglars could access nanny cameras, case an address for a preview tour and know who wasn't home.

I checked Amazon for security cameras and found it overwhelming. They had everything, from smiley face buttons that watched to cuckoo clocks with hidden cameras, and everything else one might imagine. And we thought James Bond was slick.

I decided to ask my old pal Grabich for advice. Unlike me, who got made redundant by a computer program, Grabich had been upgraded. He'd been shifted, he said, out of his catacomb to an upper floor at Krieger.

When he told me that, I had memories of his shaggy, Bigfoot appearance and asked, "Does that mean you had to get a shave and a haircut?"

"Yeh. You wouldn't recognize me, but I don't have to wear a tie.".

I personally own only one necktie and seldom wear it. "I'm thinking of installing a security camera, motion activated, with a secure password. Any suggestions?"

Harley L. Sachs

"Depends on how much you want to spend." He hesitated, remembered the bitcoin wallet. "But for you, Harvey, I realize cost is not an issue."

I detected envy in his voice. "My benefactor in Germany was kidnapped. I think maybe I need more security."

"A camera is passive. Get a pit bull."

"It might eat the baby." That shows you how little I know about dogs. I had a goldfish once, but it didn't even bark.

"Maybe ADT would be good. If your alarm is set off, they come."

"Don't I have to call them first?"

He remembered. "They call you to make sure they're not sending a swat team for a false alarm."

"Doesn't help if I'm not at home."

Grabich was getting impatient. "What's going on, Harvey? You got a siege mentality?"

"Why not? You remember our place got shot up. The FBI installed a bulletproof picture window and hardened the walls."

He admitted I might have a good reason and made a recommendation. Amazing how you can buy everything on line, even order a bunch of carrots for home delivery.

Grabich was interrupted. His promotion deprived him of the solitary, hermit like existence he used to have in his warren of computers and wires. I didn't envy him.

Of course, the minute I went on line looking for the security system the search was added to my metadata. I would now get ads on Facebook, etc. for security gear of all kinds. I wasn't surprised. That was my job at Krieger. Trouble is, you don't know who is accessing your big data.

A person with Harvey Goldstein data access would know what we'd bought to furnish the nursery, our choice of wallpaper, where Ursula bought her expandable maternity dress, etc. down to the last personal detail of our lives.

In fact, the last bastion of privacy we had left was the bitcoin wallet out there in the dark web. I hoped.

Grabich was right when he mentioned a siege mentality. We'd already insisted that the FBI replace the shot up picture window with something bullet proof. After all, it was their misuse of my portal password that drew the ire of some violent crooks and got us a drive by shooting.

They couldn't drive by our patio. What good was an armored front door if all anyone had to do was walk around to the back of our condo and break the sliding glass door?

I'd seen houses in bad neighborhoods. They were like jails. People put bars on their windows and resistant storm doors only to be trapped indoors in case of fire.

So what was I supposed to do? Put up an eight foot fence with electrified concertina wire?

What would Ursula think of that?

I decided not to bother her with the details of replacing the sliding patio glass doors. Agent Walker would know who the contractor was who did our window. I called him.

I didn't bother to connect to his office surveillance camera. He didn't like that intrusion and my remark about his choice of neckties.

Before I could get beyond the usual pleasantries, he jumped in with "I heard what you did about the kidnapping in Amsterdam."

"Who told you?"

"We have our ways."

I had never revealed Gulli's real name. He knew her only from the photo we used to track her and her numerous aliases. "It looked to me like my angel slipped the net."

"What about you, Harvey? Will they be after you next?"

"That's what I'm calling about. Who did the picture window contract? I need to replace the patio door."

"You afraid of home invasion?"

I had to admit I was.

I could almost imagine him shaking his head. Maybe I should have got into his office camera. Body language says so much. "If they want to kidnap you, they'd catch you on the street. The KGB would wait until their mark was sitting on the beach in a bathing suit by the Black Sea on vacation. Catch him by surprise. No phone, no gun, no body guard."

"Now you're making me nervous."

"Get a bathing suit with a holster and a Glock."

"You know how I feel about firearms."

That was enough banter. Walker's gun was a part of his uniform as much as his belt and his socks. He had no patience for a civilian like me. He found the address of the contractor who could install a bulletproof glass door and wished me luck. Before he rang off he asked, "Did you get a call back from the CIA?"

"Nope."

"Remember, we can still use you as our internet cop. Think about it."

"I will." But I remembered how my job at Krieger was made redundant by an AI program. Technology was moving too fast. It was getting to the point where all you would have to do was feed the face of a crook into the system. It would find him and send a robot to make an arrest. Robots don't take bribes or fake evidence. They don't need health insurance or a pension plan.

I called the contractor. It was called Armor Auto. Normally they upgraded cars with bulletproof glass and armored door panels. Those jobs were ordered by nervous politicians and big time Mafiosa. A patio door, like all their jobs, would be a special order. Triple Lexan layered with smoked film also provided some privacy. They'd send someone out to take measurements.

The result would be heavy, several hundred pounds with the frame.

They didn't do bulletproof Kevlar bathing suits to protect the family jewels.

While all this was happening Ursula was busy setting up a baby shower. I had never been to a baby shower, but then, I never had a baby. Guys don't go to those. What would they bring? If the anticipated baby was a boy, would they bring baseball mitts? Footballs?

I wondered who Ursula would invite. When we were both working we had little social life. I would not have invited Boss Margaret. Ursula's only meeting with her had been at a Krieger Christmas party and was mutually hostile. Grabich no longer had that Iranian girl friend. There were the neighbors, of course, but we never saw them. The most I ever saw of my neighbors were the guys when they took the garbage and recycling out to the curb.

It was different in the olden days, like they say. Before air conditioning people sat on their porches on hot summer nights and talked to neighbors who took an evening walk. Now everybody stayed inside with their televisions. There was no sense of community.

Ursula did know the other teachers at her old k-12 school. They'd meet in the break room and in the hallways, at meetings and when they monitored the school cafeteria to prevent food fights. That was it. People had their own lives, their own kids. No after school socializing.

If they shopped at Krieger I knew more about them than Ursula did. Anyone who understood metadata might be leery. Best that I stayed out of it. A baby shower was a girl thing.

I should have paid more attention.

Chapter twenty-four

Ursula busied herself with making our condo presentable for guests. She put out guest towels and fancy soap in the bathroom, even a new roll of TP.

She gave me a list to buy and sent me out as Mr. Step'nfetchit. I brought back pretty paper plates and, since we knew it was to be a girl, a white cake with pink frosting, no gender bias intended.

Her guests arrived. Ursula had invited a dozen but only ten came, which was more than we could seat. I hadn't met any of the women before. The only one I'd heard of was Mrs. Peach, a plump middle aged kindergarten teacher with a peachy complexion. Must have been her karma to look like her name.

It was crowded. As the only guy, I was distinctly out of place. Even though Ursula put me in an apron and chef's hat for kitchen duty, I felt surrounded and claustrophobic. It was her apron that said "Baby on board" which made me feel stupid or nascently pregnant. I had to escape.

I excused myself and left, decided to drop in on Armor Car for an on site inspection. That bullet proof Lexan was pretty heavy. A sample was on display, crazed by bullets that had not penetrated.

It was a chilling prospect. What kind of a world do we live in? Has the United States turned into some central American dictatorship with gangs and death squads?

When I figured that I had been away long enough, I drove home. Had to park across the street under the CCT camera the FBI had installed months before. The visitors had all the parking spaces.

Some of the guests had already left. I didn't see Ursula and assumed she was in the bathroom for another of her frequent pee breaks. The women were surprised and shocked to see me.

Mrs. Peach was flushed. "What happened? They said you had an accident."

"Who said?"

"The EMP who came by in an ambulance."

I didn't understand.

"She said Ursula should come along to the hospital."

I started to say, "I wasn't in an accident" but realized what had happened.

It was a ruse. They had been watching the apartment.

I didn't know who "they" were, but I got it. Whoever had failed to get Gulli had passed the buck to me. Agent Walker had suggested it might happen.

Thanks, Gulli. Making me the fall guy might have saved your skin, but I didn't appreciate the honor.

I rushed to the phone and was about to pick it up to call Walker when it rang.

I said "hello?" but already guessed.

The voice said simply "A million dollars or you won't see your wife again."

"Who's this?"

"Never mind."

"Let me talk to Ursula."

Now I had five school teachers crowded around me trying to listen in. Covering the receiver I whispered, "She's been kidnapped."

My called ID said "unknown caller." If I could stall him I could trace the call, but it would take a few minutes to boot up my computer.

There was a hesitation, noises of a phone being covered and muffled voices.

When Ursula's voice came on I could tell by the stress in her voice she was trying not to appear frightened. "Harvey, I've been kidnapped." Then she was gone.

If I knew enough German I'd have asked if she had her phone with her without their understanding. Then I could track her.

The voice was like a record stuck in a groove and repeating. "One million dollars."

"I don't have a million dollars."

"Then get it. One million."

With cell phone proliferation, fewer households than ever have hard wired phones. Our land line cord wasn't long enough to reach my laptop.

I covered the receiver and asked one of the guests to get my laptop out of a drawer and bring it to me. I continued to stall. "How do you want me to get the money to you?"

"We'll let you know."

"How do you want it? In used twenties, unmarked?

Now the caller was uncertain.

413

"You'll need a truck. A million in cash in twenties is pretty bulky."

I booted up my laptop. It's fast. I don't need to enter a password. It recognizes my face.

The voice reconsidered. "Maybe hundreds."

Hundred dollar bank notes have been the currency of choice for drug dealers, so much so that the treasury has considered doing away with them entirely.

"How about five hundreds?" My laptop was now awake. I entered my Harvey Goldstein password to access everything, namely where did this call come from?

"Do they make five hundred dollar bills?"

"They used to make thousands, but you could never cash one." I had seen a million dollar bank note, but it was a joke. Anyone foolish enough to try to cash one would be arrested.

"We'll let you know. You have twenty-four hours." He hung up.

I hadn't traced the call.

I stood up and tried to take command of the situation. "See our security camera on the wall above the mechanical fish?"

The ladies hadn't noticed. Since cameras are everywhere, people have stopped paying attention. Now our guests saw it. "I want you to walk up to the camera one at a time."

Looks were exchanged. They thought I was being weird. There was some milling about and inadvertent fussing with hairdos, but they complied.

I didn't think I needed each of the women to give me a description of whoever snatched Ursula. It was all on tape. I just wanted to distinguish between the faces. The face of whoever claimed to be an EMT would be on my camera record. I could run it through the facial recognition program.

I hoped that the guests would all leave and let me do my job as impromptu internet cop, but they insisted on helping clean up, put away the remainder of the baby cake, throw away the used plates and forks. I'd failed to provide coffee cups, so it was an odd assortment of mugs and souvenirs that went into the dishwasher.

Reviewing the surveillance tape I saw a person in an EMT uniform come in, speak to Ursula, and escort her out. It was a woman with dark hair and no makeup.

She had a driver's license, so was in the data base. In a minute I had her whole dossier. She was Maria Pinney, age thirty-two, shoe size nine, not a college graduate or even a nurse's assistant, but a high school drop out with a GED, home address in Cleveland, a house she shared with three other women. She'd been a meth user but went through rehab. Conviction for shoplifting at Ross. Seemed to live on pizzas delivered to her door, pepperoni. I even had her phone number.

God, I'm good.

Using Google world I saw the house she lived in, a dilapidated fixer-upper in a run down neighborhood of trash. It was a neighborhood I would avoid.

Should I go there and knock at the door? That would be a job for a Swat team with bulletproof vests and assault rifles, not Metadata Man in a red super hero jersey.

I checked the CCT camera across our street. Sure enough, Pinney had arrived in a private medical transport ambulance. I saw Ursula being put into the back of it. Saw it drive away. Got the license number and soon had the registration, the whole deal.

This was easier than the time I tracked down the creeps that shot up our condo. They hadn't shown their faces to a CCT camera until I caught up with them in the Moosehead Bar.

I phoned Agent Walker and then the police.

In a police state you are never anonymous and free for long. Now, I hoped, it wouldn't take long to catch up with Pinney and rescue Ursula.

Walker was not surprised that Ursula had been snatched. Did he have advance notice? Inside information? Or just the gut feeling of a seasoned FBI agent?

I gave him all the particulars, Pinney's description, history, address and phone.

I hadn't traced the ransom call yet. It was next.

There are hardly any public pay phones any more, everything having been replaced by cell phones that can be tracked. This call wasn't. It looked like it came from a five dollar burner. Make a few calls and throw it away. No registration, no possibility to track it.

Pinney should know who hired her.

I called the Cleveland police, gave them a description of Ursula, all the details they would need. Not familiar with my skills as Metadata Man, they were surprised at how much I'd found out about Pinney. Did I want to do a ride-along when they sent a car to pick her up?

Should be easy.

It turned out not to be.

When the police arrived at Pinney's shared house they found her unconscious from a drug overdose. She'd apparently graduated from

Meth to something stronger. Maybe, having persuaded Ursula to get into the ambulance, she'd been paid off in Chinese fatal drugs. Emergency care hadn't worked, too late, too far gone. Pinney would join the roster of Ohio drug fatalities, a local epidemic.

I'd lost my key witness.

It didn't take long to locate the ambulance. The Medical Response company that owned it said it had a GPS locator. That took me to the latitude and longitude and Google World showed me the location. The ambulance had been stolen and was abandoned at a deserted mall parking lot, one of several dead shopping centers around Cleveland with no active CCT cameras. The Cleveland police sent a crime scene crew to look for fingerprints.

I thought it would be easy to rescue Ursula. Now I wasn't so sure.

I would have to wait for a call back.

Waiting is the worst. You are helpless and afraid to leave the telephone. I could imagine this was what stressed out husbands went through, hanging around in suspense, while their wives were in labor in the delivery room.

What was the classic ransom routine? You leave the cash in a bag or a locker and make the exchange, money for abductee. Or maybe the kidnappers were seen by the victim, who could identify them. Then they simply killed their victim.

A million dollars won't fit in a bag, not even in a big roll on suitcase. The smart way was to make a wire transfer to an intermediate bank and pass it on to another.

Trouble was, I didn't have a million dollars. Ursula and I had about thirteen thousand in the credit union joint checking account. Would a kidnapper take a credit card? Check? Not bloody likely.

A million dollars ransom isn't that much, considering. Thanks to Gulli, who had used me as a stash, I sat on a million bitcoin, give or take whatever fluctuation there was in the value. In dollars, it was about five hundred million, but not my money. It was stolen from who knew where. It was all in the dark web, to me unexplored territory. The currency regulations made any movement over ten thousand dollars subject to IRS scrutiny. What's a kidnapper to do? What was I to do?

Wait.

There was still coffee left over from the baby shower party. The special cake had hardly been touched, no doubt avoided by dieters. I helped myself to a piece and between bites surveyed the chaos left when Ursula unwrapped the presents. What had she, or we, been given?

There were baby clothes, a blanket decorated with bunnies, a stuffed white cuddly polar bear, a book titled "Baby's First Year" and a couple of crib toys.

I didn't need a reminder that we didn't have the baby yet. Ursula wasn't the only Goldstein in danger.

I didn't want to leave the phone. Fingerprints taken from the stolen ambulance might lead somewhere.

Too bad nobody at the deserted mall had seen Ursula's transfer from the ambulance to whatever was used to take her away. Maybe there'd been a bystander, some kid skateboarding. I should drive over there and see if anybody was hanging around, but if I did I might miss the kidnapper's call. They only had my land line number. I didn't have one of those sophisticated and expensive I-phones.

Ursula did. Too bad it was left behind when she was rushed off or I'd know where she was.

I called Walker back. "I'm going to have to meet the kidnappers," I said. "Got to negotiate the ransom."

"You got a million dollars, Harvey?"

"I can get it."

"Oh?"

"I'm sure they're trying to get part of the bitcoin wallet I'm the, well, custodian of."

"Is it worth a million?"

"I'd rather not say. In any case, it's not mine. It's stolen from other thieves."

"So you're going to steal some of it to pay your wife's ransom?" It sounded like he was willing to arrest me.

Recalling Nixon, I said, "I am not a crook."

"So you want to negotiate with the kidnappers."

"Sure. How would you deliver a million in cash?"

He said, "I wouldn't," but offered no alternative.

"If I arrange a meeting, should I be wired, or whatever you do with witnesses?"

"We can do that."

He explained and said I shouldn't go to his office in case I was being followed. He'd arrange to meet me.

Finally the call came. "Do you have the million?"

"That's difficult. I need to meet and talk about it. I don't want to attract the attention of the IRS. You know, currency regulations. Can't attract attention with such a large amount of money."

My caller had an accent. Was it Russian? Was I dealing with the Russian Mafia? I thought the Russians had arrested Honey Bear the Hacker and killed him. Maybe they thought I had the money he'd stolen, the money Gulli intercepted. The rule was to follow the money and the trail let to me. Thanks, Gulli. And I thought she'd been doing me a favor to persuade me not to sue for the wrongful use of my photo and name in that unfortunate "Harvey Goldstein is watching you" incident. Instead she'd made me custodian of stolen geld.

If someone gives you a million bitcoin don't ask where it came from.

My caller agreed. I'd drive to a deserted shopping mall, be alone, and I would be picked up.

Just as the automobile had made it easy to live far from your job, creating strip development along highways and shopping malls had changed the character of American towns, sucking small businesses away from the center and moving them to accessible suburbs with lots of parking. Then internet shopping and free delivery killed the big keystone stores and the small shops folded. Thousands of malls across the country were now deserted, awaiting development for something new.

OK, so now I knew where to go. I alerted Walker and I met him at a parking garage downtown, top level, in a van they probably used for surveillance. It had a logo "Smith and Son: We'll Move You."

I was wired like in the movies, tested the system, and was sent on my way to the rendezvous.

I parked as instructed and waited. I saw a car approach, drive away, and come back. Got the license number for future reference. The kidnappers were cautious. It was an old model Ford Taurus, pre-GPS locator, probably stolen.

One man got out, a muscular weight lifting type with a thick neck and arms like my legs. He wore a baseball cap and a tight-lipped grim expression like he was trying to intimidate me.

My wire harness had a camera built into a shirt button. All I had to do was stand close enough for a good picture of his face.

I'd brought along an envelope and my tablet. I held it out in front of me to take his picture. I put on my most friendly face, reserved for meeting sinister people who might kill your wife. "Hi. Are you the guy who's lost a million dollars?"

He asked, "Harvey Goldstein?" and reached for the envelope. "You have million dollars in that?"

"No. That's just for show. I thought I'd write you a check, but you couldn't cash it. Besides, I don't have that much in my account."

I moved close to him so my button would get a good picture of his face. Slavic, high cheek bones, unshaven, no tattoo or scars.

Besides being wired with a camera button, I had a hearing aid in my right ear to get instructions. I stalled for time while I ran his picture through the files. I tried not to show how I was doing my Metadata Man search. "How is my wife?"

"Mrs. Goldstein is safe."

"I should warn you. She has to pee about every hour."

"What?" He hadn't expected toileting instructions.

"She's pregnant. Baby doesn't leave much room for her bladder so it fills up fast. Worse when she's nervous. Being kidnapped makes her nervous." I could imagine Ursula being tied to a chair and wetting herself. Not nice.

He wasn't interested. "Million dollars."

Clearly he had a one track mind. "You know me. What do I call you?"

"You can call me Charlie Brown. Anything you like."

By that time I already had his ID. Dimitri Birscht, Ukranian, immigrant Jew, New York Mafia.

I pretended to have a clairvoyant vision. I held the empty envelope to my forehead to pretend to clear my thoughts. "You are not Charlie Brown. You are…(pause for effect) Dimitri Birscht."

His eyes fairly popped with astonishment. With a tell like that he'd make a poor poker player.

Before he could say more I added, "What's a nice Jewish landsman like you doing in the kidnapping business?"

His cover was totally blown, always an embarrassment when you are a spy or a crook. "How you know this?"

"I'm sorry. I don't have a business card. I'm Metadata Man. I know everything about everybody. I know where you live, the names of your children, where they go to school and…" I paused. "and that your son has leukemia."

Dimitri asked, "How do you know this?"

"I'm Metadata Man. I know everything."

Now I was looking into the barrel of his gun. It's amazing how big the barrel of a pistol looks when it's a couple of inches from your eye.

I blinked and shrugged, my nebbish pose, tried to move away. "I'm not into guns."

He was thinking. He had a slow hard drive in there, but he was purposeful. "Million dollars."

I took a deep breath to reduce my anxiety. "Dimitri, if you kill me you get nothing. Put it away."

After a moment of thought, he did.

"How do you think I could have a million dollars?"

"You are American."

"You are watching too many Hollywood movies. Maybe in Brighton Beach your slum landlord Mr. Trump has a million dollars. "I've got only thirteen thousand in my checking account. I'll show you." I reached for my checkbook which I'd brought along in my jacket pocket and got nudged in the ribs by his gun. I guess he was afraid I was packing heat. "Ouch. Take it easy."

"Million dollars." He was back at it like a broken record.

I made a wild guess. "If you want the money Honey Bear the Hacker stole from the Russian bank, I think that's been recovered."

"Not all."

"You think I've got it?"

"We got tip from German lady."

"She's lying."

Lying didn't upset him. Maybe in his business everybody lies. It's SOP in Brighten Beach Mafia country.

"You want your wife?"

"Sure, I want Ursula."

We were at an impasse. Finally I offered, "I don't have a million dollars, but I think I can find out how to get it. You just have to be patient."

Dimitri shook his head. "Have only three days."

I saw the anxiety in his face and understood. "I see. You're just a contractor. If you don't get the million your son dies of leukemia. He's their hostage."

I had guessed right. Dimitri sighed. The gun went back in his waistband. The starch had gone out of him. Now his face showed pain and desperation. "What can I do?"

"Come back to my place. We'll have coffee. I have some baby cake. Oh, and bring my wife. You know the address. We'll work something out."

He seemed to agree.

I got back in my car, hands shaking, and, after some fumbling with the ignition key, started the engine. I am not used to having a gun in my face. Maybe in time I might get used to it, but not yet.

Alone in the car I spoke up so Walker could hear. "Don't rush in and arrest this guy. We need him to lead us to his employers, whoever they are."

My earpiece said Walker would be ready in case. He didn't say in case of what.

"If you come by the apartment afterwards, I've got cake. Pink icing. You'll love it."

Walker made a sound like maybe he wasn't into cake. If he was diabetic it'd be in his dossier, but wasn't. I knew what he ate, but not what he didn't like. Even Metadata Man has limits.

I continued. "Did you see how desperate he is? I don't think he's going to hurt Ursula. I think he's being squeezed. They've got a contract on him. He'll do anything to get out of it."

"So you're going to pay him?"

I was almost home. "I haven't figured that out yet." I thought, if only Gulli were here. She'd know what to do. I was afraid if I paid up, that would be only the beginning. They'd want more. My best bet was to convince them that I couldn't pay.

I had an idea.

Chapter twenty-five

Back at my condo, eerily empty without Ursula there, I logged onto my email account and waited, getting more nervous by the minute. What if he didn't show up? What if Dimitri changed his mind? Didn't bring Ursula? What if Walker got over zealous and surrounded my place with a swat team?

I stood by our now bullet proof picture window and waited.

Finally I saw the car. It circled the block before finally parking in front of our condo. I couldn't see how many were in the car, but Dimitri was driving. He got out, opened the back passenger door and helped Ursula out.

She was obviously shaken, off balance. Anxiety and baby had done their thing. As I feared, she had wet herself. Frankly, in her position, I might have pooped my pants.

I opened the front door for them, took Ursula in my arms. "It's OK. Why don't you go and change?"

She sniffled but didn't bawl. Bawling could come later. Right then we had to hang onto ourselves.

I said to Dimitri, "Come in the kitchen. I need to get you your million dollars."

"You have million dollars in kitchen?"

"No. I have my laptop." We settled down, Dimitri across from me so he couldn't see the screen. "I don't know when I can get an answer, but I need your bank information. Do you have a checkbook?"

He was reluctant, but handed over a battered check holder. There were not many checks in it. The check register was a mess. It looked like Dimitri lived, like many Americans, from paycheck to paycheck. I got to the bottom of the blank checks and pulled out a deposit slip for the routing and account number.

Then I sent Gulli a message. Ursula had been kidnapped. It was a Russian Mafia shakedown. They want a million dollars ransom.

"I can't guarantee this can happen immediately," I explained. It may take awhile before my contact opens the mail. Then it can take awhile to arrange the money for you."

Dimitri was impressed. "Getting million dollars just for sending an email?"

"You understand, Dimitri, this is not my money. It takes time. I cannot guarantee you will get it."

I was trying to buy time. He wanted the ransom in twenty-four hours. That wasn't possible. But he had a deadline, too. His bosses gave him three days. What would happen if he didn't deliver?

I had visions of Dimitri standing in a bucket of concrete at the end of a dock in New Jersey. As concrete sets, it generates a lot of heat around the ankles. I didn't want to go there.

My suggestion to Gulli was to steal a million from Trump's account in the Deutsche Bank. He's borrowed three hundred million, but it was guaranteed by the Russian KGB bank which meant Putin. Russia was run by criminals. The New York Russian Mafia was just a branch. It would be ironic to steal their money and give it back to them via Dimitri.

That would appeal to Gulli's sense of humor. She could hack into any bank, but why get the million from someone in the American one percent's stash hidden in the Bahamas? Let Dimitri's ransom come out of the Mafia's own account. I loved the idea.

It was only an idea. There was no certainty that Gulli would open my email in time. I didn't know where she was hiding. I could imagine her in some internet café, hunkered over a terminal, wearing a hoodie and with an umbrella folded beside her for when she went out on the street and avoided CCT cameras.

I was sure she would like my random suggestion. She could do it.

I sent the routing number and account for Dimitri. What he would do when the money showed up in his balance was his problem.

I hit the send button and turned to him. "Coffee?"

He was too nervous.

"How about a Sam Adams?"

"Sam Adams?" He didn't know the brand.

"My favorite beer."

He shook his head.

"I'm sorry, I don't have any vodka."

"What do you do now?" He asked, licking his lips. He, too, must have dry mouth from all this stress.

"Wait. If this works the million dollars will show up in your account. Now I think you should get out of here. I'm afraid your car has been followed by the police."

I went to our bullet proof picture window to check the street. The car he'd arrived in had left. Now what? Maybe the driver was just going around the block to avoid suspicion.

He thanked me. The handshake turned into a Russian hug. The poor guy was desperate.

I let him out and locked our front door. As I closed it I saw that Walker had not waited.

There was a Swat team out there covering our condo.

Those guys are stressed out, too. One false move and they shoot.

The ideal is to arrest their guy and get him to talk, find out who hired him, get the whole story..

Dimitri must have panicked.

I heard a muffled command to put down the weapon.

Then there was a volley of shots hitting our armored front door. I jumped back, relieved that nothing had penetrated or I would have been ventilated.

I staggered back and fell onto our Ikea couch. I didn't want to look. The stress of all this was too much. I felt sick to my stomach, rushed into the bathroom and threw up.

Even so, I couldn't resist going to the window and looking out on the street. An ambulance was taking away a body bag. There was no sign of the car he had arrived in.

A few minutes later there was a knock at the door. When I opened it I saw the impact of many bullets and blood spatters. My condo was a crime scene. Poor Dimitri.

What about his partner or partners? Would they be back? I doubted it. With Dimitri dead, it would be too dangerous.

Walker was in my open doorway. He avoided touching the blood smears and the bullet marks. He had a grim look. "You all right, Goldstein?"

It was Goldstein again. This was an official call.

"I'm OK. Just shaken."

He examined the inside of our front door and was impressed. "Works well. I might get one for my own place."

All could do was nod. I was still in shock.

"What about your wife?"

"Ursula is taking a shower. She wants to wash away the whole business." I motioned for him to come into our kitchen. The laptop was still on. No reply from Gulli.

I offered Walker a Sam Adams, which he accepted. After a good swig he asked, "What did you do about the ransom?"

I opened by shirt to takeoff the wire harness, plucked the earpiece out of my ear and set it on the table. I didn't answer.

"Your kidnapper doesn't need it now. He's DOA."

I was sorry about that. Really sorry. He might be a Mafia kidnapper, but he had his problems. "If the ransom is paid, it'll be to his account. He has a sick kid. His family will need the money."

Walker was puzzled. "Where do you get a million dollars?"

"I haven't yet. Don't know for sure. If it goes through, I think maybe the Deutsche Bank, taken out of the Trump account. It's Russian laundered money anyway."

We both laughed. We needed a good laugh. Broke the tension. His laugh wasn't just because he thought it might be funny. Robbing the Deutsche Bank of Russian Mafia money might have its ironic twist, but it was still bank robbery. It made me what in his business was called a person of interest.

As for the kidnappers, I had won this round, but I was afraid there might be others. Some people are vengeful. I didn't need to alert the cops. I was wearing a wire and they followed every word. I wasn't exactly innocent in his death. If Dimitri's pals came after me, I didn't have much of an alibi, that is, if my protestations would have made any difference.

Chapter twenty-six

Walker had hardly left when the local press swooped in like a flock of vultures. This time the Plain Dealer sent a real reporter, not an intern. There was even a TV truck parked out on the street in front of our apartment, the satellite antenna on its roof aimed somewhere in space. Two people lugging TV cameras on their shoulders were aimed at me when I came to the door.

A couple of microphones were thrust at my face. Question: "How did it feel when your wife was kidnapped?"

How did it feel? What was this high school reporting? Where did they get these questions? How did they expect me to feel? Elated? Excited? Thrilled at the publicity?

I was furious. I turned the question back at them. "How would you feel if your pregnant wife was abducted? The kidnappers want a million dollars in ransom. What do you do? Call your folks for a down payment? My checking account has only thirteen thousand in it. What do you expect? Set up a monthly payment plan? For God's sake…"

I would have gone on but the interviewer was abashed by my outburst.

A more sensible interviewer, I think from the local homeless weekly, asked "How is your wife bearing up?"

I took a deep breath to ease my blood pressure. "We'll be OK. Look, we just had a man shot to death on our doorstep." I gestured at the blood and the bullet marks. I didn't want to mention that we have an armored front door, that the FBI had turned our place into a fortress. You can't tell a bulletproof picture window just by looking at it.

My gesture diverted the cameras to the bloody front door. No doubt the pictures would go viral.

What was missing was any compassion for Dimitri, his wife and sick kid. I had negotiated a deal with him and it had gone wrong. I guess he drew his gun out of panic. Never show a Swat team that you are armed. They are scared, too.

"That's all I have to say." I retreated behind the front door. The vultures flew off.

Ursula and I were both badly shaken by the whole business. She was very seriously upset, alternately crying and laughing out of relief. As I'd feared, she hadn't been able to get to a toilet. When I hugged her her bottom was damp. I thought she'd had to pee. I was wrong.

She was eager to change clothes and wash. Only after she came out of the bedroom, after Walker and the reporters had left, did she explain. What with all the stress of the kidnapping and some rough handling, her water had broken. It was baby time. Maybe that was why Dimitri had been so willing to return her. They weren't prepared for home delivery.

That threw all thoughts of the million dollar ransom out of my head. We had been reading up on babies, at how frequent contractions were when delivery was eminent. There's a huge difference between a dry passage in a book and the real thing. How do words describe the agonies of labor? How soon did we have to get to a hospital?

I had read that first babies generally take a little longer in labor, which can go on for many hours. Having a baby is dangerous. Some women die.

We had a doctor and a hospital, had done prenatal care. I had been along for the class as the only male observer.

I didn't want to wait. She had contractions and real pain I, as a guy, could only imagine. The male skeleton doesn't have a pelvis shaped like a basket, nor are we built with a nascent birth canal that has to be opened up for a baby to pass through. Major ouch.

Ursula had already packed a bag of things she'd want at the hospital. Off we went.

When we checked in the clerk, like any American medical person, wanted to know about our insurance. My post dismissal grace period for insurance after I was fired from Krieger had lapsed while we were in Switzerland. In Switzerland they have a National Health. In the states it's a socialist pipe dream.

Of course, I had to get an insurance policy after we got back to Cleveland, but there was a hitch. Because Ursula was already pregnant when I got the policy, her pregnancy was a preexisting condition. Our policy didn't cover preexisting conditions. Come to think of it, once I read the fine print of the policy, it covered little more than catastrophic events, like an auto accident, as long as it wasn't our fault. Pregnancy was certainly our fault.

So we weren't covered.

Ursula wasn't supposed to be due yet, so the baby would be premature, with the additional hospital expense impending, explained in language only a lawyer could cook up. What would this all cost? Over ten thousand dollars on our checking account balance of, thanks to my ten thousand from the bitcoin wallet, thirteen thousand.

At least, if the bitcoin wallet didn't disappear as quickly as Gulli set it up, we could pay the bill. Thanks to Gulli, we were lucky. I couldn't help but wonder what people did who had no insurance. That explained why the American infant mortality rate was as poor as Nigeria.

Agent Walker tracked us to the hospital and insisted on a debriefing. I did not want to see him. Not then. Answering questions about the kidnapping was the last thing I wanted to talk about. Ursula was in no condition to be interviewed, either. Those contractions can distract you from invasive questions.

Walker cornered me in the fathers' waiting room, a rather shabby place with tired Naugahide furniture that smelled of anxiety and boredom.

There were two other men there. One was a kid young enough to be waiting for his mom to have his baby sister, except he was the father to be. He had been shotgunned into the wedding and was about to acquire a responsibility he was not prepared for. The second was the father of a daughter who was unwed. His wife had disowned the daughter. He'd wanted her to get an abortion. She refused and would not adopt out her baby. I couldn't refuse looking at her picture in her father's wallet. She was not pretty. Not all babies are welcome, a sad start to a new life. So I was sitting in a room full of unhappy stress and didn't welcome Walker.

Walker wanted every detail about the kidnapping, the names of the women at the baby shower so he could interview each of them. I didn't even have the guest list. It had been Ursula's thing and I hadn't even been introduced to all of the women. I was just the errand boy. He would have to get that from Ursula.

He wanted to know how many had been involved in the kidnapping,, what happened when Pinney had put Ursula in the ambulance, where they had gone when they switched her out of the GPS tracked ambulance, how many were there, could she identify them, and on and on. His fear was that labor pains and delivery would wipe out her memory. It was not a good time.

Walker took me to the hospital café. We found a table out of earshot of interns in lab coats. Walker bought the coffee and, true to cop practice, a stale donut, chocolate covered with sprinkles. I had no appetite.

I insisted my role in the kidnapping was minor. There was nothing to add. After all, I'd been wired. The FBI had a complete transcript of everything I said. What more did he expect?

I soon found out. It wasn't just the Russian Walker wanted to know about. He was hot for my knowledge of how to wrest a million bucks from a foreign bank, something I had never done and knew nothing about.

As for the ransom, that was different and I didn't want to tell all or make up a story. When I mentioned Gulli I called her only "Angel" which was, in spite of all her false identities, the only one that felt authentic. I did not know her full real name. If she told me I couldn't trust it.

She had good reason to hide. Her hacking, her self-appointed role as some sort of Robin Hood, was dangerous. Of course, in some countries hacking is not a crime, but international theft is.

I was on a thin edge of being a criminal myself. As recipient of her stash of a million bitcoin I could be seen as a co-conspirator in her thievery. That's why I insisted on a low profile. We could have acted like wealthy billionaires. After all, a million bitcoin was worth about five hundred million. We didn't have any need for a yacht or a private jet or houses around the world. Warren Buffet was a billionaire and still lived in a modest house. A Mafia don might show off in a sharkskin suit, but people with real wealth and power could come to the office in a tee shirt and jogging shorts.

I called anything we took from the bitcoin wallet a management fee. I had no knowledge of where it came from, presumably from someone who moved so much money, trillions probably, that a million bitcoin would hardly be missed, or written off as sloppy bookkeeping.

I knew that an auditor is satisfied to be within five percent of accurate. With a trillion dollars, five percent would slip through without notice.

Contrast that with Dimitri, a low level footman living from medical bill to medical bill in a country with no National Health. There just ain't no justice.

Did Gulli get my message? I didn't know. She might be using several email addresses under several names. I had only one.

I think I satisfied Walker that I was an ignorant stooge, a part I can play with skill and experience. He still wanted me on board, but not as a bone fide FBI employee. With my shady connection to Gulli I could never get a security clearance. To the FBI I would at best be an occasional resource, like a criminal who sometimes provides information for a favor or a fee, the favor, like Whitey Bolger, who bought a modicum of immunity from a bent agent, time enough to disappear.

Walker knew I was holding back on the ransom business. We would have to wait and see if the million dollars showed up in Dimitri's checking account.

As for the getaway car and whoever had driven it off, that was the FBI's job. I'd had done more than enough. Dimitri's blood on my front door turned me off. The moment the photo I took with my tablet yielded his dossier, I had sympathy for the guy. Now he was dead, and in a way I was complicit. I hated that. Next time I might be the victim, or Ursula. I was not on the payroll to serve and protect and defend the Constitution against all enemies, foreign or domestic.

I managed to get rid of Walker and returned to the Dad's waiting room. The teen aged girl had delivered, a boy. What would his new grandma say? Would she forgive?

The unwilling boy-dad looked like he'd been condemned to the gallows. At least he hadn't just run away. Maybe that would come later as too many fathers had--just deserted their families without the legality of divorce, the mothers left with kids? There just ain't no justice.

At last, hours and several cups of coffee later, a nurse came into the waiting room and asked me if I wanted to see my daughter.

Ursula in that hospital bed looked like a wrung out wash cloth, but she had a smile on her face, a look that she was glad it was all over. She cuddled a tiny swaddled creature to her breast. No matter how painful labor had been the memory disappears with the appearance of the infant child.

I'd had no experience with babies. All I could think was of awe and wonder. Such tiny fingers.

Ursula was discovering, too, that the baby's cry was like a signal to mother's breasts to start making milk. Amazing.

Now we were three. It was going to be a major life change for all of us.

We hadn't even thought of a name. Naming a child is serious business. Somehow, your name is your karma. Giving a child an unfortunate name can doom it to a lifetime of ridicule, like in that hillbilly western song where the guy complains that his dad named him Sue on the conviction that he'd have to defend himself all his life and be tough.

It's bad enough to be given a stupid nickname. I'm Harvey and always rejected any attempts for people to call me Har. Ursula was Ursula, not the German diminutive Uschi which sounds a bit like Ucky..

So what should we name our daughter?

Three days later, before they would discharge Ursula and the baby, they insisted on presenting us the with bill. Without insurance we owed over four thousand dollars. A thousand a night for the room. Separate bills for the delivery room, the doctor, and supplies. The itemized list included every Band Aid and aspirin. So much for medical care in America.

What did the poor do? Have baby at home? No doctor, no midwife, no support. No wonder the American infant mortality rate was so poor.

You don't name your kid "Bankrupt." I thought of Gwendolyn which would be Gwennie for short, and was an homage to Gulli. We talked about that.

Ursula wanted our daughter to be named Sarah, a good biblical name. I suggested Gwendolyn as a middle name. Life is full of compromises. At least her birth certificate has me as the dad, not father unknown as happens all too often.

Naming our daughter was more important to us than whether or not a million dollars went into the late Dimitri's bank account.

Still, that was where Metadata Man had a thin advantage over the FBI. They needed a warrant to get into his account. I could get into Dimitri's bank records, his kid's medical records, anything digital.

To my astonishment, the million showed up. Gulli had come through. Did she know Dimitri had been killed? I had the address for Dimitri Birscht and the phone number in Brighton Beach. I debated whether I should call his wife.

I asked Walker for advice. Ursula was still in the hospital. Could I stop by the FBI office? I did, stopping first at a florist for a dozen roses for Ursula.

Walker had moved his desk so he wouldn't be in direct view of the security camera. I guess he hadn't appreciated my comment on his awful necktie.

"For me?" Walker asked, pretending it was a joke.

"I could buy you a little teddy bear with an FBI badge for Christmas." Gratuities to FBI men are not appropriate, even when they've come to your rescue.

He shook his head.

"Maybe for one of your kids." I'd think about it.

Walker was all business. "So the million was paid to Birscht's account?"

I nodded.

"We've sent someone to interview his wife. We can provide her with a security camera. We can tap her phone and put a stakeout on her place. But I have an assignment for you, Goldstein. Find out where the money came from. You can track it."

"It's laundered money."

"Then find out where the laundry is."

The rule was "follow the money." I could see there had to be a chain of contacts. Who hired Dimitri? Probably someone local in the New York Russian Mafia. They would have orders from elsewhere, probably Russia or Ukraine. It might lead to Putin or some oligarch.

What would the FBI do then? They were limited to domestic crime. Foreign stuff was for the CIA and, if cooperation could be trusted, Interpol. I didn't think the CIA trusted anybody. They hadn't called me back.

The sanctions imposed on Russian investments in the United States were a thorn in President Putin's hide. They were imposed by congress after the Ukrainian annexation. The million dollar ransom might have been a down payment to get around the restrictions. There was always a nefarious fiddle if you were a good enough fiddler.

But a mere million? Putin was reputed to be worth two hundred trillion, the lifeblood sucked out of the Russian people. If they wanted more they'd have to kidnap the president, not Ursula.

Someone knew that I had a connection to the purloined wealth of the criminals and one per centers. Gulli had palmed me off to get off the hook of her kidnappers in Holland. Thanks, Gulli, such a pal.

That was the price I was paying for the million bitcoin. It was like being struck by lightning and then being charged for the electric bill.

I hoped Dimitri's family could keep the money. Since he was the unfortunate fall guy, they deserved a pension. Wasn't that organized crime practice? While one of their own did prison time, the family wasn't left destitute. Even criminals had a code of ethics. I wasn't that sure about the Russians.

With all that in mind, I returned to the hospital with the dozen red roses. Ursula looked rested after the ordeal of delivery. Holding the baby I couldn't imagine how a woman's pelvis could be forced open enough to push a baby out. No wonder women died in childbirth! And here she was, a miracle, a sleepy little thing about to discover the world, God help her.

I had brought my digital camera for selfies we could send to our parents. There would be phone calls and letters. None of our family were anywhere near Cleveland. My parents were in LA on that kosher street. Ursula's folks were in Florida, her father at the fishing pier when they weren't off to the early bird special. Photos and calls would have to do for the time being. My mother didn't Skype or I'd bring my laptop to the hospital for face to face kvelling.

At least, without the Krieger job, I could be a stay at home dad with Ursula and the baby while I did my detective work on line for Walker, no Boss Margaret watching over me from her glass office.

It felt strange, returning home alone. It was empty without Ursula. The yellow crime scene tape had been taken down. Remembering to wear rubber gloves, I scrubbed the bloodstains off the door with bleach, but didn't know what to do about the dents from the bullets. At least the SWAT team hadn't used armor piercing shells. If they had, standing behind the door, I might have been punctured.

Would Bondo stick in the dents? Maybe, for advice, I should ask the guy at Armor who was doing the patio doors. Then I'd have to repaint the door. Maybe I'd just leave it and have the dents as a souvenir. Our condo would look like something in a war zone, or some bullet riddled house in Syria.

Before you dig into a difficult job there's a certain inertia before you are mentally prepared. As Pirsig wrote in "Zen and the Art of Motorcycle Maintenance" you had to be in a certain frame of mind.

I wasn't ready to take on the Russian Mafia. Instead I printed pictures of Ursula and the baby, sent out copies, cobbled together a baby announcement which would no doubt be seen as an invitation for more presents. That could all be stretched out to take up quite a lot of time.

Then, of course there was house work, tidying up after the party, putting away the assorted cups and mugs, taking out the garbage, anything to postpone what I really should be doing.

The night before Ursula was to come home with the baby, I settled down to the task.

Of course, there was the email, another excuse to not do my job. At last came a response from Gulli. It was a one word apology: "Sorry."

My response to her response was "Thanks."

Then I had to send another. "Where did you get the ransom?"

I could almost see her twisted grin. "Trump's line of credit at the Deutsche Bank."

Was that true or was she joking? I knew the Deutsche Bank was the only bank left that would loan money to the Trump gang of con artists and thieves. Even the Deutsche Bank, already fined big time for shady operations, wouldn't take the risk without some guarantees. That came from the Russian bank run by Putin's own KGB manager.

The Deutsche Bank was out of bounds for Agent Walker. FBI was for domestic crime, not foreign banks.

The thing about money is it is fungible. It has no loyalty and can be spent anywhere. International corporations live outside the law, willing to move their headquarters on short notice to some country that doesn't tax or can be bribed. So Apple or whoever moves to Ireland to avoid US taxes. Catch me if you can.

What I needed was the Russian link between Moscow and Brighten Beach.

Except to change planes I had never been in New York. With me, a secular Midwesterner, I couldn't imagine a city with so many Jews. My only concept of New York was old documentaries showing push carts and lots of shops with signs in Hebrew or Yiddish. I couldn't tell the difference.

In those days that spawned gangsters like Meyer Lansky there were few Russians, lots of Poles and Lithuanians. Since the Soviet Union collapse where was a flood of Russian Jews familiar with the shady grey market and deals you had to make to survive in the old Police State.

I didn't want to be a statistic in a gang war. People who were not bought off used to end up hanging from a bridge in London or at the bottom of the Moscow river, or poisoned with some radioactive substance slipped into you tea in a London café.

I told myself I had no political axe to grind. I was not a big player. I was just a nebisch computer jockey with special access as Metadata Man, Internet Cop. You couldn't bribe me, I was already filthy rich in bitcoin.

After considerable sighing and head scratching I went after all of Dimitri's emails, phone calls, and activity in view of the CCT cameras on his street. This was going to take time.

The FBI was running street surveillance. My advantage was I could get into Dimitri's bank account. The banks always send out privacy notices to gullible customers, but no place is safe from a skilled hacker. What I was looking for was a pattern of regular deposits, like a payroll, and regular withdrawals.

The ever widening ripples when you drop a stone in a pond, the deposits led to the accounts of payers. This was going to take time.

Then, surprise, surprise, I got a call from the CIA.

This was a voice I didn't recognize and I didn't trust it. Could be anybody calling to trap me. The last time I had a face to face it was with someone with the cover name Gordon Moxon, assigned to make the contact, not some higher up. We went through the little song and dance routine. I said, "Hello, who's this?"

The answer was Gordon Moxon.

That was the guy I'd met before. I asked, "What's the code word?"

He sounded puzzled and maybe irritated because I was being so cagey. "Code word?"

I remembered the code name from before, Hatchet Job. "Let's do this like a charade," I suggested. "Sounds like Axe."

Moxon thought a moment, may have been asking for help from some one listening in. Finally, "Hatchet Job."

"OK. You're in. What's this about?"

"The FBI says you're investigating the connections to the Russian Mafia in New York."

I hadn't felt like I wasn't making much headway so said, "It's a slow process."

"We'd like you to take on another little job."

"What sort of a job?"

"North Korea."

This they called a little job? What did they expect me to do? Parachute into a prison compound and rescue a detainee? That was Seal Team Six stuff, not Harvey Goldstein Metadata Man. "What about North Korea?"

There was a pause. I think this Gordon Moxon was trying to work up the courage to ask without revealing any CIA secrets. We both knew the phones were not secure.

"You know about Ransom ware?"

Grabich had warned me. You get a red flag on your computer screen that says if you don't pay three hundred bucks within 72 hours all your files would be encrypted beyond any recovery. Payment in bitcoin. "Yes."

He explained, "North Korea, to get around the sanctions, has a thriving Ransom ware business to extort money from companies around the world."

"I'm not into Ransom ware."

"Do you think you could break into the North Korean Ransom ware account and steal the money back?"

What? The CIA, NSA, and any one of our many clandestine organizations must have teams of experts trying to do that. And they're asking Harvey Goldstein? What do they think I am, some super hero to save the world from Bad North Korea? Just because Ursula made me a Metadata Man shirt? I had to laugh.

Maybe they were trying to trap me into admitting I was an internet thief.. "You think I can do stuff like that?"

"We think you know someone who can."

Ah. That was it. They were after Gulli. "It's possible. My contact doesn't like police. What could you offer for the services?"

"No guarantees. How about immunity?"

I realize that they must have monitored my email and that brief exchange with Gulli. She might be evasive and hard to locate, but even with Tor I was not hiding at all. "How about a Green card and safe residence in the USA?"

"Certainly."

Now I was faced with a dilemma: pass on my contact with Gulli and be out of the loop, unaware of anything the CIA arranged with her, or remain part of the chain with the advantage of the knowledge and the disadvantage of the risk. Passing on the information about her would not only be a danger to her but a possible invitation to some North Korean assassin who would wipe my face with a deadly nerve agent.

I had to be non committal. "I'll make inquiries."

Chapter twenty-seven

Ursula was nursing the baby when I came into the bedroom to tell her the latest development. Seeing that little person suckling at Ursula's breast was a distraction. It was so wonderful, how could hacking North Korea be of any interest? A guy can't nurse a baby. It's a bonding advantage no father can share. I think, in spite of the excruciating pain of birthing, which nobody would really want to experience, guys miss out. The mother not only grows the child inside her body but feeds it with her own milk. No man can share that experience. I was feeling left out.

Finally I pulled myself together and explained, "The CIA wants to break into the North Korean Ransom ware treasury and steal the money.

She looked up at me too surprised to be dumfounded. The idea was too outrageous. "How are you going to do that, Metadata Man?"

"I'm not, but Gulli might."

"Why should she?"

"Good question. Maybe among the hacker community there's a resentment between the people who started doing that stuff for fun and the rotten criminals who have no respect for people's files."

Could be like the early days when programmers made freeware only to find others wanted money. Greedy bastards. Everybody wants to be a millionaire.

I should talk.

Ursula smiled and wiped baby's drool with a cloth. "Which side do you think she's on? She's a big time thief. Just because she steals from thieves doesn't make her an honest player."

"You mean, there's a difference between stealing from a bank robber and stealing from a thieving bank?"

She laughed. "You got it."

She moved baby to the other breast. I guess you have to keep a balance.

"I think we all live in a grey world," I admitted. "We say we respect privacy but at Krieger I knew everything every customer bought. I exploited that information for advertising purposes. So much for the sanctity of privacy."

Ursula shook her head. Getting baby attached to the breast occupied her attention. "See what she says. I'm busy."

"And I'm jealous," I joked. I didn't envy baby's suckling, well, not very much, but I already sensed that in the pecking order in our new household arrangement I was the help.

Back to the computer.

I called Grabich. He has caller ID and sounded irritated. "Now, what, Harvey?"

"Not to be a pest, but there must be a way to hide my surfing the way Tor redirects my email."

Turns out there is, except I'd forgotten. It's for devious people, the really secretive and evasive people use, maybe seekers of kiddy porn or snuff movies. There was a small fee. He had told me before but I hadn't done it. He explained how to set it up.

He wasn't going to give out that tip for nothing. "What's this about."

"It's a CIA thing. They want me to overthrow the government of North Korea."

He knew I couldn't do that and laughed, but stopped laughing when he realized there was something to what I'd said but wouldn't explain. "My grandfather was in Korea. Never talked about it except it gets pretty cold there. Better pack your woolies."

"Not to worry about that. I'm staying in Cleveland."

We ended on a tentative invitation for him to come by and see the baby.

One thing I'd read in the baby manual. Don't expect to sleep much for the first six months.

Just for convenience, we moved the crib beside our bed to save getting up again and again all night. This way Ursula hardly had to wake up, just reach over, get the kid and put her on a breast until they both conked out. Once she settled down we'd move the crib back to the nursery.

Of course, that meant I didn't sleep much either. Awakened at three I the morning, I retreated to my computer and explored. "Gulli, where are you? Our government will provide you with safety so you don't always have to be on the run. They just want this teensy favor: steal North Korea's Ransom ware account."

To my surprise she didn't say it was impossible or that she'd even try. She just asked, "Where do I move the money?"

Like I knew what I was doing, I called Gordon Moxon back. "Where do you want the money moved?" Like I already had it.

For the United States to pillage North Korea's Ransom ware account and move it to, say, the US treasury, would be an act of cyber war. Retaliation might come in the form of a nuclear ICBM.

Maybe Gulli should redirect the money so it looked like the Russians had stolen it. Like my mother used to say, "Let's you and him fight." Ah, but nukes dropped on Russia had a habit of drifting downwind radioactive rain on the rest of us.

Moxon actually believed it was a done deal. I protested. "Maybe we should send a private jet to Germany or wherever my contact is and get her out of there."

"Can't do that if you don't tell us who she is and where."

Now I had a dilemma. I didn't know where Gulli was. With the internet she could be anywhere. I didn't want to go back to Germany and look for her. Stuttgart was out. Her safehouse in Amsterdam was blown.

She would need a visa. Normally that meant multiple trips to a US embassy or consulate.

Moxon wasn't the one to make those decisions. Ordering charter jets and green cards was above his pay grade.

I would have to wait until the request filtered upward.

Of course, I expected that the CIA spooks would be tracking me. They don't trust anybody, especially each other. You never knew who might be the next whistle blower or mole, or wannabe Chelsie who decides something isn't kosher and he/she has to take the initiative, even if it means jail time.

As long as nobody knew who Gulli was or where she was hanging out, she was temporarily safe. I suppose they'd give her a top secret code name like Ivana or Vladimir or Deep Throat. Those have been used.

So if Gulli did hijack North Korea's Ransom ware loot, where should she put it? We're talking potentially billions here. Even if you put it in a very big pocket it would make a revealing bulge. A billion is hard to hide, at least in my world. What did I know? I was challenged enough to balance my check book.

Chapter twenty-eight

Now I had to wait.

I felt like a sitting duck, hunkered down behind my bullet proof picture window and front door. The New York Mafia knew where I was, but they had lost their errand boy, shot dead on my door step. Maybe they would feel I was too well protected to extort money from, even by kidnapping wife and baby. Nature always follows the path of least resistance. It's easier for a bear to get into your garbage can than rip the bark off a rotting log to get at the grubs inside. Maybe the Mafia would look for an easier target.

In the meantime I continued my probing of Dimitri's bank records. I'd hoped he got regular deposits, but those were the kind of people who paid cash for everything. They carry their dollars in their pockets in rolls held by a thick grocery store rubber band.

The CCT camera across his street showed a steady stream of visitors, no doubt mourning relatives. I wondered what the procedure was for delivering his body to a funeral home. There would be a ceremony. Dimitri was perhaps nominally a co-religionist, but did Russian Jews sit shiva, the traditional period of mourning? That meant a feast of food brought in by relatives and friends.

I had a vision of the family sitting in their stocking feet in a darkened apartment, the mirrors covered.

I worked on a list of all the recognizable faces that turned up at his address. Each face had been digitized, turned up in the data base, and with each face a dossier of personal information, Metadata Man's specialty. It was becoming a catalog that grew and grew. What was unknowable was which one was important and which was just a delivery boy bringing kosher pizzas.

Cross referencing with a list of known shady characters might narrow the field, get to whoever ordered Dimitri to kidnap Ursula. I still didn't have the driver of the getaway car.

It doesn't pay to fail an assignment. Whoever had picked up Gulli in Amsterdam had not fared so well either.

Would they keep trying?

Did I have to become someone with agoraphobia, a stay at home forced to go on line to order groceries? I preferred to pick out my own bananas. Would I have to go to the internet for my supply of Sam Adams beer? Maybe that carton of delivered groceries would have a bomb in it.

It's easy to scare yourself.

I felt like Alfred E Newman of Mad Magazine. What? Me worry? YES.

Ursula was settling into the role of stay at home mom. She didn't have to get dressed, padded around in her bunny slippers, a pair of panties and a bathrobe. I could get used to that, except her always ready outfit was always ready to nurse baby Sarah.

I'd found the hidden camera in the TV and put a bit of tape over it, but now the picture had a permanent black spot where the tape was. If we turned on the TV to watch the news it was all chit chat, the unknowing blathering with alleged experts while the country floundered under a confused, conflicted administration.

If we watched a Netflix spy movie it was all shoot 'em up car chases, explosions, and murder, too close to home for us.

Baby Sarah Gwendolyn was too young for Sesame Street. I already knew the alphabet and how to count to ten.

Finally, after several days we got two messages.

Email from Gulli. She enjoyed the challenge of breaking through North Korea's firewalls. She was having fun. She was splitting up the Ransom ware. Bangladesh had lost sixty million to hackers. She replenished their treasury. She put more Korean loot into the pillaged pension fund of Alibaba, that Chinese mail order company. There was more left over.

Moxon, my CIA contact, had his own resources. Intercepted messages revealed a shakeup in the cyber war center in North Korea. Arrests and executions. A police state can be so unforgiving.

When we did turn on CNN we learned that the US state department had denied any knowledge of a cyber attack on North Korea. Who us? I guess for once we were innocent.

That still left Gulli vulnerable to avengers.

CIA wanted to pick her up and interrogate her, find out how she did her thing. She would be so skittish that only I could identify her and get her aboard an airplane. That meant they wanted me to meet and identify her, wherever she could be found. What would they do then?

Treat her like some suspected terrorist and park her in Bulgaria where torture was OK? No way.

That gave me mixed feelings. After all, Gulli had fingered me to divert the attention of her kidnappers in Holland. Yes, I was the depository of her million bitcoin, but was it necessary to send the Russian Mafia after us?

Domesticity took priority. I didn't want to leave Ursula on her own with baby Sarah. I couldn't do the nursing thing, but I'd taken on the role of house husband, cooking, laundry, that stuff.

As for Gulli, what was I supposed to do? Wait on the rainy tarmac of some obscure airfield in Germany and welcome Gulli into the arms of the American secret police? That's how she saw the CIA and all the rest. She hated police.

This was going to take some negotiation. How would they appeal to her? Money was no object. She was not loyal to the United States or anybody else. She was Gulli, a free agent, like Robin Hood, except she didn't steal from the rich and give to the poor. She stole from the thieves.

That was her life. I could hardly imagine her with a boy friend or married. Hacking must have been a hobby at first, then an obsession, the sort of thing that takes over your life, like hoarding. It was also a challenge and her special talent.

That's what we had in common, except with me it grew out of the Krieger coupon job until I wanted more and more data and was overwhelmed. I guess Gulli and I were both obsessive. My job had taken hold of me. Gulli had to be like a gambler who simply can't stop. The challenge of outwitting thieves was too great.

She would make a great detective. That would have to be the angle the CIA played upon to get her to cooperate. Safety and a level of legitimacy in exchange for her expertise.

I needed confirmation from Moxon and his CIA superiors. Moxon said something about a background check, lie detector test, and the Secrets Act. I was familiar with that and had signed it myself. How could you run a background check on Gulli, who assumed several identities and was always on the move? She was hard to pin down, a category of one.

I guessed it would take another attempt on her life to persuade her. If her opposition succeeded, she'd be dead, end of story. If not, maybe she'd come along.

Harley L. Sachs

Gulli was a little bit of a thing, crippled, hobbling around on an orthopedic shoe, hiding from CCT cameras under an umbrella. To a mugger she was easy prey.

Then I got an actual phone call from her.

My first questions were, "Where are you?" and "What name are you using?"

"Hilda Schweinfurt. I am in Frankfurt University Hospital. I was robbed. They took my purse."

She never had to carry much money. What was the risk?

"They got my papers."

Frankfurt has many hospitals, about two hundred if you counted all the clinics and private ones. While I held our hard wired phone between my cheek and shoulder I did a quick computer search. I got the particulars for the University Hospital, looked for Hilda Schweinfurt, connected to the security cameras.

There she was, a pitiful, bruised figure with tubes.

I watched her on the security camera. She was trying to smile through swollen lips. She had a black eye and her face was bruised.

I can't read German but again I called on Ursula for help. "I've got Gulli on the phone. Can you read her chart for me?"

A medical report is a bit beyond Ursula's vocabulary need for teaching high school German, but she worked it out. A broken rib, possible concussion.

Gulli was worried. "They took my papers. I had six identities in it. They will think I am a spy."

"That depends on who mugged you."

"I think Turkish."

Germany was full of scurvy foreign immigrants. The Turks, brought in as guest workers who stayed, had spawned a generation of misfits. If you are born in the USA you are an automatic citizen. In Germany the kids of a Turk are still Turks, misfits, often angry, like the children of Algerians resettled in France.

I did not think her assailant would be connected with her internet crimes. Most likely her robber would take money and credit cards and toss the purse in the trash.

I called Moxon. "My contact is in the University Hospital in Frankfurt, Germany, using the name Hilda Schweinfurt. It's another of her aliases. She's always changing identities. We'd better get her out of there."

443

Moxon had to confer with someone while I squirmed at our kitchen table, wishing I hadn't run out of Sam Adams. Coffee didn't settle my nerves.

When he called back he had a proposition of his own. "You'll have to pick her up."

"What? Me?"

"You're the only one who knows her and she trusts."

"When?"

"Next flight to Germany."

"What?"

Moxon's voice was serious. "Mr. Goldstein, this Hilda whatshername is a valuable resource. If we can get her over here she can be a great benefit to our country. This is priority."

He sounded like she was as important as Niels Bohr, the Danish Jewish nuclear scientist who got smuggled out of Denmark in World War II in the back of a fighter plane and nearly froze to death.

My brain whirled, mostly with Ursula and the baby Sarah.

Ursula had finished translating what she could of Gulli's medical record. She was called away from my computer for diaper duty. Nothing like a dirty diaper to bring you down to earth.

I explained, "The CIA wants me to fly to Germany to pick up Gulli and bring her here."

"Why you?"

"Because I'm the only one she knows and trusts."

"Do you trust the CIA?"

That was another issue. "I trust them more than the Russian Mafia."

Ursula actually laughed, showed her teeth. "You call that a recommendation?"

"What about you?"

"What? You think I'm going along? No way. I'll ask my mother to stay with me and Sarah while you're gone. She can't wait to see the baby."

She always makes such good sense. She's my pillar of stability.

I called Moxon back. He had an odd question. "Can you handle Mach-2?"

"What is that? A hamburger?"

"No. It supersonic speed. You get to Washington and we'll have you in Frankfurt in a couple of hours. Don't worry about your passport. You won't be going through customs."

444

The fun began. Before Ursula's mother could even make a plane reservation to Cleveland I was in a private turbo jet owned by some corporate donor to a congressmen in a quick flight to Washington. Now I saw how the one per-centers live. Plush leather seats, me the only passenger, no flight attendant, just a serve yourself bar and a box lunch, turkey and mayo sandwich, chips and a can of soda.

I should have taken advantage of the flight time and napped but was too nervous. Like most people, I like to be in charge of my life. Here I was being steered by who knew who?

That was only the beginning. I arrived at Reagan airport and took a cab to Andrews, the military airport eleven miles away. Getting past the guarded gate was a bit tricky. I didn't have my passport, just an Ohio driver's license. My brief notoriety as a public figure with my face on all screens had faded into a forgotten short term public memory. I no longer felt miffed if not recognized as Harvey Goldstein Metadata Man.

Moxon's people in the CIA had prepared the way. Like some VIP I was hustled to a hanger and zipped into a flight suit like a cocoon, all those olive drab pockets. Bewildered, I felt dizzy. Too many stimuli. I instinctively tried to identify every face, read every CCT camera. I was on my way again to a nervous breakdown from the overload. When that happened at home I could retreat to bed with my blanky over my head. Not so here.

Before I boarded a flight to Germany they made me take the battery out of my little ten dollar track phone. Didn't want me tracked.

They had to help me up the ladder into the back seat of some sort of grey, radar evading stealth bomber. The worst was when they buckled me in and put an oxygen mask on my face. Instant claustrophobia. It didn't give me any comfort to be shown the ejection button. If I pushed it I'd be blasted out like out of a cannon, seat and all, with the parachute built in, to land where? In the ocean? Greenland? As polar bear bait?

The pilot looked like a high school kid. They're the only ones with reflexes quick enough for planes like that. Probably got practice playing computer games.

I think I passed out from acceleration when we took off like Evil Kaneval being shot out of a cannon. When I finally dared open my eyes we were half way across the Atlantic and slowing down to refuel in mid flight.

When we disconnected from the tanker plane we were off again, whoosh, minutes away from Frankfurt on Main. We landed in the dark.

My knees were weak when I was helped out of the plane. The pilot cautioned me, "Don't remember anything you saw. It's all classified."

"So am I," I joked. "You never saw me."

They say the military is hurry up and wait. After a supersonic flight to Germany all I could do was sit in an Air Force waiting room with a cup of coffee, jet lag, and wonder what time it was in Germany. Should I bother to reset my watch?

Someone from an American consulate office that served as cover for the CIA was supposed to meet me, but it was the middle of the night in Germany, or more correctly very early in the morning, like two thirty.

Finally I saw a civilian come in. He was wearing a winter jacket with a fake fur hood and hadn't shaved. He knew who to look for. Just in case, he asked, "Harvey Goldstein?"

I nodded, already wise enough not to ask his name while I sifted through my memory for his digitized face. I told myself I don't want to now who this is. What I don't know I can't confess if the kidnappers get me this time. In any case, I didn't trust anybody from the CIA to give me his real name. I wondered if his wife knew it.

"We've organized an ambulance to pick up your contact, get her out of that hospital. It's not secure."

"OK. Then what?"

Without answering, he sighed, obviously in great need of coffee. Like a hound dog after a coon he followed his nose to the machine, dropped in some Euro coins, and got himself a cup. Stirring the powdered creamer with a ball point pen he took a tentative sip, found it gulpable, and recharged his batteries. "We'll bring her back here and medivac her to Walter Reid. Her cover is she's wounded military from Afghanistan. You'll accompany her."

"As what? I'm not a doctor."

"I'll get you a white coat."

I wondered if it came with a diploma.

I was guided to an ambulance with one of those multi-syllable German names that sounded like some sort of a hospital. Off we went through the very early morning to the University Hospital, a very modern building.

Whoever tried to snatch Gulli in Amsterdam could be replaced by another team. After all, when millions, even billions of redirected treasury wealth was at stake, money was no object. The risk of Gulli being in a public hospital was that the next batch of kidnappers might catch up with her.

My guide spoke what sounded to me like fluent German. There was some flashing of documents, real or forged I wouldn't know, before I was led to Gulli's room.

It was typical hospital, not a private room, but with privacy curtains drawn. I peeked in. She was asleep. Seen in the flesh she looked even worse than on the security cameras. I pulled the visitor's chair beside the bed and, careful of the butterfly bandage and tube taped to her wrist, took her hand.

She stirred.

"Gulli?"

Her eyes opened, uncertain, afraid, then recognized me. "Harvey."

"It's me." Like who else?

"How did you get here?"

"Like Superman, faster than a speeding bullet." Pretty close to the truth. "We've come to get you out of here."

She looked around, helpless, saw that I had someone with me, which alarmed her.

My guide was still holding his paper cup of coffee like a security blanket.

I explained, "He's from the American Embassy. He's OK." Not as if he really was, or maybe the consulate, or some secret cover organization. Was he really? Was he OK? I sincerely hoped so, but I was no longer sure of anything.

"Where are you taking me?"

"To someplace safe." I didn't think she would know Walter Reid, the famous Washington, DC hospital for our wounded veterans.

Safe was what she needed. It was what she always needed. Unintentionally or unwittingly, she had made herself a target. People don't like it when you steal their money, even if it isn't theirs.

Orderlies had to lift her onto a gurney and trail along with the intravenous drip on its wheels. Out to the exit and another transfer, on the count of one two, three into the ambulance, the drip following.

The door slammed and we were off, me in the back with Gulli, holding her free hand for assurance. She was sedated and compliant.

At Rhine Main one of those enormous cargo planes was waiting. It was already being loaded with other patients, a real hospital ward, a flying ambulance with wings and jet engines. They actually did give me a white coat, this time with a surgical mask. After all, there were sick and wounded aboard.

I was buckled into a jump seat, no parachute this time. I guess if the plane was going down we would go along with those poor guys and women strapped in their gurneys.

It was a long flight to Washington. This time, totally weary from stress and exhaustion, I did sleep, slumped, held up by my seat belt.

When we did land in Washington, same air field where less lucky GI's were delivered in their flag draped coffins, Gulli was unloaded along with the other wounded.

Several ambulances were waiting, even a special bus for those who could sit.

I didn't want to leave Gulli. I felt totally responsible for her well being. Who else did she have? I was it.

The same man who had seen me strapped into the stealth bomber was waiting. He introduced himself, a name that might actually have been genuine.

I thought I was done. "Do I get to go home now?"

What? Like I was a free person?

"We'd like you to stay a day or two until we can get her settled. When she's out of the hospital we'll set her up in a safehouse and orient her."

"Where will that be?"

He gave me a stony look like if I tell you I have to kill you.

"Sorry I asked."

"You understand, Mrs. Schweinfurt or whoever she says she is, is a valuable asset."

"It's important that she is safe. She hates police and has made many enemies, so she's been on her own. She has a sister who keeps her distance, probably for her own self-preservation."

He didn't know she had a sister. "Her sister?"

He was waiting for an explanation. "It's a need to know thing. You don't need to know."

"Suit yourself."

"What now? I need to call my wife." I showed him the phone and the battery I had taken out.

"Just be discreet."

My call was as innocuous as possible. I was in Washington and would be back in a couple of days. When was her mother arriving? That afternoon?

With a shock, I realized I'd been gone hardly more than twenty-four hours, to Germany and back.

Harley L. Sachs

They didn't tell me how things went with Gulli. I figured, when she got out of Walter Reid, they set her up in a safe house. I was sure they would get her into a secure office and track every key stroke she made to find out just how she did it. Gulli was what they call humint, human intelligence. Once they knew her system, her tricks, they'd be done with her, squeezed like some defecting Russian who had nothing more to reveal and could be put out to pasture. That's what happened to me at Krieger. Outsourced by a computer program. We are all dispensable, disposable, whatever.

I hoped with Ursula I was worth keeping, not like some honeybee drone who, once the queen is fertilized, is killed or kicked out of the hive. After all Sarah Gwendolyn is my baby, too. Once we got used to being parents we might want more.

I knew no one in Washington. I did not feel like a tourist. I did go to the Holocaust Museum, cried for unknown lost relatives. Being under cover I felt like an interloper in a strange house. If someone asked me what I was doing in the District I could only say I was visiting a sick friend. I couldn't wait to get home.

I knew that, like my job at Krieger, Metadata Man could be outsourced by an IA program. The only limit was the computing capacity of the combined clouds. Given enough computing power, every face could be tracked all the time, every bank and medical record screened for inconsistencies and illegalities. Big Data, unleashed and in the wrong hands could control everything and everybody. Then nobody needed me. We, the unwitting public, could blithely go about our business, as Uncle Julius had said, in la-la land.

About Harley L. Sachs:

Though born in Chicago and raised in Indiana, Harley L. Sachs considers himself an international, having lived in Germany, Sweden, Scotland, and Denmark. He earned a degree in English at Indiana University, then served in the US Army in Germany. After getting his Master's degree at I.U. he returned to Europe and worked under cover for several years. He met and married Ulla in Stockholm, Sweden and they spent a year's honeymoon in a Scottish castle. Returning to the USA, Sachs taught English briefly at Southern Illinois University then moved to Michigan Technological University in the Upper Peninsula where he and his wife raised three daughters. He took early retirement and now lives in Portland, Oregon.

Upd 1/2018
Here's a catalog of books by Harley L. Sachs:

MYSTERY NOVELS

The Mystery Club Series

THE MYSTERY CLUB SOLVES A MURDER
First and most popular of the Mystery Club series. Mary Higgins finds the body of Dora Reed on the roof of the Plaza retirement building, notifies the police, then tells the Mystery Club. They assume several suspects: the manager of the Plaza, Dora's son Donald, or a Plaza employee. Dora's husband, Ed Sutherland, is in Hawaii on board the yacht Miss Chief with an all girl crew. Carrying on their own investigation, the Mystery Club finally suspects Sutherland, though he seems to have a perfect alibi. If they can prove it to their satisfaction, will a court ever convict him-- if he can be found somewhere in the Pacific?

THE MYSTERY CLUB AND THE DEAD DOCTOR
Second in the Mystery Club series. The Mystery Club consists of five elderly women who live at the Rose Plaza and discuss mysteries written by women. The Mystery Club ladies have no idea of the consequences when Viola Cartwright, their blind member, asks them to go over her Medicare bills. That leads to suspicion about the identity of her personal assistant, Dorothy Anderson, who turns out to be using a stolen identity. Viola's doctor runs a phony clinic owned by a member of the Russian Mafia. Soon the investigation of Medicare bills leads to murder and tragedy, stopped only by the courage of Mary Higgins.

THE MYSTERY CLUB AND THE HIDDEN WITNESS
Third in the Mystery Club series. The ladies of the Mystery Club discover one of the residents is a crook under WITSEC, the witness protection program. He apparently keeps dipping into the employee gift fund. The Mystery Club bands together to track down the missing money, but what they discover is danger.

THE MYSTERY CLUB AND THE SERIAL WIDOW

Fourth in the Mystery Club series. Caroline Kostinsky, new resident at the Rose Plaza, is a widow four times over and she's looking for a fifth husband in retired General Hardcastle, but when drunk she says she killed all of her husbands. Except for her confession, there's no evidence. Now what?

DELIVER ME FROM EVIL

Responding to a posted invitation for new members for the Mystery Club, Judge Ira Kahane and Ursula Besette show up. Ursula, at a turning point in her life as a new Rose Plaza resident, is interested in Wicca and Kabala. Roberta Nelson believes one should not suffer a witch to live. Judge Kahane tries to lead Ursula on the right path, but there is conflict and tragedy coming.

WHITE SLAVE

Sequel to *The Mystery Club Solves a Murder*. The appearance of Ed Sutherland's gold bracelet in a Portland pawn shop revives retired detective Casey's interest in the cold case. He doesn't know that Sutherland has been picked up and is a slave on a Korean fishing boat. Sutherland, penniless, .without clothes or identification, is stranded in New Zealand. Can he find his way back to Portland and be somehow redeemed or face a death sentence for first degree murder?

The Irwin Glass Series

BETRAYAL

Prequel to *Retribution*. Irwin Glass, BA in Russian, MA in International Relations, has a promising career in the Foreign Service in Moscow until he is snared in a classic "honey pot" seduction. He's young and naïve, honest, always wants to do the right thing, but at every turn he is betrayed. The incident in Moscow destroys his career. He is accused of being a paid Soviet agent and is pursued by the consequences of his encounter with the KGB twenty years later. Some enemies never let go

RETRIBUTION

Sequel to *Betrayal*. Newly married to Ivy Hartshorn, Irwin Glass gets a dunning letter from the IRS for taxes on interest at the Washington, DC account he didn't think he had. It's a joint account with his missing birth daughter and the balance is huge. Assuming it's money Katya's KGB

Harley L. Sachs

father of record, Vladimir Putinsky (now Putin) deposited for her living expenses, Irwin moves it to force her to contact him. But Ivy warns him that he is laundering money and the people it belongs to will come after him. Irwin's complicated life is catching up with him, but this time he will find retribution.

BURNT OUT
Irwin Glass is approached by FBI Agent Wilkins who asks for Irwin's lists of foreign students. Not satisfied he wants more and is looking for potential terrorists among the Moslem students. Gradually Irwin is sucked into the role of FBI informant on the Michigan Institute of Technology's Muslim Students' Association and the results are tragic.

THE IRWIN GLASS TRILOGY
All three Irwin Glass books in one package deal. The Irwin Glass Trilogy combines all three of the Irwin Glass Mysteries: "Betrayal," "Retribution," and "Burnt Out," following the chaotic career of Irwin Glass who began, in "Betrayal," as a state department clerk in Moscow only to be caught in a classic honey pot seduction. Betrayed at every turn, he was sent back to the United States in disgrace to try to start a new life. No such luck. His teaching career is upturned by the revelation that the Moscow seduction had a consequence in the form of a beautiful student Katya who claims to be his daughter. In "Retribution," Irwin's KGB nemesis is in the United States seeking political asylum, but in fact is fleeing the Russian Mafia with Irwin as quarry. After "Retribution," Irwin thinks he is home free of all that intrigue, but the local FBI agent has a hold on him and wants information about potential terrorists among Irwin's students at Michigan Institute of Technology. There are risks to being a reluctant FBI informant, and Irwin's reports may be misconstrued with tragic results. What Irwin and his wife really want is a normal life, but his mysterious Russian birth daughter Katya remains an enigma. Is she or isn't she?

Other Mysteries

MURDER BY MAIL (Scratch--Out!)
German exchange student Klaus Hitz is more interested in making money than in asking questions about his work assignment. He doesn't know that the industrialist father of his punk girl friend is using him in a terrorist conspiracy to kill everyone in the United States with a mass

453

mailing of a scratch and sniff virus. The plot begins to unravel when a Polish nurse brings blood samples from Libya and alerts a CIA agent. While the CIA and FBI track down the terrorists, Klaus Hitz gradually figures it out. How can he avoid being murdered or imprisoned for being naive?

MURDER IN THE KEWEENAW

CIA agent recovering from Post traumatic Stress after failed missions in Finland and a divorce is fishing in Lake Superior when he snags a corpse. He thinks he has seen the girl before and his attempt to identify her leads him to a ring of deadly pornographers. It almost costs him his own life.

CONSPIRACY!

Technical writer Tom Godot can't believe his luck when CONSPIRACY!, the book he has co-written with the elusive Harold Stevenson, is a hit. The book details a plot to hijack communication satellites. As Tom crosses the country on his book tour, he is disturbed by people interested in early drafts and dogged by an NSA agent. Communicating by fax with his editor and by encrypted e-mail with the mysterious Stevenson, Tom reaches out in his loneliness to his California girl friend Sylvia Hanson who turns out to be a pivotal figure. There is another conspiracy, and Tom is part of it

THE GOLD CHROMOSOME

When Adam Rottman's childless Aunt Sadie Gold died, the eight cousins learned her estate was in an irrevocable trust, the proceeds going to Adam's sister Sarah while she lives. After Sarah's death, the money would go to the last surviving cousin. It's a fatal tontine Adam's lawyer brother Harold set up. Would the cousins kill each other for one million dollars? Sarah's car is found in the river, but not Sarah. That begins a series of mysterious deaths. Coincidence? Or Murder? Who will be next? Adam and his psychologist wife Deborah must stop the chain before he, too, is eliminated.

BEN ZAKKAI'S COFFIN

Born of a Jewish father and a Catholic mother, Herman Bachrach insists he has no religion, but he is drawn by circumstance into a holocaust vendetta over gold stolen by a Swiss bank from Jewish depositors. Seduced by a woman who calls herself Diana, no last name, Herman is

Harley L. Sachs

suspected by detective Sheehan to be her murderer.   Someone else wants him dead.   His Jewish boss provides him with a lawyer, but sends him to Switzerland to finish the job "Diana" started.   It's an assignment he can't refuse.   The result is an epiphany of identity that changes Herman's life forever.

THE LOLLIPOP MURDER

A warning for wannabe novelists! What happens when a stable of neurotic novelists who live in their pseudonyms and are bound by iron clad contracts are invited aboard their miserly Florida publisher's yacht for the Miami Book Fair only to find that they have no hope of ever earning a dime of royalties for their books? All this as Hurricane Gerta threatens to sink the yacht at the dock.   It's grounds for murder

DEAD MEN DON'T BLEED

Being transgender is tough. A grisly murder of a Vietnam vet on the top floor of the Rose Plaza retirement building is a challenge for Detective Carol, previously Caryl. As a ransgender person she is not accepted by the Portland police, nor is a vice cop convert to Islam. The pair team up to solve the crime and prove they have what it takes to be respected on the force..

NOVELS

SAM IN LOVE

A coming of age romance for mature young adults. U.S. Army life in Europe in the 1950's was an equivalent of the Grand Tour of the eighteenth century when young men traveled and sowed wild oats. Marty, roommate of Sam Logan, a PFC draftee serving in the US Army in Munich, Germany, says all Sam needs is to get laid. Sam is not a virgin, but has a Midwestern ethic and believes in love. He doesn't know quite what that is. No Casanova, Sam, through a series of tentative encounters, thinks he's found the love of his life.

STOPRAPE.COM

Kerstin Mikkola, a young TV reporter at KDUP in Marquette, Michigan has hopes of a better network job. Her interview with a marine victim or rape might be just the ticket. Her interview about the web site

StopRape.com goes viral on U-tube and Kerstin finds herself in the thick of consequences she did not anticipate.

THE ACCIDENTAL COURIER

A romance, road trip, and mystery all in one. Charles Kosko, retired orchard owner from Oregon, decides to take a bus trip in Europe and finds himself involved in a whistle-blower's scheme to discredit an American cell phone company that uses rare earths mined by slaves in the Congo. Unable to speak any foreign language, and without his US passport, he is picked up by a beautiful Israeli woman who says she is his driver. But is he really her prisoner? They are pursued by an African mining engineer, who hopes to intercept the delivery of stolen rare earths,

The Metadata Man Series:

THE SEVENTH PARADIGM:

Harvey Goldstein does the grocery coupons for the Krieger grocery chain and wants to know everything about everybody.. On a visit to Hamburg with a distant Uncle Julius, ex stasi secret policeman, Harvey is warned about the Seventh Paradigm. It all has to do with metadata. By the time he finds out what it is, it may be too late.

THE METADATA CURSE

Harvey has a "gift" of a million stolen bitcoins from the mysterious "Angel," but he is afraid the owners will want it returned or at least revenge. But who gave it to him? And where did it come from? He might be Metadata Man, but he is no super hero? He and Ursula try to track down the elusive "Angel"

INTERNET COP

Returning to Cleveland after decompressing in Switzerland, Ursula is pregnant with their first child. They cannot separate from their past, however, as Gulli, Harvey's hacker benefactor, is kidnapped and gives his name to her abductors. FBI Agent Walker has his own plans for Harvey as a paid informant. Being a detective comes naturally to Metadata Man, but not confronting his wife's kidnappers. There is one solution: find the elusive Gulli again Baby's coming!.

.

Harley L. Sachs
SCI-FI AND FANTASY

NEVER TRUST A TALKING HORSE
The narrator of this dystopian novel escapes preventive detention into a world he discovers has gone mad. Hungry, he is told he can eat for free at Lachumba's supper club, only to discover that he might be the main dish. He rescues Iris I. Iris from the ovens and in a series of episodes explores the insane world in search of a livelihood. He gradually realizes why he was incarcerated in the first place, but by then it is too late. His and Iris's roles have been reversed. Arrested, they are given a sadistic sentence which is their final challenge.

THE SEARCH FOR JESSE BRAM
Jesse Bram, the young hero of this metaphysical science fiction adventure, is unaware of his Jewish roots. An Eldre of mixed breed, he is marooned on the post apocalyptic shunned planet URth where technology and books have been destroyed. The URthlings variously view Jesse as a bringer of cargo for the half-breed prefect Hrod, as the reborn Savior by crypto-Christians, and as a link to the past by a remnant of Jews. The Galactic Federation suspects him of treason and he is pursued by an enigmatic Trinian policeman. If Jesse survives, will he be convicted? If acquitted, what next?

SHORT STORIES

THREADS OF THE COVENANT: THE JEWS OF RED JACKET
A collection of twenty-one short stories about Jewish life in small town America centering about two main characters, David Katz, the only Jewish boy in Red Jacket, and Richard Goldman, the only Jewish professor at Copper country Community College. Each story depicts another aspect of what it means to be a Jew in a small town as each character comes to realize his own identity.

MISPLACED PERSONS
Though set in different locales what these stories have in common is a central character who is out of his element, in the wrong place, coming to grips with cultural, generational, or physical displacement. In PROBLEM FOR THE TEACHER an expatriate fumbles for a living; in LIMBO an ex-G.I. is adrift in Copenhagen; in TRIUMPH OF THE WILL a nervous wreck seeks recuperation; in MISCALCULATION a

would be tax evader succumbs to his own fears; in THE LIE a drunk gets himself into difficulties, and in THE GIRLS OF FREDERIKSHAVN an old man is trapped by girls looking for action.

YOOPER TALES AND OTHER FUNNY STUFF
Extracted from the massive volume of Sachs's published Essays and Columns: 1992-2011, this collection of stories related to Michigan's Upper Peninsula, known as the UP, home of Yoopers, reveals the truth about snow fleas, ice worms, the humungous fungus (world's largest living thing) and the rigors of winters in the remote north woods. You can also learn how to catch and cook the Mosquito Giganticus and why visitors won't come. Sachs has several awards for his humor.

AHOY! QUARTERDECK!
Originally published as IRMA QUARTERDECK REPORTS but re-released with new illustrations and, in the paperback edition, with sea shanties, this funny book is a series of boating anecdotes about Irma and her bumbling husband Ralph ("I can't believe I lost the anchor") Quarterdeck in their many boating adventures and mishaps.   One reviewer says the book is as informative as Chapman's famous manual, but more fun.   Readers will find plenty of laughs in this book and at the same time learn a great deal of boating fundamentals.

ANNA-LENA'S TROLL AND OHER STORIES
Each of the three Sachs daughters has a story in this children's book. "Anna-Lena's Troll" explores the nature of trolls, which represent the dark side of human behavior as Anna-Lena's nasty letter to Santa is rewarded by the gift of a nasty troll. "The Return of Baby Suzy" is the true story of Cynthia's worn out doll and its resurrection. "The Stars for Christmas" is the remarkable surprise Belinda got along with her new eye glasses. Other family stories are Christmas related.

NON-FICTION

THE MISADVENTURES OF CPL. SACHS
Adrift through college at Indiana University, author Sachs was drafted at the end of the Korean War. Physically unfit for combat, he was sent to Queer Company for basic training, then by a fluke was shipped out to

Germany instead of Korea. Thus began his own version of the traditional Grand Tour.

FREELANCE NONFICTION ARTICLES
This third edition of a monograph on freelance writing first published by the Society for Technical Communication is newly updated. This little manual provides tips for interviewing, article structure, article preparation and submission, photography, and business practice.

CHILLY-CHILLY-BANG—HOW WE FREELANCED THROUGH EUROPE'S COLDEST WINTER IN A VW WITH A KID
Companion piece to *Freelance Nonfiction Articles*. The former is a how to book. This is a "how we did it" memoir. The author knew nothing about Volkswagens when they set off, but as they worked from VW dealer to dealer getting the old Combi fixed, he learned! It's as much a book for VW enthusiasts as it is for writers.

Both FREELANCE NONFICTION ARTICLES and *Chilly-Chilly-BANG! How we Freelanced Through Europe's Coldest Winter in a VW with a Kid* are combined in a double volume, *The Writing Life*.

THE 1957 SACHS ARCTIC EXPEDITION
After military service in Germany the author took the GI Bill to Sweden. With no income in the summer, and not even sure there was a road to the far north, he set off hitchhiking to North Cape, the northernmost point in Europe in search of the midnight sun. Illustrated.

FROM TENT TO CASTLE: MEMOIR OF A YEAR LONG HONEYMOON
Setting off from Stockholm, Sweden on rebuilt one speed bicycles, Harley and Ulla embarked on an open-ended honeymoon with no fixed destination and equipped with a tent, a thin double sleeping bag, a tiny gasoline stove, and $3000. After arriving in Britain, Ulla discovered she was pregnant. Tired of unrelenting rain, they advertised for a cheap place to spend the winter. They were offered the gatehouse to Borthwick Castle outside Edinburgh, Scotland for $25 a month by British author Theo Lang.

"IS"
As Bill Clinton said, "It all depends on what the meaning of "is" is."

A problem we all have is distinguishing between what is real and what is not. This is in fact an age-old question. This volume switches between classical instances of the problem to the author and his psychiatrist and his wife. What is real? That all depends on the meaning of "real."

QUEER COMPANY

Not a gay novel, this is a fictionalized memoir of an experimental basic training unit at the end of the Korean War. All the draftees were physically unfit for combat but the army didn't want to discharge them. Instead they got modified training in a company unfortunately designated Q. In the Army phonetic alphabet Q is Queen, but Q company was called queer. A copy is in the US Army historical archives.

www.ingramcontent.com/pod-product-compliance
Lightning Source LLC
Chambersburg PA
CBHW071341020726
47502CB00001B/202